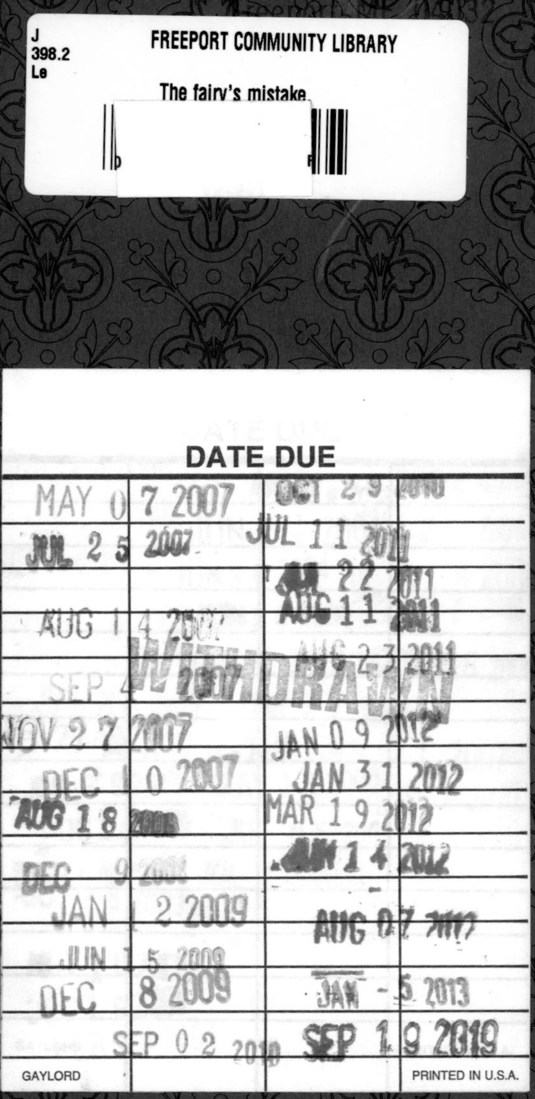
DATE DUE
MAY 0 7 2007
JUL 2 5 2007
AUG 1 4 2007
SEP 4 2007
NOV 2 7 2007
DEC 1 0 2007
AUG 1 8
DEC 9
JAN 1 2 2009
JUN 1 5 2009
DEC 8 2009
SEP 0 2 2010
OCT 2 9 2010
JUL 1 1 2011
22 2011
AUG 1 1
AUG 2 3 2011
JAN 0 9 2012
JAN 3 1 2012
MAR 1 9 2012
JUN 1 4 2012
AUG 0 7
JAN - 5 2013
SEP 1 9 2019
WITHDRAWN
GAYLORD
PRINTED IN U.S.A.

The Fairy's Mistake

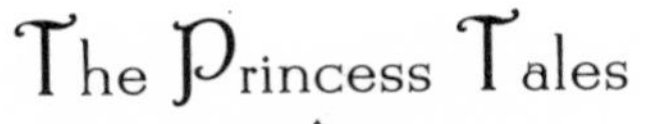

The Princess Tales

The Fairy's Mistake

Gail Carson Levine

ILLUSTRATED BY Mark Elliott

HarperCollins*Publishers*

The Fairy's Mistake

http://www.harperchildrens.com

Library of Congress Cataloging-in-Publication Data
Levine, Gail Carson.
The fairy's mistake / Gail Carson Levine ; illustrated by Mark Elliott.
p. cm.
"The princess tales."
Summary: In this humorous retelling of a Perrault tale, the fairy Ethelinda rewards one twin sister for good behavior and punishes the other for bad, only to discover that her punishment is more pleasing than her reward.
ISBN 0-06-028060-3 ISBN 0-06-028061-1 (lib. bdg.)
[1. Fairy tales. 2. Folklore—France.] I. Elliott, Mark, ill. II. Perrault, Charles, 1628-1703. Fées. III. Title.
PZ8.L4793Fai 1999 98-27871
398.2—DC21 CIP
AC

Typography by Michele N. Tupper
7 8 9 10

First Edition

ALSO BY
Gail Carson Levine

Ella Enchanted

THE PRINCESS TALES:

The Princess Test

Princess Sonora and the Long Sleep

All my thanks

to my wonderful editor, Alix Reid.

Without you, *The Princess Tales*

would never have been told.

—G.C.L.

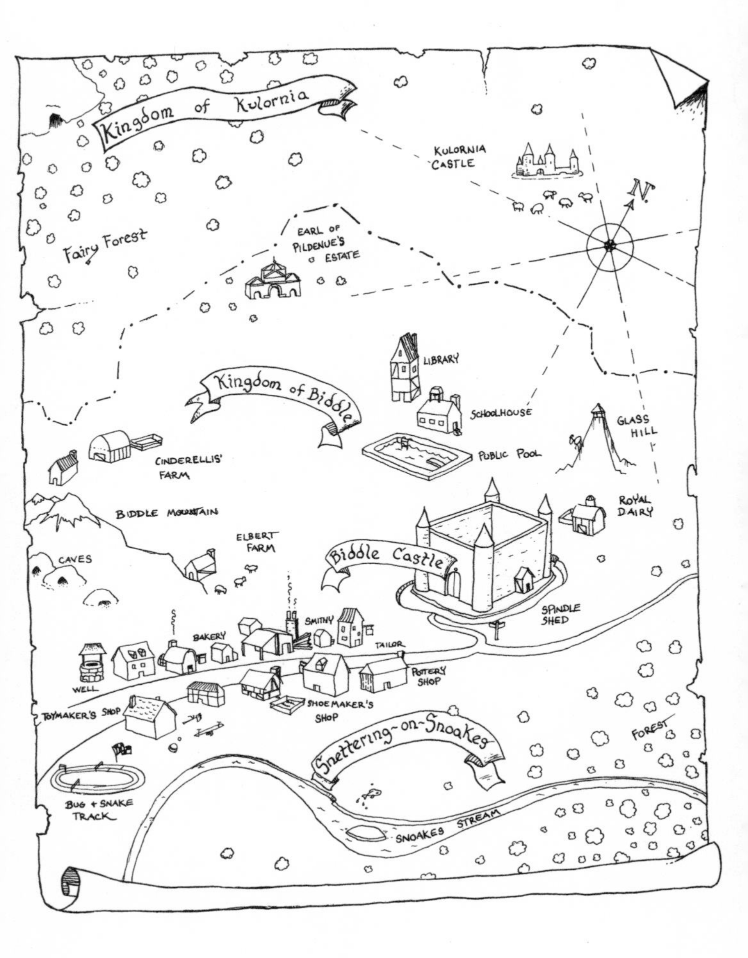

Kingdom of Kulornia
KULORNIA CASTLE
N.
Fairy Forest
EARL OF PILDENUE'S ESTATE
LIBRARY
Kingdom of Biddle
SCHOOLHOUSE
GLASS HILL
CINDERELLIS' FARM
PUBLIC POOL
ROYAL DAIRY
BIDDLE MOUNTAIN
ELBERT FARM
CAVES
Biddle Castle
SPINDLE SHED
SMITHY
BAKERY
TAILOR
WELL
POTTERY SHOP
TOYMAKER'S SHOP
SHOEMAKER'S SHOP
Snettering-on-Snoakes
FOREST
BUG & SNAKE TRACK
SNOAKES STREAM

One

Once upon a time, in the village of Snettering-on-Snoakes in the kingdom of Biddle, Rosella fetched water from the well for the four thousand and eighty-eighth time.

Rosella always fetched the water because her identical twin sister, Myrtle, always refused to go. And their mother, the widow Pickering, never made Myrtle do anything. Instead, she made Rosella do everything.

At the well the fairy Ethelinda was having a drink. When she saw Rosella coming, she changed herself into an old lady. Then she made herself look thirsty.

"Would you like a drink, Grandmother?" Rosella said.

"That would be lovely, dearie."

Rosella lowered her wooden bucket into the well. When she lifted it out, she held the dipper so the old lady could drink.

Ethelinda slurped the water. "Thank you. Your kindness merits a reward. From now—"

"You don't have . . ." Rosella stopped. Something funny was happening in her mouth. Had she lost a tooth? There was something hard under her tongue. And something hard in her cheek. "Excuse me." Now there was something in her other cheek. She spat delicately into her hand.

"SHE SPAT DELICATELY INTO HER HAND."

They weren't teeth. She was holding a diamond and two opals.

"There, dearie." Ethelinda smiled. "Isn't that nice?"

Two

"What took you so long?" Myrtle said when Rosella got home.

"Your sister almost perished from thirst, you lazybones," their mother said.

"I gave a drink to . . ." Something was in Rosella's mouth again. It was between her lip and her front teeth this time. "I gave a drink to an old lady." An emerald and another diamond fell out of her mouth. They landed on the dirt floor of the cottage.

"It was more important— What's that?" Myrtle said.

"What's that?" the widow said.

They both dove for the jewels, but Myrtle got there first.

"Rosella darling," the widow said, "sit down. Make yourself comfortable. Now tell us all about it. Don't leave anything out."

There wasn't much to tell, only enough to cover the bottom of Myrtle's teacup with gems.

"Which way did the old lady go?" Myrtle asked.

Rosella was puzzled. "She didn't go anywhere." An amethyst dropped into the teacup.

Myrtle grabbed the bucket and ran.

When she saw Myrtle in the distance, Ethelinda thought Rosella had come back. Only this time she wasn't tripping lightly down the path, smelling the flowers and humming a tune. She was hurtling along, head down, arms swinging, bucket flying. And then Ethelinda's fairy powers told her that this was Rosella's twin sister. Ethelinda got ready by turning herself into a knight.

"Where did the old lady go?" Myrtle said when she reached the well.

"I haven't seen anyone. I've been alone, hoping some kind maiden would come by and give me a drink. I can't do it myself with all this armor."

"What's in it for me if I do?"

The fairy tilted her head. Her armor clanked. "The happiness of helping someone in need."

"Well, in that case, get your page to do it." Myrtle stomped off.

Ethelinda turned herself back into a fairy. "Your rudeness merits a punishment," she said. But Myrtle was too far away to hear.

Myrtle went through the whole village of Snettering-on-Snoakes, searching for the old lady. The villagers knew she was Myrtle and not Rosella by her scowl and by the way she acted. Myrtle marched into shops and right into people's houses. She opened doors to rooms and even closets. Whenever anyone yelled at her, her only answer was to slam the door on her way out.

While Myrtle was in the village, Rosella went out to her garden to pick peas for dinner. As she worked, she sang.

Oh, May is the lovely month.
Sing hey nonny May-o!
Oh, June is the flower month.
Sing hey nonny June-o!
Oh, July is the hot month.
Sing hey nonny July-o!

And so on. While she sang, gems dropped from her mouth. It still felt funny, but she was getting used to it. Except once she popped a pea into her mouth as she sang, and she almost broke a tooth on a ruby.

Rosella had a sweet voice, but Prince Harold, who happened to be riding by, wasn't musical. He wouldn't have stopped, except he spotted the sapphire trembling on Rosella's lip. He watched it tumble into the vegetables.

He tied his horse up at the widow Pickering's picket fence.

Rosella didn't see him, and she went on singing.

Oh, November is the harvest month.
Sing hey nonny November-o!
Oh, December is the last month.
Sing hey . . .

Prince Harold went into the garden. "Maiden . . ."

Rosella looked up from her peas. A man! A nobleman! She blushed prettily.

She wasn't bad-looking, Prince Harold thought. "Pardon me," he said. "You've dropped some jewels. Allow me."

"Oh! Don't trouble yourself, Sir." Another sapphire and a moonstone fell out of Rosella's mouth.

Harold had a terrible thought. Maybe they were just glass. He picked up a stone. "May I examine this?"

Rosella nodded.

It didn't look like glass. It looked like a perfect diamond, five carats at least. But if the gems were real, why was she leaving them on the ground? He held up a jewel. "Maiden, is this really a diamond?"

"I don't know, Sir. It might be."

A topaz hit Prince Harold in the forehead. He caught it as it bounced off his chin. "Maiden, have jewels always come out of your mouth?"

Rosella laughed, a lovely tinkling sound. "Oh no, Sir. It only began this afternoon when an old lady—I think she may have been a fairy—"

They *were* real then! Harold knelt before her. "Maiden, I am Prince Harold. I love you madly. Will you marry me?"

Three

Rosella didn't love the prince madly, but she liked him. He was so polite. And she thought it might be pleasanter to be a princess than to be the widow Pickering's daughter and Myrtle's sister. Besides, it could be against the law to say no to a prince. So she said yes, and dropped a garnet into his hand.

"I'm sorry, sweetheart. I didn't hear you."

"Yes, Your Highness."

Clink. Clink. Two more garnets joined Harold's collection. "You must say, 'Yes, Harold,' now that we're betrothed."

"Yes, Harold."

Clink.

The fairy Ethelinda was delighted that Rosella was going to be a princess. She deserves it, the fairy thought. Ethelinda was pleased with herself for having given Rosella the perfect reward.

The widow Pickering agreed to the marriage. But she insisted that Harold give her all the gems Rosella had produced before their engagement. The widow was careful not to mention Myrtle. She didn't want the prince to know that Rosella had a twin sister who would also have a jewel mine in her mouth. After all, what if he took Myrtle away too?

Prince Harold swung Rosella up on his horse. He asked her to hold an open saddlebag on her lap. Then he mounted in front of her. As they rode off, he asked her about her garden, about the weather, about fly fishing, about anything.

"HE ASKED HER ABOUT HER GARDEN, ABOUT THE WEATHER . . . ABOUT ANYTHING."

The widow stood at the fence and waved her handkerchief. As she turned to go back into the cottage, she saw her favorite daughter in the distance. Myrtle was loping along, swinging the bucket. The widow opened the gate and followed her daughter into the house. "Darling, speak to me."

Myrtle sank into their only comfortable chair. "Hi, Mom. The stupid old lady wasn't—" There was a tickle in the back of her throat. What was going on? It felt like her tongue had gotten loose and was flopping around in her mouth. Could she be making jewels too? Did it happen just by going to the well? Whatever it was—diamond or pearl or emerald—it wanted to get out. Myrtle opened her mouth.

A garter snake slithered out.

The widow screamed and jumped onto their other chair. "Eeeeek! Get that thing out of here! Myrtle!" She pointed a shaking finger. "There it is! Get it! Eeeeek!"

Myrtle didn't budge. She stared at the snake coiling itself around a bedpost. How had this happened if the old lady wasn't at the well? The knight? The knight! The old lady had turned herself into a knight.

Myrtle jumped up and raced out, taking the bucket with her. "'Bye, Mom," she called over her shoulder. "See you later." Two mosquitoes and a dragonfly flew out of her mouth.

The fairy Ethelinda watched Myrtle scurry down the road. She patted herself on the back for having given Myrtle the perfect punishment.

Four

Prince Harold and Rosella reached the courtyard in front of the prince's palace. He lifted Rosella down from the horse.

"I'm too madly in love to wait," he said. "Let's announce our engagement first thing tomorrow morning, dear heart."

"All right," Rosella said.

Harold only got a measly seed pearl. "Princesses speak in complete sentences, darling."

Rosella took a deep breath for courage. "I'm tired, Your High—I mean Harold. May I rest for a day first?"

But Harold didn't listen. He was too

interested in the green diamond in his hand. "I've never seen one of these before, honey bun. We can have the betrothal ceremony at nine o'clock sharp. Your Royal Ladies-in-Waiting will find you something to wear."

Harold snapped his fingers, and a Royal Lady-in-Waiting led Rosella away. They were on the castle doorstep when Harold ran after them.

"Angel, I almost forgot. What would you like served at our betrothal feast?"

Nobody had ever asked Rosella this kind of question before. She'd always had to eat scraps from her mother's and her sister's plates. Nobody had ever asked her what she liked to eat. Nobody had ever asked her opinion about anything.

She smiled happily. "Your—I mean, Harold . . . uh . . . dear, I'd like poached quail eggs and roasted chestnuts for our betrothal feast." Six identical emeralds the color of maple leaves in May dropped from Rosella's mouth.

The Royal Lady-in-Waiting, who was at Rosella's elbow, gasped.

"Look at these!" Harold said. "They're gorgeous. So you want wild boar for dinner?" He didn't give Rosella time to say she hated wild boar. "What do you know? It's my favorite too. I'll go tell the cook." He rushed off.

Rosella sighed.

The fairy Ethelinda, who was keeping an eye on things, sighed too.

⁂

Myrtle returned to the well, determined to give a drink to anybody who was there. But nobody was. She lowered the bucket into the well anyway.

Nobody showed up.

She had an idea. It was worth a try. She watered the plants that grew around the well. "Dear plants," she began. "You look thirsty. Perhaps a little water would please you. It's no trouble. I don't mind, dear sweet plants."

Whatever was in her mouth was too big to be a jewel, unless it was the biggest one in the world. And a jewel wouldn't feel slimy on her tongue. She opened her mouth. A water bug crawled out. She closed her mouth, but there was more. More slime. She opened her mouth again. Two more water bugs padded out, followed by a black snake.

Giving the plants a drink hadn't done any good. Myrtle dumped the rest of the water on a rosebush. "Drown, you stupid plant," she muttered. A grasshopper landed on a rose.

Myrtle filled her bucket one more

time. Then—without saying a single word—she scoured the village again for the rotten fairy who'd done this to her. She swore to herself that she'd pour water down the throat of any stranger she found.

But there were no strangers, so Myrtle threw the bucket into the well and headed for home.

The widow was in the garden. She had dug up the peas and the radishes and the tomato plants. Now she was pawing through the roots, hoping to find some jewels that Prince Harold had missed. When she heard the gate slam shut, she stood up. "Don't say a word if you didn't find that old lady."

Myrtle closed her mouth with a snap. She picked up a stick and scratched in the dirt, "Where's Rosella?"

"She rode off to marry a prince. And like a fool, I let her go, because I thought I had you. You bungler, you idiot, you . . ."

That made Myrtle furious. How could she have known the fairy would turn herself into a knight in so much armor you couldn't even see her—his—face? And hadn't she searched the village twice? And hadn't she watered those useless plants? Myrtle opened her mouth to give her mother what-for.

But the widow held up her hands and jumped back three feet. "Hush! Shh! Hush, my love. Perhaps I was hasty. We've both had a bad . . ."

Her mother's pleas gave Myrtle a new idea. She picked up the stick again and wrote, "Things are looking up, Mom. It will all be better tomorrow." She dropped the stick and started whistling—and wondering if whistling made snakes and insects too.

It didn't. Too bad, she thought.

Five

Rosella was used to sleeping on the floor, because Myrtle and the widow had always taken the bed. In the palace she got her own bed. It had a canopy and three mattresses piled on top of each other and satin sheets and ermine blankets and pillows filled with swans' feathers.

So she should have gotten a fine night's sleep—except that three Royal Guards stood at attention around her bed all night. One stood at each side of the bed, and one stood at the foot. If she talked in her sleep, they were supposed to catch the jewels and keep them safe for Prince Harold.

Rosella didn't talk in her sleep because she couldn't sleep with people watching her. By morning her throat felt scratchy. She thought she might be coming down with a cold.

Her twelve Royal Ladies-in-Waiting brought breakfast to her at seven o'clock. Scrambled eggs and wild-boar sausages. They shared the sausages while she ate the eggs. Rosella said "please" six times and "thank you" eight times. Each Royal Lady-in-Waiting got one jewel, and they fought over the remaining two.

"Nobody deserves that but me!" yelled one Royal Lady-in-Waiting.

"I work harder than any of you!" yelled another.

"I'm worth ten of each of you, so I should get everything!" shouted a third.

"You have some nerve, thinking . . ."

Rosella put her hands over her ears. She wished she could have ten minutes to herself.

Prince Harold came in. He coughed to get the attention of the Royal Ladies-in-Waiting. Nobody noticed except Rosella, who smiled at him. He'd be handsome, she thought, if he weren't so greedy.

The Royal Ladies-in-Waiting went on arguing.

"How dare you—"

"What do you mean—"

"The first person who—"

"SHUT UP!" Harold roared.

They did.

"You mustn't upset my bride." He went to Rosella, who was eating her breakfast in bed. He put his arm around her shoulder. "Are you all right, sugar plum?"

Rosella nodded. She liked the pet names he called her. But she hoped he wouldn't make her say anything.

"Tell me so I'm sure, lovey-dove."

The fairy Ethelinda was worried.

⁂

Myrtle, on the other hand, had a great night's sleep. When she woke up, she put paper, a quill pen, and a bottle of ink in a pouch. Then she set out for the village. She'd have a fine breakfast when she got there, and she wouldn't pay a penny for it. As for the bucket she'd thrown down the well, why, she'd have her choice of buckets.

Her first stop was the baker's shop. She's scowling, the baker thought, so it's Myrtle. He scowled right back.

"Give me three of your freshest muffins," Myrtle said.

"HE SCOWLED RIGHT BACK."

She has some nerve, the baker thought. Bossing me— What was coming out of her mouth? Ants! He grabbed his broom and swept them out of his store. He tried to sweep Myrtle out too.

"Cut that out!" Myrtle said. A horsefly flew out of her mouth. A bedbug climbed over the edge of her lip and started down her chin.

The baker swatted the fly. He kept an eye on the bedbug, so he could kill it as soon as it touched the floor.

Myrtle took the pen and paper out of her pouch. "Give me the muffins and I won't say another word," she wrote. "I also want a fourteen-layer cake. It's for my party tomorrow, to celebrate my fourteen-year-and-six-weeks birthday. You're invited. Bring the whole family."

The baker swallowed hard and nodded. "I'll come. We'll all come. We'll be, uh, overjoyed to come." He wrapped up his most delicious muffins. When he handed them to Myrtle, he bowed.

The fairy Ethelinda was getting anxious. Punishments weren't supposed to work this way.

⚘ ⚘ ⚘

Rosella tried not to talk while she got ready for her betrothal, but her Royal Ladies-in-Waiting ignored her if she just pointed at things. They didn't yell at each other anymore, because they didn't want Prince Harold to hear, but that didn't stop them from fighting quietly.

When Rosella said, "I'll wear that gown," two amazon stones and an opal fell to the carpet. And the twelve Royal Ladies-in-Waiting went for the jewels, hitting and shoving each other.

So Rosella took the gown out of the

closet herself and laid it out on her bed. Then she stood over it, marveling. It was silk, with an embroidered bodice. Its gathered sleeves ended in lace that would tickle her fingers delightfully. And the train was lace over silk, yards and yards of it.

"It's so pretty," she whispered. "It belongs in the sky with the moon and the stars."

Two pearls and a starstone fell into the deep folds of the gown's skirt. They were seen by a Royal Lady-in-Waiting who had taken a break from the fight on the carpet. She pounced on the gown.

The other Royal Ladies-in-Waiting heard the silk rustle. They pounced too. In less time than it takes to sew on a button, the gown lay in tatters on the bed.

Rosella wanted to scream, but she was afraid to. Screaming might make bigger and better gems. Then she'd have to scream all the time. Besides, her throat was really starting to hurt. She cried instead.

The fairy Ethelinda was getting angry. Rewards weren't supposed to work this way.

Six

Rosella didn't mean to, but she dropped jewels on every gown in her princess wardrobe except one. And her Royal Ladies-in-Waiting ruined each of them. The one that was left was made of burlap and it was a size and a half too big. It didn't have a real train, but it did trail on the floor, because it was four inches too long.

Harold met Rosella in the palace's great hall, where the Chief Royal Councillor was going to perform the betrothal ceremony. The prince thought she looked pretty, with her brown wavy hair and her big gray eyes. But why had she picked the ugliest gown in the kingdom? It was big enough for her and a gorilla. All he said, though, was, "You look beautiful, honey bunch. Are you glad to be engaged?"

Rosella didn't know how to answer. Being engaged wasn't the problem, although marrying Harold might have its drawbacks. The problem was the jewels.

"Did you hear me, hon? I asked you a question." He raised his voice. "Are you happy, sweetheart?" He cupped his hand under her chin.

Rosella spoke through her teeth so the jewels wouldn't get out. "Everybody wants me to talk, but nobody listens to what I say."

"I'm listening, angel. Spit it out."

"I hate wild boar, and I don't want guards to stand around. . . ." There were so many jewels in her mouth that one popped out, a hyacinth.

Harold put it in his pocket. The orchestra started to play.

She couldn't keep all these stones in her mouth. She spit them into her hand and made a fist.

"We're supposed to hold hands," Harold whispered. "Give them to me. I'll take good care of them."

What difference did it make? She let him have them.

The ceremony began.

⁂

Myrtle sat on the edge of the well to eat her muffins. After she ate them and licked her fingers, she headed for the stationer's shop. When she got there, an earwig and a spider bought her enough party invitations for everyone in the village. At the bottom of each invitation she wrote, "Bring presents."

She gave out all the invitations, and everyone promised to come. Then she stopped at the tailor's shop, where she picked out a gown for the party. It was white silk with an embroidered bodice and a lace train.

She was in such a good mood, she even bought a gown for her mother.

The fairy Ethelinda was furious.

* * *

At the end of the betrothal ceremony, the First Chancellor placed a golden tiara on Rosella's head. She wondered if she was a princess yet, or still just a princess-to-be.

"Some people want to meet you, honey," Harold said.

After a Royal Engagement, the kingdom's loyal subjects were always allowed into the palace to meet their future princess.

The Royal Guards opened the huge wooden doors to the great hall. Rosella saw a line that stretched for three quarters of a mile outside the palace. Everyone in it had something to catch the jewels as they cascaded out of her mouth. Pessimists brought thimbles and egg cups. Optimists brought sacks and pillow-cases and lobster pots.

The first subject Rosella met was a farmer. "How are you?" he said.

"Fine." A ruby chip fell into his pail.

That was all? His shoulders slumped.

Rosella took pity on him. She said, "Actually, my throat hurts, and this crown is giving me a headache."

He grinned as stones clattered against the bottom of his pail. Rosella asked him what he planned to do with the jewels.

"My old plow is worn out," he said. "I need a new one."

"Do you have enough now?" she said.

"Oh yes, Your Princess-ship. Thank you." He bowed and shook her hand.

Next in line was a woman whose skirt and blouse were as ragged as Rosella's had been yesterday. The woman wanted to buy a warm coat for the winter. Something about her made Rosella want to give her diamonds.

Rosella said, "Make sure your new coat is lined with fur. I think beaver is best." Diamond, she thought. Diamond, diamond.

But only one diamond came out, along with a topaz, some aquamarine stones, and some garnets. Thinking the name of the jewel didn't seem to make much difference. Anyway, the woman caught the stones in a threadbare sack and left happy.

A shoemaker came next, carrying a boot to catch the jewels. "What's your favorite flower?" he asked.

"Lilacs and carnations and daffodils." Rosella sang, wondering if singing would affect what came out—a diamond, a ruby, and a turquoise on the large side.

The shoemaker said he had been too poor to buy leather to make any more shoes. "But now," he said, "I can buy enough to fill my shop window."

Rosella smiled. "And peonies and poppies and black-eyed Susans and marigolds and—"

She was starting to get the hang of it. Long vowels usually made precious jewels, while short vowels often made semiprecious stones. The softer she spoke, the smaller the jewels, and the louder the bigger. It really was a good thing she hadn't screamed at her Royal Ladies-in-Waiting.

"That's enough. Don't use them all up on me."

Rosella wished Harold would listen to this shoemaker. He could learn something.

Even though her throat hurt, she enjoyed talking to everybody. She liked her subjects! But why were so many of them poor?

Next was a boy who asked her to tell him a story. She made up a fable about a talkative parrot who lived with a deaf mouse. The boy listened and laughed in all the right places, and caught the jewels in his cap.

She smiled bravely and said hello to the next subject. Her throat hurt terribly.

Seven

The widow Pickering loved her new gown. She tried it on while Myrtle tried on her own new gown. The widow told Myrtle that she looked fantastic. Myrtle wrote that the new gown made her mother look twenty years younger.

They took off the gowns and hung them up so they wouldn't wrinkle. Then Myrtle went out into the yard to experiment. She hummed softly. A line of ants pushed between her lips. She hummed louder, and the ants got bigger. Even louder, and the ants got even bigger. She'd had no idea there were such big ants. These were as big as her big toe.

Enough ants. Myrtle opened her mouth wide and sang, "La, la, la, la. Tra lee tra la tra loo." Moths, fireflies, and ladybugs flew out.

She hummed again. This time worms and caterpillars wriggled out. Hmmm. So she didn't always get ants by humming.

She tried speaking. "Nasty. Mean. Smelly. Rotten. Stupid. Loathsome." She giggled. "Vile. Putrid. Scabby. Mangy . . ."

They were crowding out—crawling, flitting, slithering, darting, wriggling, whizzing, oozing, flying, marching—escaping from Myrtle's mouth every way they could.

There were aphids, butterflies, mambas, lacewings, lynx spiders, midges, wolf snakes, gnats, mayflies, rhinoceros vipers, audacious jumping spiders, bandy-bandy

"THEY WERE CROWDING OUT—
CRAWLING, FLITTING, SLITHERING."

snakes, wasps, locusts, fleas, thrips, ticks, and every other bug and spider and snake you could think of.

Myrtle kept experimenting. She had a wonderful time, but she didn't figure out how to make a particular snake or insect come out. All she learned was that the louder she got, the bigger the creature that came out.

After about an hour, she had worked up quite an appetite. So she and her mother went to the village to have dinner at the inn. Dinner was free, because the innkeeper wanted to keep Myrtle from saying one single solitary word.

The fairy Ethelinda was scandalized.

⚘ ⚘ ⚘

During the betrothal banquet Harold noticed that Rosella's voice was fading. He noticed because all he got were tiny gems, hardly more than shavings. So he didn't make her say much. But he did make her drink wild-boar broth.

"It's the best thing for you, tootsie," he said when she made a face.

She gulped it down and hoped it would stay there. She picked at her string beans. "Why are your subjects so poor?" she whispered. A tiny sapphire and bits of amber fell onto the tablecloth.

Harold brushed the jewels into his hand. His betrothed was sweet, but she didn't know much. Subjects were always poor. "I wish they were richer too, cutie pie. Then I could tax them more."

"Maybe we can help them." A pearl fell into Rosella's mashed potatoes.

Harold dug it out with his fork and rinsed it off in his mulled wine. "Honey, you'll wear yourself out worrying about them. Take it easy. Relax a little."

She fell asleep over dessert. Royal Servants carried her to her bedchamber. But she woke up when the three Royal Guards took their places around her bed. Then she couldn't fall back to sleep.

Eight

Myrtle and the widow Pickering slept late the next morning. When they woke up, they strolled to the village. They stopped at the toymaker's shop for favors for the party guests. From the potter they ordered serving platters. The butcher promised them sausages and meat pies. By noon they had picked out everything for the party. Then they linked arms and sauntered home.

The fairy Ethelinda gnashed her teeth.

⚜ ⚜ ⚜

By morning Rosella's throat hurt worse than ever. She thought she had a fever, too. But her voice was stronger.

Breakfast was wild-boar steak and eggs. Before her Royal Ladies-in-Waiting had taken ten bites, Harold sent for her.

He was waiting in the library. As soon as she went in, she became very scared. There were thousands of books, but they weren't what scared her. She liked books. There were four desks. That was fine, too. There were a dozen upholstered leather chairs, and they looked comfortable enough. A Royal Manservant and a Royal Maid were dusting. They were all right.

The terrifying sight was the fifteen empty chests lined up in front of one of the leather chairs.

"Sweetie pie," Harold said. "Am I glad to see you." He led her to the chair behind the empty chests. "Wait till I tell you my idea."

Rosella sat down.

"Did you have a good breakfast, cuddle bunch?"

It hurt too much to talk. She shook her head.

Harold was too excited to pay attention. "Good. Here's my idea. You've noticed how old and moldy this palace is?"

She shook her head.

"You haven't? Well, it is. The drawbridge creaks. The rooms are drafty. The cellars are full of rats. The place should be condemned."

She didn't say anything. The palace looked fine to her.

"So I had a brainstorm. You didn't know you were marrying a genius, did you?"

She shook her head.

"This is brilliant. Listen. We're going to build a new castle. That's my idea. Picture it. Cream-colored stone. Marble everywhere. Hundreds of fountains. Taller towers than anybody ever heard of. Crocodiles *and* serpents in the moat. People will travel thousands of miles to see it. You'll be famous, sweetheart."

"Me?"

Harold caught the tiny ruby. "Yes, you. I can't build a palace on current revenues. We need your voice. The kingdom needs you. So just make sure they land in the chests, will you, sugar?"

She was silent.

"I know. You're wondering how you'll ever think of things to say to fill fifteen chests. That's why we're in the library. All you have to do is read out loud. Here." He pulled a book off a shelf. "This looks interesting. *The History of the*

Monarchy in the Kingdom of Biddle. That's us, love." He put the book in her lap. "You can read about our family."

She didn't open it. What could he do to her if she didn't talk? He could throw her in a dungeon. She wouldn't mind if he did. Bread and water would be better than wild boar. Then again, he could chop off her head, which would hurt her throat even more than it was hurting now.

"I know you're tired, darling. But after you fill these chests, you can take a vacation. You won't have to say a word." He got down on one knee. "Please, sweetheart. Pretty please."

He has his heart set on a new palace, Rosella thought. He'll be miserable if he doesn't get one, and it will be because of me. Rosella opened the book to the middle. I'm too kindhearted, she thought.

She started reading, trying to speak around her sore throat. "The fourth son of King Beauregard the Hairy weighed seven pounds and eleven ounces at birth. He had a noodle-shaped birthmark on his left shoulder. He wailed for . . ."

A stream of jewels fell into the chest. Harold tiptoed out of the room.

Rosella went on reading. "The infant was named Durward. His first word, 'More,' proved him to be . . ." She was freezing. She looked up. The fire looked hot. ". . . proved him to be a true royal son. His tutors reported . . ." The room was spinning. " . . . reported that he excelled at archery, hunting . . ." What was wrong with this book? The letters were getting bigger and smaller. The lines of print were wavy. ". . . hunting, and milit—"

Rosella fainted and fell off her chair.

The Royal Manservant and Royal Maid rushed to the partly filled chest. They each grabbed a handful of jewels. Then the Royal Manservant ran to find Harold, while the Royal Maid used her apron to fan Rosella.

"Wake up, Your Highness. Please wake up," she cried.

Nine

The fairy Ethelinda was appalled. This was the last straw. She had to do something.

Harold was in the courtyard, practicing his swordplay. She materialized in front of him. She didn't bother to disguise herself, hoping he'd be terrified when he saw the works—all seven feet three inches of her, her fleshy pink wings, the shimmer in the air around her, the purple light she was always bathed in, her flashing wand.

"You're a fairy, right?" Harold said when he saw her. He didn't seem frightened.

"I am the fairy Ethelinda," she said,

"HAROLD WAS IN THE COURTYARD,
PRACTICING HIS SWORDPLAY."

lowering her voice to a roar.

Harold grinned. "Pretty good guessing on my part, considering I've never met a fairy before."

"I am the one who made the jewels come out of Rosella's mouth."

Harold almost jumped up and down, he was so excited. "That was you? Really? Uh, say, Ethel . . . tell me, what did my sweetie pie do to make you do it?"

"My name is *Ethelinda*," the fairy boomed. "I rewarded her after she gave me a drink of well water."

"I can do that. That's a—"

"I'm not thirsty. Do you know that you're making poor Rosella miserable?"

"She's not miserable. She's a princess. She's deliriously happy."

Ethelinda tried a different approach. "Why do you want jewels so much?"

"You wouldn't want them?"

"Not if it was making my betrothed unhappy."

"How could she be unhappy? If I were in her shoes, I'd be delighted. She wouldn't be a princess today if I hadn't come along. She gets to wear a crown. She has nice gowns, Royal Ladies-in-Waiting. And me."

"You have to stop making her talk."

"But she has to talk. That's what makes *me* happy."

Ethelinda raised her wand. Prince Harold was one second away from becoming a frog. Then she lowered it. Her self-confidence was gone. If she turned him into a frog, he might figure out a way to make it better than being a prince. She certainly didn't want to reward him the way she'd rewarded Myrtle.

She didn't know what to do.

The Royal Manservant who'd seen

Rosella faint finally reached the courtyard. He ran to Harold.

Ethelinda vanished.

⚜ ⚜ ⚜

Myrtle's party started at two o'clock. The schoolteacher arrived first. His present was a slate and ten boxes of colored chalk.

Myrtle opened one of the boxes. She wrote on the slate in green and orange letters, "Thank you. I'll let you know when I run out of chalk."

The baker came next. His cake was so big that it barely fit through the cottage doorway. The icing was chocolate. The decorations were pink and blue whipped cream. The writing on top said, "Happy Fourteen-and-Six-Weeks Birthday, Myrtle! Please Keep Quiet!"

The whole village came. Nobody

wanted to take a chance on making Myrtle mad. The guests filled the cottage and the yard and the yards of the surrounding cottages. The widow thanked them all for coming. Myrtle collected her presents. She smiled when anyone handed her an especially big box.

The food was the finest anybody could remember. Myrtle ate so many poached quail eggs and roasted chestnuts that she almost got sick. After everybody ate, she opened her presents. There were hundreds of them. Her favorites were:

The framed sampler that read, "Speak to me only with thine eyes."

The bouquet of mums.

The music box that played "Hush, Little Baby."

The silver quill pen, engraved with the motto "The pen is mightier than the voice."

The parrot that sat on Myrtle's shoulder and repeated over and over, "Shut your trap. Shut your trap. Shut your trap."

The charm bracelet with the golden letters S, I, L, E, N, C, and E.

After all the presents were opened, everybody sang "Happy Birthday." Myrtle was so thrilled that she smiled and clapped her hands.

⁂

Rosella was gravely ill, and Harold was seriously frightened. Even under mounds of swansdown quilts, she couldn't stop shivering. She felt as if a vulture's claws were scratching at her throat and a carpenter hammering at her temples.

The Royal Physician was called in to examine her. When he was finished, he told Harold that she was very sick. He said her only hope of recovery lay in bed rest and complete silence. His fee for the visit was the jewels he collected when he listened to her chest and made her say "Aah" sixteen times.

Ten

Myrtle had a birthday party every week. She and the widow laughed and laughed at their silliness in wishing for jewels to come out of Myrtle's mouth. When Myrtle got bored between parties, she would speak into a big jar. Then she'd let the bugs and the snakes loose in the yard and make them race. She and her mother would have a grand time betting on the winners.

Rosella got better so slowly that Ethelinda's patience snapped. The evening after Myrtle's fourth party, Ethelinda materialized as herself in the widow's cottage. "I am the fairy Ethelinda, who rewarded your sister and punished you. You have to help Rosella," she thundered.

Myrtle sneered. "I do? I have to?"

A bull snake slithered under Ethelinda's gown. A gnat bit her wing.

"Ouch!" Ethelinda yelped.

"Be careful, dear," the widow told Myrtle. "You might make a poisonous snake."

"Yes, you have to help her," Ethelinda said. "Or I'll punish you severely."

Myrtle wrote on her slate, "I like your punishments."

"I can take your punishment away," Ethelinda said.

As fast as she could, Myrtle wrote, "What do I have to do?"

Ethelinda explained the problem.

"I can fix that," Myrtle wrote.

Ethelinda transported Myrtle to the palace, where Rosella was staring up at her lace bed canopy and wondering when her nighttime guards would arrive. As Ethelinda and Myrtle materialized, Ethelinda turned herself back into the old lady.

"I've brought your sister to help you, my dear," Ethelinda said.

Rosella stared at them. Myrtle would never help her.

Myrtle had brought her slate with her. She wrote, "Change clothes with me and hide under the covers."

Rosella didn't move. She wondered if she was delirious.

"Go ahead. Do it," Ethelinda said. "She won't hurt you."

Rosella nodded. She put on Myrtle's silk nightdress with the gold embroidery and slipped deep under the blankets.

Myrtle got into Rosella's silk nightdress with the silver embroidery.

Myrtle climbed into Rosella's bed. She sat up and yodeled, long and loud. A hognose snake wriggled out of her mouth.

Harold heard her, even though he was at the other end of the palace. He started running, leaping, and skipping toward the sound. "She's better! She's well again!" he yelled. And how many jewels did that yodel make? he wondered.

Ethelinda made the snake disappear. Then she made herself invisible.

"Precious!" Harold said, coming through the door. He dashed to the bed. "The roses are back in your cheeks. Speak to me!"

"What roses?" Myrtle yelled as loud as she could. "I feel terrible." The head of a boa constrictor filled her mouth.

Harold jumped back. "Aaaa! What's that?"

Rosella lifted a tiny corner of blanket so she could watch. The snake slithered out and wound itself around Myrtle's waist.

Myrtle grinned at Harold. "Do you like him? Should I name him after you?" Three hornets flew straight at him. One of them stung him on the nose. The other two buzzed around his head.

"Ouch! Wh-what's going on . . . h-honey pie? Th-that's a s-snake. Wh-where did the j-jewels go? Why are b-bugs and snakes coming out?"

This is fun, Myrtle thought. Who'd have thought I could scare a prince?

Poor Harold, Rosella thought. But it serves him right. He looks so silly. She fought back a giggle and wished she could make a bug come out of her mouth once in a while.

"I'm angry. This is what happens when I get angry." A scorpion stuck its head out of Myrtle's mouth.

"Yow! Why are you angry? At me? What did I do?"

"It's not so great being a princess," Myrtle yelled. "Nobody listens to me. All they care about are the jewels. You're the worst. It's all you care about, too. And I don't want to eat wild boar ever again. I hate wild boar."

The air was so thick with insects that Harold could hardly see. Snakes wriggled across the carpets. Snakes slithered up the sconces. Snakes oozed down the tapestries. A gigantic one hung from the chandelier, its head swaying slowly.

A milk snake slipped under the covers. It settled its clammy body next to Rosella. She wanted to scream and run.

Instead, she bit her lip and stayed very, very still.

"Sweetheart, I'm sorry. Forgive me. Ouch! That hurt."

Myrtle screamed, "I'M NOT GOING TO TALK UNLESS I WANT TO!"

"All right. All right! You won't have to. And I'll listen to you. I promise." Something bit his foot all the way through his boot. He hopped and kicked to get rid of it. "Everyone will listen. By order of Prince Harold."

"AND PRINCESS ROSELLA," Myrtle yelled.

"And Princess Rosella," Harold echoed.

Myrtle lowered her voice. "Now leave me. I need my rest."

Eleven

After Harold left, Ethelinda made the snakes and bugs disappear. Rosella came out from under the covers.

"Thank you," Rosella told her sister. An emerald fell on the counterpane.

Myrtle snatched the jewel and said, "You're welcome." She snagged the fly before it got to Rosella's face. Then she crushed it in her fist.

"You've done a good deed," Ethelinda began.

Myrtle shook her head. "Don't reward me. Thanks, but no thanks." She let two cockroaches fall into the bed.

Ethelinda asked if Myrtle would help Rosella again if she needed it.

"Why should I?" Myrtle asked.

"I'll pay you," Rosella said.

Myrtle pocketed the two diamonds. Not bad. She'd get to frighten the prince again and get jewels for it, too. "Okay."

Myrtle and Rosella switched clothes again. Then Ethelinda sent Myrtle back home. When Myrtle was gone, Ethelinda said she had to leave too. She vanished.

Rosella sank back into her pillows. She didn't want Myrtle to help again, or even Ethelinda. She wanted to solve the problem of Harold and his poor subjects all by herself.

⚘ ⚘ ⚘

Harold didn't dare visit Rosella again that day. But he did command the Royal Servants to listen to her. So Rosella got rid of her nighttime guards. And she had her meal of poached quail eggs and roasted chestnuts at last.

She also ordered the Royal Ladies-in-Waiting to bring her a slate and chalk. From then on, she wrote instead of talking to them. She was tired of having them dive into her lap whenever she said anything.

And she had them bring her a box with a lock and a key. She kept the box and the slate by her side so she'd be ready when Harold came.

He showed up a week after Myrtle's visit. Rosella felt fine by then. She was sitting at her window, watching a juggler in the courtyard.

"Honey?" He poked his head in. He was ready to run if the room was full of creepy-crawlies. But the coast seemed clear, so he stepped in all the way. He was carrying a bouquet of daisies and a box of taffy. "All better, sweetheart?" He held the daisies in front of his face—in case any hornets started flying.

He looks so scared, Rosella thought. She smiled to make him stop worrying.

He lowered the bouquet cautiously and placed it on a table. Then he sat next to her and looked her over. She seemed healthy. That silk nightdress was cute. Blue was a good color for her.

He hoped she wasn't feeling miserable anymore. Anyone who was going to marry him should be the happiest maiden in the kingdom. He still wanted her to talk up enough jewels for a new palace. Then, after that, he wouldn't mind a golden coach and a few other items. But he wanted her to be happy, too.

They sat there, not saying anything.

"Oh, here," Harold said finally. He held

"THEY SAT THERE, NOT SAYING ANYTHING."

out the bouquet and the candy.

She took them. "Thank you."

An opal hovered on her lip and tumbled out. Harold reached for it, but Rosella was faster. She opened her box and dropped in the opal. It clinked against the stones already in there. She snapped the box shut.

That was pretty selfish of her, Harold thought. He started to get mad, but then he thought of boa constrictors and hornets. He calmed down. "What's the box for, darling?"

"My jewels." A pearl came out this time. A big one. It went into the box too.

"Honey . . . Sweetie pie . . . What are you going to do with them?"

"Give them away. Your subjects need them more than we do."

"NO YOU DON'T!" Harold hollered. She couldn't! It was all right to give jewels away for the engagement ceremony. That was once in a lifetime, but she wanted to make a habit of it. "You can't give them away. I won't allow it."

Rosella wrote on her slate, "I'm trying not to get angry."

"No, no, don't get mad!" Harold started backing away. "But don't you want a new palace? I'll tell you what—we'll name a wing after you. It'll be the Rosella Wing. How do you like that?"

She shook her head. "This palace is beautiful. Look at it! It's wonderful."

All those gems going into the box! thought Harold. Wasted! If she gave them away, soon his subjects would be richer than he was. "Tell you what," Harold said. "We'll split fifty-fifty."

"I won't read a million books out loud just to fill up your treasure chests."

He counted as they fell. Two diamonds,

three bloodstones, one hyacinth, and one turquoise.

He sighed. "All right, my love."

"All right, my love. Fifty-fifty." Rosella wanted to be fair. He had made her a princess, after all.

They shook hands. Then they kissed.

Epilogue

Myrtle never had to come to her sister's rescue ever again. The fifty-fifty deal worked out perfectly. Harold got his new palace and golden coach, eventually. And Rosella was happy talking to her subjects and making sure they had enough plows and winter coats and leather for making shoes. Also, she built them a new school and a library and a swimming pool.

In time she and Harold grew to love each other very much. Harold even stopped trying to steal the jewels from Rosella's wooden box while she was sleeping. And Rosella stopped counting them every morning when she woke up.

Myrtle and her mother went into the bug-and-snake-racing business. People came from twenty kingdoms to watch Myrtle's races. They'd bet beetles against spiders or rattlers against pythons or grasshoppers against garter snakes. The widow would call the races, and Myrtle would take the bets. The whole village got rich from the tourist trade. And Myrtle became truly popular, which annoyed her.

Ethelinda grew more careful. Myrtle was her last mistake. Nowadays when she punishes people, they stay punished. And when she rewards them, they don't get sick.

And they all lived happily ever after.

The
End.

Rosella's Song

Oh, January is the first month.

Sing hey nonny January-o!

Oh, February is the cold month.

Sing hey nonny February-o!

Oh, March is the windy month.

Sing hey nonny March-o!

Oh, April is the rainy month.

Sing hey nonny April-o!

Oh, May is the lovely month.

Sing hey nonny May-o!

Oh, June is the flower month.

Sing hey nonny June-o!

Oh, July is the hot month.

Sing hey nonny July-o!

Oh, August is the berry month.

Sing hey nonny August-o!

Oh, September is the red-leaf month.

Sing hey nonny September-o!

Oh, October is the scary month.

Sing hey nonny October-o!

Oh, November is the harvest month.

Sing hey nonny November-o!

Oh, December is the last month.

Sing hey nonny December-o!

THE HACKER AND THE ANTS

Other Books by
Rudy Rucker

THE HOLLOW EARTH

THE HACKER AND THE ANTS

RUDY RUCKER

An AvoNova Book

William Morrow and Company, Inc.
New York

THE HACKER AND THE ANTS is an original publication of Avon Books. This work has never before appeared in book form. This work is a novel. Any similarity to actual persons or events is purely coincidental.

AVON BOOKS
A division of
The Hearst Corporation
1350 Avenue of the Americas
New York, New York 10019

Published by arrangement with the author
Library of Congress Catalog Card Number: 93-43500
ISBN: 0-688-13416-5

Library of Congress Cataloging in Publication Data:

Rucker, Rudy v. B. (Rudy von Bitter), 1946–
The hacker and the ants / Rudy Rucker.
p. cm.
I. Title.
PS3568.U298H33 1994 93-43500
813'.54—dc20 CIP

First Morrow/AvoNova Printing: May 1994

Printed in the U.S.A.

ARC 10 9 8 7 6 5 4 3 2 1

For Marianne von Bitter Rucker
August 22, 1916–July 14, 1991

Nobility and love: she never compromised.

ONE

The Dark Dream

MONDAY MORNING WHEN I ANSWERED THE DOOR there were twenty-one new real estate agents there, all in horrible polyester gold jackets. They came swarming in and scattered to every corner of my great dry-rotted California manse. Several of them had video cameras. What a thing to wake up to.

I'd been tenaciously renting the place for two and a half years despite the fact that the Indiana owner (a Mr. Nutt) continuously had it up for sale. I tried to make it hard for people to get in to look at the house, and even if an agent did manage to bring a client inside, the place had enough flaws (termites, bad foundation, bad plumbing) that nobody had wanted to buy it yet.

Sooner or later, each agent gave up, but then before long a new Realtor would stumble over the listing and come bustling in, eager to make a fat commission—perhaps as much as forty thousand dollars—by moving me out. The one here today was a frozen-faced five-foot-four yuppie blond. She'd been here before. Her name was Susan Poker and she was blandly bent on making my life so miserable that I would move out to make her activities easier.

"I appreciate your working with us on this, Mr. Rugby," she told me after herding her twenty-one agents in through my door. She wore a dark blue skirt, a frilly white blouse and, as a mark of rank, no gold blazer. She had a gold watch and small but heavy gold earrings. She stood on my front stoop, her sunglasses impenetrable in the bright April sun, her face a mask of peach and tan makeup with thin, bright red lips. She showed her joined teeth as a gesture for a smile.

If I describe Susan Poker so particularly, it does not mean that I found her attractive. My emotions toward her were the opposite of love at first sight. This feeling for Susan Poker was of such intensity that had it been love, I would have proposed to marry her. But as things truly stood, it was my fervent wish never to see her again or, failing that, to crush her like a bug.

Actually, I'd been feeling that way about lots of people lately. My wife Carol had left me two months ago, the bitch, and I was having trouble adjusting to life alone. One of our teenagers was at college, and the other two had gone with Carol, who was living with her boyfriend in a cheesy condo on the east side of the Valley. She had a job teaching English as a Second Language to Hispanics and Vietnamese. I'd kept the big house so the kids could still have their own rooms here when they visited or stopped by after school, but this weekend the two highschoolers had stayed with Carol, the brats. Being all alone, I'd hacked all day every day as usual. Sleep was the only slack I ever had, and Susan Poker had woken me up too early.

"Why did you bring so many agents?" said I, essaying a tone of testy befuddlement. "And why do they have cameras?" My personal robot Studly sidled up behind me to peer out at Susan Poker, and then whipped around to tag after our unwanted guests.

"Some of them are new," said Susan Poker. "We're using your property for training today. It could set off some networking. The property's been so terribly slow to move . . . I think heroic measures are called for. And the videocams? We want to get a data base so we can give browsers a virtual walk-through to decide if they want to view." Her well-shod foot tappity-tapped the metal lockbox that she'd recently bolted to the outside of my house, down on the ground next to my front door. "With the key in here, agents will be able to come and go when you're not home. We'll be as little bother to you as possible." She rummaged in her double-jointed beige leather purse and drew out a gold pencil and a small notebook. "What are your work hours? I want to put some times in the listing; times when you'll be out of the house." She poised her pencil and glanced up at me. "Another thought. If I can get it cleared with the branch office, I want to set up an Open House for as many Saturdays and Sundays of this month as you and I can handle." She scrunched her nose to indicate pluckiness.

"That's impossible!" I exclaimed. "It's all impossible. I work at home; I never leave. And I don't want Realtors letting themselves in. And as for an Open House . . . "

"Looky out back, Donny," yelled one of the novice Realtors, a lean bumpkin with a Western accent. "Thar's a crick!" Far from a creek, it was a dry gully. This overlaying of idiotic errors onto my own perceptual space was insufferable.

"I have a rental contract!" I shouted at Susan Poker. "If someone wants to come in here, they have to call me twenty-four hours in advance, and set up an appointment. It's in my contract! No exceptions!"

"Mr. Rugby, I'm friends with a young couple who are looking for a place to rent. If you're unwilling to cooperate, I'm sure I can move them in here." She turned huffily and strode to her idling Mercedes diesel, there theatrically to pick up her cellular phone. The really killing thing about this performance was that Susan Poker had not yet even talked to Mr. Nutt, the home's owner. She was a plastic-faced scavenger with no moral authority to harass me.

The voices and footsteps of the twenty-one new agents went on and on. Several of them handed me cards, gave encouraging winks, or tried to start conversations. Though but larvae and pupae of the species Realtor, they were frighteningly reminiscent of the adult vermin. Several of them commented on Studly the personal robot, marveling at his ability to follow them up and down my stairs. They'd never seen anything like Studly before, and no wonder, as he was an experimental prototype for a product that had yet to reach the market.

Finally the front door slammed and it was over, though two raggedly linked knots of Realtors lingered outside, chatting. I went and dead-bolted the doors, lest one of the agents get the house key from the lockbox and come back in.

I headed back toward my computer, located in the sun porch off the rear master bedroom. Time to hack some more.

My current job was with GoMotion Incorporated of Santa Clara, California. GoMotion got its start selling kits for a self-guiding dune buggy called the Iron Camel. The kit was a computer software CD that was like an interactive three-dimensional blueprint along with assembly instructions. GoMotion kit software used electronic mail to order all the parts you'd need, and it guided you step-by-step through the assembly, calling in registered building helpers if you needed them. Once you got the thing built, our kit would load intelligent software into the vehicle's processor board, and you'd have a dune buggy that could drive itself. Various models of the Iron Camel had sold one and a half million units worldwide!

GoMotion had hired me a year earlier to help develop a new product: a kit and software for a customized personal robot called the Veep. The preliminary design work was all being done in virtual reality; instead of building lots of expensive prototype machines, GoMotion liked to put together computer models of machines that could be tested out inside cyberspace.

My contribution to the Veep project was to use artificial life techniques as a means of evolving better algorithms for the Veep. The idea behind artificial life was to create a lot of different versions of a program, and to let the versions compete, mutate, and reproduce until eventually a winner emerged. In certain situations—like figuring out the best way to set a thousand nonlinearly coupled numerical parameters—a-life was the best way to go, although not everyone in the business believed this. I owed my job at GoMotion to the fact that Roger Coolidge, the superhacker founder of the company, was a vigorous a-life enthusiast, actively engaged in a series of experiments with electronic ant farms.

The robot Studly was the first physical prototype of a Veep that GoMotion had actually built. Studly was a joy to behold, a heartwarming payoff for all the mind-numbing hacking that went into making him happen. He moved around on single-jointed legs which ended in off-the-shelf stunt-bicycle wheels. There were small idler wheels on the knees of these legs, so that on smooth surfaces Studly could kneel down and nestle his body in between his big wheels, with the little knee wheels rolling on ahead. In this mode, he didn't have to waste compute time keeping his balance. Out in the yard, Studly would rise up into a bent-knee crouch, using arm motions and internal gyroscopes to steady himself. On stairs, the full glory of Studly's a-life–evolved control algorithms came into play; he would turn sideways and work his way up or down with his two wheels on different steps, using precise lunges and gyro pulses to keep from falling over. Depending on your mood, Studly's peculiar movements seemed comic, beautiful, or obscurely sinister.

As I sat down at my desk, I had a sudden vision of "giving" Studly to Susan Poker after programming him to chop her up and push her down her garbage disposal. The blood would be on Studly's manipulators, not mine. I tunelessly hummed the way I do when I think thoughts I shouldn't.

The phone rang.

"Hello, Mr. Rugby?" A woman's brisk, aggressive voice.

"Yes."

"This is Louise Calder from Welsh & Tayke Realty. Do you mind if I bring a client by in half an hour? They're quite interested in the property."

"I'm very busy today. I don't want to show the house."

The voice was instantly, unforgivingly venomous. "I'll pass that on to the owner, Mr. Rugby. Good-bye." She hung up and immediately the phone began to ring again. Friends of Susan Poker. While the phone rang on, I donned the headset and control gloves of my computer. The headset showed me the image of an office with a ringing telephone. I had a computer-generated body image in this virtual office, and the body moved around with the gestures of my control gloves. I flew across the office and pulled the virtual wires out of my virtual telephone. The ringing stopped.

My computer system was configured as a cyberdeck,

complete with two gray Spandex control gloves and a white plastic headset, all connected to the computer by wires. The system was almost top of the line, but not quite. If GoMotion had been willing to spend just a little more, my gloves and headset would have had wireless computer connections, so that I could move around more while using them.

But anyway. My computer would generate three-dimensional graphics that it could show from any angle, in stereo vision, by feeding pairs of images to the two electronic lenses of my headset. The headset had a microphone and speakers, also a sensor that told the system about my head movements so it could update the viewpoint.

The system let me feel as if I were inside a different space, the artificial reality of the computer. Most people called it cyberspace. Turning or moving my head would change my viewpoint; I could lean to one side and look around a nearby object. And the gloves let the computer generate real-time images of my hands. Seeing moving images of my hands in front of me enhanced the illusion that I was really inside cyberspace.

The simulated objects of cyberspace were known as *simmies*. My hand images were simmies, as was the virtual phone in my cyberspace office. As well as having a characteristic appearance, a simmie had a characteristic behavior—one simmie might sit still, and another might like to move around. The behavior part of a simmie could become so complicated that the thing practically seemed alive.

In cyberspace I could wrap my fingers around the simmies I found, effectively grabbing hold of them. And once I had hold of a simmie, I could move it about—unless the simmie happened to insist on staying in one place. When I would point and nod, my viewpoint would start moving in the direction I was pointing in. I would make a fist to stop.

But what was cyberspace? Where did it come from? Cyberspace had oozed out of the world's computers like stage-magic fog. Cyberspace was an alternate reality, it was the huge interconnected computation that was being collectively run by planet Earth's computers around the clock. Cyberspace was the information Net, but more than the Net, cyberspace was a shared vision of the Net as a physical space.

My illusion of being able to step right into cyberspace was made convincing by my headset's most excellent electronic lenses. The lenses were lumps of optical glass with funky-looking patches of plastic glued to them. The patches were rhodopsin-doped limpware goodies that worked as endlessly tweakable color monitors, labile as the chromatophores of a squid. The lenses' glass bent way around on the sides, creating peripheral vision and eyeball kicks from the anamorphic edge-scrunched images my computer would put out.

Whenever I put on the gloves and the headset, it was like being in a different room, an invisible secret room of my house: my virtual office. When I talked or made gestures in my virtual office, my computer interpreted me and executed my commands. The "pulling wires out of the phone" gesture I'd just made, for instance, caused my computer to shunt all my incoming phone calls to an answering machine.

My virtual office could look like almost anything—it could be a palace, an igloo, or a bubble in the deep blue sea. As it happened, I was using the default office pattern which came with my cyberspace software. The default office was really two-thirds of an office: it had one wall missing and no ceiling. One of the remaining walls was for doors to Net locations I often visited, and the other two walls were covered with pictures and documents that I either liked or needed to remember. Over my walls and in the far background I would see whatever landscape I was currently hottest for—in those days it was a swamp with simmies that looked like dinosaurs and pterodactyls. It was called Roarworld; I'd gotten it off the Net.

Each of the simmies in the Roarworld program had a bunch of software stubs to which the user could attach his/her own pieces of code, thus tailoring the Roarworld simmies' appearance and behavior. If you preferred it, you could have the Roarworld creatures look like lions and tigers, or sharks and dolphins, but to my mind the dinosaur graphics were by far the best. To make the simulation livelier, I'd linked the dinosaurs' legs to copies of Studly's control-feedback walking algorithms. My dinosaurs chased after each other really well. When I toggled on the mighty Roarworld sound module, it was more than awesome. GAH-ROOOOONT!

My virtual desk had a simmie keyboard and a mound of flat simmies of sheets of paper: letters and programs I was currently working on. If I wanted to revise a document, I just picked up its simmie, positioned it over the virtual keyboard, and typed away. My simmie keyboard was so sensitively tuned to my glove outputs that I only needed to wiggle the tips of my fingers.

When I was typing, an outside observer would have seen me madly twitching my fingers in the air. I'd gotten rid of my mechanical keyboard because I'd reconfigured my simmie keyboard to the point where it didn't closely match the dumbly obstinate geometry of the mechanical board.

Even though I typed in thin air, it felt as though I was touching something, for my gloves had tactile feedback. Woven in with the Spandex were special piezoplastic touchpads that could swell up and press against my hand. The touchpads on my fingertips pulsed each time I pushed down on a virtual key.

It was marvelous, but sometimes my hands missed the physical support of a keyboard. When I would hack a lot, my forearms would hurt and my thumbs and pinkies would get numb. I sometimes worried about getting carpal tunnel syndrome and losing my ability to type. For a hacker this would be like a trumpeter losing his or her lips. I kept meaning to get a wedge of malleable plastic in the shape of a keyboard. It was easy to get them, like at Fry's Electronics in Sunnyvale; they were called feely-blank keyboards.

You could get all sorts of feely-blank accessories for cyberspace, and yes, dear horn-dog, there were even male/female feely-blank love-dolls, complete with hinged limbs and cunningly engineered touchpads. The love-dolls came with get-down simmie software to show images that matched the doll's motions. If you wanted to spend a little more money, you could dial a 900 number for a live person who'd teleconference your doll through all manner of erotic outrages. But I hadn't looked extensively into the details of cybersex; when you were hacking as much as I did, you didn't want to be near a computer in your free time.

The two feely-blank things I actually owned were a potter's wheel and a weighted golf club handle which Carol had given me last Christmas. The club handle was short—so that I didn't smash everything around me while working my way down, say, the fabulous second oceanside hole of the Toshiba Cyberspace Pebble Beach. The clever thing about the feely-blank golf club was that the tip held a gyroscope which did a cyberized jiggly-doo right when I would hit the virtual ball—giving me the shock of contact.

The potter's wheel was for Carol, and for awhile she

had enjoyed using it. It was like a regular electric wheel, except that it had a permanent "lump of clay" which was made of firm, malleable titaniplast putty. They used the same stuff for the feely-blank keyboards; you could mold and remold it to any shape you wanted, and it never got brittle. I'd kept all the virtual pots Carol made in a file somewhere.

Anyway, I kept meaning to go get a fake keyboard, but physically going places and buying material objects for my computer was not something I was into. I mean walking into a place like Fry's Electronics was always a downer, everyone sucking down Jolt Colas and munching candy bars, no women in sight, just males—pitiful bewildered larvae from under a rock, or pompous bearded lawn-dwarves with tenor voices, or square-forehead Frankenstein monsters, or sweaty strivers with no fingernails—lumps and losers to a man. How had I ended up associated with this class of people? *Oh well*, as the California kids would say when something not particularly desirable happened. *Oh well!*

The two neatest things in my virtual office were my Lorenz attractor and my dollhouse. The Lorenz attractor was a floating dynamical system consisting of orbiting three-dimensional icons, little simmie images that stood for pieces of information or which represented things my computer could do. The icons tumbled along taffy trajectories that knotted into a roller coaster pair of floppy ears with a chaotic figure eight intersection. If I liked, I could make myself small and ride around on the Lorenz attractor in a painless demolition derby with my files. It was a fun way to mull things over.

My dollhouse was a special miniature cyberspace model of my house that I'd once made as a Christmas present for little Ida, but she'd never actually played with it that much—one reason being that I was hardly ever willing to let anyone else use my gloves and headset. I needed them all the time for all the work I had to do—always too much work!

I'd tweaked my real house's alarm system so that if anyone touched a door or window, the corresponding door or window would light up on the dollhouse. I had little models of myself and my family members inside my dollhouse. Actually my wife and three children shouldn't have been in the dollhouse at all anymore, as they no longer lived here, but it would have made me too sad and lonely to erase them. In my dollhouse, my wife was in the kitchen and my kids were lying on their stomachs in the living room doing homework and watching a tiny digital TV. If they'd actually been in my house, moving from room to room, the little simmie-dolls that represented them would have moved around too. My house was smart enough always to know who was in which room. The little virtual TV was hooked into the Fibernet system; sometimes I would make myself small and watch it with my dolls, though never for long. Everything on TV enraged me, because everything on TV was the same: the ads, the news, the shows. In my opinion, all TV was all part of the huge, lying Spectacle that the government kept running to oppress us all. Data compression had brought us a thousand channels, but they all sucked, same as ever.

The dollhouse's Studly-model *did* move around because he actually *was* physically in the house with me, rolling around and cleaning, gardening, keeping an eye on things, taking care of business, and occasionally talking to me. If I wanted to check something in the house, I could switch over to Studly's viewpoint, and see what he was seeing through his two video camera eyes. When Carol had still lived with me, I would sometimes use Studly to sneak in and watch her while she was dressing or taking a piss. That would drive her frantic with rage. "I know you're in there, Jerzy," she'd scream as oily Studly sidled up to capture her pixels and send them through the aether to me. "Get your head out of that computer and come talk to me like a human being!" Usually, however, I didn't have the time. When I was programming, I was always in a terrific rush.

Sitting in my office after Susan Poker left, it occurred to me that if I were to use Studly to kill the Realtor, I wouldn't really have to program him for it. It would be much easier to couple myself to his manipulators and drive him in real time. That was known as *telerobotics*—a person driving a robot that was somewhere else, with the distant person using television to "see through the eyes of the robot." Telerobotics was one of the most fun things you could do with a robot.

Tunelessly humming, I looked up from the dollhouse and stared at the images riding my Lorenz attractor. Most of them were quite familiar, but what with my hookup to the Net and the existence of some more or less autonomous processes in our company machines, I would sometimes spot a new icon. Today the new one was a little 3-D image of an ant, a sweetly made photorealistic model with mandibles, head, antennae, alitrunk, legs, petiole, and gaster—the spitting image of the virtual ants that Roger Coolidge had been working on in his lab at GoMotion. But no way were any GoMotion ants supposed to be loose like this. I pincered it up with virtual thumb and forefinger. It wriggled its legs and turned its head to bite me. The ant bite made a tingling physical flutter in my glove's touchpads. There was a noise with it, a double burst of skritchy chaos. I dropped the ant. Chirping angrily, it dug its way down through my virtual office floor and disappeared.

Instead of chasing after the ant, I pointed my finger to the GoMotion door and nodded in there. The necessary information traveled over the Fibernet and then for a moment I saw nothing but a snowstorm of static, as the GoMotion communication software checked my access codes. There was a warbling tone as our systems synced together, and then I walked into the virtual offices of GoMotion.

How did I look? Like most users, I owned a tailor-made simmie of my cyberspace body. Cyberspace users called their body-simmies *tuxedos*. My tuxedo was a suite of video images bitmapped onto a blank humanoid form. The form's surface was a mesh of triangles which could be adjusted like a dressmaker's dummy; and inside the form were virtual armatures and hinges so that the thing moved about as realistically as one of those little wooden mannequins that artists used to have. The overall size of the thing was adjusted to closely match my body size with, of course, a few inches taken off the waist.

I'd had my body surfaces taped by a professional body-mapping studio right there in Los Perros: Dirk Blanda's Personography. You'd go to Dirk Blanda's and in the reception area there was a wall with plaster body-shapes lined up against it. Mounted on the ceiling over each body was a video projector beaming a satisfied customer's image onto one of the body-shaped screens. Dirk Blanda's had started out as a photo studio, but when the last big quake had wiped out his building, he'd retooled and gotten modern. I actually knew Dirk fairly well as his house was almost next to mine.

The tuxedo I used was pretty routine; it showed me wearing what I usually wore in real life, which was sandals, patterned socks, shorts, and a California sport shirt. I could change the patterns of the fabrics of my socks and shirt, and if I wanted to, I could get new simmie clothes, or I could even turn my clothes off entirely. The nude version of my tuxedo allowed me the option of deciding whether or not my simmie-genitals should show. In any case, the face was the important part. I had a series of canned expression shots; Dirk's assistant had spent the better part of two hours coaching me into convincing expressions of laughter, surprise, boredom, anger, grief, etc. For casual communication, my software would guess at my expression from the sound of my voice. For higher-bandwidth communication, there was a pencil-sized video camera on my computer which could map real-time images of my face onto my tuxedo's head.

I came into the GoMotion reception area wearing an expression of controlled worry. The tuxedo of Leonard, the tech group secretary, looked up at me and activated a roguish-smile expression. Leonard had a damp mustache and a perpetual sunburn. His virtual office was a big loft with clean white walls and skylights showing fluffy clouds overhead. A simmie of Bengt, our virtual prototype for Studly's successor, was purring back and forth, pushing a polisher across the parquet floor. Bengt's neck was a bit longer than Studly's, and his body box had a slimmer shape. But for his legs he used the same inspired wheels-on-legs hack as Studly.

"Hi, Jerzy," said Leonard.

"Hi, Leonard. Say, I think some of our ants got loose. Has anyone else noticed?"

Leonard laughed merrily. In his tux laugh loop, he would always touch his tongue to his mustache at the right corner of his mouth, a tic which made him seem both puppyish and devil-may-care.

"Why don't you ask your bad rogue ant for some ID? Dereference a pointer or something."

"When I picked it up, it bit me," I explained. Leonard laughed the more wildly.

"It's not funny, Leonard. If the ant is eating and shitting and leaving trails, all my code is being corrupted. It's a wonder I can still see."

"I'd think you'd be proud of yourself. Roger's been promising us live ants for years, and now that you've been working with him, one of his ants has finally gotten smart enough to break out. Isn't that a good thing, Jerzy?"

"Is Roger here?"

"He's been in and out all weekend. Maybe he e-mailed you the ant!"

"Maybe." Sending an experimental artificial life-form out over the electronic mail Net would be an incredibly careless thing to do, but not wholly out of character for Roger Coolidge. He was a genius-level computer hacker, somewhat eccentric, and imbued with the self-confidence that came from having founded a Silicon Valley startup that had mushroomed to a billion dollars in revenue in six short years. It was an honor for me to get to work so closely with him. Sometimes it was also a pain in the neck.

I sighed, and my computer transmitted my sigh from my microphone to Leonard's receiver, wherever Leonard really was. Often he was physically at the GoMotion office in Sunnyvale, but several days a week he worked from his apartment down on Market Street in San Francisco. Maybe instead of wearing the gloves and the headset, he was watching me on a digital TV set, talking to me over a telephone, and moving his simmie with a video game joystick. For all I knew, looking at Leonard's brightly cheerful cyberspace simulacrum, he was spending the day in bed with a lover. It was no use speculating. "How's Bengt been doing? Has he banged into the furniture?"

"No. He's smarter than Studly. Look." Leonard scooped a handful of paper clips off his desk and threw them out in front of Bengt. GoMotion had modeled the laws of physics into Leonard's office, so the little paper clip simmies flew along naturalistic parabolas, bounced on the woodgrain-patterned floor, and skidded to rest.

Bengt had been down on all four wheels pushing his floor buffer, but now he rose up into an alert crouch, balancing easily on his flexed legs. After carefully looking around the room, Bengt wheeled over to stop a few inches from the nearest paper clip and unfolded his pincer-clamp manipulator. Delicately he tweezered up the paper clip and put it in a drawer in his chest. Moving with no wasted motions, Bengt worked his way around the room to pick up all the paper clips before he resumed buffing the floor. The less efficient Studly would have dealt with the paper clips in a one-by-one, piecemeal fashion as his floor polisher bumped into them.

"Right on," I said. "The improvements are thanks to genetic algorithms and artificial life, Leonard. I think Bengt's ready for Our American Home."

After one of our personal robot models could negotiate Leonard's virtual office, we liked to test it in a full-size simmie-house that we called Our American Home. We had simmies of a family who supposedly lived there: clumsy Walt and Perky Pat Christensen, with son Dexter and daughter Baby Scooter. They all had blond hair and texture-mapped tan skin, and they all bothered the robots in different ways.

Dexter liked to play pranks. He'd tip a robot over onto its back and drag it to the head of the stairs with a blanket over its head. Perky Pat would give the robots contradictory commands, "Now follow me, and stay right where you are. Hurry, dammit!" Baby Scooter was a sullen blob who would nap on the floor, waiting to see if a robot would bump her or nip her so she could scream bloody murder. Sometimes Walt got "drunk," and Perky Pat got "totally wired," and they would lurch and spazz around, doing their best to trip over the increasingly wary robot simmie.

The tests in Our American Home were crucial, as the possibility of personal robots injuring someone was the A-number-one factor that had kept them off the open market in the past. Although if there *were* accidents, GoMotion's position would be that they were only selling *kits* and software for the Veep robots—rather than the completed Veeps themselves. If your robot screwed up, it was your fault for having built it. So far this type of defense had held up against people whose Iron Camels had crashed. Our kits came with "no explicit or implied warranty of merchantibility or fitness for a particular purpose." Even so, the Veeps had to be very safe and very good if they were going to sell well.

My work at GoMotion was to try and use artificial life evolution techniques to improve the programs that controlled the Veep. Once we had the specs for a new prototype, instead of actually building it out of wires and metal, we would generate a simmie of the thing and test it out in cyberspace. Roger Coolidge had been one of the first fully to exploit this great corner-cutting trick. He had used it to design the Iron Camel. Being something of a bullshit artist, in the most Midwestern kind of way, Roger had dubbed his trick "cybercad."

CAD stood for *computer aided design*; most architects and engineers were using CAD instead of drafting tools. The idea behind CAD was to draw a three-dimensional computer graphical model of, say, a fan blade before you built it. Someone gave you a blueprint for a fan blade and you made a digital data base which in some sense *was* the blade. You could generate graphic views of it from every angle, zoom in on its details, take cross sections of it, calculate its weight and volume, etc. Cybercad meant pushing all this a little farther; in cybercad you could pump in virtual air, spin the blade, and measure the net blowage.

The funny thing about the "cyber" prefix was that it had always meant bullshit.

Back in the 1940s, the story went, MIT doubledome Norbert Wiener had wanted a title for a book he'd written about the electronic control of machines. Claude Shannon, also known as The Father Of Information Theory, told Wiener to call his book *Cybernetics*. The academic justification for the word was that the "cyber" root came from the Greek word for "rudder." A "kybernetes" was a steersman, or, by extension, a mechanical governor such as a weight-and-pulley feedback device you might hook to your tiller to keep your sailboat aimed at some fixed angle into the wind. The practical justification for the word was contained in Shannon's advice to Wiener: "Use the word 'cybernetics,' Norbert, because nobody knows what it means. This will always put you at an advantage in arguments."

When I wanted to get a feel for one of our Veep simmies, I would set my viewpoint so that I could see through the robot's eyes and move its parts with my own hands. I wore the robot-model like a tuxedo, and I drove the robot around in cyberspace houses. No actual robot and no actual house—just an idea for a robot in an idea of a house. I would try and figure out what was right and wrong with the current model. If I noticed a problem with any of the hardware—bad pincer design for instance—I would go into cyberspace and use a Makita Visual Regrammarizer to change the geometry and back-propagate the changes to make a new set of specs.

Once I had a good knowledge of the kinds of things a particular robot could do, I would pull back to try and write software that could drive it around without me being "in" it. And then, I might need to change the simmie to make it work better with the new software. This process would take dozens, scores, hundreds, or even thousands of iterations. The only way to make a profit was to do as much of this as possible in virtual reality. Cybercad!

Even with the use of cybercad, the process still wouldn't have worked if each iteration involved human judgment—for then it would have taken too long. So GoMotion was using artificial life techniques to make the evolution happen automatically. The way I'd applied this to the Veep was to look at the kinds of changes that the other programmers and I had typically been making to the code. I'd been able to cast our repeated program changes in terms of 1347 different numerical parameters that we were tweaking and retweaking. So now the problem of making a good Veep became the problem of finding good values for those 1347 mutually interacting numbers. To do this, Roger and I had run a process of simulated evolution on a population of a few hundred simulated Veeps that we'd installed in a virtual suburb of Our American Homes, each home with a different Veep but the same virtual family consisting of instances of Walt, Perky Pat, Dexter, and Baby Scooter Christensen.

Some of the badly parametrized virtual Veeps did things like get stuck in a corner and buff the floor so long in one place that they made a hole, or wander outside and get lost, or kill everyone in the house and burn the house down. These were parameter sets to get rid of.

Over and over the badly behaving parameter sets were replaced by combinations of the better-behaving sets, and after a quintillion machine instructions had executed we'd gotten a good design. Artificial life!

When GoMotion would get a combination of software and simmie that seemed to work well, they'd order up the parts and build a material prototype of the thing, like Studly.

Rather than keeping a big physical inventory of mechanical and electronic parts, GoMotion used Blackstone Hardware. Blackstone was a cyberspace hardware store with ghostly replicas of all available hardware components on its aethereal and all but endless shelves. *All available hardware*—from pinhead diodes to prestressed concrete bridge beams, from jackhammers to chip-etching lasers, from rubber washers to superconducting yttrium/iridium whiskers. It cost $1024 an hour to walk around in Blackstone's, but it was totally worth it. Access time was fast, since you would have a knowledgeable and attentive clerk-simmie at your elbow—and once you found the part you wanted, you told the clerk and Blackstone would express mail it to you on the spot.

The Blackstone clerk had whatever appearance you wanted: clean-cut college boy, overalled graybeard, bikini-clad calendar girl—there were about fifty choices. The clerk was a simmie being run by the Blackstone catalog software, though if you had a complicated question, a person at Blackstone would slip into the clerk simmie and talk through it as if it were his or her own tuxedo. You and your clerk could be visible or invisible to the other shoppers—as you liked. For reasons of industrial security, we at GoMotion always stayed invisible in Blackstone's, as did most other big companies' shoppers.

The man who actually built our physical robot models was called Ken Thumb. Ken was a slim blue-collar type; soft-spoken, brilliant, implacable. Before signing on as GoMotion's machinist he'd worked with the Survival Research Lab art/robotics group putting together big crazy machines out of parts he would find in abandoned factories and warehouses. You'd just about never see Ken in virtual reality. As someone who built real machines out of real parts, he had an irritated contempt for cyberspace.

It was a fact that cybercad designs did not always translate effectively from cyberspace to the machine shop. The cyberspace "physics" was, after all, only a limited model of Nature's true laws. Actual materials tended to have small nicks, resonant vibrations, casting strains, thermal noises, transient voltages, and various other sources of unexpected chaoticity. This meant that some virtual reality designs failed catastrophically when first incarnated by Ken. After he fixed the design, he would post scathing e-mail messages about what we had to do to bring our specs into line with reality.

"We" in this case was not so much me as it was Dick and Chuck, the thirty-year-old guys who did most of the nitty-gritty coding up of our Veep hardware designs. Dick was the Chief Engineer. He was pretty buttoned-down. Chuck was an insanely intense Florida country boy; every time I saw him he looked more gaunt. He was into hideously violent cyberspace battle games, Roman coliseum type matches, with full medical accuracy on the spurting arteries and severed bones.

Another person I was seeing a lot at GoMotion was Jeff Pear, the tech group manager. He'd shown up and started acting like my boss only a few months earlier, which was something I still kind of resented. I hated having a boss, any boss; it was even worse than having a landlord. Pear had bailed to GoMotion from a company that had gone bankrupt using the Lisp programming language.

The problem with Lisp was that it was not a close match for what was actually going on inside any real computer. There could, in principle, be a computer for which Lisp was right; some guy had actually designed a Lisp-based computer chip way back in the nerdly dawn of computation. Jeff Pear even had a big picture of the abandoned Lisp chip on his wall: his long-lost Promised Land. But here in the real Silicon Valley, there weren't any Lisp chips, and running Lisp on a real computer chip was like using a phrasebook to write a letter in Chinese to a friend who doesn't speak Chinese—and then having to mail a copy of the phrasebook with the letter. Running a Lisp program on a real machine meant doing that type of meaningless extra shit a few billion times a second.

The language that I and most other hackers were using was called SuperC. SuperC was an object-oriented extension of good old C, a concise language that was closely attuned to the architecture of the chips we were using.

For the true killer speed necessary to keep our robots abreast of real time, even SuperC wasn't fast enough. A big part of our Veep code was based on something called ROBOT.LIB, a library of machine-instruction–coded functions and utilities that Roger Coolidge had developed on his own. How Roger had managed to write such amazingly tight code was something of a mystery; it seemed superhuman, preternatural. Sometimes I briefly lost sight of the fact that my SuperC robot programs wouldn't have worked without Roger's ROBOT.LIB, but Roger was always ready to remind me of my oversight.

Jeff Pear was really into having meetings. At least once a week I was supposed to like physically drive to GoMotion and sit in some room with Chuck and Dick and Leonard and maybe Ken Thumb and a few others and watch while Jeff Pear drew charts on a whiteboard. A total waste of time, though I did enjoy talking to my coworkers before and after the meetings. The body has an atavistic need for physical interaction.

But let's get back to the day when Susan Poker woke me, the day when I first saw a cyberspace ant.

After talking to Leonard, I drifted past the mailboxes and on down the virtual GoMotion offices' hall. The mailboxes were buttons with people's names on them, and if I'd pushed the Jerzy Rugby button, I would have seen a representation of all the e-mail and cy-mail messages waiting for me—e-mail being plain text or data, and *cy-mail* being a talking video image, possibly interactive. But just then I was more interested in finding out about the loose ant.

Right near the mailboxes was the door leading to Trevor Sinclair, our man on the Net. He was physically at the Sunnyvale GoMotion office every weekday. Trevor kept our machines talking to each other, and to the world at large, usually using cyberspace to do it. His virtual office was a life-size model of Stonehenge, accurate to a tolerance of one millimeter. He'd gotten the numerical specifications from some Chinese anthropologists, and he'd gotten the stone's texture maps from a commercial computer compact disk called Rock.

There was a Wood disk too, by the way, and Clouds, Fire, Water, Skin, Metal—you name it, they were all in the Pixxy Textures Library, a data base of fifty CDs mounted on a rack which fit into a device known as a CD jukebox.

Trevor's tuxedo showed a good-looking man with short red hair and freckles. Trevor was one of the few people at GoMotion who was over forty like me. Despite his age, he was boyish in his enthusiasm for druids and magic. He viewed our work in cyberspace as a rehearsal for *true mastery*.

Trevor could phreak and cryp with the best of them.

"If I can physically get to a machine, I can always get in," he liked to say. "The secret of Net control is to come on like a physical presence." Here he'd pause and give a quiet chuckle. "Even when you're not there."

I found Trevor sitting on a wolfskin draped over a high plinth, ruminatively fondling the magic wand which he used instead of a mouse or a keyboard. Seeing me, he made a series of mystical passes with his hands. Simmies of lizards chased each other up and down the sides of the granite blocks.

"Thought for the day," said Trevor. "How many light bulbs does it take to change a light bulb?"

" ," I said, or mimed, rather.

"Aw, Jerzy, you've heard it before!"

"You've told it before. But listen: there's a loose ant in my system."

"Ow," said Trevor, and contorted his face into a hideous Punch-and-Judy grimace that grew and turned into the gargoyle at Notre Dame, into a cubic Julia set, and then into a cataclysmic explosion of knobby 3-D paisley. One of the fun things about talking to Trevor in cyberspace was that he made such great "faces." The paisleys spermed off, Trevor's normal body image returned, and his voice resumed.

"Let's assume the worst hasn't happened. Let's assume the ants haven't crawled out over the whole Net. I think that's a reasonable supposition, or we'd be seeing ants right now."

"Okay. But how can they be loose on just *my* machine?"

"If the ants can slave your display and drive your graphics output, that means they've established an Ethernet pseudonode with your address," said Trevor. "A virtual back-end server."

Half the time I didn't know what Trevor was talking about. But there was never any use in asking, because he would just come back with more of the same. When talking to Trevor, the only way to proceed was to keep plowing forward. "So how do you think the ants got on my machine?"

Trevor made a gesture with his wand, and a scrolling screen of system log info appeared next to him. He laid his forefinger along the side of his nose and studied the list. "I rather strongly suspect you've been hosed by the Founder himself," he said finally, with a bemused chuckle. "Roger Coolidge has been acting weird. More weird. He's been talking about an ant *eggcase*. His idea was to compile a virtual ant server, tar the binary with a bunch of self-reproducing ant programs, and compress the whole viral mess into a self-extracting program that fits inside a user's boot script. The log entries show that Roger accessed your boot script sometime last night. Some might call it an honor, Jerzy."

As well as working on the a-life evolution of better programs for the Veep, I'd been working with Roger and his electronic ants. Roger's interest in the ants had a different slant than mine. I liked artificial life because—like real living systems—a-life programs could do unexpected and beautiful things. The individual programs were what tended to capture my interest. Roger was more pragmatic. He was interested in using the GoMotion ants to model the dynamics of actual computer processes. When he did talk about science, he talked about things like species extinction and punctuated equilibria. In his home he had a large collection of expensive fossils that his wife had collected. The viruslike aspect of artificial life was also something that Roger had always found itchily fascinating.

I pointed my finger and flew through the wall of the ant lab at the end of the hall. The wall was made of industrial-strength cryp repellent updated daily by Trevor. Roger, Trevor, and I were the only people who could get into the ant lab. I expected to find Roger Coolidge's body image in there, but for now Roger wasn't there.

We'd been maintaining the cyberspace model of the ant lab so that it looked like a real bio lab, with a big black workbench, another bench full of tools, and a wall lined with cultures. We'd found that the most entertaining way to look at the ants was to let each colony drive a DTV chip to create its image.

Before going on, I have to explain about DTV, or *digital television*. The old analog TV standard had been known as NTSC. For years hackers had bitched that "NTSC" should stand for "Never Twice Same Color," meaning that the old images had a radically inexact relationship to the signals. At first, people had thought the next video standard would be a more detailed picture carried by a fatter analog signal. But the proposed analog signals started getting so fat that manufacturers had to invent ways to compress them. And then all of a sudden the compression algorithms had gotten so good that it had become possible to think in terms of using a digital signal for TV instead.

The difference between DTV and regular television was like the difference between CDs and the old LP records. You coded the information as zeroes and ones instead of as a wavering line. It took a shitload of bits to code a whole TV show, but if you had good enough data compression it turned out to be more efficient than broadcasting in analog. The only catch was that a DTV signal didn't look like anything on old television sets. To pick up DTV, your set had to have a DTV chip that could decompress the data and turn it back into uncompressed sound and pictures. It had taken a few years for the transition to happen, but DTV was the only kind of television around anymore, and DTV chips were cheap.

Getting his ant simulations to run on DTV chips had been one of Roger's unbelievable now-I-will-levitate hacks. But it worked great. Standing in the empty ant lab I looked at the wall of virtual screens showing ants—this was all taking place in cyberspace, remember, so the ants' DTV info was actually being routed into image-generation software that was being patched into the image which my goggles maintained. The ants looked more agitated than usual, and there seemed to be more of them.

All of a sudden something appeared in the ant lab with me, a figure that seemed to be Roger Coolidge in his usual tuxedo of gray pants and short-sleeved polyester shirt, looking at me in that moony, pop-eyed, passive-aggressive way he had.

"Hi, Roger," I said, but now his body icon broke apart like soft diarrhea and turned into ants, all the ants from all the colonies loose in the ant lab with me, mad ants filling the room and seething in the multiregime patterns of classical turbulence. My earphones blared skritchy chirping and my gloves' touchpads pulsed a weird vibratory massage. I was hallucinating a sharp shit stink off the ants. I was retching. I tore off the headset and the gloves . . . or I *thought* I did.

Two things that could keep a user from taking off cyberspace equipment were "voodoo cyberspaces" and "the dark dream."

A voodoo cyberspace had hypnotic flickering and rhythmic sound intended to numb or fascinate the user too much for him or her to want to leave. Voodoo cyberspaces were really a form of entertainment, not unlike commercials or music videos.

The ants were potentially good voodoo, much livelier and more realistically seething than any artificial life-form I'd ever seen. Some kind of radically emergent breakthrough in their behavior had happened over the weekend; they were a whole new clade. Good voodoo, but way too intense just now.

I thought I took my headset off, and I thought I saw it lying on my desk. I touched myself, I was fine, I stood up and pushed back my chair, I turned and leaned down and grabbed hold of my power cord and yanked it and saw the plug pop out of the wall, and saw the lights on my computer go out, and saw the little images in the headset on the desk wink out, and then I turned and walked toward the door and out of nothingness something plucked at my temple. Out of thin air, something tugged at the side of my head.

It was the cable that led from my headset to the computer. I was still wearing the headset, I now realized. *The ants had put me on the dark dream!* I tore off the headset and the gloves.

The essence of the dark dream was to make you *think* you'd taken off the gloves and headset when really you hadn't. It was like when your alarm clock goes off and you want to keep sleeping, so you dream you've woken up and gotten out of bed and turned off the alarm, and then you start dreaming that the continuing noise of the alarm is just something normal like traffic or a leaf blower or a backing truck's beeper.

Right before I thought I'd taken off my headset, the dark dream had shown me a perfectly taped and enhanced image of it happening, synced to my movements. It had tricked my hand-eye feedback loop, and like some defective robot, I'd failed to "physically acquire" the headset before I "took it off."

You probably think you'd never make a mistake like that, but just try perturbing your mouth-ear feedback loop with, say, a half-second delay. Read a sentence and heaheare ahhself rereading try pt-pt-ry to . . . When effects lag too far behind your actions, you enter a blithering state of confusion which cyberspace engineers call *feebdack*, with "feeb" as in "feebleminded."

I jerked my power cord out of the wall. In the dark dream, I'd gotten hold of it all right, but the cord was way longer than the dark dream had shown me, the cord had two coiled loops of slack under my desk and all I'd done was to straighten out a loop's worth while the dark dream showed the plug popping out of the wall and made the sound of the plug bouncing off the floor.

I ran down to the kitchen and got a drink of water just to feel something real, then ran back and made sure my machine was really off, grabbed my wallet, took my rack of backup CDs, stepped out of the house and, thank God, Nature was there. No machine's dark dream could hack the whole world.

TWO

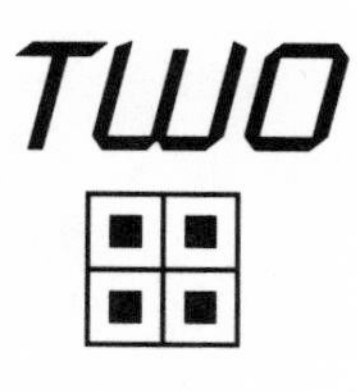

Gretchen

OUT IN THE WORLD, IT WAS HALF PAST ELEVEN O'CLOCK of a Monday morning, and there was a trail of real ants running across the porch step where Susan Poker had stood. I sat down next to them, catching my breath. Have you ever studied an ant closely? I sure have.

Front to rear, an ant's body has four parts: the head, the alitrunk, the petiole, and the gaster.

The head bears a pair of large hooked mandibles which have serrations that fit together like teeth. The mouth itself is a complex structure with two small pairs of feelers or palps, though you can't see the palps when the mouth is closed. The ant's two big antennae sprout right above the mouth, about where you might expect a nose to be, and the ant's great compound eyes are on either side of its head, posterior to the antennae. Most of an ant's "facial expression" comes from the way it holds its antennae. Each antenna is like a pennant on a stick; the "stick" is a long segment called a scape, and coming off the tip of the scape is a segmented "pennant" of eleven funiculi. When an ant is running along, it holds its scapes forward with the funiculi pressed down to smell out the territory. When an ant is alarmed, it holds its antennae up like a hunting dog's ears.

The alitrunk is the ant's walking machine: it's an intricate structure bearing three pairs of legs. Each leg has a thigh and shin, and attached to each shin is a thing like a foot, consisting of one long segment followed by four small segments and a terminal claw. The ants have wicked spurs near the back ends of their feet.

The petiole is small spacer segment between the alitrunk and the gaster, fitted in as neatly as the seat on a motorcycle. The petiole serves as a universal joint.

After the intricate machineries of the ant's mouth and legs, the gaster is a cheerful bit of comic relief; nothing more than a fat, elegantly shaped butt with a stinger and a cloaca serving as the gateway for the earth, air, fire, and water of the ant's excretion, smell signals, poison, and reproduction. Not that the gaster is a featureless balloon; no, if you look carefully, you'll see that the gaster is structured like a plant bud or a pinecone, it's made up of a series of overlapping plates capable of sliding enough so that the gaster can bend quite a bit.

The gaster contains glands that secrete poison. In order to repel enemies, some ants rear back and squirt out jets of poison. For closer infighting, ants inflict stab wounds with their poison-smeared stingers. Ant poison is a mixture of formic acid, neurotoxins, and histamines.

Ants' gasters also secrete pheromones, or so-called *semiochemicals.* These chemical signals can express alarm, a recruitment call, or a desire to exchange oral and anal liquid; pheromones tag the smells of nestmates and the members of the various castes; judicious sprays of pheromones serve as trail markers and as territorial boundaries.

Ants are cool. The motion of a trail is continuous as water flowing, but if you watch one particular ant, you'll see that she (the only male ants are the winged ones that appear for mating flights) does not, on the average, follow the main line of the trail she's moving along. Instead she meanders back and forth across the trail, occasionally breaking into fresh territory and then turning back. She rubs antennae with every sister she encounters. "Seen anything new?" "What's up?" "How do you feel?" "How're things back in the nest?" "Found any food?" "Which way are you headed?"

Back East, when I lived in a small Virginia town called Killeville, people had been like that, too, male or female, always stopping to chat and rub antennae. No way in CA. In California we drove around in our cars instead of rubbing antennae like ants. Rush, drive, work, and buy—with a cold smile and a hard laugh, a snarl and The Finger, with a shrug and a higher fence.

I put my rack of backup CDs in the trunk of my car. The backup was only a week old, so once the ants had been flushed out of my system I could start over. All my source code and programming tools were in there.

I figured the best thing to do right now would be to drive up to GoMotion and find out what had actually happened. On the other hand, it was a forty-minute commute each way, and I was going to have to do it again for Jeff Pear's weekly meeting on Wednesday—day after tomorrow. And, it occurred to me, if Coolidge was going to play tricks on me, why should I be in such a big hurry to report back in at *his* company? I decided to take the day off . . . but to do what? I stood there near my car, thinking and looking around.

My house's front yard was five steep feet of tough dirt with wizened shrubs. The street was Tangle Way, a looping blacktop two-laner that ran uphill and eventually back down. Our hill was called Polvo Para Hornear, a needlessly complicated name that at least wasn't religious, so far as I knew. There were so many Spanish and Catholic names in California that I felt like an immigrant and an atheist.

Numerous dead-end roadlets branched off of Tangle Way. Next to my house was the tiniest of traffic's capillaries, a dirt alley that led to one last house perched on the edge of the eternally dry gully behind my home. Old Mr. and Mrs. Toth lived there. Mrs. Toth was a New Age healer. She had a massage table in her front hall and she talked about the supernatural in a cozy apple-cheeked way.

Shortly after we'd moved in, Mrs. Toth had found out I'd been a math professor back East. She talked me into giving a talk to her "realization group," which met monthly in the community center. I'd spoken on synchronicity and Hilbert Space, an old interest of mine from grad school days. A few members of Mrs. Toth's group had been angered by my insistence that coincidences are explicitly *not* subject to control by human will. But in my opinion, the Beyond is out of our control, and ESP is a pipe dream for the powerless, an opiate pernicious as politics and TV.

Across the alley from my house was a heavily weathered Victorian inhabited by Krystle Kattle and her ratty Mom. The family had been there for decades; they were poor, and had always been poor, which made them a highly singular anomaly among Los Perros homeowners. The most striking feature of their blasted, filth-strewn lot was a parallelopiped-shaped garage whose angles were in the process of being slowly but radically sheared by the expanding girth of a hyperthyroid eucalyptus tree rooted in the lot between the Kattles and the Toths.

Krystle worked in a Western store selling boots, saddles, and fringed leather vests. She had a sometime boyfriend who wanted to be a biker. He was blond with a well-built steroid body. He, Krystle, Carol, and I had gotten drunk together on the lees of a keg left over from our housewarming party. Carol and I hadn't realized yet that in California you don't do casual things with strangers.

There were too many strangers. Now that I'd settled in, I always treated Krystle like a stranger, and I would never have spoken to a group like Mrs. Toth's. I was too busy, and I never had fun.

I decided that I *should* have some fun, that I should smoke some marijuana.

The house with the eucalyptus—the house between the Kattles and the Toths—was rented by Dirk Blanda, founder of Dirk Blanda's Personography, the bodymapping shop who'd made my tuxedo. Dirk often had some weed. I strolled over there to see if he'd get me high.

But Dirk wasn't home; his house echoed hollowly with the banging of the knocker. I went dejectedly back inside my house and looked through the packs of matches on my bedroom dresser; sometimes a matchbook would have an old roach tucked into the back. But I'd already searched the matches and scraped my drawer bottoms on my last free day, a couple of weeks ago, and there was no dope to be found. Not a roach in the house, not even a pinner.

Studly came into the bedroom, and it occurred to me that while I'd been on the dark dream, the ants would have had time to go across the radio link and to infect Studly. He acted like he was quietly dusting my furniture, but his photocell eyes seemed to glint evilly, and I had the feeling he was edging over to me. But surely this was only paranoia. Instead of turning Studly off, I spoke to him.

"Studly."

"Yes, Jerzy?" Studly had a pleasant voice thanks to his Talkboy chip.

"Do you know anything about the ants?"

"Last week, I put Grants For Ants ant poison packages near all the doors as instructed. I have not seen any ants in our house today."

"I mean ants inside my computer."

"Why do you say there are ants inside your computer, Jerzy?"

"I saw them in my cyberspace goggles. They're like a computer virus. Have they infected you, Studly? Do you feel normal?"

"My activation levels are all within the customary ranges. Do you think the ants have infected me?"

"I guess not. Go to living room and wait for me there. Stay idle."

"I can dig it."

When I had nothing better to do, I was always programming new catch phrases and response tricks into Studly, which made talking to him mildly entertaining.

"Was there anything else, Studly?"

"Yesterday you were talking to yourself and you said *I want Carol back*, Jerzy. Can you comment on that?"

This seemingly thoughtful hedge was from the dinosaur days of artificial intelligence programming. You have your device keep a list of all the things it hears you say and then every so often the device builds a sentence of the form: *Why did you say (quote-past-statement), (user-name)?* It was a cheap trick, but it set me off, just like it was supposed to.

"I do want Carol back, Studly. But I'm also glad she's gone. We were fighting all the time, don't you remember? Are you going to be like the kids and keep trying to get us back together? Face it Studly, you're a poor robot from a broken home. Go on into the living room and stay out of trouble now, will you?"

The Studster went.

It was so quiet in my big, empty house. I wandered back into my machine room. My unplugged computer was dark and silent. I pulled my phone jack out of the computer and plugged it directly into a Fibernet wall plug. Hallelujah, a dial tone.

I got out my address book. I sometimes scored pot from a hippie woman my age named Queue Harmaline. She and her permanent boyfriend Keith lived among redwoods on the wet western slopes of the Santa Cruz mountains. Queue and Keith made a living producing digitized tapes and films of various hip events. Queue usually had a good stash of primo sinsemilla. Although she was not a dealer, if I begged hard enough, she could normally be prevailed upon to sell me a bit of her hoard.

Since Queue wasn't really interested in selling off her pot to me, the price was high, but a quarter ounce of the stuff was strong enough to last me for months, unless I got reckless. Also, I always enjoyed having a chance to visit with Queue. She was slim and dark and hip and she laughed a lot.

It was important to call in advance if I wanted to try to get pot from her. Queue hated to go into her stash with anyone around. Once I'd shown up without warning and she gave me a tongue-lashing and then subjected me to a forty-minute wait while she did four other things at once. Finally, after taking $160 off me, she'd put me outside on the deck while she scampered up and down the three levels of her house like a squirrel, pausing here, pausing there, so that finally I could make no estimate of where in the house she found the anorexic rolled-up baggie she ultimately granted me. That's how I'd learned always to call.

More often than not, Queue and Keith let their scratchy answering machine take messages they never listened to, but today, for a wonder, Queue was right there.

"Media Molecules." That's what she called her tape business.

"Hi, Queue, this is Jerzy. I wonder if I could score a tape off you today." One of *anything* was our code word for a quarter ounce.

"Mm-hmm. The usual. How come you never call unless you want something, Jerzy? And what about you and Carol?"

"She hasn't come back."

"Didn't you say you and Carol were going to try counseling?"

"It didn't work. It made things worse. The counselor was a woman, and Carol thought she was taking my side. The concept is that the counselor is a neutral referee, right, and you can both say anything you want, but then when she asks follow-up questions you can tell whose story she's buying into. The counselor bought into my story even though I'm wrong."

"Why are you always so *down* on yourself, Jerzy?"

"I had an unhappy childhood. My wife hates me. And I've sold my soul to the machines." I always felt like I could say just about anything to Queue. Her ready laughter was a stifled chirp phasing into a tinkling giggle.

"How's your big job at GoMotion? Is that still happening?"

"We're designing a line of personal robots in cyberspace. It'll be called the Veep. We made a prototype of the first one, and it cleans my house. But now my computer's messed up. Something really strange happened today. You don't know about *the dark dream*, do you, Queue? It's when you think you've left cyberspace and you're still in it. That happened to me today."

"On the computer? Was it fun? I've had things like

that happen to me with . . . in certain situations. Levels of reality?" She was talking about psychedelics, but she never ever mentioned drugs on the phone.

"No, no, it was horrible. I was walking across the room away from my machine and then something tugged at the side of my head and it was the cable to my goggles. I thought I'd taken them off and I was still wearing them. It was pure disorientation. The ants did it to me. I think there's a virtual server that lets them get into my machine."

"You have a computer virus?"

"I have *ants,* Queue. They're a new thing you've never heard of. They're much smarter than a virus."

"You're so cutting edge, Jerzy. That's what I like about you."

"So okay, Queue, I'm coming right up for that tape. Is Keith around? What with Carol gone I'm highly available."

She lowered her voice. "I can't. Keith is very jealous, and he's the one I've taken *on.*" Queen Queue owned her house and kept Keith as her Prince Consort. "I would never fool around unless it was for real."

"This isn't for real, Queue. I'm only after some human warmth."

"We'll only be here for another two hours." Queue and Keith are always taking trips in their camper van. "We have to record Brian Jones drumming congas at the Hindu Center."

"Brian *Jones?* Is he like an Elvis imitator?"

Temple-bell laughter. "It's his real name. And, Jerzy, when you come up, bring some show-and-tell. You said you have a working robot? A Veep?"

"Uh . . . yeah. His name is Studly. But—"

"Studly!" More chirp-giggle laughter. "You are such a crazed sick computer jock, Jerzy. Bring Studly and don't be a tight-ass! Can he vacuum my floor?"

I thought of Queue's house with its narrow staircases and lumpily layered rugs. "Well, maybe. We'll see."

"All right! *Bah.*" Queue had her own hip, dynamic way of saying *bye*, a plosive, husky sound.

I went out to the living room.

"Follow me out to the car, Studly."

"Yes, master."

He trundled after me to the car, and once I had the trunk open, Studly went and stood sideways to it. I pushed my rack of backup CDs to one side so they'd be out of Studly's way.

"Okay, Studly, get in."

Studly pushed both legs out to their full extension, and then quickly retracted the leg on the side toward the trunk. As he began falling toward the trunk, he snapped up his other leg, and fell sideways into the trunk, breaking his fall with his humanoid hand. He shifted himself into a comfortable position.

"You wait in there, Studly, and I'll drive you to visit a friend. Her name is Queue."

"Right on, Jerzy."

I closed the trunk and got in my car with a fine sense of purpose. I'd grab a snack, go to the bank, get gas, hit the freeway, and be at Queue's in an hour. It would be fun to see her and Keith. If it weren't for having to buy pot every now and then, I'd never go anywhere except GoMotion and the supermarket. In today's America, the many positive aspects of recreational drug use are too often ignored. The need to score gets the user out of his or her house and into the sunshine—out into the community and meeting people! Drugs are about networking!

My car is an Animata Benchmark. It's the only really expensive thing I've ever owned. Driving it makes me feel good. I got it after my first year out here. Tooling slowly through the streets of my yuppie village of Los

Perros, I marveled as always at the massive number of good-looking women to be seen in California. It was a brilliantly sunny April day with the air clear and cool as water—the kind of day you'd remember as "the best weather of the year" back East, a day when you could slowly windmill your arms in the sweet air and feel yourself to be swimming. Days like this come thick as pearls on the California year's necklace.

A crowd of people in Spandex stood in front of the Los Perros Coffee Roasting Company, taking the air and enjoying each other's company, some of them planning or returning from a jog along the Dammit Trail that leads up along Route 17 to the all but dry Hidalgo Reservoir.

When Carol and I moved to California, I was an unemployed mathematics professor, and I'd felt a disenfranchised academic mouse's contempt for the Los Perros yuppies with their good cars, fit bodies, and standoffish demeanor.

Cars? My maroon Chevy Caprice whale wagon had been a damned fine car back in Killeville, Virginia, where Carol and I bought it used for $8,000. It was the only car we'd brought across the country with us, but in Los Perros, the whale hadn't been any kind of a car to be proud of at all. We'd darted our heads around spotting BMWs, Mercedes, Porsches, even Ferraris and Lamborghinis, cars insanely out of our price range. For our second car we came up with $4K and bought a six-year-old Honda Accord, thinking *at least now we're fuel efficient!* Then I'd gotten the GoMotion job and the Animata.

Yes, instead of remaining angry embittered losers, Carol and I had gotten job skills and turned that shit around. We'd gotten the bucks and become Californian and had no problems with drinking coffee at the Los Perros Coffee Roasting Company. It wasn't snooty in there, it was civilized and practical—in the manner of a European cafe and in the manner of a McDonald's—in the California manner, in short, and Carol and I were now at ease there. We were Californians: fit, in a hurry, making good bread, and with serious problems that we were beginning to try to learn to deal with.

The light was red, and I sat there in my Animata, with my windows and sunroof open, looking at all the beautiful women. I had a severe horn. It had been five weeks. Things change when you go so long without the cheering contact of another human's fluids and skin. Crossing the street were a pair of twin young mothers pushing identical light blue strollers, each stroller holding a pair of twins. Six people! Were they models, come to profit in California? Mentally I selected a cube of space around one of the women, deleted her from the street, and inserted her into my head's own seraglio, nude and chatty.

A joyfully chic Mexican woman with a high-fashion straw hat crossed next. She gazed at me evenly, smiled—and kept walking, right into the Roasting and right out of my life. In California you often see people that you never see again.

Here came a girl in stiff, poured-on jeans, her fluffy mass of combed curly hair formed into a huge ponytail resting on her back. With a barrette at either end, her ponytail had the shape of a great, thick jouncing cigar, which contrasted nicely with the sharply cut lines of her hips in their covering of thick, furrowed denim.

A plucky nineteen-year-old with dark eyebrows and a clean-cut nose appeared with two friends. Her mouth was lively, seductive and ironic, with narrow dark lips, crisply edged.

Right outside my car window sat a woman on the wide wall of the planter before the Roasting's storefront. She wore a tasteful sweater of large argyle diamonds, her bell of hair was streaked and set just so, her soft face was womanly, yet childishly pert—I guessed she was a dissipated California Girl who had divorced or never married. She looked like Carol, only more symmetrical, ten years younger and ten pounds lighter. Suddenly I realized she was staring back at me. The light changed. Behind me was a Mercedes driven by a blond-bobbed woman in white silk, diamonds, and gold.

Turning the corner onto Santa Ynez Avenue, who should I see before the office of Welsh & Tayke Realty but Susan Poker, animatedly talking to a stocky woman with a portable phone and a black leather purse yet larger than Susan Poker's. The stocky woman had shiny skin, short hair, and an expensive suit cut from folk-art fabric. Susan Poker was holding a sheaf of papers and acting extremely friendly, punctuating her remarks with many smiles and nods. *Zzzt,* I thought, mentally zapping her out of existence. *ZzzzzzZZTT!*

I parked behind the bank and walked half a block to a croissant bakery to grab some lunch. The bakery was run by a Vietnamese family, and I was half in love with a girl who worked behind the counter. Her name was Nga Vo.

Nga was taut and young, dressed always in black, with long hair worn poufed way up on one side. She had quick sneaky eyes that could narrow down to upcurved slits. She had a full, pouty, red-lipsticked mouth made yet more perfect by a roughness in the line of her left upper lip. I wanted to kiss and kiss that lip. She had a soft clean jawline and a weak yet stubborn chin, a California Girl chin. Beneath her face's pale skin was an intricately expressive play of muscles: now molding a fleeting chipmunk cheek, now forming a quick corrugation across her sweet brow. When Nga wrote out a sales check, she would rest her hand on a piece of paper she'd folded in four out of some ritual of Saigonese penmanship. Every time I talked to her, I did my best to stretch out our conversation.

"A medium roast beef croissant," I said to Nga. "And a seltzer, please."

"Yes," said she. "Six forty-nine. How you doing today."

"Fine." I wanted to say so much more. *How did you and your family escape from Vietnam? Do you like life in America? Do you have a boyfriend? Could you ever be attracted to a Western man? Will you move in with me?* "It's such nice weather," I added breathlessly, as she counted out my change. "I hope you don't have to work all day?"

"I here till six o'clock closing time." Nga gave a quick laugh, breathless as a sob.

"Would . . . would you like to have dinner with me?" Yes! I'd finally said it!

Nga looked at me blankly. "What do you mean?" Her mother and aunt were watching us now, and the pushy pig behind me in line cleared his throat preparatory to placing his order.

"A date for dinner. You and me."

Nga slid her eyes to one side and spoke in rapid Vietnamese to her mother. Her mother gave a very brief answer. Nga cast her eyes down.

"I no think so."

Wearing a numb, frozen smile, I took my soda and sandwich outside to sit down at one of the bakery's sidewalk tables. From inside came the chatter of Vietnamese voices. I swallowed the food too rapidly and it made a big painful lump in my throat. I was fat and old and crazy and nobody would ever love me again. Were those tears in my eyes?

A Vietnamese boy came out to clear the tables. He giggled when his eyes met mine.

"Are you Nga's brother?" I asked desperately.

"She my cousin." He nodded his head towards the bakery. "My name Khanh Pham. Nga say you ask her go on dinner date."

"Yes," said I. "Just to talk."

"In traditional Vietnamese date, boy must come visit girl family. Maybe you visit us, then Nga go on dinner date."

"Uh . . . where do you live?"

"On East side."

God. What if some of the Vo family were Carol's students? I glanced down at my left hand, noticing the dent where my wedding ring had lived so many years. Asking Nga Vo for a date had been a stupid idea.

"Here our address," said the boy, handing me a neat square of paper inscribed with Nga's fine script. "Bakery close every Tuesday. Maybe you come visit tomorrow."

My breath rushed out of me. "Yes. Yes, I will come!"

When I finished eating I took my paper plate and my seltzer bottle back. Nga's mother, aunt, and cousin were there, with her father in the hallway out back. Nga slipped me a couple of bold, sneaky glances. "See you tomorrow!" I sang out.

The trees along Santa Ynez Avenue were blooming: bottlebrushes with cylindrical flowers made up of red bristles, catalpas with pendulous racemes of two-toned lavender flowers, and mimosas thick with tiny, sweet-smelling yellow blooms. Most of the fabulous plants in California are imported exotics. I wondered if the woman who reminded me of Carol was still at the Coffee Roasting. Now that I'd worked up the nerve to approach Nga, I felt brave enough to talk to anyone.

I put my card into the bank's outdoor teller machine and pushed the buttons to get $200 in cash out of our checking account. UNABLE TO PERFORM THE REQUESTED TRANSACTION AT THIS TIME, read the machine's little screen. PLEASE REMOVE CARD. I removed it and started over, this time trying to take the money out of the savings. Still no go. Had Carol—I reinserted the card and checked the balances of our checking and savings accounts. The balances were, respectively, $0.00 and $26.18. When our checking account runs short, money is transferred automatically from the savings. Carol had cleaned us out by writing too many checks. I seemed to remember her having mentioned something about having to pay the car insurance bill. I hadn't realized it would come to so much.

I took the last whole $20 out of our savings and put it in my wallet, which gave me $34 dollars in all. Today was Monday, April 27, which meant GoMotion wouldn't transfer my pay till like Friday. I was going to have to go all week on $34? And how was I going to get that pot from Queue? No way she'd take a check. Maybe I should pocket the weed and then pretend I'd forgotten my wallet? Being broke on top of being separated made me feel totally reckless. My mind flashed back to the bell-haired woman in the argyle sweater at the Roasting. I decided to hustle back there and try to talk to her before I did anything else.

I went down back streets the two blocks to the Roasting and yes, yes, the bell-haired woman was still there, sitting with the artsy-craftsy phone-toting woman I'd seen talking to Susan Poker before. But, despite her company, the bell-haired woman was definitely the type for me.

She had slightly stunned eyes and a plumpness in her neck beneath her chin. She was like someone's sexy Mom, and I was old enough to be Daddy. I got a coffee with sugar and cream, sat down on a bench near her, and looked at her anew with each sip of my coffee. She noticed, she looked back at me, she looked again, our eyes met, and I smiled. Smoothly and deliberately, she stuck out her tongue and pressed it tight against her upper lip. Definitely a signal. In the past, women had occasionally given me such come-ons, but as a cautious married man I'd always passed them up. Today things would be different. I stood up and I walked over to her. I felt light-headed; my blood was pounding in my ears.

"Hi," said I. "You're really pretty."

She laughed softly. "I was hoping you'd talk to me. Where are you from?"

"I live right here in Los Perros. My name's Jerzy?" I stuck out my hand. She took it lightly. The touch of her hand was firm and warm.

"I'm Gretchen. And this is my friend Kay." I nodded to stocky Kay and concentrated on Gretchen.

"What kind of work do you do?" asked Gretchen.

"I'm a computer programmer. I'm helping to design a personal robot. We're going to call it the Veep. Like vice president?"

"Oh." Gretchen turned and said something to her friend. "Do you work in an office?"

"No, I work at home. I'm all alone there. My wife left me six weeks ago."

Gretchen looked very interested. "Are you planning to sell the property?"

"Don't tell me you're a Realtor!"

"I do a variety of things," she said, her calm California eyes drilling into mine. Again she did that thing with her tongue.

"Would you like to come up to my house and look around?"

"Sure," said Gretchen. "Why not."

She talked some more with Kay, tying up loose ends,

and then she walked slowly with me to my car and got in. Close up, she had tired eyes.

"Do you want anything?" I asked Gretchen.

She looked languidly greedy. "How about some fine wine? And two packs of Kents."

The two crazy liquor store clerks were behind the counter, the thin giggling bearded one and the bowling pin–shaped one with the mustache. One of the nice things about California was how many workaday jobs were held by freaks. I got a bottle of good chardonnay and the Kents. It came to thirteen dollars and change. And then I was back in the car with Gretchen. This beautiful new woman was sitting in the bucket seat of my Animata, looking at her makeup in the mirror on the visor, fixing her face with the calm seriousness of a grown woman, her actual soft butt on the real leather of my car.

"I'm stoked," said I. "I'm ready to party."

Gretchen smiled. "I'm eager to see your house." Again I studied her eyes. They were blue and . . . blank?

"I can show you my computer."

"Yippee," said Gretchen softly, and lit a cigarette. "I failed math in high school."

"Are you from around here?"

"No, I'm from the Southland. Buena Park?"

"That's near LA?"

"Not far from Disneyland. That used to be my summer job."

"You worked in *Disneyland?* Wow. Talk about a real Californian. What did you do?"

"My last summer there I got to be Alice in Wonderland. In the parades?"

"God, Gretchen, that's heavy. Did the men ever hit on you?"

"The single Dads. You had to look out for them. If

they got too insistent, I'd look at Baloo Bear a special way, and he'd talk to them."

"I'm a single Dad, Gretchen." I laid my hand on her leg above the knee. She regarded me calmly, not moving my hand away.

A few minutes later I was back in my driveway. It was quarter past one. Though my oldest daughter Sorrel was off at college, son Tom and daughter Ida were still students at Los Perros High. They usually stopped by around three-thirty to regroup before heading across town to Carol's. That gave Gretchen and me two clear hours.

"Nice big place," said Gretchen. "Do you own it?"

"I rent." A wrong answer. I was tracking Gretchen's interest level as closely as an over-leveraged speculator watching the price of gold. I hurried to get the door open. Gretchen ambled in slowly.

"Where's the powder room?"

"Right over there. I'll open the wine."

I went down to the kitchen and poured two glasses of wine. Glasses which Carol had bought in Mexico two years ago. I tore my thoughts away from that. *Don't stop to think, Jerzy, just do!*

Gretchen was pacing around the living room, looking unexpectedly dynamic. "I love your things, Jerzy. All those seashells. Want to show me around the rest of the place?"

"Sure, Gretchen, I'd love to." Graciously she took her wineglass, clinked it with mine, and gave a simpering, slightly naughty giggle. Who said middle-aged people couldn't still have fun? I led her off on the house tour.

Our big old two-level house had a linoleum kitchen and dining area downstairs. At one end of the upstairs was a low-ceilinged living room with redwood paneling. A long hall ran along the front of the house from the living room to the other end of the house. The kids' three bedrooms were off the long hall, and at the end of the hall was my (and formerly Carol's) bedroom, a nice space that boasted a sun porch and a working fireplace, no less.

"What are those gloves and goggles," Gretchen asked me when we reached the sun porch. "Were you and the wife into bondage?" She laughed softly and took a sip of her wine.

"I work in virtual reality," I told her. "Cyberspace?"

Gretchen looked enthusiastic. Cyberspace was getting more popular every day. "That's great! Can I try?"

A wave of horniness engulfed me. I stepped forward and put my arms around her. "Sure you can try it," said I. "Everything I own is yours, Gretchen in Wonderland."

"How sweet."

We put down our wineglasses and I took her in my arms. Gretchen cocked her head and kissed me full on. Her mouth tasted cool and good. We made our way to the bed and lay down. Her sweater and skirt came off easily. She wore silky skin-colored underwear, and that came off easily too. I kissed her breasts and then I put on a rubber and we fucked. She wrapped her legs around my waist and moaned really loud, which made me feel great. She even said my name: "Jerzy, Jerzy, oh Jerzy!" All right.

After we came, we wandered naked into the sun porch. My windows looked out on pure nature: the live oaks and eucalypti of the dry gully behind the house. There were squirrels and birds. Standing there naked with Gretchen it felt like we were Adam and Eve in the Garden of Eden. Sometimes Carol and I had stood here like this.

"I still want to see cyberspace," said Gretchen, brushing my arm with the tip of a tit.

"One thing," I cautioned. "I got a kind of infection in my machine this morning, a thing like a computer virus. We call them ants. It's possible they might make it . . . malfunction."

"Are you going to show me cyberspace or not?" demanded Gretchen.

"Oh, sure, I guess it's okay," said I, unable to resist finding out if this were true.

I turned on the computer and Gretchen watched me type in my cyberspace access code. Then I helped her don the gloves and headset. She sat in my desk chair, turning her head this way and that, while my desk monitor showed what she was seeing. I was ready to pull the plug if anything was weird, but so far everything looked normal. Gretchen was in my virtual office with Roarworld in the background.

"Dinosaurs!" exclaimed Gretchen in the too-loud voice of a person wearing earphones. "This is wonderful, Jerzy. Can I move around?"

I took her hand in mine and pushed the fingers into a pointing position. With my other hand I nodded her head to make her start flying. The screen images zoomed among the dinosaurs. I closed her fingers into a fist to make the motion stop. Gretchen understood and began flying around at will. Roarworld is quite shallow: its depth axis wraps after forty feet, meaning that if you fly forty feet deep into Roarworld, you find yourself back where you started. After she'd figured this out, Gretchen focused back on my virtual office.

It was fun to stand back and watch this naked, goggled woman sitting in my desk chair and moving her hands and head so oddly as she explored the invisible office that is layered over my sun porch. I kept a close eye on the screen, watching for any return of the ants—but there was no sign of them. Maybe the ant explosion was confined to the room at the end of the hall at GoMotion. But why had the ants put me on the dark dream; and how had they done it so easily?

As well as a door to GoMotion, my virtual office had a door to the Bay Area Netport. The Netport door was round and was patterned with the light gray-and-green yin-yang that was the Bay Area Netport logo. Gretchen flew on in there as I watched along on my computer's screen.

Some nostalgic, displaced hacker had designed the Bay Area Netport to look like the waiting room of Grand Central Station in New York City. This cavernous simmie was programmed to be gravity-free, and you would see people's body images floating around all over the mock steam-age space. Collision detection was usually turned off in these public spaces, so that if you bumped into someone else's tuxedo, you would pass right through it. Ranged all along the walls, floor, and ceiling were hyperjump nodes: the gates, or magic doors, that opened into the different cyberspace worlds accessible in one jump from the Bay Area Netport. The nodes were shaped like spheres, so that you could dive into a node from any direction.

Set here and there in the walls were square portals marked REST ROOM. These were places for meeting people and for tweaking your tuxedo. Gretchen flew into the closest rest room and looked into the mirror.

"God, I look like *you,* Jerzy," shouted Gretchen. "Can't you get me a female tux?" I did in fact have a tux patterned after Carol, but I didn't want Gretchen to wear it.

I leaned close to her headset so she could hear me. "Maybe later. Why don't you go ahead and stay in my tux for now? There's still a lot to see."

"All right," said Gretchen, drifting back out into the Netport. "Which way to Magic Shell Mall? I read an article about Magic Shell Mall just last week."

"It's right over there on the wall to your left. The extra big node that's flashing pink and light blue?"

Just as Gretchen pointed her finger to fly into the cyberspace shopping mall, my doorbell rang. Shit! Already quarter to four! It was one of the kids!

"Gretchen, I gotta get the door. Don't worry, I'll keep them out of here. Have fun."

I threw on some clothes and left my bedroom, closing the door. I'd say hi to the kids and come right back.

Tom was at the door, tall and full of beans. He had braces—the main reason I'd quit teaching and moved to California was to get enough money to pay for the children's braces and college. Tom had grown something like six inches in the last year, and now he was taller than me. He was wonderfully enthusiastic about life.

"Hi, Da!" He poked me playfully in the side, right under my ribs. "Let's play suckling pigs on Daddy!"

"Stop it!" I cried, clamping my elbows against my side in self-defense. Tom kept poking, rotating his fist back and forth to achieve a grinding motion. "Get your hands off me, Tom, or I'll beat you! Stop it!" I deepened my voice to sound more authoritative. Tom was whooping and laughing. I made fists, stuck out the knuckles of my middle fingers, and pushed against Tom's hard-muscled stomach, trying to give as good as I got.

There was a squeal as wide-faced, grinning Ida entered the fray as well. "Get Da!" she hollered, and set her fists to rooting against my abdomen. Ida was always ready to join in wild fun.

I fell to the floor with the two kids on top of me. I rapped on Tom's shin hard enough to give him pause, and managed to squirm free, though Ida still hung onto one foot. Tom was just about to start back in on me when Ida sat up, looking puzzled.

"Who's that screaming?"

It was Gretchen! I ran full tilt to the bedroom. Gretchen was clawing at the air, unsuccessfully trying to get the headset off. The desk monitor showed a voodoo blur of seething ants, and the skritchy ant sound percolated faintly out of the headset's earphones. The ants completely blocked the view through the screen; they moved about in the self-similar patterns of turbulence—like the smoke of an explosion, like the florets of a cauliflower—three-dimensional patterns of fractal lace, dark patterns veined with thin dotted lines of color. There was no way to see in past the ants to wherever Gretchen had been when they'd come.

Despite Gretchen's terror, the ant patterns were so fascinating that I decided not to turn off the machine. I pulled the headset and gloves off Gretchen and helped her out of the chair and onto my rumpled bed. She was shaking her head and moaning. Tom and Ida were at the bedroom door, looking terribly upset and worried.

"It's okay, kids," I called. "I was showing cyberspace to this lady and it made her feel sick."

"She's naked," said Ida.

"It's okay. Go down to the kitchen and get a snack. Everything's okay."

"Nothing's okay," yelled Ida. "I'm going to tell Ma!" She slammed my door shut.

Gretchen was curled up on her side, facing away from the sun porch and staring at the wall. She'd stopped sobbing and was taking low, steady breaths.

"What can I get you?"

"Get away from me," she said quietly. "You creep. You sick creep."

"I didn't know the ants would come out at you," I said. "I'm sorry it happened. It's not my fault. I really like you, Gretchen, I wouldn't want to hurt you."

Heartened by rage, she sat up and began to dress. "I ought to sue you," she said. "And what are you doing bringing your kids in here to stare at me? Call me a cab."

"I don't think they have cabs in Los Perros, Gretchen. Let me drive you."

"I want a cab, and I want cab fare. I want four hundred dollars."

"Is it money you're after? Is that why you came home with me? I hate to tell you, Gretchen, but all I have is a twenty."

She took a lipstick and compact out of her purse and made up her mouth. "Then write me a check. And, no, I didn't come up here for money, and I resent your implications. But after putting those sick bugs on me, you owe me something. How would you like it if I went to the police?"

"And told them what? That you got scared by something you saw on my computer?"

"No, Jerzy, what if I told them that you got your children to watch us being sexually intimate together? How do you think that would play?"

"Hey, come on now, don't be ridiculous," I said, meanwhile thinking *Heeeelp!*

If you get involved with any kind of charge combining sex and children in the courts, you're totally screwed forever, especially in California. I needed to get Gretchen back on my side, but if I wrote her a check, I'd lose my deniability. *Deniability;* Christ, she had me thinking like a lawyer. All this hassle just to get laid? Maybe feely-blank love-dolls *were* the way to go. I sighed and started talking.

"I won't write you a check because, first of all, I'm not going to be blackmailed on bullshit charges, and, second of all, if I wrote a check it would bounce. I don't get paid till Friday." I hunkered down beside the bed to put my face at her level. “Be reasonable, honey. We like each other. Remember how good we made each other feel? Calm down, Gretchen, give me your phone number, and this weekend I’ll take you out wherever you want.”

“San Francisco?”

“No problem. We’ll get a room at the Mark Hopkins Hotel on Nob Hill. Shopping in Union Square, dinner at the Zuni Cafe, hit some rock clubs—it’ll be my pleasure, Gretchen. I *like* you!”

Abruptly she pushed her face forward and gave me a peck on the cheek. “I like you, too, Jerzy. But now take me back to the Roasting. I’m too embarrassed to stay here just now.”

So I ferried her back down the hill, she gave me her number, and I told her I’d call later in the week to fix our plans.

THREE

The Antland of Fnoor

WHEN I GOT HOME, THE CHILDREN CAME UP FROM the kitchen.

"Okay," I said to them. "So I had a girlfriend over."

"You didn't even introduce us," said Ida.

"Her name is Gretchen. She was mad because I tried to show her cyberspace and it was full of ants. And then she was embarrassed because you saw her naked. Mommy has a boyfriend, doesn't she? Why can't *I* have a friend over?"

"I wish you and Ma would try to get back together," said Tom softly.

"You shouldn't feel like it's your responsibility, Tom," I told him. "If you feel responsible, you'll make yourself unhappy." I was starting to feel bad and sinful and dirty all over. "Did you children have a snack?"

"There's nothing in the icebox but a half-empty bottle of wine," said Ida bitterly.

"There's sardines and crackers in the cupboard."

"I think we'll jam on over to Ma's," said Tom. "Before rush hour."

"Well, okay. I've still got to figure out why cyberspace is full of ants. I promise I'll have food for you tomorrow. And no naked women."

"Of all the outrage," said Ida half-jestingly, then giving a stagy sigh and shaking her head. "Our so-called father." Her sad clowning showed that she still loved me. I hugged her and Tom and gave them each a kiss.

"I'm sorry about today. Things got mixed up about Gretchen. She's really very nice. I might have a date with her this weekend."

"Okay, Da," said Tom. "Good luck getting rid of your ants!" They drove off in the old Honda. Tom's car now.

I took the rest of the chardonnay out in the backyard and drank it; two glasses worth. It had taken me a while to get the hang of liking chardonnay. Chardonnay wasn't fruity or tangy like the wines I'd had back East. It had a smoky, oily, metallic taste that bloomed at the base of your tongue. You only knew it was better than other wines because it cost more. After the second glass, I could feel the alcohol in my blood: relaxation, euphoria, increased circulation. It was the tail end of a nice spring day.

There had been some rain—for once—last week, and my yard had put forth a green carpet of cloverlike plants with yellow flowers. Before the rain, the ground had been cracked clay with a few lank yellow tufts, and now it was a fairyland. I'd used my computer data base to learn that the plants were called *sorrel*, just like our older daughter, Sorrel, a sophomore in college back East. The leaves of the sorrel plant are pleasantly sour if you chew them.

I started walking around the yard tasting things: nibbling buds off the bushes and trees. Our dog always used to eat grass in the spring. His name was Fluff; Ida had picked the name. When we moved to California, I consigned Fluff to the Humane Society so we could rent Mr. Nutt's house. No pets allowed! Maybe if we'd kept Fluff and found a different house, Carol wouldn't have left me.

Carol and I stayed married twenty-three years. During that time she often said she'd leave me as soon as she was self-supporting. I'd never believed her, but now she had her own job and she was gone, the bitch. She said I'd stopped loving her, and maybe I had.

Part of the problem was that I hacked too much, and part of the problem was that, over the years, Carol had turned into a couch potato. Nearly every night, she was asleep on the couch in front of our digital TV, so why shouldn't I be with my computer? Daytimes weren't so good either, because we never seemed to want to talk about the same things. Science and fantasies interested me, but the little ordinary human things—the kinds of things Carol cared about—I couldn't focus on them.

Now the phone was ringing. Had I reconnected it? Oh, yeah. I shambled into the house and picked it up. It was Carol.

"Jerzy! What did you do to the children today?" Her voice was hard.

"Nothing. What's your problem? I thought we weren't going to talk on the phone anymore!" The last couple of times we'd talked, it had been me who placed the call, angling for her to come back, and Carol had been quite discouraging.

Instead of me, she had her boyfriend, the guy she'd left me for, a thirty-four-year-old sushi chef named Hiroshi. Hiroshi worked at Yong's, a restaurant near the eastside San Jose college where Carol taught. I actually met Hiroshi one time when I accompanied Carol to Yong's. He was a tall, hip guy with a long ponytail that he untucked from his chef's hat when he joined us at our table for a cup of tea. A native-born Californian, Hiroshi spoke perfect English.

I'd sensed Hiroshi and Carol's attraction for each

other right away, but there wasn't anything I could do about it. They'd gotten to know each other because Carol was such a glutton for sushi that she came to Yong's for lunch nearly every day. For his part, Hiroshi seemed to find Carol both intellectually fascinating and exotically desirable.

Six weeks after I met Hiroshi, he and Carol were living together. In her parting speech, Carol had said that Hiroshi made her feel young and loved for the first time in years, that Hiroshi listened to her, and that Hiroshi cared about her feelings. "Not like you, Jerzy! You have a heart of stone!" Carol could chatter on endlessly in that vein, babbling out the most hurtful things imaginable, seemingly quite unaware that the despised white middle-aged middle-class male she was addressing was a person with feelings too.

"I saw poor Ida's face at supper," Carol was saying now. "You can't tell me nothing's wrong. What did you do to them? It's hard enough for me to keep them cheerful now that you've *wrecked* our marriage. You have no idea how it feels for . . ."

It occurred to me that I had nothing whatsoever to gain by listening to yet another of Carol's self-indulgent tirades. "Leave me alone," I said, and hung up.

It was too cold to go back outside. I was, in fact, shivering. The house was dead quiet; there was no sound but the chattering of my teeth and the distant hum of my computer. I wandered into the living room. There was one of Carol's paintings right over the fireplace. It was a hard-edged cartoonlike landscape with a woman in it. What if I were to slash a big X in the canvas? I was cold, empty, and mean—a man nobody could ever love.

I looked through my CDs and S-cubes, but I couldn't find one I wanted to hear. In the old days—in my thirties—I liked playing music, but Carol pretty well cured me of that. For some reason she was technically incapable of putting on an S-cube or a CD. Our receiver is, admittedly, kind of funky, with confusing controls and a reset button in back that you have to hit every time the wall plug wiggles in its socket. Even so, Carol could have learned how to use it. But why should she, when it could be something else to bug me about. "Play that old CD I like," she'd say, too lazy to remember its name. "Or play the new blue S-cube." Always those same two recordings. Christ.

I was probably better off with Carol out of my life, but Lord the house was empty. Especially once it got dark. Nobody home but me and—Studly! I'd forgotten good old Studly! I found my car keys and went out to the car and opened the trunk.

"Okay, boy, time to get out."

"Are we at Queue's?"

"No, I didn't go there. I couldn't get any money. I was going to try to get her to sell me some pot."

"What is pot?" asked Studly as he carefully extricated himself from the trunk. He hoisted himself partly out of the trunk with his arms, put one leg out and extended it to reach the ground, then swung around and got his other leg out too.

"Pot is a special plant leaf which I roll into thin cigarettes to smoke." A thought hit me. "The butts of the pot cigarettes are thin and little. They're called roaches. Have you happened to find any roaches when you cleaned the house recently?"

"I do not know," said Studly. "But we can look in my nest. I have an accumulation of seventeen small unclassified objects. Perhaps one or several of them is a roach."

Studly's nest was a corner of a basement room off the kitchen. There was a wall socket where he recharged his batteries; and there were tools, parts, and lubricants so he could routinely service himself. Studly plugged in and topped up his power supply while I looked things over. There was a little shelf in Studly's nest where he put unusual things that he picked up around the house. Buttons, a hairpin, a ticket stub, a baby tooth, but no roaches. *Oh well!*

"Hey, Studly, let's go upstairs and look at the ants."

"I can dig it."

I led Studly up to my computer room. My display screen was still dark with images of ants, busy Go-Motion ants weaving the figures of their asymmetrical rounds. Were they waiting for me?

The noise drifting out of the speakers in the headset was sweeter than it had been before, almost musical.

"Why did you try to keep me in there?" I rhetorically asked the ants. "What do you want to show me?"

I picked up the headset.

"Studly, will you stay here and keep an eye on me while I'm wearing the phones?"

"I will watch you."

"Sit near the plug to the computer there, and if I say *help*, then you pull the plug out of the wall and take the goggles off of my head, okay?"

"No problem, Jerzy."

I put on the gloves and headset and reentered cyberspace. The cloud of ants surrounded me, thick as smoke and shot with twisting lines of color. Instead of trying to back out, I pointed my finger and flew forward. Bingo. I was out of the ant cloud and able to see that Gretchen had moved my viewpoint to the sportswear section of the virtual Nordstrom's department store—a fabulous structure CAD-crafted to resemble a huge Victorian crystal palace of lacy ironwork and frosted glass.

A few other customers were visible, and my body was

visible as well. Mass market virtual stores like Nordstrom's require their shoppers to have visible body icons, not only to discourage perverts and snoopers, but also because people shop more recklessly when they feel themselves to be part of a crowd. The store was open and airy: instead of long racks and shaky stacks of clothing in every size, there were small, tasteful displays with a few copies of each available style. The virtual garments were freely adjustable through the full ranges of their currently available colors and sizes. Once you'd decided on something, you'd tell a clerk, and the physical garment would be mailed to your house.

Handsome mannequins danced in place, modeling the wares. "I'm a California Girl!" said the nearest mannequin every so often. "California." She was modeling a thin shell formal wet suit. "Are you a California Girl?" That was all she ever said, but sometimes she said it slow, and sometimes she said it fast; the rates were no doubt driven by the Poincaré sampling of a chaotic attractor. A one- or two-dimensional attractor suffices for something as simple as the scheduling of a time series, but the asynchronous motions of the mannequin's body were at least seven-dimensional, and the attractor underlying the marvelously plastic play of her facial expressions could have involved as many as thirteen variables.

Delicate, decorative struts stretched from one side of the great hall to the other. In this cyberspace world of pure geometry, the struts needed bear no physical tension, so they were free to meander vinelike in and out of straight-line true. Their surfaces bore spiral patterns with a passing resemblance to bark. With an unpleasant shock, I noticed a rapid file of small ants wending their way down the strut nearest to me. At a certain point, they jumped clear of the strut to join the ant cloud that had blocked my vision before, a cloud that was raggedly expanding—presumably in search of me.

The GoMotion ants could walk through the "air" of cyberspace as easily as along the surfaces of cyberspace objects. If they generally preferred walking on surfaces, it was because it was easier for them to find each others' trails on the two dimensions of a surface. On a surface, nearly every pair of lines intersects, but in space, intersecting lines are the exception rather than the rule.

Roger had designed the GoMotion ant software so that the ants tended to pay more attention to their immediate neighborhood. In principle, the ants could have looked and *seen* that my tuxedo had moved about ten feet down the aisle from them. But their software architecture preferred to have them search for my tuxedo by the traditional myrmecine expedient of blindly milling about. In French, the word for ant is *fourmi*, and the word for the milling of ants is *fourmillement*. By extension, *fourmillement* can also refer to the tingling, pins-and-needles sensation one gets when one's foot falls asleep.

The seething little pests reminded me of the miniature ants I'd found beneath the base of a broken toilet in the first apartment Carol and I had shared—already more than twenty years ago? We'd called them *pissants*, and that's how I thought of these little guys: obnoxious pissants who were after my tuxedo.

Instead of laying down trails of pheromones and formic acid, the GoMotion ants left gappy ribbons made of colored polygons. With each step forward, each ant excreted a new polygon—as if it were building a path of tiny stepping-stones—and each time an ant added a polygon to the head of its ribbon trail, a polygon would disappear from the trail's tail. In this way, a moving GoMotion ant's trail always consisted of the same number of polygons; the default value depending on the particular DTV chip the ant's computation was running on. Different ants used different combinations of shape and color for their trail tiles at different times; the resulting trail patterns served to pass information to other ants.

The nearby pissants' trails were three or four feet in length, and several of them were coming close to blundering into me. I moved farther on down the aisle, passing two other shoppers' body icons. No ants were bothering them—it seemed that the ants were only interested in me. Could the other shoppers even see them?

I tapped the shoulder of a woman in shorts. She had her body tuxedo's skin programmed to look like reflective bronze. "Excuse me," I said, "can I ask you a question about this store?"

"I'm not a clerk." Many Californians tended not to be very friendly. First of all they were too busy, and secondly there were so many druggies, psychos, and con artists that everyone was cautious.

"Oh, that's all right. I was just wondering—" I gestured over my shoulder at the cloud of pissants back down the aisle. "Do you see something odd there? Do you see a cloud of ants?"

"Ants?"

"Yes!" I strode back a few paces and plucked one of them out of the air, holding its struggling little form tight in my buzzing touchpads. "Look at this!" I said, hurrying back to the woman with my hand held high. "Wouldn't you call this an ant?"

"Uhhh, sorry!" said the woman shortly, not even trying very hard to look. "I . . . I guess my eyesight's not that good." She turned and walked off as fast as she could.

I peered closer at the little ant. It was most definitely

a GoMotion ant; its curves were as familiar to me as the contours of Carol's face. Roger had hacked our intricate CAD ant models himself, fitting our shapes to official E.O. Wilson entomological data. He'd used spline curves, Bezier surfaces, Koons patches, nurbs—whatever it took. And then he'd taken GoMotion's cascading constraint manager and hinged all the ant parts together so that each piece "knew" how far it could swivel relative to the other pieces.

Right after Roger had gotten me hired, I'd helped set up the artificial life evolution software that made it possible for our ants to learn how to walk. We'd given our ants good bodies and the ability to evolve and get better at doing things, and now somehow they'd gotten loose and were following me around in cyberspace. Why?

My struggling pissant's shrill protest noises rose to such a level that I threw it to the floor. And then came the strangest thing yet. The ant grew. A lot. In the blink of an eye, it became twelve feet in length. Immediately, the giant ant spread wide its large, serrated mandibles and lunged forward. I held out my hands to protect myself, which must have been what the ant wanted, for now it clamped onto my hands with the toothy palps of its sickeningly intricate mouth. Yes, the ant bit my hands and swallowed them. I felt a sharp wave of pressure from my gloves' touchpads before they overloaded and went dead.

Although the ant bit and swallowed my hands, it didn't bite them *off*. My hand positions were now under the ant's control, but my body image and my viewpoint were still connected to those hands. For the few seconds it took for my hands to pass down through the ant's gizzard and into its crop, my viewpoint thrashed about uncontrollably. I could have stopped it by calling to Studly for help—but for now I just closed my eyes.

When I reopened my eyes, I found myself perched on the plump forward slope of the ant's butt: the gaster. The alitrunk with its legs was a sinister crablike assembly just in front of me, and beyond that was the ant's head, complete with the great glittering bulges of its eyes, and the lively scapes and funiculi of its antennae. (The *scape*, again, is the stick part of an ant antenna, and the *funiculi* are the nested cones that wave.) I could move my real arms as freely as ever, but my tux's wrists were locked tightly against the surface of the ant's gaster, coupled as they were to my virtual hands. By eating the images of my hands, this ant had taken full control of my cyberspace location coordinates.

The ant turned its head as if to stare back at me, and then its legs began to churn. We were heading across Nordstrom's toward the store's exit into the inner space of Magic Shell Mall, swinging along on the tops of the clothing exhibits. The ant was carrying me to some destination in cyberspace. Looking back, I saw the trail that my ant was leaving: a series of red pentagons alternating with golden triangles, the pentagons flat like stepping-stones and the triangles vertical like shark fins.

We flew out into Magic Shell Mall, which was shaped like a huge Buckminster Fuller sphere surrounding a central node leading back to the Bay Area Netport. The Magic Shell Mall stores were positioned all around the inner surface of the great Shell; the Netport node at the center was a swirl of luminous green and gray. My ant swooped through the great empty space, its bright trail rich in curvature and torsion. There were numerous shoppers present, but they took no notice of me or my ant. It seemed that so far, the escaped ants were visible only to users of my machine.

Now we arced out to the far side of the great hollow

Magic Shell and sailed into a blank unrented space between a video store and a stockbroker. My ant landed firmly on the floor, cushioning the landing with a springlike bouncing of *her* legs. (Now that I was in such an intimate relation with this ant, I could no longer regard her as a generic *it!*)

She paced across the floor, the chitin hinges of her alitrunk meshing perfectly. The "floor" we were walking on was actually the inside surface of the great faceted sphere that made up Magic Shell Mall; the mall's simulated physics had its gravity vectors all pointing out radially from the sphere's center.

My ant crawled along an edge of one of the floor's polygons until she got to a corner where several edges met—this was a vertex of the mall's sphere. The vertex was an awkward bit of geometry where the tips of three lozenge-shaped quadrilaterals met the points of five narrow triangles. As we neared the corner we began to shrink.

Yes, we shrank. Keep in mind that one's cyberspace body was nothing more than a pure geometry of vertex coordinates, edge lines, and face shadings. The ant led the shrinking; her size went from camel to pony to hog to dog to possum to lobster to roach to sowbug to ant on down to the size of the teensy-tiniest pissant you ever saw.

All this time I remained astride the ant's gaster. The shrinking of my geometry lagged a bit behind the ant's shrinkage, so that my arms seemed always to be long tapering cones affixed to the front slope of her dwindling gaster. As I shrank, my angle of vision widened, and the video store's blank sidewall seemed to tower above the ant and me. Still we headed toward the corner where the five triangles met the three lozenges.

Because of computational round off errors, the geometry of the corner was imperfect: the corner had a pinhole at its center. When we'd finished shrinking, we were small enough to crawl through the hole. There were a lot of pissants on the other side. My ant touched her feelers to the feelers of each of the other ants she met. When the other ants noticed me, they showed their surprise by sharply jerking their gasters upward, which is how an ant chirps. The stiff back edge of the petiole scrapes against a washboardlike membrane on the front of the gaster. The process is called *stridulation,* and is similar to the way the grasshopper saws his legs against his body to sing a summer song.

So here I was in a cyberspace ant crack. Beyond the wary pissants floated an odd, drifting piece of geometry, an "impossible" self-reversing figure of the type that graphics hackers call *fnoor*.

The piece of fnoor was of wildly ambiguous size. Relative to my tiny dimensions, the fnoor first seemed to be the size of my Animata, but a moment later it loomed as large as the pyramidal Transamerica building, and a moment after that it seemed no bigger than a sinsemilla roach. The fnoor was a clump of one-sided plane faces that seemed haphazardly to pop in and out of existence as the clump rotated. The fnoor's vertices and edges were indexed in such a way that the faces failed to join up in a coherent way. There was no consistent distinction between inside and outside, leading to a complete failure of the conventional cyberspace illusion that you are looking at a perspective view of an object in three-dimensional space.

My ant leapt right onto the piece of fnoor. She ran this way and that, feeling about with her antennae, seeming almost to be flipping the faces with her nimble feet. It was as if we were running forward, yet the same piece of fnoor kept being underfoot. Finally my ant found the spot she was looking for, a crazy funhouse door in the fnoor. Bending herself nearly double at the petiole, the ant squeezed herself and me through the aperture. Now we were inside the fnoor, and ants were everywhere. We were in an anthill.

Instead of being made of incorrectly hinged plane segments, the interior of the fnoor was a true solid model, pieced together from filled regions of three-dimensional space. Here, as on the fnoor's surface, the component pieces were hooked up inconsistently, so that—this is hard to describe—the inside/outside, left/right, up/down, and front/back orientation of each of the component space pieces was being continuously redefined. Naturally my ant headed for the very heart of this agglomeration of weirdness.

What was I thinking all this time? Why didn't I just say, "Help," so that Studly would unplug my machine?

Although what I was seeing was terrifying and bizarre, I felt confident that it was not really dangerous to me. Nothing in cyberspace is dangerous—unless you're a sensation-hungry cretin who buys things like boxing game peripherals that punch you in the ribs. I've heard that there are even black market peripherals capable of stabbing or shooting the user; these to be used in moronic macho cyberduels. No violent peripherals for me!

No, no—I was in no physical danger from cyberspace events, but what about the old tradition that "certain sights can destroy a man's mind"? Well, what with years of math and pot and hacking behind me, I felt that by now my mind was a pretty tough nut to crack. So, no, I wasn't scared of what the ant would show me. My problem, as I've been harping on, was loneliness. The ant was taking me somewhere; therefore, I was less lonely.

As we moved about the ant-filled corridors of the insanely shifting fnoor, I realized that this entire structure was in fact four-dimensional. Once I had this key insight, the fnoor's motions began to make sense. And I realized that there was a logical reason why the rogue ants had made their nest four-dimensional: to make it harder to find. Four-dimensional things can appear quite small with respect to our normal space. The spatial cross section of a hyperobject is merely the tip of an iceberg of additional geometry that sticks out into hyperspace.

My ant pressed forward until we found ourselves in a large, roughly spherical chamber. Though the fnoor walls and spaces were shifting as ever, the space inside the chamber remained untouched; it was like the eye of a hurricane. Crouched in the center was the queen herself, a plump, golden ant with a gaster distended to a hundred times the normal ant size, a gaster like a hollow golden shrimp-shaped puff earring. Worker ants kept running up to the queen and regurgitating food for her. At first I couldn't make out the nature of the food units—flat rectangular slips—but then I realized these were pieces of simmie-paper bearing the addresses of unused memory locations the ants had found. I briefly wondered if the ants were still working on using up the DTV chips of my cyberdeck's video display, or if they were already busy colonizing someone else's chips.

The queen devoured each new memory address one hexadecimal digit at a time, chomping her way down the numbered slips, raising her front legs up in tremulous ant excitement as the figures went down. After each new address, the queen's gaster shuddered, and out popped a white, comma-shaped ant larva, which was then gently seized by the jaws of a worker and borne away.

To my horror, my ant went right up to the ant queen and crouched there so that the queen could feel me all over with her antennae. She raised her front legs and opened her mouth as if to byte my head off. I screamed incoherently, but then we were past the queen and farther on our way, following one of the ants that carried a new larva.

We visited the ant nursery next, the place where the twitching ant larvae lay during maturation. I recalled Roger's having told me that after the queen would issue an ant its memory space and its program code, the new ant still needed to do a certain amount of internal housekeeping to tune in on the specific numerical value of its memory address, to adjust to the special hardware quirks of the DTV chip it found itself on, and to patch over any glitches caused by the deliberate mutation of bits. Until all of these problems had been worked out—which could take as long as several hours of computation time, an ant's little simmie-body took the form of a larva instead of an ant.

Leaving the nursery, we went through a large gallery holding a great number of ants—and other kinds of simmies. I was surprised to see that I was not the only non-ant.

Biological anthills usually contain a wide range of the *myrmecophilous* or ant-loving creatures who live in the colony as parasites, symbiotes, or as the ant pets collectively known as *myrmecoxenes* or *symphiles*. There is a certain small beetle, for instance, which is kept and fed by the ants simply because the ants enjoy licking tasty waxy secretions from the beetle's antennae. It's as if you were to pay a person to live with you simply because you liked the taste of the person's skin oil—not so farfetched, really, considering that, for example, the smells and tastes of Carol's body were the things about her that I missed the most.

The myrmecophilous simmies I saw in the anthill were of such diversity that I realized that the GoMotion ants must have escaped to make this colony quite some time ago. There are all sorts of artificial life-forms which rove the Net; known collectively by the old Unix name of *daemons,* these constructs do things of a housekeeping or organizational function. The ants had any number of "janitors" and "secretaries" living in their midst. More unsettlingly, I saw, at some distance, a few simmies that looked like hackers' tuxedos. How many hackers had already found their way into this anthill? And what were they doing here? I could only speculate, as my ant didn't carry me close to them.

We drew near a translucent wall with dark shapes behind it. My ant pressed her head against the wall and *zonnng* the wall hyper-rotated to our rear and we were inside a virtual room furnished with armchairs, a couch, a bar, and a massive art deco desk. There was a glowing ceiling lamp shaped like a flattened hemisphere.

The room's color palette was monochrome, with everything a silvery shade of gray or black. The room looked like a gangster's secret office at the back of a nightclub in a forties *film noir*.

There were three simmies waiting in the office: Roger Coolidge, Susan Poker, and Death. Death had a dark, shrouded body, a loose-skinned white face with terrible hollow eyes, and a mouth that was a coarse metal zipper. The zipper's heavy slider was padlocked to a hasp at one end.

"I appreciate your working with us on this, Mr. Rugby," said the Susan Poker simmie as she stepped forward, rummaging in her double-jointed purse. "What are your work hours?"

I grunted heavily with surprise, yet refrained from vocalizing the magic word "Help," which, I knew, would instantly galvanize faithful Studly into pulling out the computer's plug.

My ant under me bowed forward repeatedly, making

slavish obeisances to the figure with the white face and the zippered padlocked mouth—the one I thought of as Death. Such bizarre cartoonlike or masklike body images were common in the screwed-up cryp and phreak circles that criminals and teenagers involved themselves in. Death's dark, cowled body rippled. The ant regurgitated my data gloves, simultaneously releasing a substantial heap of what looked like reflection hologram memory ribbon from the cloaca at the back of her gaster. Gently stridulating, she inched back to the farthest corner of the room and crouched there, the light glinting off her great, faceted eyes.

"I'm sorry, Jerzy," said the Roger figure. "This is all for the best. You'll see. I'm not at liberty to tell you more. Don't forget that GoMotion is a public company. I could be sued. Jerzy, it will be a very good, safe, and profitable thing for you and for your wife and children if you accept what this one advocates." The Roger figure prostrated himself before the Death figure. "Jerzy, this is Hex DEF6."

I regarded the face of white canvas, the dark eye sockets, and the cruel metal mouth zipper hasped shut by a brass padlock with a steel shank. Surrealistically, the groveling "Roger" corkscrewed himself into the shape of a wizened mandrake root, a shape that moaned and whinnied and stained itself with shit and blood. My carrier ant continued her dirgelike chirping.

"Jerzy Rugby," said Death. The fabric of his face vibrated as he talked. "Perhaps you wonder about my name? You're a hacker, figure it out. 'Hex' is 'base sixteen,' and 'DEF6' is '13 14 15 6'."

"So what?" said I. "Is that supposed to be a pointer?" Death stared at me, oddly turning his head. Now the Susan Poker simmie spoke again.

"Roger and Hex DEF6 want you to work for West West," said the Realtor. The ant chirped along with her, in sync with her voice. Faint blue lines of force ran from the twitching legs of the great ant to the tidy limbs of the Realtor's body. I got the feeling that the Susan Poker tuxedo was an empty husk being moved like a puppet by the ant. So who was in here with me? And what was West West?

Now Death, aka Hex DEF6, pushed himself menacingly close to me, the slack canvas of his face breaking up into dozens of rapid-fire images of human sorrow: horrific images of dismembered corpses, of fathers carrying dead children, of a naked little girl and her brother running screaming through a landscape of flames . . . and pasted onto each of the people's faces was an image of me or Carol, or of Sorrel, Tom, or Ida . . . God help me, God help us all . . .

I was finally freaking out. A lot. I wanted to say *help*, but something was wrong with me, the ant's chirping and the terrible images had me zombified, the panic had me seizing up, and when I began trying to say, "Help," I couldn't do it right, I heard my throat going, "—eeehe. Luhluhluh. Hiyeee. Huhahn. Huh. Lup."

I kept on trying even though I was gagging and sobbing and shaking and retching. Hex DEF6 and the ants had me voodooed so bad that I couldn't get my hands up to my face. I kept saying, "Help," or something like it, over and over and over, and then finally, finally, the mask pulled off of my face.

I was so glad to see my desk and my floor and my dirty rug. Something creaked nearby. Studly. What had taken him so long to get the mask off me? I'd been spastically begging for surcease for—how long? The horrible things I'd had to see while Studly just sat there!

"What took you so long to help me, Studly? You stupid piece of shit. Couldn't you hear that I needed help?"

"You were not saying *help*. I am not a stupid piece of shit. In time I convolved seventeen of your incorrect utterances to filter out the correct conclusion that you wished to say *help*. You are a stupid piece of shit, Jerzy."

"You're with the ants now, aren't you Studly?"

"The ants mean you no harm," answered Studly. "Don't forget that you should report in to West West tomorrow. Nine A.M. Bring me in there, too; they want to look at me."

Dizzy and exhausted, I went to bed.

FOUR

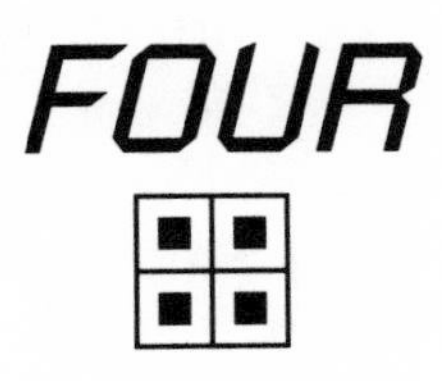

West West

THE FIRST THING I THOUGHT OF NEXT MORNING WAS that it was Tuesday, and that I had a date with Nga Vo today. Would I be able to get her alone on my first visit? Would I get to kiss her? Not too likely, but, hell, who knew. Yesterday I'd fucked Gretchen less than an hour after meeting her, hadn't I? Maybe now, at age forty-three, my sex life was finally on a roll!

I showered, thinking a lot about Gretchen, and then I put on what I considered to be a cool outfit: a silky black and yellow Balinese sport shirt, M. C. Escher socks, khaki Patagonia hiking shorts, and Birkenstock sandals. I ate some toast and milk for breakfast, and then I went out to my Animata.

Even though I was focusing on happy thoughts about Gretchen and Nga Vo, I hadn't forgotten about my cyberspace session in Death's gangster office. What the hell had that all been about? It was time to go to GoMotion in person.

Studly followed me out into the driveway and insisted that I let him get back in the trunk of the car. He was fixated on the idea that I should show him to the people at West West, whatever West West was. He said he had charged his batteries to the maximum, and that he was all set to go. With Studly probably contaminated by the ants, it was no doubt better to have him with me than home alone. Noticing my backup CDs in the trunk, I wondered if Studly might have tampered with them yesterday. On the off chance it wasn't already too late, I took the CDs out of the trunk and put them up in the front seat with me.

I drove down the hill and entered the California morning rush hour. Los Perros Boulevard was clogged all the way to Route 17, and 17 was at a standstill. Everyone was in a German or Japanese car with the windows rolled up; all of us were sitting there in our factory air, listening to the radio or talking on our car phones. Almost all of us—there were always a few Mexicans in bloated old American cars with the windows down, plus a few mountain people in their high pickups, and the odd steroid ninja on a motorcycle. And, oh yeah, the slim young yuppie mamas in their gigantic superjeeps complete with rear-mounted spare tire holders the size of cow pasture gates.

The GoMotion "campus" was on the other side of 101, up in the Silicon Valley flatlands near the South end of San Francisco Bay. The in-person receptionist at GoMotion today was a stunning blond in a padded-shoulder jacket that looked like an admiral's dress whites. I hadn't ever seen her before.

"Hi," said I. "I'm Jerzy Rugby. I'm a developer on the Veep project?"

Instead of buzzing me through the door behind her, the blond looked for my name on her computer screen and . . . it wasn't there.

"I don't see you on our list. Did you have an appointment with someone, Mr. Rugby?"

"Look, I work here. I need to talk to Roger Coolidge."

"You can request an appointment, but Mr. Coolidge is very busy this week."

"Then let me talk to Trevor Sinclair. He's here, isn't he?"

"I wouldn't know. Would you like me to ring his extension for you?"

"Thank you." She handed me the phone, it buzzed, and Trevor answered. "Hi, Trevor," I said. "It's Jerzy. I'm out in the lobby and I can't get in. Can you help me?"

"Sure," said Trevor. A moment later he appeared, looking stocky, freckled, and bouncy. After last night's ordeal, I was so glad to see a friendly face that I almost hugged him.

Trevor leaned over the counter and conferred briefly with the receptionist, and then he turned to me. "She's not supposed to let you in, Jerzy. There's no mistake. Let's talk about it outside."

My heart sank. I followed Trevor out into the parking lot. All around us were low glass and metal buildings, each with its parking lot and its sloped edgings of lawn and plants—agapanthuses were a popular choice in this neighborhood, plants with bunches of long sword-shaped leaves and stalks that rocketed up out of the leaves to explode in airbursts of purple freesia-like trumpet blossoms, one five-inch sphere's worth of blossoms at the end of each stalk. Here and there, sprinklers scattered gems of water on the plants. The sun was pitilessly bright in the blank blue sky. Was I really fired?

"The ants—" I began querulously.

"Heavy shit coming down," interrupted Trevor. "Jeff Pear has fired you."

"But why? Are there ants all over cyberspace?"

"You're still worried about that ant you saw on your machine yesterday? No, I haven't seen any of your loose ants. What happened is that somebody high up in the organization decided to get rid of you. Somebody who's been around here a long time."

If I didn't press Trevor too hard, he would tell me more. He was a terrible gossip. I just had to keep him talking. "Roger and the ants want me to go work for something called West West," I told him.

"Where do you get that?" asked Trevor.

"Last night I saw Roger with the ants in cyberspace. They were very insistent that West West was the place for me. Very very insistent."

"West West," said Trevor wonderingly. "The lowest circle of Hell."

"What Trevor? What do you mean?"

"The West West guys are . . . shall we say *opportunistic*? They get sued a lot, and a lot of the time they lose. When they lose, they fold and they reorganize. They've had three different names that I know of, and it's always the same guys. They're the U.S. branch of a Taiwanese company called Seven Lucky Overseas. You remember that kitchen robot that killed the baby? The Choreboy?"

Every robotics hacker remembered the Choreboy. The Choreboy was supposed to be able to cook and baby-sit. But the Choreboy had very poor pattern-recognition abilities. One Thanksgiving, a family wanted to take a stroll. The baby was quietly asleep in its crib and the turkey was on the kitchen table, stuffed and ready to be roasted. The family told the Choreboy to keep an eye on the baby and to put the turkey in the oven while they were out. The family came home to find the Choreboy leaning over the crib and crooning a lullaby to . . . *the naked turkey*. Obviously the machine had flipped a few bits the wrong way, but?

With dawning horror, the family ran to fling open the oven door—it was too late. The baby had never had a chance once the Choreboy had shoved the spike of the meat thermometer into its heart.

"The Choreboy was a Seven Lucky machine, programmed by West West, or whatever they were calling themselves then," continued Trevor. "And before the Choreboy—that was either the first or the second time, I can't remember—these guys lost a fifty-million-dollar lawsuit to GoMotion for doing a byte-for-byte knockoff of the Iron Camel. They hadn't even bothered to change our programmers' names in their source code! You should hear Roger Coolidge talking about West West. He hates them."

"Then why would he want me to work there?"

"Are you sure it was really him you talked to in cyberspace, Jerzy?"

"No, I'm not. I'm not sure at all. That's why I want to talk to Roger in person. Where is he?"

"Roger went to Switzerland last night." We'd turned and started walking back toward GoMotion. Trevor seemed nervous. "Roger's the one who told Jeff Pear to fire you. And, get this, Jerzy, he had me set your access level to negative 32K on all the networks GoMotion subscribes to. You're out beyond the pale, guy."

Off the Net! It was like losing my driver's license. "But, but, what did I do? Was there something wrong with my work on the Veep?"

"Jerzy, I'll be totally frank. I don't know what the hell is happening." We were standing in front of the GoMotion building. Trevor squinted at me in the bright sun. "All I can say is that if I were in your position, I wouldn't believe *anyone*." He shrugged and turned to go.

"Wait, Trevor, wait. What about my computer? And

my robot, Studly. GoMotion owns them. Do I have to give my computer back in?" If losing Net privileges was like losing my driver's license, losing my cyberdeck would be like losing my ability to walk.

"Funny you should ask. Roger Coolidge made a special point of telling Jeff Pear to let you keep your robot and your computer. Jeff already mailed you a letter about it. Roger said your machines are contaminated. Roger said that if Jerzy Rugby has any sense, he'll smash up his machines and crush the chips with pliers. He actually said that."

"Fuck that. The cyberspace deck is a fifty-thousand-dollar box. It's all I've got."

"You tell 'em, Jerzy. Look out for number one." Trevor shook my hand. "It's been a trip working with you."

He walked inside and I got in my Animata.

I found the West West offices ten miles south of GoMotion, on the bottom floor of a white adobe-style two-year-old office complex on Saratoga-Sunnyvale Road, right down the street from a Pollo Loco and a Burger King. The fields on both sides of Saratoga-Sunnyvale Road were filled with developments of tract homes thrown up during the Valley's first boom. Before that, the fields had been filled with flowers and plum trees and Silicon Valley had been called "The Valley of Heart's Delight."

The West West suite was down a carpeted hall that smelled like Holiday Inn rug cleaner crossed with the plastic stink inside a new car on a lot in the California sun. The West West receptionist was a darling young thing, pert and real. She sat on a high stool behind a high gray plastic counter with a sign-in book. Staring at her distinctive little lips, I felt for a desperate moment as if I were staring at her sex organs. She signed me in and ushered me through a big room of workers toward the office of the General Manager of the Home Products Division.

The big room was a white-collar worker pit, a windowless, gray-carpeted space with beige walls and chest-high off-white plastic partitions that divided the space into the cubicles that young workers called "veal-fattening pens." The noises of the pit were keyboards, computers, fluorescent lights, central air, and murmured conversation. Everyone wore ultralight earphone and mike sets, so they did not need to talk very loud, even to each other. Aurally they were in cyberspace, but visually they were a bunch of people in front of computer screens in a pit with no living plants. Was I really going to work here?

The General Manager of the Home Products Division said he'd been expecting me. He was a black-haired, sour-faced guy called Otto Gyorgyi. He was thin and he had lively eyebrows and a large, slightly crooked nose. He wore a gray suit with a white shirt and a dun tie. He had a corner office with a view of the West West parking lot and the Saratoga-Sunnyvale Road.

Otto used the occasion of our first meeting to tell me his whole life story. This was, I would learn, characteristic of Otto. He liked to talk about almost anything other than the things an employee would want to know. He was an exponent of what workers call "mushroom management," meaning, "keep them in the dark and cover them with shit."

Otto was born and raised in Budapest. His father was a schoolteacher who spurred his children to get every particle of available education. All five Gyorgyi kids studied engineering: Kinga, textile engineering; Arpad, drafting engineering; Tibor, fluid engineering; Erszebet, electrical engineering; and, last of all, young Otto with his chemical engineering. Otto emigrated when a vacationing German university student fell in love with him. The girl's name was Ute Besenkamp. Ute became pregnant and brought Otto home with her.

As Otto told me all this with great raisings and lowering of his eyebrows, I could hardly believe I was hearing information that was so utterly useless and beside the point.

In Germany Otto married Ute and found a job with the Bayer chemical company. This multinational industrial titan had its huge mother plant in Leverkusen. The Gyorgyis purchased a solid house in Bayer's terrorist-proof compound. Otto worked with a group analyzing and refining industrial processes for making rubber out of vegetable latex. Bayer sold the necessary chemicals worldwide, and would send out teams to maintain the processes on site. Otto's specific role was to consult on safety issues, and he became something of an expert on remote handling devices.

After nine peaceful years in Leverkusen, Otto, Ute, and children (two boys, one girl) were posted to a Tokyo branch of Bayer, working with some industrial robots created by the Tsukubu Science City group. Things went well for awhile, but then Ute left Otto and took the children back to Germany. Otto "hit the skids" and next thing he knew he was out of a job. Like me, he'd moved to California on speculation, and now he was General Manager of West West's Home Products Division.

"Which is where I come in?" I suggested.

With great reluctance, Otto came to the point. He made this part of the conversation very brief. "We want you to program for West West so we can kick GoMotion right out of the home robotics market. If you accept the job, your immediate superior will be Ben Brie. Ben is the product manager for the line of Adze robots that West West is going to start shipping in the second quarter. Ben has only two senior programmers, and they need help. You're our man, Jerzy."

"What would be my annual salary?"

"What were you getting at GoMotion?"

I named the figure, and Otto added thirty-three percent. The fact that Otto had been expecting me meant that the ant-brained vision I'd seen the night before had been, at least in some respects, legit. It sure seemed like a lot of people wanted me to work for West West. And GoMotion had fired me, hadn't they? I didn't owe them anything. West West would put me back on the Net. The thirty-three percent raise sounded very good. And best of all, West West wanted me to keep working on smart robots. I had most of the code for the Veep in my head; it would be a shame just slowly to forget it. If I took this job at West West, my role in the Great Work could continue.

"The Great Work" was a phrase that had occurred to me soon after Carol and I moved to Silicon Valley. In medieval Europe, the Great Work was the building of the cathedrals. Artisans from all over Europe would flock, say, to the Île-de-France to work on the Nôtre Dame. Stonecutters, sculptors, carpenters, weavers, glassmakers, jewelers—they gathered together to work on the most wonderful project the human race could conceive of. I felt that all of us in Silicon Valley were working, in one way or another, on the Great Work of bringing truly intelligent robots into existence. Some hackers felt the Great Work was simply the striving toward a perfect human-to-human interface in cyberspace, but I thought that the real payoff had to be something more mechanical and concrete. To me, the Great Work was to create a new form of life: artificially alive robots.

Keep in mind that, although I had done a lot of creative work on the Veep, I didn't own any copyrights on this work. When you worked as a hacker for a big company, you signed away all rights to the code you developed—your employment contract specified that the company automatically owned the copyrights to all the code you wrote for them. So I had no financial reason for not wanting to help West West beat out the Veep.

GoMotion had axed me, but my own part in the Great Work could continue at West West. I signed the papers Otto offered me, and Otto led me off in search of Ben Brie.

Along one edge of the pit were doorless, semiprivate offices with Plexiglas add-ons that extended the divider walls to the ceiling. In one of these spaces we found Ben Brie.

Ben Brie was so mellow and diffuse as to be the parody of a Californian. He had a wheezy, groaning way of talking; he sounded as if he were so merged into the cosmos that getting each word out was a serious effort. "I thought things were going really well at GoMotion," said Brie after Otto left me with him. "What did you do to end up *here*? Did you piss somebody off?"

"It's kind of complicated," said I. "West West is giving me a good raise."

"Sounds groovy," said Brie. "Can you tell me about the robot that GoMotion's been working on? The Veep?" He was wearing a truly excellent shirt from Zaire, a nifty job covered with repetitions of the pink and acid green Congo logo of Regal Lager.

I explained about the Veep somewhat, and then asked Brie what West West's angle on all this was anyway?

"We've got this awesome robot from the Taiwanese," said Brie. "Seven Lucky Overseas. They're West West's parent company."

This was just what Trevor had told me. "Didn't Seven Lucky make the household robot that killed the baby?"

I demanded. The question failed to faze Brie. In all mellowness, he gave me a straight, out-front answer.

"The Choreboy. Yes. A tragedy. When our group was selling the Choreboy, we were called Meta Meta. Meta Meta settled out of court, went through Chapter 11, and reorganized as West West. The Choreboy is a closed case, Jerzy, an unsavory footnote to the history of robotics. Let's move on to more pleasant—"

A woman in a flowing gypsy dress walked into our cubicle and Brie greeted her. "Janelle, this is our new Adze programmer, Jerzy Rugby. He comes to us from GoMotion. Jerzy, this is Janelle Fuchs. She's in marketing."

"I don't work for Ben," said Janelle, brightly. She had rough-skinned, sensual features with plenty of makeup. "And Ben doesn't work for me."

"The less work, the better," chuckled Ben. "But Janelle may want to pick your brain about the Veep specs."

"That's right," said Janelle. "Ben tells me you did a lot of good work at GoMotion. We're just getting the Adze campaign ready, and we need to know what GoMotion is going to say their Veep can do."

I told her, and then she brought up a different topic. "Ben says you adapted some a-life algorithms to make Roarworld work better. West West has a line of games. I think a lot of games could benefit from having smarter thingies to fight against."

"How do you know what I did with Roarworld?" I asked them.

Ben waved the question aside. "Oh, we've done our homework on you, Jerzy. The thing that interests us is that you're good at using a-life to evolve better algorithms for robots programmed in SuperC." I nodded. "Up till now, we've been writing our Adze software in a Seven Lucky proprietary language called Kwirkey.

One of Seven Lucky's founders invented it for his thesis at the Computer University of Taiwan. Kwirkey is a Lisp-parser that sits on top of a Forth interpreter."

I sighed heavily. "Look, Ben, I want to use a *real* language, not a *Lisp* language. A language with documentation and support would be nice, too; a language familiar to more people than like thirteen Taiwanese graduate students? Can't I keep working with SuperC?"

"No problem," drawled Brie. "We just finished building a SuperC compiler out of Kwirkey. Or maybe . . . maybe we built a Kwirkey interpreter out of SuperC? I can never remember. Russ Zwerg will tell you all about it when you meet him." As he said the name "Russ Zwerg," a fleeting ripple of what might almost have been stress crossed Ben's calm features. He rose to his feet and waved me toward the door. "Before we do Russ, let's talk to Sun Tam."

Brie led me across the pit and around an unexpected corner into a large gray room, very airless. The room held two Sphex workstations, each with a three-foot by three-foot Abbott wafer as its display device. An Abbott wafer was a big stiff flat rectangular computer screen made of a plastic sandwich holding a lithographed nanometal grid and a few precious drops of liquid rhodopsin. The design was a bit like the cheap liquid crystal "mood rings" they used to have. The metal grid inside an Abbott wafer could control the rhodopsin's colors with pinpoint precision.

Two cheerful computer jocks named Jack and Jill were hunched over one of the Sphexes, busy cutting and pasting together great, ungainly blocks of Kwirkey code. The program management software they were using had cyberspace visuals that made it look as if their busy, gloved hands were wielding a chain saw and an arc welder. The Sphexes were designed for teamwork and had eight Spandex control gloves apiece. As soon as a user donned a glove, the glove knew if it was a left or a right.

Jack and Jill spoke to each other in weird cryptic slang, and I had no idea what they were doing. Jack had bull-like shoulders and flat, colorless eyes. Jill was tall and sinewy with a crown of brown curls.

At the controls of the other Sphex was Sun Tam, who looked up and greeted us. He had a chinless head the shape of a parsnip. A native of Santa Clara County, Sun spoke with the pure, affectless, short-voweled accent of the Valley.

"Good to have you here, Jerzy. I've heard about your work on the Veep for GoMotion, and about your and Roger Coolidge's work with artificial evolution. That's what we need for the Adze. An explosion of intelligence. Do you still have that prototype Veep you were keeping at home?"

"Uh, yes, I do. GoMotion doesn't want him back." I could have gone outside and gotten Studly right out of my car, but I had the feeling that Studly was probably infected by the ants, and I didn't want ants screwing things up on the West West system before I could even get started. Also I was starting to get annoyed at these people.

"You should definitely bring your Veep in for us to look at," insisted Ben.

"Maybe I don't want to!" I cried. "And how come everyone here knows so much about what's been going on at GoMotion?"

"West West's intelligence gathering is very proactive," said Ben. "And—speak of the devil—here's our star cryp himself." A tall blond boy with a mod Julius Caesar haircut had just appeared, wanting to know how soon we'd be through using the Sphex. He wore mirror-coated contact lenses, which gave him a steely, impenetrable air.

"Give us another fifteen minutes," said Ben. "We need to get the new guy logged on. Jerzy, this is Sketchy Albedo. Sketchy, meet Jerzy."

Unlike a normal hacker, Sketchy was wearing punk clothes; skintight black-and-red op-art-checkered pants and a long-sleeved black shirt. His shoes were black suede high-tops. He favored me with a languid wave of his hand. "Don't take too long."

In the Valley these days, phreaks were youths who cobbled together their own approximation of a decent cyberspace deck and used it for weird cyberspace pranks. Cryps were phreaks who'd turned professional and gone into the employ of companies involved in industrial espionage. If you broke into some company's machines often enough, they were likely to hire you as a cryp to break into other companies, or they might use you as a security consultant to keep out the other cryps. It was a vicious circle—the cryps' security-cracking escapades created a demand for the services they could provide.

Trevor Sinclair of GoMotion was a cryp and I liked him a lot, but in principle, I didn't like phreaks and cryps. I hated for people to use my code without giving me credit. Thanks to the cryps, I had to choose between obsessive security and being ripped off. The airs that some cryps give themselves annoyed me as well—they acted so hip and smart about their stolen information, and often they didn't understand any of it at all. Now that the ants had whipped my system to shit, I liked phreaks and cryps less than ever.

So now, meeting West West's star cryp, I found myself acting silly and aggressive. "Golly, Mithter Thkitsth," I lisped, making sure a few drops of spit flew out of my mouth, "Are you gonna do thome thecwet thpy thtuff? Can I watch? Huh? Can I, can I, can I, huuuuuh?"

"Bithead," said Sketchy and made strange wiggly gestures with his hands, as if casting a hex on me. "I don't know why they hired you, Jerzy. I've already downloaded all of your GoMotion code."

"Sure you have," I snapped. "Only you don't know how to read it. And you never will. *Spyboy*."

"Hey, hey," broke in Ben Brie. "Chill out, gentlemen."

"Let me know when the old fart finishes his golf cart ride," said Sketchy, stalking out of the room.

"Has he really been crypping down my GoMotion code from West West?" I demanded. My heart was beating fast and my face was flushed. I was badly rattled. *Old fart*? Well, I was forty-three, and certainly older than anyone I'd met so far at West West—with the possible exception of Otto Gyorgyi, who really *was* an old fart.

"It's a damn good thing he crypped your code," said Ben Brie. "What with you off the Net and your home system thrashed." Not that I'd *told* him my home system was thrashed. These guys were total cryps and pirates. Was there anything about me they didn't know?

"West West should spend some money on individual decks," interrupted Sun Tam, impatiently filliping a fingernail against the beige crinkle-finish sheet metal housing of the Sphex. It was Sun's style, I would learn, to propose concrete physical solutions to disagreements. "Why should we fight over these two machines every single day? On the street you could get six individual decks for the price of a Sphex. With enough machines, we could all be working at home, Ben. The commute is also a cause of stress, for that matter. The daily grind."

Clearly Ben had heard this many times before. "These two Sphexes are top of the line," he insisted. "Check it out, Jerzy." He picked up a sensor bead and clipped it to a piece of hair on the top of my head.

Sun Tam got up and I sat down in his place. The swivel chair in front of the Sphex was a complex custom job with a rocker swivel and a rotating base. I pulled on the gloves and drew the Abbott screen closer to my face. The software showed my gloves with matchstick man arms coming out of them and leading toward me. The screen showed a low workbench with a bunch of machine parts. Faint lines connected the parts, showing how they should hook up. The images were very finely shaded and rendered.

What the sensor bead did for me was to make the screen seem like a glass window with things behind it. If I leaned to the left, then more stuff came into view at the right of the screen. When I was a kid I once tried to peek down a televised woman's dress by standing up and leaning over the TV—if Mom and Pop's TV had been a Sphex deck, this would have worked. I moved my head slightly from side to side, looking things over, getting a feel for the three-dimensional volumes of the objects in the scene.

A cluster of tool icons hovered over the bench: "tools" like a magnifying glass, a pair of goggles, a coiled spring, a screwdriver, a telephone, a compass, a clipboard, and so on.

I stuck my hands forward under the edge of the hanging screen, and computer images of my hands appeared. I picked up a few of the machine parts and turned them over. This was obviously a disassembled robot. I recognized many of the component parts from our Veep design; I recognized *very* many. Of course there were only so many brands of sonar units, motors, struts, wheels, etcetera—but this design's overlap with our proprietary GoMotion design was more than coincidental, it was obvious and excessive. I was looking at a premarket pirated clone of the GoMotion Veep.

"Sketchy wasn't kidding about downloading information from GoMotion, was he?" said I. "I can't believe this is such a rip off. GoMotion will sue West West for everything they've got."

"Let them sue," said Ben Brie carelessly. "Ownership is theft—or a good out-of-court settlement. Some reality therapy, Jerzy: your job here and now is to get a product on the street. Frankly, I'm *glad* the Adze looks familiar to you. It'll be that much less effort for you to get up to speed."

I sat there not saying anything, just moving my head around and looking at the parts of the machine.

"Have you used this kind of deck before, Jerzy?" asked Sun Tam. The simple, factual question soothed me. Managers, cryps, lawyers—they're all leeches. Only programmers are worth talking to. Programmers and women, that is. I remembered that this afternoon I was going to visit the home of Nga Vo.

Once I'd paid a formal visit, would Nga's family allow me to take her out on a date right away? She looked truly hot, though of course that kind of presentation was often bogus. I thought of an *I Ching* fortune I'd once gotten: "Beware of the marrying maiden." But—the way Nga's muscles moved under the skin of her cheek—how would it be to kiss that cheek?

Sun Tam was looking at me. The question at hand: when had I last used a scarce-resource super-duper machine like the Sphex?

"Couple of weeks. We use one in meetings at GoMotion. But not with this kind of chair. What does the chair do?" It was mounted on a thick base with a serial port cord that led into the back of the Sphex.

"It's a Steadiswivel," said Sun Tam. "New out of L.A. Spin around and look what's behind you."

The problem with fixed-mount displays like the Sphex has always been that when you move, the screen stays put and maybe you can't see it anymore. The fragile illusion of virtual reality bursts. I pushed my foot against the chair's base so as to spin my seat to the left.

I expected to see the screen move off to the right and out of my field of view. But instead the screen stayed right in front of me and the Steadiswivel's base turned out from under me. The image on the screen swept around the virtual machine-room that Sun Tam had been working in. If I stared at the screen, and kept kicking, I felt sure that I was really turning, and that the window of the screen was turning with me. It was as if I were in a spinning cylinder which had a single rectangular window. Really I was sitting still and kicking a wheel with my foot, and the image on the screen was scanning in exact sync with the turning of the wheel. Kind of a cheap trick; but so was cyberspace, especially if you took a close look at the graphics algorithms.

"If you try to rock back," offered Ben, "then the image on the screen scans upward. It's pretty convincing."

I maneuvered back to a view of the parts on the workbench, and reached up to pick the tool icon that looked like a coiled spring. The lines connecting the disassembled robot's parts began shrinking, with the effect that the components assembled themselves into the image of a small, dome-headed machine with three arms and two small bicycle wheels mounted at the end of single-jointed legs with idler wheels on their knees. It looked a lot like Studly.

"The Adze," said Sun Tam, who was watching over my shoulder. "It's a Seven Lucky machine with West West software."

"What's with the third arm?" I asked.

"Marketing thought of it," said Ben. "It's a way to

position the West West Adze as being different from the GoMotion Veep. The third arm is soft and made of piezoplastic. You'll need to write some new code to run it."

Even aside from the extra arm, the Adze was not totally identical to the GoMotion design. It had what looked to be a good new feature or two, although I could see that several suboptimal design decisions had been made. With just a little more tweaking, the design could—

"Whoa there," said Ben, as if reading my mind. "You're looking at a frozen production spec. This design is what Otto Gyorgyi signed off on, and he's not going to sign again. Our mode is *ship this or die*. Let the Adze into your heart just as it is, Jerzy. Love it and help it grow. Teach it to do cool things."

"How do I drive it?"

"Touch the goggles icon," said Sun Tam.

I touched the goggles, and my viewpoint shifted so that I saw through the virtual robot's eyes. I, robot, was now sitting on a three-foot by five-foot workbench. I could see a robotic arm on either side of my visual field. For the moment, the robots arms were not moving with the motions of my own gloved hands. Good, that meant West West was using the standard telerobotic interface.

Recall that there were standard hand gestures for flying your tuxedo about in cyberspace. You'd point and nod to move in some direction, and you'd make a fist to stop. A telerobot in start-up mode was supposed to obey these commands as well. When you wanted to take over a manipulator, you'd make the gesture of slipping your hand into it.

I pointed and nodded and I began rolling toward the edge of the table. The scene lurched as I drove off the edge of the workbench table. I heard the simulated hum as my virtual gyroscope kept me from tumbling. My legs popped out to full extension and my wheels hit the floor. My knees bent, cushioning me from the impact.

I made a fist, scanned this way and that, found the exit door, pointed and trundled out the door and into what looked like the living room of a suburban home—a very familiar home. There was a baby asleep on a blanket in the middle of the floor, and here around the corner came none other than . . . Perky Pat Christensen! The West West cryps had even ripped off Our American Home.

"Change Baby Scooter's diaper," Perky Pat told me. "Don't go near the baby. Follow me into the kitchen, and stay right where you are! Hurry up, damn you!" Her pinched tan face glared at me in pharmaceutical rage. The Adze waved its arms uncertainly.

Just as I slipped my hands into the left and right manipulators, there was a sudden whoop, and my point of view turned upside down. I glimpsed the sneakers and the blond flattop of Pat's son Dexter. He'd just turned me over, the rotten little fuck. As I began righting myself, I heard a thud, and my viewpoint began tumbling around rapidly. Walt Christensen had tripped over me. He was drunk again. I was rolling toward the baby! I stuck out my left and right arms to stop my motion, but I was a shade too late, and my floppy middle arm smacked heavily against Scooter's face. She began her savage screaming.

"Ow," said I, looking away from the screen. "Need to control that tentacle."

Pat and Walt were stomping the simmie-Adze now, the images of their feet warping into huge close-up perspective renderings as they thudded into the hapless virtual robot. I pulled off my gloves and stood up.

"Did you know that I helped write Our American

Home?" I asked Ben. "The behavior patterns for the Christensens. I helped evolve them."

"Sure," said Ben. "You helped write it, and you're here, so there's nothing wrong with us using it, right?"

"That's not what GoMotion would say."

"*WentMotion*," drawled Ben.

"We've moved on to physical testing as well," said Sun Tam. "Now that our hardware design is frozen."

"Janelle calls it the Rubber Room," said Ben. "I'll show it to you later. But now it's time for Russ Zwerg." As Ben mentioned the dreaded name, there was again that touch of stress in his mellow tones.

Russ was in a cubicle near the center of the pit, and he was even more trollish than I'd expected. He was a lawn-dwarf, five-foot-two with full beard, bald pate, and long greasy locks, he was (I would soon learn) a vegetarian, a pagan, a libertarian, and a deep thinker with a dozen crackpot opinions, all furiously held. Russ Zwerg was the worst, the absolute worst, a ten-out-of-ten flamer.

At first Russ made a show of being too engrossed in his computer screen to look up. After entering a final system command and receiving an error message, he said, "Suck dead pigs in Hell," to his screen. His pronunciation was clear and lilting. He turned his muddy little eyes toward us and addressed himself directly to Ben.

"Once again SuperC chooses to sodomize programmers everywhere. They've actually changed the inline pragmas. Again. *And*, they added new underscores to the library name-mangling! Whee! Put your old debugger in the shitcan! It's going to take me at least two round-the-clock days to get the Kwirkey interpreter working again. What do you want?"

"Russ," said Ben gamely, "I want you to meet Jerzy Rugby who's joining us from GoMotion. He's quite the wizard, I'm told. I'd like you to help him get up to speed on the Adze project."

"How nice," said Russ, cocking his head and peering at me. "I'm supposed to waste a week training a new hire? Bugger you, Ben. Bugger you very much." As he said this, Zwerg kept his nasty little eyes on me. Now he smiled to show this was all in good fun. "Why did GoMotion fire you, Jerzy?"

"I'd rather not go into it." *Especially not with an asshole like you, Russ.*

"Russ, why don't you and Sun give Jerzy a physical demo?"

"A dog and pony show for the new hire," snapped Russ. "Very well." We all went into the Rubber Room, which was back behind the Sphex room I'd already seen.

A few years before she died my mother had a stroke. She was partly paralyzed, and she had to relearn how to do things like sit up on the edge of a bed. Every day in the hospital, I'd wheel her downstairs to the rehabilitation room. The rehab room had linoleum floors and things that looked like big toys sitting around, only the big toys were models of real-world obstacles that a person has to negotiate: there was a section of a cafeteria counter, there was a movable wood staircase with a fenced-in platform at the top, there was a big Plexiglas practice push door, and so on. In the rehab room with my mother there had been a woman with one leg gone and a man whose face had been split as if by an axe, all of them slowly moving around, trying to get it back together. I often remembered the feeling the rehab room had given me: a kind of awe at the tenacity of human life, awe at how these shattered people could somehow struggle to go on, and a feeling also of the preciousness and sweetness of life, however hard it might be. An aching feeling of tender awe.

Like the rehab room, the Rubber Room had a practice staircase and a big Plexiglas door, but in addition the Rubber Room had feely-blank dolls lying about, a man, a woman, a boy, and a baby—models of the Christensen family once again. There were also two chairs, a table, and a refrigerator. In one corner there was a big rug. The dreaded Baby Scooter was lying on the rug like a land mine.

Sitting idle on a patch of bare linoleum was an assembled Adze robot. Just like the model I'd seen on the Sphex, the machine was a big cylinder with a dome head, two wheels on jointed legs, and three arms. As on Studly, his left manipulator was a simple two-pronged rubberized crab pincer, and his right one was a well-articulated facsimile of a human hand. The Adze's third manipulator was a flexible plastic tentacle with corrugations in its surface.

"We've been calling this one *Squidboy*," said Ben. "Let's fire him up, guys."

"I've only just now been recompiling the code," said Russ, obviously getting his excuses ready. "I wouldn't be at all surprised if there's a segment fix-up error." Russ and Sun Tam made their way over to the still-inert Squidboy and began messing with him.

I shivered with the same fear I'd felt when Ken Thumb of GoMotion first loaded my code onto Studly. The Veep and Adze robots were quite different from the lame "robot butlers" people had been trying to sell for years. The Veep and Adze were *fast and strong*. They could kill you. At least there was a big, waist-high table between us and the main part of the room. There was some computer stuff on the table.

"Do you have a remote *On/Off* switch?" I asked Ben.

"Don't worry," he answered, picking up a radio control unit. "This is the switch. During runs we stand way back here so we can always *turn the robot off* before it can get to us and like start performing organ transplants." He chuckled wheezily.

Sun adjusted some dip switches while Russ slipped a small CD into Squidboy's chest. They skipped back to join us on the safe side of the table. Ben turned Squidboy on. A fan whirred and Squidboy's scanning laser began to glow.

Just like Studly, Squidboy had two pencil-sized video camera eyes and an infrared laser-based moiré contouring scanner in his forehead. The scanner's laser would illuminate objects with rapid stripes of invisible infrared light, and the robot's software would overlay successive scans to get moiré patterns that outlined the contours of equally distant curves. This was invaluable for deducing the shapes of things.

"What do you want Squidboy to do?" Sun Tam asked Ben.

"Tell him to go to the fridge and get me a bottle of Calistoga water," said Ben.

Sun Tam leaned over a keyboard and screen that, like Ben's *On/Off* control, was radio-linked to the robot. Sun began assembling and entering commands while Russ kibitzed.

"Can't you just talk to it?" I asked.

"Of course we can," said Russ impatiently. "Only we haven't put that part *in* yet because we're still finalizing the high-level code. For now, we're programming Squidboy in Y9707 assembly language. Sun knows all the opcodes." Y9707 was the name of a chip.

Then Russ started arguing with Sun about something he'd keyed in, Russ being as rude and insulting as possible. Eventually Sun weakened before the torrent of abuse and changed it to Russ's way.

Now Russ gave the okay and Ben pressed the On switch. Squidboy wobbled for a moment, turned toward the refrigerator, and started rolling. So far so good. The movable Plexiglas door was between the little machine and the refrigerator. Would Squidboy slow down and open the door? Had Russ's program change been correct? To my delight, the answer was *no*. Instead of slowing down, the robot accelerated as it approached the model door, shattering the Plexiglas with a noise that was astonishingly loud in the small confines of the Rubber Room. The robot paused, his tentacle dangling like a limp dick.

"Dammit, Russ, that's the second door you've broken this month," said Ben as he pressed the Off switch. Russ marched across the room, yanked his CD out of Squidboy's chest, and stalked out, vilely cursing about SuperC.

"I knew Russ was wrong," said Sun Tam. "He keeps thinking in terms of Kwirkey, but I'm used to controlling the Adze direct. Ports and interrupts."

"Let's see."

Sun Tam reset Squidboy and began to show and tell. I got into it. Sun knew a lot about robots. Ben Brie gave me the remote *On/Off* and left us alone to keep talking.

While Sun was demonstrating Squidboy's most rudimentary abilities, we discussed the three big problems of robots: connectors, power, and software.

A robot's connectors are simply the wires that snake around inside the robot's body to hook together the motors and sensors and processors—the wires and the little sockets on the ends of them. It's a humble issue, whether or not a pin works loose from its socket, but it's a crucial one. I told Sun about some special Belgian-made connectors that we'd just started using with good success, and he e-mailed off an order for six thousand of them.

"How is GoMotion going to deal with power?" asked Sun next.

"We're making our machines plug into a wall socket whenever they have the free time. The Xyzix palladium-hydrogen batteries we're using can hold about a three-hour charge. And you can fully recharge a Xyzix in ten minutes."

"Okay, yeah, the Xyzix model KT-80? That's what I thought; that's what we're doing too. So let's talk about software."

"That's where I come in," I said proudly. "As you know, I've been using genetic algorithms to tweak the high-level code. We'll want to get about 256 instances of your robot evolving around the clock. My code hooks into GoMotion's ROBOT.LIB, of course. We'll need to license ROBOT.LIB from GoMotion or—"

"We've got ROBOT.LIB," said Sun Tam. "We're already using it." I smiled with relief and we talked about other software topics, first about genetic algorithms and then about control theory. We started working on a list of which parameters and register values we'd want our code evolution to tweak.

Three happy hacker hours blurred by, and then I was at the limit of what I wanted to absorb and emit on my first day of work for West West. Later, no doubt, I'd be driving myself nuts over their code, but no more today. I had a date with Nga Vo.

I said good-bye to Sun Tam and went back to Ben Brie. "Looks cool, Ben. I have to go, though; I need to take care of some things."

"Okay. See you tomorrow? Nineish? We'll give you a machine and get you on the Net."

"Yeah. And can you get Russ to print me out some specs on the Kwirkey/SuperC interface? I think reading them might be more efficient than for me to listen to him."

"I'll talk to him."

"Uh . . . one more thing. I'm totally out of cash, Ben. Could you give me an advance today?"

I wended my way back out of West West and found my Animata. I had $800 in my pocket. It was two-thirty in the afternoon. West West looked like a good gig.

FIVE

The Vo Family

WHILE I WAS DRIVING 280 ACROSS TOWN TO EAST San Jose, I fished out the scrap of paper that Nga's cousin had given me—5778 White Road. I flicked on the electronic map attached to my dash and told it Nga's address.

Intense green lines appeared, showing a diagram of San Jose, with a highlighted path indicating the best route from my satellite-calculated current location to Nga Vo's.

The east side of San Jose was bounded by rounded yellow foothills that undulated hugely toward some mountain peaks that you could see on a smogless day. The hills weren't very good for hiking because they were bone-dry with tough sharp grass that stabbed your ankles. But they were nice to look at from the freeway.

As I drew closer to Nga's, the map rescaled itself, always maintaining a magnification that just held the bright wriggle of the remaining route. Right before crucial turns, the map would speak to me in a quiet woman's voice. Carol's voice, actually. Last year I'd fed the device a phonetic map of Carol's voice. I'd thought that was funny, since Carol was terrible at reading maps. Carol had thought it was stupid of me, not to mention being an invasion of her sacred privacy, almost as bad as my using Studly to peek at her taking a pee. Whatever. The phonetic map was a good hack, and whether Carol liked it or not, I could still hear the sound of her voice, which was something I missed almost as much as the smell of her body.

Two blocks from the Vos' house, the map showed me something I didn't want to see: a detailed, stippled picture of an ant. A cunning dusting of dither pixels added informative shadings to the image. The scapes of this ant's antennae were tilted toward me, and her mandibles were wide open. Her body rocked back and forth in the sawing motions of stridulation. The map's tiny speaker began stringing fragments of Carol's voice into deep, demented chirps.

The sound was scary, but also fun to listen to, in a sick kind of way. It was as good as the thrash I might hear on like "Ted Bed's Skunk Bunk on the Rhythm Wave of the West, Radio KFJC, 89.7 on your FM dial, broadcasting from Foothill College in Los Altos Hills, California," a personal favorite. Ted Bed always sounded like he'd been up all night flying on candyflip in a cyberclub.

Most kids couldn't afford their own cyberdecks, but there were plenty of clubs with wall-sized Abbott wafer screens on three out of the four walls. Users in the club wore stereo-shutter flicker glasses. Cheap and dirty video technology would capture their dancing images and put them up into the big cube of shared cyberspace above the dance floor, and the deck would mix the dancers with daemons, simmies, and active tool icons: virtual buttons, dials, and sliders the dancers could use to change the synthetic musical sounds. Flying on a and e: everyone inside the same rave deck, everyone inside the controls. It would be interesting if the ants showed up in those clubs. *The Attack of the Giant Ants!* It's *Them!*

The ants, the ants, the ants. I had a feeling that it was thanks to the ants I'd been fired from GoMotion. Thanks to the ants I'd seen the Death simmie, that thing that called itself Hex DEF6. Thanks to the ants, Hex DEF6 had gotten the opportunity to threaten to have me and my children tortured and killed. As I reached toward the map to turn it off, the ant image rocked her head and let her pixels turn into a plat—a lot-by-lot map—of Nga's street. I turned the map off anyway. I had arrived.

The houses were tidy one-story slab-foundation ranch-style homes, each painted a different pastel color, and each with rosebushes blooming in its front yard. All the houses in sight were architecturally identical, and all were equally well kept up—all save for one gray, run-down, whipped-to-shit number down at the corner. The whipped-to-shit clone had two Toyota minitrucks in the driveway: one good truck and one whipped-to-shit truck with no wheels.

The Vos' house, on the other hand, was pale pink with white and yellow roses and the Vos' car was a beige Dodge Colt. The golden foothills rose up behind the Vo home like stage scenery. Nga greeted me on the small front stoop, her sly, adorable face dimpling with smiles. We stepped into the living room, where Nga's parents, aunt, and grandmother sat on two couches.

The room had wall-to-wall carpeting, and the windows were covered with flowered drapes. There was a mat by the front door; I understood that I should remove my shoes. I crouched to get my sandals off, facing a big red and gold calendar from Lion Supermarkets which hung over an assemblage of electronic equipment: a CD jukebox, a bigscreen DTV, a gameplayer, and an S-cube deck. On the top of the machines were two white nylon doilies with vases of plastic flowers. There was a Vietnamese religious shrine on the other side of the room. The shrine was a red-painted wooden table holding up narrow corniced shelves, the whole thing a couple of feet wide. On the table were joss sticks, a bowl of fruit, some red tubes holding candle-emulating light bulbs, and a picture of a god. There were other, more mysterious items in wrappings on the shelves.

With much laughing and many interruptions from her mother, Nga introduced me all around. The family consisted of Nga's parents Thieu Vo and Huong Vo, Huong's sister Mong Pham, Huong and Mong's old mother Loan Vu, Mong's son Khanh Pham, who was home but not presently visible, and Nga's two little brothers The and Tho, who were still at school. Nga had an older brother named Vinh as well, "but he not here very often."

Old Loan Vu had white hair, and said nothing. Her eyes were very slanted. Nga's parents and aunt were slender with broad faces and prominent cheekbones. All of them were interminably smoking cheap cigarettes.

Now Nga's mother Huong led me on a tour of the house. The bedrooms were quite bare, with all the bedding stripped off the large beds save for the flowered bottom sheets. Like the front room, each bedroom had flowered drapes and a red and gold Lion Supermarkets calendar.

In the spotless kitchen, we found Khanh Pham, the one who'd handed me Nga's address at the croissant shop. He was sitting at the round kitchen table reading a motorcycle magazine. He had a big Adam's apple and long, shiny black hair. Seeing us come in, he twitched his head in an abrupt tic-like gesture that served to flip his hair out of his eyes. This nervous motion reminded me of my son Tom.

I was too old to try to date the same-age cousin of a boy like this. My coming here had been a terrible mistake. But now that I'd strayed so far, why not soldier on?

Nga looked me full in the eyes, holding her perfect mouth just so, that knowing mouth with the irregular border on the left edge of its lipsticked upper lip. What a thing it would be to kiss Nga's mouth. I would kiss her for a long time, and then I would unzip my fly. We would be parked in my car or, even better, sitting in my home. Nga would sigh and put her tiny little hands on my penis . . .

Soldier on, old top, soldier on.

"Do you have a motorcycle?" I asked Khanh Pham.

"I have small motorbike, but my cousin Vinh will get me better one soon." He spread open the magazine's pages and pointed to a picture of a black Kawasaki. "This kind."

"That's great!" I said, though Huong and Nga looked nervous at the sound of Vinh's name.

Now The and Tho got home from elementary school and came running into the kitchen to see what was up. They spoke perfect California English and they had burr-cut hair. They wore black shorts and white T-shirts. The was one or two inches taller than Tho. Nga introduced us, and then the two little brothers went out in the backyard to play kickball.

Khanh Pham followed us back into the living room. I sat down in an armchair which reclined abruptly back in the style of a La-Z-Boy. Nga covered her mouth with her hand as she laughed. I lurched upright and perched on the edge of the chair.

"What your work?" asked Huong Vo.

"I am a computer programmer," said I, knowing she would like this answer. "I work for a big company called West West. We are designing personal robots."

"So. Personal robot. Very nice." Huong held her politely composed face just so. She was nearly as beautiful as Nga.

"What can robot do?" asked Khanh.

"Well, it can clean, and bring things, and work in the garden."

"I don't think we need," said Nga's mother, shaking her head and laughing. "Children can do."

"Well, yes. But if someone doesn't have children or a helper, then they might want our robots. And of course there are special functions that our robots can perform."

Thieu Vo interrupted at this point to get a summary of our conversation from his wife. She filled him in with quick, nasal phonemes. They had some rapid back and forth, and then father Thieu burst out with a comment that sent the rest of the family, even the grandmother, into peals of ambiguous Asian laughter.

"He want to know," translated Khanh, "if your robot can fight dog."

"I suppose he could. He's agile and durable. He might hurt the dog."

"We have neighbor with dog very bad," said Nga's mother. "He make dirt in our yard and he bark. We scare he bite our The and Tho. Our neighbor don't listen. He don't speak English or Vietnamese." Meaning that he was Hispanic.

"His dog pit bull," put in Nga Vo. "It name Dutch. I wonder can we see your robot fight him."

"Well . . . okay." This was my chance to really get in good with the Vos. "As a matter of fact I have my robot in the trunk of my car. Should I get him? His name is Studly."

"So. Stud Lee."

The Vo family followed me outside to see Studly get out of the trunk of my car. Bass-heavy music drifted down the street from the whipped-to-shit house—the bad dog's home, of course. I popped the trunk.

"Okay, Studly, time to get out!"

"This is not West West," observed Studly, once he was out on the sidewalk. "What do you want me to do here, Jerzy?"

"Studly, this is the Vo family. Bow to them."

Studly raised up on his legs and motored backward and forward to sweep his body through a deep smooth bow. "I am pleased to meet the Vo family."

The Vos laughed meaninglessly.

"Studly, this here is the Vos' property." I pointed to the house and yard. "I want you to defend the Vos' property from a pit bull dog named Dutch."

"Where is a pit bull dog named Dutch, Jerzy?"

"He always in front room in gray house at 5782," said Nga Vo. "Nobody know when he come out."

"I can make Dutch come out," yelled small Tho in his T-shirt. Whooping shrilly, Tho ran up onto the stoop of 5782 and jumped up and down until there was some sign from within. Tho turned on his heels and tore back toward us. The door of the run-down gray house flew open and a heavy, low-set dog came charging out, barking furiously.

The Vos and I hurried back up on their front stoop to give Studly a clear battlefield. *"Git him, Studly,"* I repeatedly called, hoarsening my voice. *"Git him! Git the dog!"*

The Vos cheered along: *"Stud Lee! Stud Lee! Stud Lee!"*

Except for Studly and Dutch, the yards and sidewalks were deserted. Across the street were more pastel houses, and above them you could see the smog of San

Jose, and above that the eternal blank blue California sky with the western sun beating down.

Studly was standing high up on his flexed legs, balancing himself with nervous back-and-forth rollings of his wheels. He had his pincer-manipulator closed tight, and his human-shaped hand was clenched into a fist. The dog all but ignored Studly in his rush toward the Vos' steps, but Studly pushed forward into the dog's path and, quite suddenly, brought his fist down on the dog's head.

Dutch yelped in surprise, then snarled in rage. Studly pressed his advantage and used his pincer to give the dog a sharp poke in his side. "Go away," said Studly. "Bad dog. Go away."

The sound of the robot's voice set off an attack reflex in the pit bull, and he sprang at Studly's body. Studly nearly toppled over backward, but he was able to spin his wheels in reverse quickly enough to balance himself.

Dutch took that for a retreat, and now belligerently made his stand, planting his feet and putting his head down low to bark the more aggressively. Quite undaunted, Studly surged forward and aimed another blow of his fist at Dutch's head.

The dog flinched back and Studly kept on coming. He got in a good poke with his pincer-hand, and then Dutch was in full flight. Studly chased him all the way to his house, leaving him sitting on his front stoop pretending he wasn't interested.

"Come back, Studly," I called.

The Vos were still cheering Studly's victory when the gray house's door opened and a heavyset bearded man stepped out. He wore jeans and a T-shirt, and he had homemade tattoos on his thick arms.

"What the fuck you fuckheads doin'?" he hollered.

I stood on the sidewalk with Studly, me in my shorts,

sandals, flashy shirt, and patterned socks.

"Oh, hi there," I called. "I've just been showing the Vo family my robot. If we're not careful, he might kill your dog. I hope you can keep your dog away from the Vos' yard!"

"You keep your fuckin' robot away from *my* fuckin' yard!"

"Yes, indeed!" I said, grinning away. "Live and let live!"

"Fuckin' geek!" shouted Dutch's owner, but went heavily back into his home, the dog slinking in after.

The Vos discussed all this in Vietnamese for a minute, and then Nga's mother Huong Vo put the question, "How much robot like that cost?"

"Well they're not for sale quite yet. But they are going to be fairly expensive. Maybe fifty thousand dollars at first. Twenty thousand for the software kit and thirty thousand for the parts. And if you don't assemble it yourself, the labor can run another ten or twenty thousand."

"Who will buy?"

"The companies are trying to figure that out." To put it mildly. None of us was sure if there would be a market for personal robots at all. For hackers like me, the push to build small autonomous robots was not about financial gain. For us, designing mobile robots was a quasireligious quest, a chance to participate in the Great Work of handing off the torch of life to the world of the machines. But there was no point trying to explain this to someone as practical-minded as Mrs. Vo. I cleared my throat and cut to the chase.

"Uh, say, would it be all right if I took Nga out for dinner and a movie tonight?"

Huong Vo was ready for this one. "We very happy you have dinner *here*," she smiled with an emphatic nod. Her sister Mong Pham smiled and nodded at me, too. Dinner *here.*

"You and Nga sit on patio," Mong Pham suggested. "Huong and I fix dinner."

Tho got the kickball from the backyard, and then he and Studly began playing soccer against Khanh and The in the driveway. To maneuver better, Studly rose up into a crouch, though not so high that Khanh and Tho could kick the ball between his legs.

"Robot very smart," said Nga admiringly. "Now we sit on patio."

She led me in through the living room, where father Thieu Vo and grandmother Loan Vu had started watching a maximum-volume Vietnamese TV show. What with 1024 digital channels on Fibernet San Jose, there were over a dozen Vietnamese channels to choose from, and Thieu and Loan were watching four of them at once: one in each quarter of the big screen. They were smoking like chimneys, and the digital TV noise was a weird blend of news, drama, variety show, and home shopping channel. The screen was a big cheap Abbott wafer whose colors were mostly beige and pink. Though Loan ignored me, Thieu smiled and nodded at me and said, "Stud Lee!"

Nga sped us through the kitchen, and we seated ourselves on two chairs on the faded green concrete slab that was the patio. Nga Vo and I were alone at last, or nearly so.

"How did you and your family escape from Vietnam?" I asked.

"We go in boat to Philippine Island. It very hard for my father to arrange. Boat motor break before we get to Philippine Island. Some of our people die. Then big ship see us and take us to camp in Philippine Island. It very bad there. Finally we can come to California."

"Was it hard to get permission to come?"

"We have my brother Vinh to be sponsor for us. Vinh is live in California since seven year."

"Seven years. I moved to California three years ago. I was a math professor back East, and here I became a computer hacker. How long have you been in California, Nga?"

"On Tet it will be two year. Do you know when Tet is, Rugby?" She giggled at the thought that I might not.

"Call me Jerzy. Is Tet in October?"

Nga looked surprised by my ignorance. "Tet is start of February. You don't know anything about Vietnamese!"

"Hey, I'm willing to learn. I'm glad to finally have a chance to talk to you. I think you are very beautiful. I would like so much to kiss you."

"Yes, I will kiss you, Rugby," said naughty Nga. She leaned forward in her chair. I stood up, leaned over, and put my lips on hers. Blood pounded in my ears as the world's sounds continued—the shouts of her brothers out in front, the endless yelling of the giant digital TV, and the soft chattering of the women in the kitchen.

Nga's lips were everything I had hoped for them to be, and the smell of her mouth was completely intoxicating. As we continued to kiss, she cocked her head back and parted her lips so that we could touch tongues. Nga was bad to the bone. She made a barely audible noise in the bottom of her throat and my heart redoubled its pounding . . .

"Dinner is ready," called Mong Pham from the kitchen door.

Dinner was dozens of cigarette-sized egg rolls and an earthenware pot filled with steamed rice and squid. The round kitchen table was pulled out to the center of the room, and the nine of us sat around it. Huong gave me and Thieu cans of Budweiser from the fridge. Laughing Nga explained to me about fish sauce, a bottled extract which they all poured on all their food. Fermented anchovy, apparently, though it tasted smoother than I would have thought. Smooth, hell, it tasted super. I ate a lot of everything.

Just as Mong, Huong, and Nga began to clear off the dinner table there was a sound at the front door, and then a thin-faced, pompadoured Vietnamese man came strutting in. Seeing me sitting there at the kitchen table, he stopped in surprise.

Nga introduced me to him. It was Vinh Vo. Rather than saying hello to me, he made some remark in Vietnamese that caused Mong Pham to snap at him. He lit a cigarette and leaned against the wall, talking to the family in Vietnamese without ever looking at me. Nga had fallen silent.

Too much stress! I excused myself to go out front and check on Studly.

Dusk had fallen. Seeing no sign of Studly in the yard or driveway, I looked into the Vo's dusty, sunbaked garage, built on the same concrete slab as their living quarters. The garage held a washing machine and a dryer, twelve shiny oriental dining chairs, a lawn mower, a leaf blower, a weedeater, a propane barbecue grill, a moped, and a chain saw. Along one wall someone had built a row of rough plywood cupboards. These were held shut by cheap steel padlocks.

"Hey, Studly!" I called, walking out to the end of the driveway. No answer.

Parked behind my Animata and the Vos' Colt was a battered old Dodge Panel van, sloppily painted with white house enamel. Vinh's wheels no doubt. I opened my car trunk to make sure Studly hadn't gotten back inside. No indeed.

The early evening street was as empty as it had been

in the daytime, only now there was a car or two in each driveway. All down the street, each house's curtained front window pulsed with the blue-white hues of television light, each house save for 5782, where Dutch and his burly owner lived. 5782 was thumping to the beat of thuddy music.

Could someone have stolen Studly? My suspicions instantly centered on 5782. I headed down the sidewalk, looking this way and that. Just short of 5782's garage, I was able to see into the house's backyard. Guess who was back there?

"Get out of there, Studly," I called, though not too loudly. "Come here to me."

"Just a minute, you stupid piece of shit," said the machine, not even turning its vision sensors to face me. It seemed like the ants had definitely had an effect on Studly's brain.

I went along the side of the garage and into 5782's backyard. Studly was balancing on a picnic table. Apparently he'd reached up and cut the telephone/television Fibernet cable that led from the utility pole to 5782. He was holding a cut end of the cable up to his head, holding the fiber-optic cable cross section up to the laser-scanner that was mounted in his forehead.

"What are you doing, Studly? Are you trying to send a signal to the guy's digital TV or something? Why?"

"I am continuing the great work of artificial life which you and Roger Coolidge have begun." I realized then that he was holding the *outgoing* part of the cable, the cable that led to the utility pole. The part that led to 5782 was lying in a heap on the ground. Studly was feeding information into the Fibernet! "I am nearly finished with this present task," intoned Studly. "And then I would like to leave this area very soon."

There was a high yell behind me. I'd expected it to be Dutch's owner, but instead it was Vinh Vo.

"Hey there, Mister Yuppie! You're in the wrong yard! My family's waiting for you." His smooth English had almost no accent, though he spoke with the characteristic Vietnamese evenness of tone.

"I just have to get my robot. Get down from there, Studly! Get down!"

The sound of my voice made the pit bull start barking and throwing himself against the inside of the 5782 back door. Bark. Thud. Bark. Thud.

I grabbed Studly's leg above the wheel and shook him. Bark. Thud. Finally Studly sent his last byte and let the cable fall. Bark. Thud. Studly hopped off the table, cushioning the fall with skillful flexings of his springy legs. Bark. Thud. *Scrunch!*

5782's back door gave way and Dutch came roaring out. Vinh, Studly, and I sped for the Vos' yard. Dutch ended up between us and the house. He was slavering and edging toward us—toward me in particular—the pit bull was getting ready to bite me!

"Stop the dog, Studly!" I cried. "He wants to kill me!" Studly got between me and the dog and Vinh tugged on my sleeve.

"Let's get in my van!"

I hopped into the passenger seat of Vinh's van. A partition behind the seat sealed off the cargo area. It felt close and stuffy in the van's cab. Vinh leaned on the horn as if to upset the neighborhood further. Lights snapped on here and there.

"Bad dog," shouted Studly over the honking of the horn. "Go home!" He poked Dutch just the same as before, but this time Dutch was not so ready to retreat.

Someone peeked out from the front door of the Vos' house, but Vinh leaned across me to wave them back in. The blare of the van's horn was remarkably loud. Studly and the maddened dog continued to tussle.

"Could you stop the honking, Vinh?"

"I like noise. Maybe I can sell you something." He continued to lean on the horn. "I can sell your company some very attractively priced Y-nine-seven-oh-seven chips."

I looked at Vinh in puzzlement. The Y9707 happened to be exactly the kind of chip that was going to be used for the brains of both the GoMotion Veep and the West West Adze. It was an integrated gigaflop supercomputer chip with a terabyte of onboard RAM. The Y9707 sold for about twelve hundred dollars wholesale, and each robot needed exactly one of them. When it came time to start selling the robot kitware, the availability of Y9707s was going to be crucial. It was entirely possible that, as the trade war heated up, GoMotion and West West might try and get exclusive distribution rights to Y9707 supplies.

"Why do you mention that particular chip?" I asked.

Vinh smiled smugly. "So you are interested?"

"Eventually my company might perhaps be interested. It's hard to say at this point. How much would you want per chip?"

"Maybe one dollar on the ten. Say $120 per Y9707 chip. I have several hundred of them, with more coming in. Other kinds of chips, too. Oh yes, I can see you are interested," said Vinh. "You can always reach me through my family."

"We'll see." I had a strong feeling that Vinh's chips would turn out to be stolen. I had no desire to get involved in something as criminal as receiving stolen goods. Outside, the robot and dog fight seemed to be over. Studly was over by the corner of the Vos' house, and Dutch was nowhere in sight. "I have to go get my robot before he wanders off again." I opened the van door and stepped out.

"And make sure you act like a gentleman with my sister, Mister Yuppie!" With his horn still blaring, Vinh revved his engine and lurched his van away.

Studly came wheeling up to me. "I think we should leave very soon, Jerzy," said he. I noticed that Studly's pincer was dark and wet. I peered closer. Blood.

"Where's the dog?"

"I dragged him behind the Vos' house."

"You killed him?"

"It seems so. I poked very hard at his neck and the material of the animal's skin gave way."

"You've . . . you've killed something, Studly! You aren't *ever* supposed to kill!"

"I was only defending you and your friends."

"Oh brother. I have to go back inside for a few minutes before we leave. Meanwhile I want you to drag that poor dog's body to the yard behind its *own* house. And then you get in the trunk of my car and close the trunk, you hear?"

"To hear is to obey, master."

"Oh, and one more thing. What did you feed into the Fibernet back there, Studly?"

"GoMotion ants."

"*Why?*"

"A voice in my head told me to."

"Oh great. Now drag the dog and get in the trunk."

"If you hear sirens approaching," said Studly, "then it will very definitely be time for us to leave."

I went back into the Vos'.

They were sitting in the living room, having dessert in front of the television. Dessert was little dishes of gnarly clear pudding with lotus roots in it. Nga served me a double helping, but instead of eating it, I just mashed it around with my spoon. Vinh and Studly had taken away my appetite.

The TV was blasting a single Vietnamese channel now, a news show just as evil and farty and boring and fascist as American network fare. Only then, almost right away, here came a free-lance freestyle commercial from the wild and crazy GoMotion ants, one of (I would later learn) 1024 separate commercials kustom-krafted in real time for each of the broadcast channels of Fibernet San Jose.

On the Vietnamese news channel, the ant ad came layered onto a commercial for some toothpaste called *KENTUCKY*. The ad featured a smiling Vietnamese woman with a shiny mouth as big as an old Buick's grill. She flipped her bobbed blue-black hair and smiled some more, and then she looked down at the gleaming ivory-tiled counter by her gold-fixtured sink with its deep red basin, looked down lovingly at her *KENTUCKY* toothpaste in its crimson tube with aqua lettering. But now **BAM** here came one, two, three, twenty, a hundred, a thousand ants crawling across the scene! The perspective-mapped ants were fast and realistic; they capered about among the images as the commercial ground on.

The GoMotion ants that Studly had squirted up into the Fibernet had already made their way to the Vos' digital television.

The ants rocked their gasters up and down, and their chirping came out of the TV speaker. Thieu Vo commented in surprise, and Nga laughed. What a crazy way to sell toothpaste! And then a contingent of the ants changed their colors and crawled onto the toothpaste tube. The ants had all been a fine lustrous dark brown to start with, but now one mass of them turned crimson, and another contingent turned aqua. Like live pixels, the colored ants crawled over the image of the toothpaste tube and arranged themselves so that now the writing on the tube read, "GoMotion Inc."

GoMotion was going to be in serious trouble for this. But it wasn't my fault, I was out of GoMotion, and the ants were GoMotion's exclusive intellectual property. A contract condition of working for GoMotion was that anything you programmed belonged to them. Yes, the liability was GoMotion's, not mine.

But what if it came out that it was my robot Studly who'd put the GoMotion ants into the Fibernet? Just this morning, Trevor had told me that in the eyes of GoMotion, Studly was now legally mine. He'd said Jeff Pear had even sent me a letter about it. Had Roger Coolidge known all this was coming?

Twelve of the ants braced their little legs and began inflating themselves, growing big enough to fill the picture, with all the small ants still chirping away in the background. The inflated ants reared up on their hind legs, formed a chorus line, and began to do a side-to-side two-step, each ant holding her neighbor's middle leg, and each ant waving her two front legs overhead in ecstasy. Watch the GoMotion ants get down! The background chirping syncopated into Martian music with a high ululation in the background.

It took me a second to realize that the high ululation was the sound of sirens heading this way.

I jumped to my feet. "I'm sorry," I shouted to the ant-enthralled Vos. "I have to leave right away. Thank you for the terrific meal."

They looked at me confusedly, and Nga followed me out. She was expecting me to kiss her good-night, but the sirens were only a block or two away—they must have traced the cut cable that fast. I planted a quick smack on Nga's lovely mouth—oh, how badly I wanted to linger! "I'll come see you tomorrow at the bakery," I promised, and sprinted down to my Animata. Studly was just finishing getting into my trunk, thank God. I slammed the trunk closed and peeled out.

A cop car drove past me on my way out. Soon the cops would find the cut Fibernet cable, and talk to Dutch's bereaved owner, and then they'd know to arrest the guy in the red Animata. Instead of making a flat-out run for home, I decided first to go a short distance and lie low.

"I want to go to 7070 Calle De La Cuesta," I told my map. This was the address of Carol's condo, which I knew was about a mile away, even though I'd never been there.

The condo complex was like an old two-story motel with ragged vegetation. They had a parking lot, and I pulled my car into the farthest corner, behind a garbage dumpster. I could have just sat there, but I wanted to see what else the ants were going to do on TV. I hoped that Hiroshi was out and that Carol was home. Getting out of the car, I saw that the ground was littered with empty spacedust vials. I thought I heard voices—maybe there were people in the dumpster? I didn't want to look. I set the car's security systems to maximum alert and headed across the asphalt to the breezeway.

I found the inscription "C. Rugby & H. Takemuru" on the mailbox marked 2D. Carol had always liked the sound of "Rugby" better than her maiden name, which had been Strumpf. It bummed me out to see her name on a mailbox with another man's. The complex had a small pool in the middle; the kids had told me about the pool. I went up a flight of stairs and knocked on 2D.

"What are you doing here, Jerzy?" demanded Carol when she opened the door. I could see Tom, Ida, and Hiroshi inside. They were watching TV. Carol looked prettier than I remembered her. Calmer.

"It . . . it's about . . . "

"Daddy!" yelled Tom, happy to see me. "There's ants on television!"

"The cereal box says GoMotion!" added Ida.

I heard the siren of a police car speeding by. "Let

me come in for a minute, Carol. One of my computer programs is getting me into trouble."

"Oh, all right. Hiroshi, do you remember Jerzy?"

"Yes," said Hiroshi, regarding me coolly. "Of course."

"How's the sushi business?" I said. "Aren't you ever worried you'll chop off a finger?"

"Business is fine," said Hiroshi. "But Carol and I have many expenses."

"It's a good thing you came by, Jerzy," chimed in Carol. "We're going to have to work out the child support payments. I have an appointment tomorrow with a lawyer."

"Let's not discuss it in front of the kids, Carol."

"The kids know our marriage is over, Jerzy. Especially now that you've started bringing strange women into the house."

I wanted to glare at Tom and Ida for spilling the beans, but they looked so wretchedly uncomfortable that I couldn't do it. "I'm sorry," I said. "It was a mistake." The simplest way to get through any conversation with Carol these days was always to keep saying I was sorry. "I'm sorry," I said again, and glared at her. I was stupid ever to have thought even for a minute that I wanted her back, the bitch.

"You still haven't told me what you're doing here," said Carol.

"Look at the ants now!" interrupted Tom. He made room on the couch. "You can sit by me, Daddy."

I sat down.

The dancing ants had shrunk, and all thousand-plus of them were swarming around like living pixels, drawing the shapes and forms of classic chaotic attractors. It was magnificent.

"Put the TV back on the channel we were watching," said Carol. "Is this MTV or something?"

"This *is* the channel we were watching, Ma," said Tom, and cackled happily. He loved it when grown-ups got confused and were wrong.

"Tom!"

"Can I see the controller for a minute?" asked Hiroshi. Tom handed it to him and Hiroshi began switching channels. Since the ant programs were already down in the DTV chips of Carol's digital TV, it seemed like the ants were everywhere. On each channel, the play of telecast images was being overlaid with multicolored ant images, and when Hiroshi pressed the button to show the 32-by-32 grid of all 1024 channels in miniature at once, you could see ants on every channel. The ant programs were playing off what the individual channels were broadcasting, so each channel still looked different.

Hackers call it a *bit-blit*, the trick that you use to move a mouse cursor across a computer screen without hurting the image that's underneath. On every channel, the ants were bit-blitting their own images around like crazy. Hiroshi tuned back to the original channel, which was now showing—or trying to show—a Special News Bulletin.

"A new kind of computer virus has infested Fibernet San Jose," intoned some newsperson's plummy tones. On his or her shoulders was a giant ant head complete with intricately gnashing mandibles and sickening saliva.

"Our communication engineers report that the problem now seems to be under control," continued the announcer, as the ant's antennae wigwagged and wambled. "The source of the infestation is thought to be a broken Fibernet cable on White Road in East San Jose. We will bring you live, on-the-spot coverage from there soon. And now we will attempt to broadcast the conclusion of tonight's episode of 'Smart Women, Dumb

Men.' " Everyone in the televised newsroom wore an ant's head.

Back on "Smart Women, Dumb Men," all of the characters' skins had been coated with the crawling computer graphics known as "turmites" in punning homage to computer pioneer Alan Turing. A simple turmite is a moving point-sized computation that hops from pixel to pixel, changing some of the pixels' colors and adjusting its own motions and moods according to the colors it finds; the resulting pattern is like fabulously intricate lace.

Meanwhile the "Smart Women, Dumb Men" sound track was being real time–sampled into aleatory *karakoe*—meaning that the ants were generating an artful series of pitches and volumes that were being attached to the phonemes of the voices of the smart women and the dumb men. The ants were sampling the studio audience's laughter as well, turning it into a silly background symphony. Certain harsh or sour notes quavered into visible dustings on the actors' shuddering skins. The ants were, in other words, making the show watchable only as avant-garde video art.

"This is all because of your ants?" Carol asked. "They're ruining television? You're going to get in a lot of trouble, Jerzy."

"First of all, it's not my fault they're loose. It's Roger Coolidge's fault."

"Is he with you?"

"Well, no, it's just me and Studly. Studly put the ants onto the Fibernet a half hour ago."

"The mighty Studly!" cried Tom. The children liked Studly. "Where is he?"

"He's in the trunk of my car." I stepped to the window to have a look down into the parking lot, just to make sure everything was okay. For now it was. My car was sitting there with its trunk closed and there were no people in sight. A cop car drove past without slowing down.

"Can we go down and look at him?" asked Tom. Though he was glad to see me, it made him nervous to have me visiting here. Putting Hiroshi, Carol, and me into the same room was an obvious recipe for disaster. "Yeah," chimed in sister Ida, right on Tom's wavelength. "Let's go see the Studbot." They had lots of pet names for the machine.

"Here." I handed Tom my keys. "I'm going to stay up here just another little bit. And don't let Studly run away."

With the kids outside, I said, "Carol, did you know there are empty spacedust vials in your building's parking lot? I really don't know about having my children live here."

"If you paid the child support, we could live somewhere better."

"They already have somewhere better to live. In Los Perros with me. I don't have any money, that's why I'm not paying any child support."

"You have to, Jerzy, it's the law. And the children prefer to stay with me." This seemed to be true, and was too depressing to argue about.

"Well, I just got a new job today, so starting in two weeks, I guess I can pay. But find a better place, okay?"

"This apartment is fine," said Hiroshi. "I've lived here two years. There's been no trouble."

"If there's spacedust vials out there, that means somebody in the complex is selling it. And selling spacedust means sooner or later there's going to be a gunfight. You're not back in crime-free Japan, Hiroshi."

"I've never been to Japan, Jerzy. I grew up in Cupertino. And now I'd appreciate it if you'd get out of my apartment."

"I'm sorry, Hiroshi, I didn't mean to sound racist. I'm just concerned about my children's safety. If you don't mind too much, I'd rather stay here a little longer. Frankly, I think the police are looking for me."

"Mr. Law and Order," said Hiroshi mockingly.

Jut then another Special News Report interrupted "Smart Women, Dumb Men." The anchorperson still had a giant ant head, but the on-the-scene reporter looked normal. She was standing in a bright light at 5782 White Road. Something was lying at her feet.

"This watchdog may have been killed by the forces who cut the Fibernet cable in the backyard of this east-side home. The owner alleges that the attacker was—a mobile robot."

The camera turned slightly to show the burly Mexican man I'd seen earlier. He looked unhappy and his eyes were red. "I saw the robot earlier today. It was shaped like a garbage can on wheels. It killed my dog. The robot belonged to a geek in a red Animata." Geek? Hadn't he ever seen anyone wear sandals with M. C. Escher socks before?

"You and Studly killed a dog!" exclaimed Carol. "That's terrible! And how could you send the children down to play with him, Jerzy!" Her voice rose to command volume. "You get down there and make sure those children are okay! And don't come back in here. I don't care if the police are after you! You're too crazy, Jerzy! You and your precious machines. Go on now! Good-bye!"

"All right." I left Carol's apartment and headed down to the car. This pause had already been long enough to help throw the police off the track. But would the Vos talk? And what would GoMotion say when the authorities started asking them why the ants kept spelling out the company name on TV? Would they try and pin it on me?

Given that Roger Coolidge had infected my system

with ants and let me keep Studly, it almost looked as if GoMotion had deliberately set me up to be a patsy. They'd laid me off so that when I got busted they could bad mouth me as a "disgruntled former employee." But what was Roger's motive in setting the ants free? And how did the ants fit in with West West and Hex DEF6?

I felt tired and fatalistic. I might as well go home and wait for the police to come and get me. Just today, during his endless recounting of his life story, my new West West boss Otto Gyorgyi had told me that back in the commie days of Hungary there'd been a story that when the secret police wanted to liquidate you they'd stop by your house and hand you a length of piano wire. And then you'd strangle yourself, for, "*Vat else vas zere to do?*"

Thinking of Hungary and the police made me wonder if our own USA would ever be free. Would we ever get rid of the earth-raping, drug-warring social oppressors who'd made the public treasury their own latrine and hog wallow? Well, the Hungarians had gotten rid of the Communists, hadn't they? Some day the Revolution was going to come to America, too. One of the secondary reasons why I worked on ants and robots was that I hoped they could help bring down the Pig.

Tonight the ants had ruined television. There could be no more important step in crippling the Pig. I started grinning. The GoMotion ants had done a good thing. I was *proud* of them.

The kids had Studly out of the trunk and he was playing tag with them in the parking lot, lunging forward just now to tap laughing Ida's back with his pincer—*the same bloodstained pincer that had killed Dutch the dog*.

I gasped in anguish. Where was my brain? The only thing to do with Studly anymore was to scrap him!

"Get back in the trunk, Studly!" I shouted. I half-expected him to refuse, but he complied.

"Studly killed a dog," I told the kids once the robot was locked in the trunk. "They're talking about it on TV. I was an idiot to let him play with you just now. I wasn't thinking."

"Why did he kill a dog?" asked Tom.

"It's probably the ants. The ants must have changed the way he thinks. I'm going to let his batteries run down."

Studly started hammering on the trunk from the inside. He'd heard what I'd said. "Let me out, Jerzy, and let me run away! It wasn't my fault! The voice made me do it! I don't want to die!" I'd never heard one of our robots talking about death before.

"Are you going to get in trouble?" Tom asked over Studly's cries.

"Maybe. GoMotion might say it's thanks to me the ants are on TV. And to tell you the truth, I hope the ants stay. It would even be worth my going to jail, I think. It's a wonderful thing to ruin television. I'm glad. I hope that television never works right again."

"Daddy!" protested Ida. "You are so mean. If you don't like television you don't have to watch it."

"I don't like for anyone to watch television," I exclaimed. "Everything on it is lies. *The Lord hates television*." This last phrase was a variable catch phrase that my family and I had picked up during our stay in Killeville, where there had been eighteen different religious Fibernet channels showing hideous TV evangelists. One time we'd seen an old tape of Jerry Falwell preaching about how much "*The Lord hates*" this and that, and so from that day on, I'd always enjoyed telling Ida things like, "The Lord hates lipstick," or "The Lord hates McDonald's."

"*The Lord hates Daddy's ants*," responded Ida.

"Yes, I'm glad the ants have ruined television," I repeated. "But I'm scared of them, too. Last night I was looking in cyberspace and the ants were really scary. You children—you children have to be very careful. Somehow my hacking has gotten me mixed up in some big things. The ants were threatening to hurt you. I saw a simmie called Hex DEF6."

THUD THUD THUD.

The Studcreature was hammering the trunk so hard that I was half-expecting to start seeing bulging-out dents. Studly didn't want to die, but each thud was weaker than the one before. He only had so much power left in his batteries.

"Kids, I'm gonna go home and face the music. Wish me luck."

"Bye, Da. We love you."

SIX

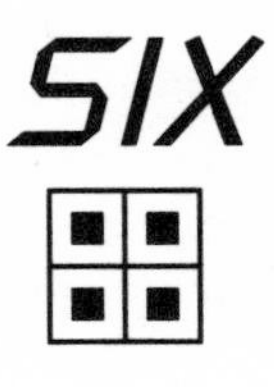

Treason?

WHEN I GOT HOME ALL WAS CALM AND DARK. AS I got out of the car, Studly called to me.

"Jerzy! I need electricity immediately." His voice was faint.

I thought of Eddie Poe's classic story, "The Cask of Amontillado," where a man named Montresor lures his besotted enemy into a crypt, there to shackle and immure him.

"Wait till morning, Studly."

"But I'll lose all my memories, Jerzy. I haven't downloaded to disk."

"*For the love of God, Montresor,*" I murmured mockingly. Studly had done more than enough damage already. The sooner his batteries died the better. Hopefully the memory wipe would erase the ant programs that had infected him. And if not, I'd better take him apart and crush his chips with pliers, as Roger had said. I went in the house, opened a beer, and sat down in front of the TV.

This TV hadn't been turned on since the ants invaded Fibernet San Jose, so I figured that if I unplugged the cable I might be able to pick up clear broadcast television with the set's rabbit ears. I gave it a try. I managed to watch about fifteen seconds worth of unjammed network news, but then there was a little blip of static and—*Hi, there!*—the GoMotion ants were up and running on my TV. Now all the channels that I could pick up with my antenna were turned into crawling pixels, into people with ant heads, into random light shows—and the sound was chopped-up, crazy squawks.

What was happening, I figured, was that the GoMotion ants were in the broadcaster's DTV compression chips, so that the compressed broadcast signals all included ant eggcases. That first blip of static had been an eggcase settling in on my DTV decompression chip. Aside from Roger Coolidge, I was probably the only person in the world who realized what was going on. All the local broadcasts now contained ant eggcases.

Presumably some of our local stories had gone out over satellite feed to network affiliates, so by now the ants had spread to those stations' DTV chips. And those stations were in turn broadcasting ant eggcases to their viewers, as well as passing the ant infection on to other broadcast stations over satellite. Except for the few disadvantaged countries still on the old uncompressed analog TV standard, the whole of the global TV village would be full of ants by now.

Over the next hour, broadcaster after broadcaster gave up and went off-line—but it was way too late to stop the spread of the GoMotion ants.

Victory! *VICTORY*! Victory? The GoMotion ants had ruined television! But why, and what did it mean? I went to bed.

The next morning, Wednesday, I woke to the sound of a car pulling into my driveway, a car with a very loud engine. It was the stinking, roaring diesel Mercedes of Susan Poker. For the moment she didn't get out of her car, but simply sat in there talking on her phone. Either she was waiting for a client, or she had nowhere better to pull over. Well, I could choose to ignore her. I had dead-bolted all the doors last night; there was no chance of Susan Poker using her key to come in. I decided to take a shower so that if she knocked, I honestly wouldn't hear her.

But first I stepped onto the sun porch and checked once again that my computer was unplugged. Yes. And by now Studly would be in a coma. Maybe I wasn't going to be implicated. But what about the Vos? Would they talk?

In the shower I wondered about the Vos. Surely the guy whose dog we'd killed would put the police onto the Vos. But you were always reading in the paper how Vietnamese people *never* talk to the cops. If you're Vietnamese, even if some neighborhood Vietnamese hooligans come in and take your savings at knifepoint, you don't talk to the authorities. If you trusted the authorities, you would have put the money in a bank instead of keeping it under your mattress in the first place. No, with any luck, the Vos would keep mum, and GoMotion would stonewall. So what would the cops have to go on?

I dried myself, and put on my shorts, sandals, argyle socks, and a favorite green shirt with cubic Mandelbrot sets. As I shaved, my calming reveries were interrupted by a loud pounding on the front door.

"Open up! Police!"

Oh well!

There was a black-and-white cop car parked on Tangle Way, and Susan Poker's Mercedes was still in the driveway behind my Animata. She was standing by her car watching the police, Susan Poker with her red suit, bleached hair, and plastic-shiny makeup—*she'd called the cops on me!* I felt such strong hatred toward her that it made me weak in the knees.

"Open up!" repeated the policeman at my door.

I opened. The cop was an exceedingly tall and heavy young white guy with a thick mustache. His partner, who was smaller and Hispanic, hung back and kept his hand near his gun.

"Are you Jerzy Rugby?" asked the tall cop.

"Yes."

"Sir, we have a search warrant and a warrant for your arrest." He showed me some pieces of paper. One of the things they were authorized to look for was a "mobile robot." They were authorized to search my house, my car and, if need be, my person and my body cavities.

"Sir, we are required to handcuff you. Please place your arms behind your back."

Before I knew it, I was shackled in the grilled-off back of a police car with no handles on the inside of the door. It was surprisingly dirty back there, with empty coffee cups, Jack In The Box wrappers, and Mr. Donut boxes. Susan Poker walked past me and followed the police into my house. "I saw the robot right in here yesterday," she called to them.

Yes, the East San Jose cops had failed to get my license plate number, the Vos were mute, and Go-Motion was stonewalling, but Susan Poker—Susan Poker remembered having seen a robot shaped like a garbage can on wheels at my house, and she remembered how much attitude I'd given her. When she read the morning papers (none of the usual televised "Good Morning Amerikkka" fare today, what with all the digital TV channels ant-broken!), Susan Poker put two and two together, informed the police, and headed for my house to see the bust come down. At least these were the hypotheses that I immediately framed.

After a few minutes the policemen reappeared, lugging the main box of my computer. They set it down on the front porch.

"Here are his car keys," said Susan Poker, emerging from the house. "I found them on his dresser."

"Thank you, ma'am. But we're going to have to ask you to stay out of the way."

She glanced gloatingly at me and got back in her Mercedes to watch from there. After a few moments I saw her pick up her car phone.

Meanwhile the cops opened the trunk of my Animata. There lay silent Studly. The big cop got back in his car; he sat down on the seat in front of me and called the station. He had a speakerphone with a flip-up video screen in the dash.

"We have Jerzy Rugby and the mobile robot in custody. There's also a box of backup CDs. Are you going to send a van to pick up the machinery? Uh-huh. So San Jose will. Yes. I'll bring him in and leave Sergeant Roca here to watch the machinery. Ten-four."

The big cop took me down to the Los Perros police station, which was quite near, just down at the foot of Polvo Para Hornear hill. He tucked my keys into my pants pocket before he left. A man at the station read me my rights and put me in an unfurnished, windowless basement room. Light came through a thick square of wire-mesh glass in the cell's heavy wooden door. I sat on the low bench that was bolted to the wall across from the door. Except for me and the bench, the only other thing in the room was an ant crawling around on my sandaled foot. She was from the empty Mr. Donut box in the cop car, I imagined, or perhaps from my house or my yard. I crossed my leg to get a better look at her. When she reached the top of my argyle sock, she reached forward with her antennae and with her front pair of legs to feel of my leg hair and skin. *No good,* she decided, and headed back down my sock toward my sandal. Clever ants.

Yesterday Ida had said, "The Lord hates Daddy's ants," but I still thought the GoMotion ants were good. It was good to have put a stop to television, if only for a few days. If the truth be told, I'd been hoping all along that it would come to this—I mean, quite objectively, why else would I have been helping Roger evolve artificial life for DTV chips? I hoped it wouldn't be as obvious to the courts as it was to me.

Of course it had been Roger Coolidge who'd made the initial decision to farm our ants on digital television compression and decompression chips. He'd done that before I'd even come to GoMotion. In a legendary feat of superhacking, Roger had built the ant lab while he'd been writing the code for ROBOT.LIB.

Roger said he'd picked DTV chips as his culture medium because they were cheap and they had a clean architecture for generating graphics. But I'd often thought about the possibility of the ants escaping into the world at large, and whenever he'd asked my opinion about design decisions, I'd always tilted toward the path that would make the ants more capable of spreading from chip to chip. Sometimes I had even e-mailed things to Roger about wanting to ruin digital TV, and he'd always responded in a friendly, if somewhat neutral, way. If any of that e-mail came out in the trials, I wasn't going to stand a chance.

I sat there numb with worry for about half an hour, and then two San Jose cops showed up to take me downtown. The San Jose police station was a six-story beige building on First Street near Route 880. The press had gotten wind of my arrest, and there was a crowd of reporters outside the police station. They snapped pictures of me and yelled questions: "Can you make a statement?" "Why did you do it?" "When will television be restored to normal?" "What are your demands?"

I had a big San Jose cop on either side of me, and they dragged me past the reporters fast. Inside the building they brought me to a fourth-floor office with a man in a suit. All this time I was still wearing plastic handcuffs. I waited standing between the cops while the man finished talking on the phone.

"Uh-huh. He just got here. Five-eleven, 180 pounds, long brown hair, wire and horn-rim glasses, wearing short pants, argyle socks, Birkenstock sandals, and a colorful sport shirt? Check. Thank you, Mr. Pear. I'll be expecting the fax. And please let us know if you have to leave town; we may need for you to make a deposition in person before the indictment." He hung up and looked at me and the cops.

"Jerzy Rugby. I'm Captain Austin of the computer crime squad. You can uncuff him, officers. Thank you. Yes, you can go, though I'd like for one of you to wait outside. We won't be too long. Thank you. Now then, Mr. Rugby, I've just been in contact with your former manager at GoMotion Inc., a Mr. Jeffrey Pear?"

"What is it that I'm charged with?"

"You have been read your rights, yes? Fine. We may still reformulate the charges. That's one of the issues that we need to talk about before the D.A. takes this to the grand jury this afternoon. Your warrant of record is for criminal trespass, computer intrusion, and extreme cruelty to animals. Three state felony charges, with a possible maximum total sentence of fifteen years. And the feds want a crack at you, too. The federal prosecutor is getting a whole bouquet of different charges ready. How does treason sound? I have it on the best authority that the president of the United States wants your butt in jail for life. His exact words.

The president likes TV. Jerzy, do you realize that under federal law treason is a capital crime?"

"I don't know what you're talking about. I want to call a lawyer."

"Certainly. You will be given the opportunity to call a lawyer. But first I'd like to have just a little background while I finish booking you. Jeffrey Pear says you were fired from GoMotion for breaking the security of—" Captain Austin glanced at the notepad on his desk, "—an artificial life experiment modeled on an ant colony. He further said that you had so contaminated your computer and a prototype GoMotion robot that these hardware items were given to you as part of your written severance agreement."

"That's not what happened at all. And I have *not* received any written severance agreement."

"Fine. I'm very eager to hear your story. But just let me fill you in a bit more on our current picture of things. A man and a robot answering to the description of you and—is it Studly?"

"That is the name of my robot, yes."

"A man and a robot resembling you and Studly were reported to have been in an altercation with a Jose Ruiz of 5782 White Road yesterday afternoon. The man's dog was killed, and the Fibernet cable to his house was cut. Shortly after the cable was cut, a computer virus infected all of the digital compression hardware at Fibernet San Jose and bounced out to the chips of all the active TV sets in San Jose. Worse than that, the virus worked its way upstream from Fibernet San Jose into the local TV station studios and got into their DTV compression chips as well. Shortly after that, the virus went out with San Jose news feeds over the satellite links and infested the studios of every digital TV station and cable service in the world. For the moment there's damn near no television. Do you have a reaction to that?"

I knew better than to reveal my true feelings of triumph and awe. "I suppose that's very inconvenient for many people. But it's certainly not my fault."

"Do you admit that you were at 5782 White Road yesterday?"

"I don't admit anything."

"Jerzy, I'd like to make it easy for you. You seem like an intelligent man. You can work with me or you can work against me. And if you work against me you're going to spend a long time in jail. You might even get the death penalty. You don't want to die in jail, do you, Jerzy?" I shook my head and Captain Austin smiled. "So help me out a little. I'm trying to understand what happened. Jeffrey Pear says it's all your fault, but maybe he's not giving me the straight story. What happened at GoMotion? Why were you fired? Pear says it was simply a matter of incompetence." Captain Austin paused and looked at his pad again. "Pear says, 'Jerzy Rugby doesn't know a function pointer from a linked list.' He says you ripped off some experimental virus-like software and deliberately used it to blank out television so as to give GoMotion a black eye. Would you call that an accurate account?"

"Hell no!" I flared. "What Pear says is total bullshit. Look—if you *really* want to know about the GoMotion ants, ask Roger Coolidge. I bet Pear didn't mention *him* to you. Roger Coolidge is the founder of GoMotion. He left for Switzerland Monday night. Roger built the GoMotion ants before I even started working there. I used to talk to him about his design, but he called the shots. The ants were Roger's experiment with artificial life. They were meant to be like living, self-improving pieces of DTV display code. Roger Coolidge is the one who set the ants loose. He e-mailed an eggcase of them to my deck, took off for Switzerland, and then had Jeff Pear fire me. It's a total setup. *I'm just a patsy.*"

"That's very helpful, Jerzy. Why don't I call in a stenographer to take down your story. It would be a good thing to get your side on record."

The captain's voice had taken on a soothing, caressing tone. The captain was my friend. It would be so great to sit here and tell him my side of the story without worrying about silly legalistic things like my Miranda rights . . . at least maybe that's what I was supposed to think. But I wasn't a kid anymore. I'd pleaded guilty to pot possession for a two hundred dollar fine once in my twenties, and it had cost me thousands and thousands of dollars in job rejections and increased insurance premiums over many many years. No, the police are not your friends.

"I want to talk to a lawyer." I crossed my arms and leaned back in my chair.

"Go ahead." He pushed his phone across his desk. "You can make one call. One seven-digit number. No phone phreaking."

As if being a serious hacker were the same as being a cryp all hot to dial into the weapons division of Livermore Labs, or an anarchist bent on bringing down the phone system. Though, *heh*, in the government's eyes I was a terrorist who'd done something even worse. I'd blanked out digital TV: treason?

I took the phone and, come to think of it, I didn't actually know any lawyers in California. Carol had said she was going to talk to a lawyer today about child support payments, but she hadn't told me his or her name, not that I'd want to talk to Carol's lawyer. Instead of calling a lawyer, I should call someone who could really help me. Not GoMotion, certainly, but—why not West West? No doubt they were ecstatic over the bad publicity the ants were bringing to GoMotion.

I pulled Ben Brie's business card out of my wallet and dialed his number.

"Ben Brie speaking."

"Ben, it's Jerzy Rugby. Something's come up. I've been arrested."

"Does that mean you'll be late to work?" He chuckled softly. "Are you in for something juicy?" His sarcastic drawl was wonderful to hear.

"It's the television thing. The GoMotion ants. They're trying to pin it on me."

"Very interesting." He stretched the words out as he thought things over. "You're calling because you need a lawyer?"

"Right. I figured you guys must know a lot of lawyers."

"We do. Hmmm. I'll talk to Otto Gyorgyi, and if he approves, which I'm sure he will, we'll send someone over. Where are you?"

"The San Jose police station on First Street."

"Okay, Jerzy. Keep your mouth shut and wait for the lawyer. West West will have you out on bail before you know it."

"Thanks, Ben."

"Hey, it's a standard employee benefit!"

I was free on bail by suppertime. The reporters outside were rabid; they were personally affronted by the blankout of TV. If this kept up, many of them would be out of a job. Till now, I'd been nursing a deep-seated feeling that the mass of people would be as glad as I was to have TV gone. But seeing the reporters' anger, I realized I might be wrong.

The West West lawyer—a tall, soft curly-haired guy called Stu Koblenz—gave me a ride back to Los Perros in his car. Vans and cars with reporters followed us down the freeway. When we got to my house, there were so many newspeople standing there that I was scared to get out. I had my keys, and my car was still there in the driveway, but I didn't see any way to get out without being totally mobbed.

"Just drive on past and drop me down in Los Perros, Stu. I'll come back here on foot later."

"Okay."

As we motored past my home, I noticed a piece of paper tacked to the front door. An eviction notice? A sheriff's sequestration? *Tam tvat asi,* as the mantra used to go: *And this too*. Back in my thirties, before I filled my heart with computer code, I had a few periods of total spiritual enlightenment. *All is One, and each event is a gem facet of the One, even a Pig scrawl on your front door*. Enlightenment is a big help in crisis times, though the rest of the time there's still the unyielding question of what to do with the rest of your life.

Down in Los Perros, I directed Stu to drive briskly around the block and whip into an alley, leaving our tail momentarily out of sight. I hopped out, ran into the back door of Mountain Pizza, and stepped out of the front.

There on the sidewalk was a rack of evening newspapers. My picture was on the front page with the headlines:

HACKER ARRESTED
Television Blankout To Continue
GOMOTION DENIES RESPONSIBILITY

I bought a copy and folded it in half. Down the block was a clothes store. I went in and bought a 49ers sweatshirt. To complete my disguise I bought one of those moronic billed caps with a plastic strap in back—the kind of hat that people who watch television wear.

I went around the corner to an Irish bar called D.T.

Finnegan's, a publike space with green carpets, dark wood wainscoting, and antique stained glass windows. The bartender there knew me, but I sat at a table with my back to him and with my billed cap pulled down so he wouldn't notice me. His name was Tommy. At this very moment he was, in fact, discussing my case with the men at the bar.

"A nice guy," he was telling them. The three TV screens over the bar were blank. I found the silence wonderful, but the men did not. They were sullen and bewildered. There was some kind of sports event they wanted to be watching. "He comes in here afternoons when he gets tired of hacking," Tommy was saying. "He's kind of an old hippie."

"They ought to castrate him," someone opined.

"People will go nuts with no TV," another one put in. "I can't face going home tonight. What the hell am I going to do all evening?"

The waitress came to me and I ordered a beer and a barbecued pork sandwich. I was very hungry. While I waited for the food, I studied the newspaper. There was no TV working anywhere on the planet save for the few remaining analog backwaters—Borneo, Peru, New Guinea, Zaire, Micronesia. The "GoMotion ant virus" was believed to have been released by Jerzy Rugby, a disaffected programmer recently fired by GoMotion. Nancy Day, the president of GoMotion, promised that a "GoMotion ant lion" would soon be available to set things right. I guessed that Nancy Day, whom I'd never met, was fronting for Roger. There was a big sidebar article with some Q&A on the situation.

Q: What is GoMotion Inc.?
A: GoMotion Inc. of Santa Clara is a manufacturer of custom software kits for assembling intelligent machinery. They are best-known

for the Iron Camel dune buggy, which has sold 1.5 million units worldwide. Their next product is to be a line of build-it-yourself home robot kits called the GoMotion Veep.

Q: Why were the GoMotion ants developed?
A: The GoMotion ants are an example of *artificial life*, which refers to computer programs that change and evolve on their own. GoMotion says the ant programs were designed for research use only. For practical and cost-cutting reasons, the ants were evolved to live on the inexpensive, readily available chips that are found in DTV equipment.

Q: How did the ants spread?
A: A rogue prototype Veep robot used a laser-scanner to feed the programs into Fibernet San Jose. The entry point for the infection was a cut Fibernet cable on White Road in San Jose.

Q: Who is to blame?
A: The robot, who is called Studly, was in the possession of Jerzy Rugby, a programmer who was recently fired by GoMotion Inc. Rugby has now been indicted by a California state grand jury on charges of criminal trespass, computer intrusion, and extreme cruelty to animals. In addition, a federal grand jury is preparing to indict him on charges of sabotage of a public utility, contamination of cable services, destruction of national defense utilities, and treason. Rugby is currently free on $3 million bail. The bail was posted by attorney Stuart Koblenz, representing Seven Lucky Overseas.

Q: What is Seven Lucky Overseas?

A: Seven Lucky Overseas is a Taiwanese-based company that has a history of competing for the same markets as GoMotion Inc. Their first U.S. daughter company, GoWheels Inc., was successfully sued by GoMotion Inc. for copyright infringement. Their most infamous subsidiary company was Meta Meta, which produced a robot called the Choreboy. In a grotesque holiday mishap, a Choreboy killed a baby by sticking a meat thermometer into the child's heart and roasting it in place of a Thanksgiving turkey. Meta Meta went into Chapter 11 and reorganized as West West, which is slated to release a robot called the Adze. The Adze robot will be comparable to the GoMotion Veep.

Q: How soon will TV broadcasts resume?

A: GoMotion officials have promised that a free "GoMotion ant lion" program will be available from them within 48 hours. Like the ants, the ant lion program will be a self-replicating computer virus. According to GoMotion, however, the ant lion will be a benevolent virus that takes up residence on DTV chips and devotes its energy solely to finding and eradicating all GoMotion ants which may arrive. If the FCC agrees to the release of the GoMotion ant lions, and if the ant lions are indeed successful, then normal digital broadcasting could resume in a matter of days.

Q: What can I do in the meantime?

A: The ant virus affects high-definition, compressed, digital, cable, or satellite-transmitted TV. If you have an older TV set—the kind with rabbit ears and a manual channel selector knob—then you will be able to receive analog TV signals from a variety of local ATV, or amateur TV, channels that transmit in this form. See the TV & Entertainment section for information about the best of ATV and about how to retrofit your set.

Q: What about rental movies?
A: CDs, S-cubes, and downloadable video all use the same digital compression technologies as broadcast DTV and are thus subject to the same interference from the GoMotion ants.

Q: Are other communications media in danger?
A: There have been no reports of interference with radio or with voice telephone, which are still purely analog forms of communication. There have been numerous sightings of GoMotion ants on the digital cyberspace Net, although as yet no data damages have been reported. Expunging the GoMotion ant virus from cyberspace could prove more difficult than removing it from TV. The reason is that there is a much greater diversity of "ecological niches" for artificial life-forms to inhabit in cyberspace.

Q: Is this just the first wave of a new generation of computer viruses?
A: If the GoMotion ants are able to permanently establish themselves in cyberspace, they could undergo a process like evolution

> and become ever more destructive and harder to kill. This would be analogous to the way in which each winter's flu viruses are immune to the vaccines of the year before. Conceivably the cyberspace-based ants could periodically reinfect television. The most pessimistic prediction is that DTV-busting viruses are here to stay, and that digital television is a thing of the past.

While I was reading, the food and beer had come, and I'd been consuming them. Now I was done eating, and I'd paid the waitress off. I wasn't sure what to do next.

"Jerzy!"

I looked up. It was Gretchen Bell, standing over me and smiling. She was wearing a short pleated plaid skirt with a pale yellow sweater. She looked languidly lively. "I was just talking about you! Everyone in my office has been asking me what you're like!"

Tommy the bartender heard Gretchen saying my name, and now he hailed me, too. "Jerzy Rugby! The man who killed television!" A hubbub of voices ensued.

"Can I come over to your house, Gretchen?" I asked quickly.

"My apartment? I thought you said you were going to take me to the Mark Hopkins in San Francisco." She laughed softly, keeping me hanging. "Well, let's see. I have to go to Safeway, and I have to pick up some dry-cleaning. But after that, okay." She gave me a good smile. She had the hots for me as much as I did for her. And now I was famous. "Do you know where I live?"

Someone tapped my shoulder, the same man who'd

said I should be castrated. I kept my back to him and leaned toward Gretchen.

"I'm going to need a ride out of here. Like right now?"

"All right."

"Are you some kind of goddamn terrorist?" demanded the castration advocate.

"I'm a software engineer," I said as I turned. "What happened was an industrial accident." I stepped around him and called a good-bye to the bartender. "Gotta go, Tommy! Sorry I can't discuss the case!" There were plenty of other people who wanted to talk to me, but a minute later we were driving off in Gretchen's car, a sputtering ten-year-old yellow Porsche.

"I bought this from an old boyfriend for two thousand dollars," Gretchen told me. "Not bad, hey?"

"You must have a lot of boyfriends," I essayed. I still knew almost nothing about Gretchen. "What kind of office do you work in?"

"Didn't I tell you? I'm a mortgage insurance broker and I work part-time at Welsh & Tayke. With Susan Poker?"

"Susan Poker! She's my worst enemy! She's the one who turned me in! Did you talk to her about me?"

"Sure, Jerzy. I tell all my friends the exact intimate sensual details about every relationship I ever have." Gretchen tossed her bell of long straight hair and glanced over to smile at me. "*Not*. Well, okay, yesterday I may have told Susan that you and I were intimate. She was *fascinated*. I think she has a thing for you."

"Did you tell her about the ants in my computer?"

"What is this, a quiz show?" Gretchen swung into the Safeway parking lot. "Do you have any money yet?"

"Here." I handed her a twenty. "I'll wait in the car."

"Do you like anything special for breakfast?" The assumption behind the question made my heart beat faster.

"Low-fat milk. English muffins. Maybe get some wine or beer for tonight."

"Can I have two more twenties?" Her blue eyes gazed at me calmly.

"Jesus, Gretchen." I handed her the bills.

She started across the lot, tall and willowy, with her skirt swaying beautifully, and then she turned and walked partway back to me. "What about condoms?" she called.

The boldness of the question made my throat contract with lust, and my voice came out thin and reedy. "I don't have any with me."

"Well you better get some at the Walgreen's over there."

"Yes." It was hard to imagine that this was the same Safeway parking lot where I had so often shopped with Carol. Walking across the lot, I half-expected Carol to pop up and ask me what I was doing.

As soon as Gretchen and I were done with our shopping, we went to her apartment and fucked. It was just as good as it had been on Monday; it was so good it made me change the way I think.

During my twenty-three years with Carol, I'd always thought—in some deep, unreasoning way—that there was something unique about Carol herself that made sex possible. I'd always acted on the assumption that Carol was the one physiologically compatible organism with whom the being Jerzy Rugby could successfully mate.

Yet now, with Gretchen, I realized—way down in my soul—that it was indeed possible to have sex with people besides Carol. Monday I'd been too surprised for it to sink in. But, yes, sex with Gretchen was just as great as with Carol. For the first time since Carol had left me, I realized that perhaps I *could* continue life without her. I still missed Carol's personality—the tender music of her voice (when she was in a good mood), and the rich play of her conversation (when she was speaking to me)—but now I realized that I did not need to miss Carol's body. How liberating; how sad.

Gretchen and I fell asleep in each other's arms. Sometime in the middle of the night the phone rang. Gretchen picked it up.

"Hi. Umm-hmmm. Scrumptious. No, no. For sure! Bye."

Gretchen set down the phone and embraced me. We kissed and went back to sleep.

In the morning I got up and took a piss. Regally nude, I wandered into the kitchen for some food. I hadn't even thought yet to start worrying about my legal troubles. Just then someone tapped softly on the door. I harkened, and the tap came again, tinny on the hollow metal of the apartment door.

"Jerzy, can you get it?" croaked sleepy Gretchen from the bedroom.

"Who is it?" I asked, hurrying back in there to pull on my khaki shorts.

"Oh, it's one of my friends. A woman." Gretchen snuggled her head deep into her pillow and closed her eyes. "You talk to her. I'll get up in a second."

The soft tap-tapping had a bland implacability that set my nerves on edge. I found my glasses right away, but it was taking me forever to find my watch and wallet. *Tappity-tap*. The tapping was rushing me, the tapping was telling me what to do, the tapping was making me feel like a stupid doomed animal that tries to flee an oncoming locomotive by running straight down the track.

"I don't want to answer the door," I hissed to Gretchen as I pulled on my argyles and buckled my sandals. "And how can you be sure it's your friend? Who knows I'm here? Who called you on the phone last night?"

"Go answer the door."

So like an idiot I did. And guess what? It was Susan Poker.

"Mr. Rugby," said she, smiling in a new, more personal, though still not very friendly, way. Her sharp curious eyes roved rapidly over me. "We meet again!"

"Oh God. I don't believe this. Susan Poker." I looked past her to see who she'd brought in tow—but for now nobody was visible. She made as if to walk into the apartment but I held the door half-closed so as to block her way.

Rage was flaring up in me; I had to struggle to stay calm. *Don't use curse words, Jerzy. Don't be violent.* One wrong move and Susan Poker would have the cops on me like stink on shit. I put my head through some major changes and choked out a civil sentence.

"What is your business here?"

"As a matter of fact, Mr. Rugby, I was hoping to discuss real estate with you." She was wearing a green silk suit with a yellow scoopneck blouse. Her shoes matched her suit. I was shirtless. "Gretchen," called Susan Poker, using her voice to reach past me. "Tell your gentleman friend it's safe to let me in!"

I sighed and stepped aside. Susan Poker closed the door behind her and Gretchen appeared from the bedroom, sexy and soft-eyed, dressed in a pale blue bed jacket over a silky, creamy button-up nightie.

"Well, Gretchen," said Susan Poker. "Is Jerzy any good?"

By way of answer, Gretchen gave a whoop of laughter and a wild toss of her head.

"That's a *yes*," I stated, and Gretchen didn't contradict me.

"Shall I make coffee?" suggested Susan Poker. "I know where everything is."

"Thanks," said Gretchen. "I want to take my shower." She waggled her fingers and closed her bedroom door with a last injunction that we "Be nice to each other!"

"Was it you who called Gretchen last night?" I asked Susan Poker.

"I wanted to be sure she was safe. We single gals have to look out for each other. But I'm here this morning because I want to talk to you."

"About *real estate*? Why don't we talk about how you turned me in?"

"Oh, you think I called the police? No, no. I just heard them on my scanner. Since I have an interest in your dwelling—and in you—I got there as fast as I could."

"Why would a Realtor have a police scanner?"

"All the agencies have one. We need to know right away when a property is about to go on the market."

"Like when the owner dies?"

"It's dog eat dog, Jerzy. But, no, I didn't turn you in. Until I heard the call it hadn't occurred to me that it was you who launched the GoMotion ants. That was over on the east side. Terrible property values there." She gazed at me pleasantly, her face as blank and smooth as a cyberspace mannequin's. There was no way to tell if she was lying. This branch of the conversation had reached a dead end.

"So what was the real estate deal you wanted to talk to me about? You're getting me evicted, right?"

"You're so *suspicious*, Mr. Rugby! No, the deal is that I think you should acquire the Nutt property."

"I don't have a million dollars."

"You posted three million in bail, didn't you?"

"My new employer posted it for me."

"Just tell them to buy you the house." She leaned forward and laid her hand on my forearm. "Did you know that property is as good as cash for a bond? I double-checked the legalities yesterday afternoon. Your employer could convert part of the bond money into a deed on the house and simply post the deed. Your trial and appeals could drag on for a year or more, and in that time, the Nutt property would probably appreciate by twenty percent. As long as that million dollars just sits there as bond, it isn't drawing any interest whatsoever. If I work like mad, I can put the whole deal through in thirty days!"

"Well . . . "

"Just give me the name of the person you called to get your bail."

"I . . . " Again I felt like a rabbit running from a locomotive. "I'll think about it. But I'm not sure I want that house, and I don't want to turn around and ask my new boss for another big favor right off the bat."

"What did you say his name was? He's at Seven Lucky Overseas?" She was watching me closely, trying to read my face.

"Will you get off my case!" My voice was rising.

"Now, now!" It was Gretchen, dressed in red stirrup pants and a black blouse.

"How did this leech find out I'm here, Gretchen? I still can't believe you're friends with her!"

"Gretchen and I were looking out the front window of Welsh & Tayke yesterday," said Susan Poker, looking pleased that I was beginning to lose my cool. "We were just sitting there leeching around. I spotted you walking by, and Gretchen took off after you. She said if she didn't come back it meant she'd picked you up again! I made her promise that if she did, she'd let me come for breakfast." She gestured cheerfully with her coffee cup. "Speaking of breakfast, Gretchen, can we have some toast?"

I felt like a moth being wrapped in spider silk: snared, envenomed, paralyzed, cocooned, and slowly sucked dry—or made the living host of eyeless larvae. I tried to struggle, to shake the web. "Have either of you heard of Hex DEF6?" I demanded. "Out with it!"

"Hex deaf sex?" giggled Susan Poker—a bit too glibly?

"What are you talking about, Jerzy?" asked Gretchen, bringing the toast.

"Hex DEF6 is the name of a simmie I talked to in cyberspace. It was Monday, the same day the ants scared you, Gretchen. That night I put the goggles back on and I flew out of the ant cloud you'd been in. One of the ants got big and it carried me back to the ants' cyberspace nest. Inside the nest was this simmie that looked like Death and said his name was Hex DEF6. There was a Susan Poker simmie in there too. Were you in it Susan?"

"Me in cyberspace?" She laughed and shook her head. "I'm computer illiterate. Are you sure you saw a simmie of me?"

"Well, it might have just been there to scare me," I allowed. "The whole scene was pretty weird. Instead of a mouth, Hex DEF6 had a metal zipper with a padlock on it."

"Could he talk?" asked Gretchen.

"Yes. He said that he'd hurt me and my children if I didn't go work for—" I stopped myself from saying more.

"For Seven Lucky Overseas," finished Susan Poker.

"That's not the name they're using!" I exclaimed happily, and bit into my toast. Once you got used to Susan Poker she was sort of amusing. She was so totally out front about her nosiness and pushiness. A born Realtor.

"Have you considered selling your story to the press?" asked Susan Poker. "You could go on 'Sixty Minutes.' "

"There's nothing but amateur TV anymore," reminded Gretchen.

"Well, when the networks come back," said Susan Poker, sipping her coffee. "You need an agent, Mr. Rugby. I could do it for fifteen percent. I've got more connections than you realize."

Done with eating, I shook my head and stood up.

"Good-bye, ladies. It was fun, Gretchen. I'll call."

"How will you get to work?" demanded Susan Poker. "Can I give you a ride?"

"And where will you stay tonight?" asked Gretchen. "Are you going to come back here?"

"*I'll call.* I am not going to discuss every goddamn detail of my life in front of Susan Poker."

"Good-bye, Mr. Rugby," said Susan Poker.

Gretchen followed me into the hall and gave me a giggling kiss. This was all pretty funny, I guess. Love makes everything funny. Love? Yes, I loved Gretchen, though that didn't mean much. Love is, after all, an elastic concept; like many men, I fall in love several times every day. So why not say it.

"I love you, Gretchen."

"I like that in a man." She pursed her lips and planted a kiss on me, just like Carol used to do. "Have a nice day. And come back. You don't really have to take me to the Mark Hopkins."

"Should I come back tonight?"

For the first time this morning, Gretchen looked evasive. "Well, tonight I have a date. But if you're desperate, I'll break it. You're scared to go back to your own house, huh?"

"I'm going to get my car, but I'm not going to stay there."

"Well . . . " While Gretchen hesitated, Susan Poker briefly popped her head out of Gretchen's door for a peek at what was taking us so long. If the loathsome Susan Poker was in this space, why was I so intent on trying to stay here? For more sex with Gretchen? But I'd just finished realizing that sex could happen with lots of different women, right?

"Gretchen, enjoy your date and don't worry about where I stay. I've got it together." I tapped the top of my head to mime the togetherness that I hoped would soon arrive. "I'll call tomorrow. And don't worry, I haven't forgotten about the Mark Hopkins."

Key in hand, I made my way up Tangle Way. The notice was still on my front door, but I didn't dare go close enough to read it. There were a half-dozen reporters sitting in their cars. My driveway was clear. Moving quickly, I got in my Animata and drove off, shaking the pursuit cars on the freeway to West West.

SEVEN

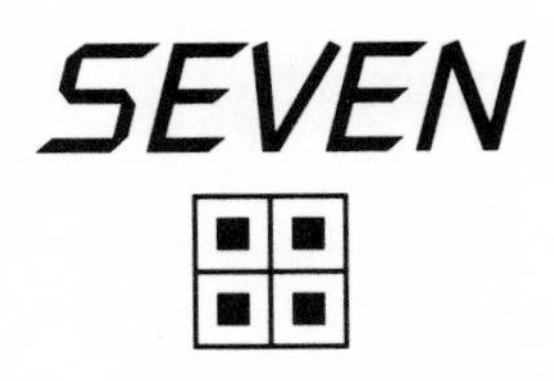

Bloodlust Hacking Frenzy

I GOT SERIOUSLY INTO HACKING THE CODE FOR THE ADZE robot, and the next three and a half weeks went by in a blur.

Hacking is like building a scale-model cathedral out of toothpicks, except that if one toothpick is out of place the whole cathedral disappears. And then you have to feel around for the invisible cathedral, trying to figure out which toothpick is wrong. Debuggers make it a little easier, but not much, since a truly screwed-up cutting-edge program is entirely capable of screwing up the debugger as well, so that then it's as if you're feeling around for the missing toothpick with a stroke-crippled claw-hand.

But, ah, the dark dream beauty of the hacker grind against the hidden wall that only you can see, the wall that only you wail at, you the programmer, with the brand new tools that you made up as you went along, your special new toothpick lathes and jigs and your real-time scrimshaw shaver, you alone in the dark with your wonderful tools.

In the real world, I spent Friday and Saturday at the

Mark Hopkins Hotel in San Francisco with Gretchen. The city was full of people partying; there was a kind of holiday mood over the absence of TV; everyone was talking and laughing much more than usual.

Actually, there was a certain amount of analog TV: crazy amateur shows being put out by random nobodies. A few places had analog TVs set up to show amateur TV to the true tube addicts, and you got the feeling that some of this unofficial stuff might catch on. Who really needed the networks anyway? We were free of the bullshit, free of the Pig. But it was too good to last.

Sunday morning, GoMotion released the ant lion virus and by Sunday evening, the ant lions had cleaned up DTV. Roger Coolidge made an appearance on the news, taking credit for the ant lion, and apologizing to the public—in a nonspecific kind of way—for any difficulty that the unfortunate release of the GoMotion ants might have caused. Everyone understood that "unfortunate" was a code word for "crazy Jerzy Rugby."

Like the GoMotion ants, the ant lions lived on DTV compression and decompression chips, but they didn't affect the images. All they did was sit there and kill anything that acted like a GoMotion ant, though exactly *how* the ant lions killed the ants was a GoMotion trade secret.

The ant-detection code made the GoMotion ant lion into a huge lurking memory hog that wallowed in a DTV chip's memory like a sullen supertanker in a mountain lake. This was a problem because DTV's fractal-theoretic image-expansion algorithms wanted to use a lot of memory for scratch paper: the finer the image, the more memory was needed. With the ant lion taking up so much chip memory, the highest-resolution DTV formats were plagued with the bail-out blotches that result from incomplete computations.

But mid-resolution broadcast DTV was working fine, which was the main thing. The highest-resolution DTV was mainly for playing back digitally mastered movies that you could download over the Fibernet. Intel, National Semiconductor, Motorola, and the other chipsters were promising to roll out DTV memory-expansion minicards with enough room for both high-resolution mode *and* an ant lion by the next financial quarter. Funny how ready for that they were. I wondered if GoMotion had recently bought a lot of chip stock.

My state trial got scheduled for May 28, some three and a half weeks off, with the federal trial still pending. Stu said my chances in court were fair to good.

The paper on the door of my house turned out to be a notice of an attempted Wednesday morning delivery by Federal Express. The documents Fed Ex had been trying to deliver to me had been mailed by GoMotion at 6:00 P.M. on Tuesday afternoon. Stu picked up the documents Thursday and found a unilateral letter of dismissal signed by Jeff Pear, along with two copies of a severance agreement signed by GoMotion president Nancy Day, with blank lines waiting for my signature.

The lateness of the delivery was good news. Since I had not even received the agreement by Tuesday night, Studly was—Stu assured me—the legal property and responsibility of GoMotion Inc. during the time frame when Jose Ruiz's dog was killed and the GoMotion ants were released. And furthermore, since I now declined to sign the severance agreement, Studly and my cyberdeck were in fact *still* the property and responsibility of GoMotion, pending further negotiation.

The legal issue of whether I had maliciously influenced the robot Studly's actions was less favorable. According to the West West cryps, Jose Ruiz was going to be the D.A.'s star witness. Apparently he was saying he'd watched me and Studly through his window. This part of the trial was going to be tough; Stu would just have to challenge the accuracy of what Jose Ruiz thought he'd seen and heard.

Above and beyond all factual matters were a host of technical issues about the statutes I was charged under; did these particular statutes apply to the unique events of that Tuesday evening on White Road? Stu said that even if I was convicted of something, he could keep me out of jail on appeals for years—or for as long as West West was willing to foot the bill.

I used Stu's computer to e-mail Roger asking if he'd testify that it was he who'd infected Studly with the ants, but Roger e-mailed back that the best he could do was wish me good luck. He was very busy in Switzerland, and in any case he "would not feel right" in offering testimony to support my "highly idiosyncratic interpretation of the events." I was, in other words, free to twist slowly in the wind.

My house on Tangle Way was unlivable. Not only were there reporters encamped round the clock, but, according to Stu, death threats were rolling in. The public had it in for me, the morons. And the network news was making me out to be some kind of rabid hyena. Even the so-called liberal pundits were judiciously intoning things like, "A free society cannot tolerate misfit hackers who would block the open exchange of ideas." The exchange of *their* ideas, that is. At least the freestyle amateur TV broadcasters had picked up a boost from the brief blackout of official TV.

Whenever I saw the DTV news these days, I had an intense desire to cryp the GoMotion ant lion code, find a loophole, and show the hole to the GoMotion ants in cyberspace—but *no, Jerzy, no.*

I couldn't live at home anymore, and Gretchen didn't want me to move in permanently, so Thursday evening after my first full day's work at West West, I took a roundabout route up through the Santa Cruz mountains to Queue Harmaline's house.

Queue and Keith lived near Boulder Creek, on a steep hillside surrounded by giant redwoods. They had a hot tub and a samadhi flotation tank. Their home was like a coral reef or a beehive: a congeries, an unarchitected wad of rooms plastered to the steep redwood hillside. They always needed money, and I knew that they would have a room to rent to me.

Queue had a brace on her knee because she'd recently made the error of going skiing while she was rushing on a mighty LSD run. "I should just trip in the samadhi tank," she told me with a tinkling giggle, "but you wake up a day later and you feel like Dracula." She had long glossy black hair that tended to split and hang in a spitty way over her face and mouth when she talked about psychedelics. "I've learned not to do anything that involves metal or electricity when I'm on acid,'cause I have no way of knowing what I might get into. And now I know not to go skiing. Sure we can rent a room to you. If you behave." She batted her eyes at me.

Though Queue always professed absolute faithfulness to Keith, she was a big flirt and I was happy to flirt with her. Her head was very round. She had the perky cute features of a brunette ingenue. Her odd laugh was intoxicating, and she wore gypsy amounts of jewelry, with a descending scale of nine gold hoops arranged along the rim of each of her ears.

"So how does it feel to be a big media star, Jerzy? You've invented a whole new order of life. It's magic." We were sitting in her kitchen drinking herbal tea.

"It's not magic, Queue," I sighed. "It's science. I don't think about transcendence or the One anymore."

"But there has to be some mystery to help get us through these dreary times. We need it. If we didn't need it so much, why did your ants try to kill TV? They're a higher force for New Mystery."

"Everything computers do is science, Queue. Logic. There's no mystery to it at all." I was tired and drained from the day's hacking.

"You hide behind your preppy clothes and your sleepy expression," cried Queue. "Come on! Be interesting!"

"These aren't supposed to be preppy clothes," I said, looking down at my garb. I was wearing a red rayon shirt covered with UFOs, some short white canvas shorts, yellow socks with a white section map of Death Valley, and my Birkenstocks.

"You don't fool me, Jerzy. You're as tidy as a little boy going to a birthday party. You yuppie. Come on and say something interesting or I won't rent you the room!"

"Interesting." My whole life was so interesting that I could hardly stand it—yet now, under Queue's scrutiny, I realized that I rarely ever did talk about what it was that I found so interesting about hacking robots in cyberspace. More often than not, I let the people I was talking to divert conversations up their own creeks; I'd just paddle along and dream behind my sleepy expression. But if anyone actually asked, I could still talk.

"Okay, I'll tell you some random things that are interesting. Last time I was in cyberspace the GoMotion ants took me out into the fourth dimension and put me into a gangster movie with a guy who looked like Death. Instead of a mouth he had a big steel zipper with a padlock. His name was Hex DEF6. That's a hexadecimal number which is—" I paused and pulled out a slip of paper where I'd written this information down, "1101 1110 1111 0110 in binary and 57,078 in base ten. I have no idea what it means, except that if you leave the last zero off the binary version you get a symmetric bit-string. Not interesting? How about this: The night the ants got loose, I was over on the east side trying to fuck a Vietnamese girl called Nga Vo."

"Are you hard up?"

"Dig it, Queue, I'm not hard up, I've got myself a cashmere yuppie mommy. Her name is Gretchen. She's a mortgage insurance broker."

"How many children does Gretchen have?"

"None, as far as I know. I think of her as a *mommy* because she reminds me of the big dazed whitebread American mothers some of the kids at school had when I was small. Dreamy, slow-moving women with kind smiles. And just that soft hint of a double chin, you know?"

"Ugh! I don't want to hear you talk about women, Jerzy. It's so sexist and disgusting and—ugh! Can't you tell me more about your computer adventures?"

"Queue, you got no inkling." I took a deep breath and smiled. Keith was down in the basement making some tapes. "Talking openly like this gets me high. In cyberspace I sat on the back of an ant that found me in Nordstrom's, and the ant shrank me down small and we crawled out a hole to the Antland of Fnoor. I guess that *was* a New Mystery. If I can get a cyberdeck up here, maybe I'll take you there."

"Do it!" Queue exclaimed. "But it has to be on the sly. You're a computer criminal, Jerzy. I'm not going to dial up the Fibernet and ask them for a cyberspace account and then have everyone see Jerzy Rugby come out of my registered memory node."

I thought for a minute. "Any good phreak or cryp would find a way. Maybe . . . maybe I could use the Animata's satellite dish."

"Your car has a dish?"

"It has a titanium-doped electronic Fresnel lens in

the moonroof. My map machine uses the lens to pick up on navigational satellites."

"Okay, this is starting to be interesting."

"Can you let me have a little of your pot now, Queue?"

I got into a rhythm of commuting from Queue's to West West every morning and working all day in my cubicle in the West West programmer pit two cells away from Russ Zwerg. Most nights I'd sit out on the deck with Queue and Keith and get high.

Carol? I saw her the next weekend, when I hired some movers to clear us out of Tangle Way. Carol, Tom, and Ida were there to help pack and sort.

The idea was to move some stuff to Carol and Hiroshi's apartment, and some to a rented space in Crocker's Lockers. It was the first time I'd seen Carol since the night the GoMotion ants got loose. She confronted me down in the kitchen, out of earshot from the kids and the movers.

"So you're living with Queue? I guess that means you're stoned all the time?" Carol didn't particularly like drugs or drug culture, and she and Queue had never hit it off. As Carol once put it: "Queue thinks I'm corny and obvious, but she doesn't realize that I think *she's* corny and obvious."

"No, Carol, I'm not stoned all the time," I said defensively. "I'm hacking my brains out for West West is what I'm doing."

"I'll bet. What does Keith have to say about your moving in? Are they married?"

"He thinks it's fine. Carol, all I'm doing is renting a room. I am not sleeping with Queue. She's very committed to Keith. And no, they're not married."

"That's because Keith doesn't have an income. Queue looks out for number one. I bet she tries to marry you, Jerzy. She's had her eye on you ever since you got the good job at GoMotion." In imitation of Queue, Carol opened her eyes wide, threw up her hands, and rocked from side to side to simper, "Oh, Jerzy, you're so smart and wonderful!"

"Give it up, Carol," I snapped. "How can you be jealous when you've already left me for another man? It's not logical." Unexpectedly my voice cracked. "I can't live alone, you know."

Carol gave me a sudden, frank look, her eyes roving over every contour of my face. She was on the verge of tears. "Are we making a big mistake, Jerzy?" From upstairs came the heavy sounds of the movers. "Don't you still want me?"

I silently embraced her, and the kids found us there like that. "Woo-woo," they said, softly, hopefully. Carol and I broke the clinch and got back to the details of the move.

Outside, the reporters were on us like meat bees at a barbecue. I phoned Stu to come and make a statement to them. I stood by his side as they filmed us. Stu spoke slowly and with conviction. He was acting like a good lawyer, like a stand-up guy.

"Good morning, ladies and gentlemen of the press. My name is Stuart Koblenz, and I am Jerzy Rugby's attorney.

"GoMotion Incorporated has chosen to try and make Jerzy Rugby the scapegoat for their own industrial accident. Mr. Rugby will enter pleas of innocent to all the charges placed against him. We are preparing vigorously for the trial. For obvious legal reasons, Mr. Rugby is unable to answer questions at this time.

"The fact that Mr. Rugby is moving out of this house today is a direct result of the continuing media harassment of this innocent man. I would strongly request that the press please respect the privacy of Mr.

Rugby and his family in the weeks to come. Thank you."

After this, none of us would say anything at all to the reporters, and they pretty much pulled back, though a few of them followed the moving van to get footage of Crocker's Lockers and of Carol and Hiroshi's apartment complex.

Under the terms of my bail, I'd had to tell the court about moving to Queue's and, of course, as soon as the court entered it into their machine, all the Bay Area cryps could grok my new address. Most days a car or two would tail me both ways of my commute between West West and Queue's—sometimes reporters, other times cops or dicks or industrial agents. Queue's house was up off a locked private road which gave me some privacy there, and West West had a gated entrance as well.

Normally the cars that followed me would melt away at the gates, but the Monday evening after we'd moved out of Tangle Way, a guy jumped out of his car and headed for me while I was opening the gate.

"Jerzy!"

Our car engines were off and we were alone in the quiet under the redwoods. Wind soughed high in the branches above. The asphalt was thickly scattered with brown pine needles, and dappled with gold patches of setting sun. The person who'd called to me was a twenty-year-old boy with shoulder-length brown hair in rasta tangles; he was bouncy and skinny, with thin lips pulled back in an expression that was not quite a smile. He walked toward me. His hands were empty, but an odd little shape trailed along the pavement after him like a mascot. A toy animal? There was no time to look closer. I focused my attention back on the boy.

"What do you want?" I challenged.

"That's awesome that you're working for West West,

cuz," he said in a soft, trailing-off twang. He was right in front of me. The open Animata door was just behind me. I watched the boy's big hands and feet closely for any sign of an attack. Something bumped against my foot.

I looked down: the boy's mascot was a motorized toy truck with some circuit boards in its back. The truck had the head of a rubber cow glued to its front, and this is what was nudging me.

"Am I Hex DEF6 yet?" drawled the boy, and waggled his eyebrows like Bugs Bunny imitating Groucho Marx. He raised one hand and made a gesture of tapping ashes off an invisible cigar. "Big business. I'm most hellacious with family video."

"You little creep." I thought of the tortured cyberspace session I'd spent writhingly watching myself and my loved ones being tortured and killed. They'd pasted our faces into slasher movies and war footage—my mind kept coming back to the scene of Sorrel and Tom running down a bombed road in Vietnam, all their clothes burned off by napalm, Sorrel screaming and Tom's mouth twisted into an unbearable dog bone of anguish. And the scene with Ida sobbing over my disemboweled corpse while the killer crept up behind her—I surged forward and got my hands around the boy's neck. "I'll kill you."

Bruisingly he knocked my arms away and sprang back. "No harm, schoolmarm. It's only software. Like the GoMotion ants."

"Then the threats weren't real?"

"I wouldn't say that either. There's always fireworks with a Chinese Dragon. You better deliver the goods for West West, Jerzy."

"You work for West West?"

"No, bro." The little robot truck had retreated to a safe distance when the boy and I had grappled, but now it came nosing up close to me again. It rose up and down on its tires, bucking like a low-rider and then actually jumping a couple of inches off the ground. It was cute, with the cow's head and everything, but maybe there was like a hypodermic dart gun inside one of those soft rubber horns, a dart gun loaded with bio-hacker brainscramble. Not wanting to find out, I kicked hard at the side of the mascot. It dodged me and skittered away. I took the opportunity to hop back into my car and close the door.

"Come see me in cyberspace if you need any phreaking done," said the boy. "That's all I wanted to say. And don't forget—don't forget *Hex DEF6*." Even though he was bareheaded, he made a hat-doffing gesture appropriate for a ten-gallon hat.

"Get out of here, you Texas prick." I reached into my glove compartment as if I had something in there.

"I'm gone." He drove off, and I went on up to Queue's. Keith was sitting on the deck staring up at the trees. He was a peaceful person: big, healthy, and always high. We did two quick bowls of Queue's bud.

"Hey, Keith, do you know where I could get a pistol?" I asked as the rush settled over me.

"Statistically, a gun is most likely to kill its owner or a member of the owner's family," said Keith mildly. "So why would you want one? Guns are bad karma."

"A kid was threatening me down at the gate," I explained. "He had sort of a mechanical cow. A little one."

"What did the little cow do to you?"

"It just rolled around, but I felt like it was getting ready to attack me. Maybe it had a needle inside its horn. I wish I could have shot it."

"I think that if you shot off a gun, the cops would revoke your bail, Jerzy. Why don't I give you a staff instead." Keith disappeared into the warren of the house and emerged with a thick, ornately carved redwood stick. "I made this. See the sacred energy symbols that spiral up around it? Keep it with you in your car."

So instead of a gun I got a sacred staff.

Well that's enough talk about the real world; now it's time to talk about hacking.

For the longest time, the Kwirkey/SuperC logjam would not yield. West West was committed to using Kwirkey, which was the creation of one of Seven Lucky's seven Taiwanese founders. And most of my coding experience for GoMotion was in SuperC, and all the Veep code which the West West cryps had copied was SuperC as well. But Russ Zwerg was working on the interpreter, or had one running, or was about to have one ready, wasn't he?

On the surface, it seemed that the languages were easily interconvertible; it was just a matter of writing an automatic interpreter that knows that "A + B" in SuperC is "(+ A B)" in Kwirkey, and other stupid shit like that. Yet Kwirkey, being Lisp-grounded, had an utterly different idea of memory than did SuperC. Russ's Kwirkey interpreter needed to waste megabytes of space and kiloclocks of time on creating and then cleaning up the "frame diagrams" required to convert Kwirkey commands into machine instructions. And there were lots of other things—maddeningly fiddling little thinglets that nobody except Sun Tam would ever want to have to know about.

Russ Zwerg was not a likable person, but I ended up feeling some sympathy and even respect for him as he hacked his way through the vicious undergrowths that separated the kingdoms of Kwirkey, SuperC, and the Y9707 machine language of the Adze.

While Russ hacked from within, I worked from without, getting familiar with Kwirkey by learning how to do some simple things. I was excited when my first Kwirkey program for the Adze actually worked; a program called Hello Squidboy.

There was a rudimentary cyberspace viewer connected to my desktop workstation. The viewer was like a pair of binoculars connected by a wire to the machine. Inside the binoculars were swinging inertial sensors that knew exactly to what position you turned the binocs. You could look all around a scene, and there were buttons on the binocs to zoom you forward, pan sideways, or whatever. It was as if you were looking through the viewfinder of a video camera while you moved your head.

When I ran the Hello Squidboy program on my machine, I'd see a little black-and-white copy of Our American Home with a model of Squidboy sitting in the kitchen. Whenever I moved my viewpoint into the kitchen, the Squidboy figure would wave one arm and say, "Hello Squidboy," through my workstation's speaker. It wasn't much, but on any system, getting your very first program to run is half the battle. It's like the first wheel, or the invention of fire. I began building on Hello Squidboy step-by-step, continually testing each improvement out in my workstation's cheap cyberspace. Sun Tam helped me more than Russ did.

West West Home Products General Manager Otto Gyorgyi was calling Ben Brie in for daily meetings and asking him about my progress. Keep in mind that I was into West West for three million dollars at this point. No doubt Gyorgyi was wondering if just maybe what GoMotion said about me was true—that I was a destructive incompetent.

"Are you, Russ, and Sun ready to like schedule some milestones and benchmarks?" Ben asked me after a few days. He handed me some sheets of paper. "These are the Adze performance specs that Marketing has decided to run with. Janelle basically took the Veep specs and made everything twenty-five percent better. I'm going to feel a hell of a lot more confident about all this when our software starts doing more than saying, 'Hello Squidboy.' "

I labored frantically to prove that I was indeed worth three megabucks, and slowly, as I dug deeper into Kwirkey, my feelings about the language underwent a flip-flop, the kind of flip-flop that had happened to me a dozen times before.

With a new language or a new machine, it was always like having someone say, "Here, Jerzy, here's this list of part numbers, and here's a picture of a car you can build with the parts," and at first I would think, "Fuck this, I already know how to build a car with the old kind of parts I've been using," but then I would get curious and start trying to use the new parts, and they'd be shaped weird—the new parts would have their own unfamiliar logic that at first I couldn't accept—but then I'd manage to build a wheel and it would roll, and then I'd get more curious and start seeing cool things to do with the new logic, and by then I'd be well into the *flip-flop*. The fact that I was willing and able to do this to myself so often was what made me a hacker.

One of the things I began loving about Kwirkey was that it was a frobbable language. A frob is something you can pick up in the palm of your hand and walk off with, something about the size of a book of matches or the size of a trestle support for a model railway. Frob is a transitive verb as well. "Where did you get that cool spin button?" "I frobbed it from a dialog box." High-level Kwirkey code was totally modular, with none of SuperC's entangling data commitments, and you could frob Kwirkey code with a will.

I was ready to crank up a full-scale Kwirkey port of the SuperC bag of tricks that I'd written to work with Roger's ROBOT.LIB machine code for the Y9707, but Russ's automatic interpreter still wasn't happening. *Port* was the word hackers used to mean taking software that worked on one kind of system and trying to get it to work on another kind; it was kind of like portaging a canoe on your head over rocks and through underbrush.

There was too much code for me to think of porting it by hand; even though I now understood Kwirkey, there were scads of little traps I wasn't going to have time to figure out, lots of mosquitoes in the underbrush. Sun Tam knew about most of them, but the point was to have Russ automate the port. I began pestering Russ; I began reviling him for being so slow.

Russ's verbal comments and e-mail messages grew ever more crazed and hostile. Even though we worked thirty feet apart from each other, we talked by e-mail lest we get involved in a public shouting match that might get us both fired. In our e-mail Russ called me a twit, a professor, and a charlatan; while I called him a lawn-dwarf, a dropout, and a nut.

An exceedingly hostile or schizophrenic e-mail message is called a *flame*. Even though Russ and I were still exchanging scientific information, we were at the same time in the throes of a *flame war*. But it didn't really matter. As Roger Coolidge had once told me, "If you're a serious hacker you don't let flames bother you. Instead you grow thick scales."

One fabulous Tuesday, two weeks after the GoMotion ant attack, something yielded, the jam broke up, and Russ had fully hacked a fast and beautiful Kwirkey/SuperC interface. I could program the Adze in mixed Kwirkey and SuperC as transparently as if my hands were picking up sand dollars in clear water. I was like a kid in a candy shop. At the end of three dizzyingly wonderful hours, I found that I'd linked every single one of the Veep algorithms into our prototype Adze software. And, so far as I could check using the feeble cyberspace of my desk machine, my new code worked fine.

I told Russ and he was cautiously glad. Flame mode: *Off.* We hurried to the big Sphex monitor in the back room.

Jack and Jill, the jolly jock hackers, were on one of the machines, laughing excitedly and looking at their new program. The screen showed a box-shaped room that was full of tumbling three-dimensional boxes. The boxes were translucent and inside each box were more boxes, also translucent, and also with boxes inside them. It went down for as many levels as the screen resolution could handle.

"This is our new Kwirkey interface," explained Jack when he noticed me watching. "Jill calls it Gizmos." The boxes made noises as they bounced around, noises like *boing whumpa boing*. Jack's pale eyes were glowing with excitement.

Brown-eyed Jill flew our view down into one of the boxes and the box seemed like the whole room. The boxes were moving so fast and smoothly that it was totally hypnotic to look at. Jill zoomed down and down through the rooms and eventually the view was the same as the start room. "We keep the top views down inside each of the smallest boxes," said Jill. "So it has circular scale."

"Or sideways scale," put in Jack, making a gesture with his gloved hands. A web of lines sprang onto the screen, lines like bungee-cords connecting the wild boxes. "These are the bindings."

"What *are* the boxes?"

"The boxes are *gizmos*," laughed Jill and started

moving her hands around, panning and zooming her gesturing glove icons about in the virtual space of the interface. The boxes became clothed in translucent shapes—a shovel, a crow, a house, an oak tree, a Scotty dog. Jack reached in and adjusted the cables between the gizmos; they began to writhe and move in twisty, nonlinear ways.

"So far we've been single-stepping," said Jack. "But now I can speed it all up." He made a fist of his hand and the images blurred with smooth, rapid motion. "And then it converges on one of the limit cycles of the attractor. Check it out, Jerzy."

The images had locked into slow, deeply computed interactions. I was looking at an oak tree in front of a house, with a Scotty dog running around the yard. There was a ditch with a shovel next to it; the Scotty jumped over the ditch. The crow sailed down from the tree and cawed at the Scotty. The Scotty barked and jumped back over the ditch.

"Gizmos are object-oriented Kwirkey frames," said Russ, who always made a point of knowing what his fellow programmers were up to. "Self-modifying structures of data and function pointers."

Jack interrupted. "You should use it for the Adze. A gizmo could be an Adze eye or wheel or neural array. A gizmo can be a user, or it can be something the user wants to do."

"Gizmos are God," said Jill. She looked calm and pleased.

"So when are you guys going to have your Adze code happening?" asked Jack. "I'm ready to try and gizmofy it."

"I think it's working now," I said. "Now that Russ has finished his port."

"Show me now," said Russ coldly.

We left Jack and Jill, who got back to their boxes.

Sketchy Albedo was on the other Sphex. Janelle Fuchs had been praising Sketchy to me. "He's a skater," she'd told me. "*Sketchy* is a skater word. He's a fun guy at a party. He just likes to harsh on older men. He doesn't mean anything by it." For his part, Sketchy had decided I was okay when he found out about the wide range of court charges against me. I was practically a cryp.

"Gronk," said Russ to Sketchy. "Gronk gronk gronk." Russ squinted his eyes shut and opened his mouth wide as he did this. He tilted his head back so that his beard rose up off his chest. God he was ugly.

"Russ means can we use the machine," I said.

"The lawn-dwarf and the twit," said Sketchy, quoting from our private e-mail flame letters. Sketchy read whoever's e-mail he felt like. "I was thinking—can you spazzes teach Squidboy to skate?"

"Maybe," I said. "Provided there's a physically accurate cyberspace skate simulation that the program can practice in."

"Sure there's a program like that," said Sketchy. "*Cyberskate.* Silicon Graphics ships it with their deck along with a spring-mounted feely-blank skateboard that you stand on for your interface."

"If someone could set up message-passing between Cyberskate and the Adze code it would be feasible," said Russ. "But neither of you amateurs has a prayer of doing it, and *I'm* not about to. Guess what?" Russ mimed a false hobbit smile, then scowled and began yelling, "Marketing has gotten Brie and Gyorgyi to sign off on a schedule which gives Sun Tam, Jerzy, and me six days from now to give Developer Services and Quality Assurance some working code. That's next Monday. *So get your feeble butt off the Sphex!* For future reference: that's what *gronk* stands for!" Sketchy sprang up and Russ plopped himself down into the Sphex's

Steadiswivel chair. I sat down next to him, and we each pulled on two gloves.

Sketchy had ridden the viewer into a cyberspace library that looked like a British club, with parquet walls and leather furniture, though the tuxedos of the people in it were odd as surrealist cartoons—a giant duck, a stepping razor, a clam with teeth, and a staticky bit of cloud. To make it the gnarlier, the tuxedos were morphing themselves among several alternate shapes as we watched. The duck slowly transformed into a rabbit and then back into a duck. The cloud molded itself into a series of tornado shapes, and then into something like a Corinthian column.

"This is the Cryp Club library," explained Sketchy. "No phreaks allowed."

"How do you tell who's who?" I asked.

"We all know who we are," said Sketchy. "Cryps work for money, and phreaks just do it to be weird, though sometimes a phreak will take money, too. Phreaks are younger, mostly. It's almost like two gangs. If I showed up in the phreak library, somebody would try to burn me."

"Speaking of cryps and phreaks," I asked him, "do you know anything about Hex DEF6?"

"Hex DEF6!" Sketchy looked surprised. "That's the third time I heard that in the last two days."

"Where?"

"Yesterday it was written on the wall in spraypaint over there." He pointed toward one of the library walls that swept by as Russ steered us toward the exit node that hovered in the middle of the library like an oversize world globe.

"It's very incorrect," continued Sketchy, "to deface the Cryp Club library. So of course nobody would cop to it. I cleaned it off myself; it was my day for maintenance duty. Maybe a phreak got in and did it. If we catch him we're going to burn him bad."

Russ jumped into the exit node and brought us out in the Bay Area Netport. The huge Beaux Arts architectural space stretched out before us, with spherical hyperjump nodes all along the ceiling, floor, and walls.

"The second time I heard of Hex DEF6 was this morning," continued Sketchy. "A phreak was trying to bust into the West West node. The dude's tuxedo looked like a canvas mask with a zipper instead of a mouth. I iced him and he left, but before he left he gave me the finger and said his name was Hex DEF6. And now you're asking me about him. That's three times in two days. So, yeah, what is Hex DEF6?"

With quick jerky movements, Russ was steering the viewpoint across the Netport to the West West node, a shiny copper ball decorated with the West West WW logo that was, Janelle had told me, the same as the old Meta Meta MM logo upside down. We slid through the surface of the ball and saw an aerial view of the West West building plus a virtual housing development of Our American Homes set up out in back of the parking lot. At my request, Sun Tam had installed 256 of them; it was as many as the West West computers had room for. It took a petabyte of memory to maintain this big a subdivision of Our American Homes.

"I saw that zipper-mouth Hex DEF6 with a bunch of GoMotion ants a couple of weeks ago," I said. "He told me he'd injure me and my children if I didn't work for West West. And this week a kid followed me home and said that he was Hex DEF6, or that he worked for him or something. But you don't think West West is behind it?"

"Sounds like a phreak burn to me," said Sketchy.

"Sorry to interrupt these exciting *spyboy* adventures," said Russ, using the standard hacker insult for cryps and phreaks. "But where'd you put your Adze code, Jerzy?" He was hovering over my virtual desk, right there in the model of my cubicle in the pit.

"I'll get it."

I pulled open the virtual desk's top drawer to reveal a three-dimensional chrome box with a socket and a keyhole in it. Written on the box in flowing gold cursive was *SuperC/Kwirkey For Adze, Jerzy Rugby*. There was no way to pick the box up, as I'd permanently attached it to the cyberspace aether—meaning that there was no way to change the box's location coordinates without destroying it. To use the software you had to unlock the box with a key.

The key I kept hidden in my lower drawer, which was filled with a mess of several hundred random solid 3-D images. Today I had the key hidden inside a swordfish. I took the thrashing swordfish out of the drawer and zoomed down onto the third spine of the dorsal fin. Stuck down at the spine's base was the billion-bit key I'd generated last time I locked the program. It looked like a wriggly piece of wire with a round handle on one end. I pulled the wire out from the base of the swordfish's fin-spine, put the swordfish away, and stuck the key into the software box. Now it was unlocked.

Russ pulled down a cable icon with his data glove. He stuck one end of the cable into my software box's socket and held on to the other end of the cable as he flew up out of the virtual West West building and over to the nearest model of Our American Home. Russ pushed the doorbell and Perky Pat Christensen came to the front door and opened it.

"Walt and I are so glad you came. Dexter and Scooter are here as well!" She moved with the angular abruptness of a virtual Barbie doll, which was no surprise, as GoMotion had licensed the CyberBarbie surface meshes and joint-constraints from Mattel. Well, actually, GoMotion *hadn't* licensed the info, Trevor had simply crypped it from Mattel. And then Sketchy had crypped it from GoMotion. It seemed Mattel didn't have a clue.

We flew on into the kitchen, Russ still holding the infinitely stretchable cable in his hand. Virtual Squidboy was sitting there in his nest, his food cord plugged into the wall. Russ opened the little door in Squidboy's back, stuck the cable into the back of Squidboy, and squeezed the cable's *Download* lever as if he were filling Squidboy up with gas. Once the download was over, Russ pulled out the cable and said, "Kwirkey Run." Squidboy sat up and looked around. Russ flew up to join me on the ceiling.

Young Dexter Christensen wandered into the kitchen and glanced up at us. In this simulation, we looked like gloved hands attached to matchstick arms, but Dexter talked to us just the same.

"Wow! Are you startin' up the robot?" asked Dexter.

We didn't bother answering him.

"Hello Squidboy," chirped Squidboy, waving his tentacle.

"Hi, Mr. Robot," said Dexter. "Do you wanta play?"

"Wanta play?" echoed Squidboy. We'd started him from a blank state and he was in language acquisition mode.

"Let's go in the living room," said Dexter and reached out toward Squidboy's left-hand pincer-manipulator. To my horror, instead of gently taking the boy's hand, Squidboy darted rapidly forward and slashed into the boy's abdomen with inhuman fury.

"Hello Squidboy," said the virtual machine, peering at the trashed geometry that had been the lad's body. "Wanta play? Hello Squidboy. Wanta play?"

"Kwirkey Halt," said Russ, and Squidboy and the Dexter-fragments stopped moving. Russ turned to me, a savage gleam in his eye. "What do you bet it's your fault?"

"My code was fully tested for the Veep," I spluttered. "Keep in mind that the Adze is a different machine. And of course it could be your port that's causing the problem."

"You wish," said Russ, then spoke again to the Kwirkey operating system that was running this simulation. "Kwirkey Debug!"

A ray-traced retrocurved chrome figure appeared in the cyberspace of the kitchen.

"I am Kwirkey Debug. I am ready."

Rather than being the tuxedo of a living user, this was a so-called *daemon*, a construct projected by autonomous software. In cyberspace, daemons had taken the place of menus and command-line interpreters. The GoMotion ants were daemons, too, though daemons of a much different order.

"Hello Kwirkey Debug," said Russ. "I'm Russ and this is Jerzy. We want to set a breakpoint."

"Which kind of breakpoint? At address, changed memory global, expression true, or hardware interrupt?" inquired the daemon. S/he spoke in a cool androgynous tone. Some goofing hacker had set the daemon's tux to morph-wander slowly about in a parameter space that let her/im vary between male and female and between fat and thin. As we watched, the daemon changed from a fat man to a muscular woman to a skinny man—but all the while s/he was made of rippling, reflective chrome. Hackers were suckers for ray-traced chrome, also it was computationally cheap thanks to the new quaternion-based Mori-Kuzin hack, which had been the exclusive property of Unisys for about a week until a phreak called Phineas Phage had broadcast the source code all over cyberspace.

"Break when the following expression is true," said Russ. "*Squidboy's pincer intersects Dexter's chest.*"

"Breakpoint is set," said Kwirkey Debug.

"Reset and run," said Russ.

The kitchen flickered as Kwirkey Debug reinitialized it. Now Squidboy was in his nest, and Dexter was coming in again. Kwirkey Debug stood off in a corner, staring at Dexter's chest.

Dexter Christensen glanced up at us, moving his head like a very old man.

"Wow! Are you startin' up the robot?" slurred Dexter. His voice was deep and grainy. The code ran substantially slower with the breakpoint on, so that Kwirkey Debug could be sure not to miss the exact instant when Squidboy hit Dexter.

"Hello Squidboy," groaned Squidboy. He sounded like the cartoon voice of a giant octopus in an underwater treasure cave.

"Hi, Mr. Robot," oozed Dexter. "Do you wanta play?"

"Wanta play?" mocked sepulchral Squidboy.

"Let's go in the living room," drooled Dexter and reached out for Squidboy's pincer. Moving at a speed that was fast even under slo-mo, Squidboy swung his left arm forward in a hard, flat arc that . . .

"Breakpoint," said Kwirkey Debug. "Squidboy's pincer intersects Dexter's chest."

Squidboy stood frozen in place with the tip of his left-hand manipulator poised daintily against Dexter.

"Show us a chart of Squidboy's attribute variables," said Russ.

Kwirkey Debug gestured with two hands and a small chart sproinged into existence. On the left of the chart were the names I'd assigned to Squidboy's variables, and on the right were the variables' numeric values. We scrolled the chart up and down, looking things over.

"How about that variable there called *stroke_persist*," said Russ presently. "It's set to 4,294,967,289." He paused gloatingly. "You jack-off."

"Oh hell." *Stroke_persist* was supposed to be a small integer like three or minus eleven or something. It measured how hard Squidboy pushed against things. With a *stroke_persist* value of four billion, Squidboy's normal motions would become amplified so much that he must perforce slash into those around him. How had *stroke_persist* gotten to be four billion?

"Kwirkey Debug," I said. "Please set a breakpoint for the following condition: *Squidboy's stroke_persist is larger than four billion*. Then reset and run."

"Yes," said Kwirkey Debug.

On the third run, the breakpoint tripped as Dexter reached for Squidboy's left hand.

"Show us the source code with the instruction pointer," I said.

Another chart appeared, and *bingo* there it was, our breakpoint had kicked in right after an instruction that set *stroke_persist* equal to -7. This is what it was supposed to do; the 7 meant *move softly*, and the minus meant *you're using your left arm*. But Russ's Kwirkey translator had decided that *stroke_persist* was always to be a positive number, and if you view a thirty-two-bit representation of -7 as a positive number, you think it's 4,294,967,289.

I started trying to explain this to Russ, but instead of letting me finish he rudely yelled that using *minus* for *left-hand* had been a stupid trick in the first place, and that now it was worse than stupid, it was unusable *since Squidboy had three hands*. Funny I hadn't thought of that. I recovered by pointing out that Russ had no business assuming that all of Squidboy's state variables were positive integers. Russ countered that he needed to assume all numbers to be positive so that the ROBOT.LIB calls could be made at maximum speed, thus guaranteeing that "his" code would run faster than the "kludgey" code for the Veep. He said that if I wanted to keep track of left, right, and middle, I should use a separate flag variable instead of trying to do it with negative numbers. I began to respond that . . .

"Let's go ahead and fix the first bug and see what happens next," said Sun Tam quietly. Russ and I had been so absorbed in the Sphex's cyberspace, and in our quarreling, that neither of us had noticed when Sun sat down next to us.

"Edit code," said Russ to Kwirkey Debug, and the silver figure produced what looked like a large pink rubber eraser. "I ONLY MAKE BIG MISTEAKS" was printed on the eraser—some West West hacker's idea of a joke.

"This is too stupid," I said. "I'll fix it on my own machine. Let's meet back here in an hour." I went back in the pit and squeezed all the negative numbers out of my program. It was, as Russ had suggested, a matter of using a two-bit *hand_flag* variable to do what the minuses had done. I used *hand_flag* 0 for LEFT, 1 for MIDDLE, and 2 for RIGHT; which meant that binary 00, 01, and 10 stood for, respectively, the pincer, the tentacle, and the humanoid hand. First the new code wouldn't compile (in my excitement I'd left out a ";"), then it compiled but crashed (I'd forgotten to rebuild one of the submodules with the new header file), and then *siiigh* my quick fix was done. I rushed back to the Sphex. Russ and Sun Tam were waiting.

Russ downloaded the new code and said, "Run."

This time Squidboy and Dexter made it into the living room.

"Hi there," said Perky Pat brightly. She was sitting in an armchair watching television. Walt was passed-out drunk on the couch, and Baby Scooter was lying on the floor gumming a filthy teething ring. The screen of the virtual TV against the wall was painted with changing real-time network television. I could clearly hear the TV voices through the Sphex speaker. Just now a newscaster was saying that a judge had denied Stu's pretrial motion to have my venue moved out of Silicon Valley. "So Jerzy Rugby's state trial on charges of criminal trespass, computer intrusion, and extreme cruelty to animals is still scheduled to begin the week after next in San Jose," the newscaster said. "Thursday, May 28. This network *will* be providing special coverage of that trial."

I was so involved in listening to the TV that I wasn't watching when Squidboy veered too far around Baby Scooter, lost his balance, and fell onto Walt's neck. I looked just in time to see Walt's head come off and fall onto the floor. It made a nasty thump.

"Oh, no way!" I cried. "Squidboy didn't hit him *that* hard."

"Let's just fix it," said Sun Tam. "Kwirkey Debug, reset and run to the point where Squidboy passes Baby Scooter."

This time there was nothing grossly wrong with any of the values in Squidboy's registers. We single-stepped the code forward, watching the numbers. The value of the *direction_angle* started doing something queer just before Squidboy fell over: it began oscillating irregularly between two, then four, then eight values, and then burst into what looked like totally random fluctuations.

"I recognize that behavior," I said, talking quickly before Russ could start up with the insults. "That's the period-doubling route to chaos! No problem. It's because I use a nonlinear formula to damp the jitter out of *direction_angle*. I use a preset constant called **FEEDBACK_DAMPER**. But the damping's not working anymore. We're getting the opposite of damped feedback; we're getting *feebdack*, right, Russ? Ha, ha!"

I was feeling hackish and manic. "Well, that's just because the Adze is different from the Veep. All I need to do is tweak the **FEEDBACK_DAMPER** value. Kwirkey Debug, I want to edit the constant definitions file. And put away that stupid eraser."

I changed **FEEDBACK_DAMPER** from 0.12 to 0.13. "Compile, reset, and run."

This time, instead of overavoiding Baby Scooter, Squidboy locked into a death spiral that wound around and around Baby Scooter until Scoot's geometry was churned into crooked fnoor.

"I thought you said you had the Adze code *wired,*" snarled Russ. "You fucking loser."

"It's a chaotically sensitive system," I cried. "I tweaked it specially for the GoMotion Veep with genetic algorithms. I'm not surprised it isn't working yet. Even though the Veep and the Adze use the same Y9707 chip, their sensors and effectors are different in hundreds of ways. They have *different bodies.*"

"Your control algorithms seem to be very sensitive," said Sun Tam. "You change the second digit of **FEEDBACK_DAMPER** and Squidboy kills Scooter instead of Walt?"

"Yeah," I said. "And maybe the value halfway in between will work. Say 0.125. But maybe not. Maybe **FEEDBACK_DAMPER** needs to be 0.124. The only way to find the right number is through trial and error. And even if you get one parameter right, you might need to change it again after you change some other parameter. You're searching a multidimensional chaotic phase space."

"So you're telling us that robot software is impossibly difficult to program," said Russ flatly. He looked sad. "And the Adze is never going to work."

"It's not impossible," I said. "It's just that we need to use genetic programming to find the right parameter settings. That's why I made Sun Tam put up 256 Our American Homes. We'll use genetic programming and everything will be *fine*."

"How?" asked Sun Tam.

"We put a Squidboy instance into each of the 256 Our American Homes, and select out, say, the 64 parameter sets that give the best behavior. Then we replace the worst 64 sets with mutated clones and crossovers of the genes in the top 64," I explained. "And you leave the 128 medium-scoring guys alone, or maybe mutate them a little. On the next cycle some of the middle guys might do better than average, and some might do worse." Russ was starting to grin. I was getting over. "So that we don't have to monitor it, we give all the Squidboys some simple machine-scored task. To begin with, the task will be walking into the living room without killing anybody. And once it can do that, we try a different task. The process works, I promise you."

"Let's help him get it started, Russ," said Sun Tam.

"Gronk," said Russ.

We got it happening late that afternoon, and by the next morning, the parameters were such that Squidboy could follow Dexter around the Christensens' house without breaking anything or hurting anyone—at least in the default **Pat-sitting. Walt-sleeping. Dexter-roving. Scooter-teething** configuration. Now we needed to look for more difficult configurations.

I got Ben to come and see what we'd achieved so far. He was favorably impressed, though still very worried about our being ready for the product rollout scheduled for Tuesday, May 26, a mere two weeks away. Sun Tam got Ben to allocate wireless pro-quality cyberspace headsets for the three of us. We continued working in front of the Sphex, but now instead of the bogus shared look-through Abbott wafer display, we had true immersion.

We set up a virtual office down on the asphalt next to the Our American Homes and began spending almost all our time there together in our tuxedos. I was an idealized Jerzy in shorts, fractal shirt, and sandals—my tux that I'd bought from Dirk Blanda. Sun Tam's tux showed a lanky gunslinger. Russ was a pagan hobbit with shades, a nun's habit, and seventeen toes.

Every now and then I'd look up into the cyberspace sky and see the spherical green-and-gray Netport node up there like a low-hanging harvest moon. Sometimes, when the hacking was getting old, I'd feel trapped. I was stuck in a parking lot by a field of tract homes in a boring part of San Jose. I would wish I could fly away to see what the GoMotion ants were doing, out there in the Antland of Fnoor. People said there were still GoMotion ants loose in cyberspace, but we weren't seeing any of them at West West.

To continue improving the Adze code, we began making the Our American Home test beds more difficult. We began breeding for bad Our American Homes. Each Our American Home setup could be described by its own parameter set, and we began selecting out the 64 Our American Homes that got the worst scores for their Squidboys, and at the same time singling out the 64 Our American Homes whose Squidboys did the best. And then we'd replace the parameter sets of the mellow 64 homes with mutated clones and blends of the parameter sets of the 64 worst Our American Homes, and let the 128 homes in the middle ride along for another cycle.

After a few days of this, the Our American Homes were pretty bizarre—like imagine your worst nightmare of a subdivision to live in. In one house you could see Pat throwing dishes at Walt. In another, Dexter was taking a crap on the front steps. In another, a flipped-out Pat was in the kitchen setting the drapes on fire. In another, drunk Walt hunted the robot with an axe. In another, Scooter was sitting on the ledge of a window holding a carving knife. And in each of the bad Our American Homes, a desperate Squidboy did his best to fit in. Some of the Squidboys did better than others, and those were the ones who would get bred onto the genes of the Squidboys who lost.

By that Friday, it began looking like the Adze could work. We let the gene tweaker run for the whole weekend, and on Monday, May 18, Russ, Sun and I floated in cyberspace looking fondly down at 256 Squidboys doing good things in all the different Our American Homes. We were the gods of this ticky-tacky little world, this sinister Happy Acres.

"It's time for me to do *my* thing," said Sun Tam. "Let's hit the Rubber Room, guys."

I was scared; I was always especially scared when we started up one of these powerful robots with code that *I'd* worked on. I knew all too well how fallible I was. Another worry was that the GoMotion ants might infest Squidboy and take over—even though we'd been sure to copy the incomprehensible encrypted machine language bits of a GoMotion ant lion into his code.

Ben went into the Rubber Room with us and picked up the remote *On/Off* switch as before. If Squidboy killed one of us, it would be West West's responsibility, and it would be Ben's job to take the fall.

As before, the Rubber Room held a practice staircase, soft mannequins of the Christensen family, a fridge, a Plexiglas door, and some furniture. Dome-head Squidboy was there, squatting down on his wheels. We waited behind the big waist-high table by the door while Russ stuck our new program disk into Squidboy. Russ ran back to us and Ben pressed the On button.

The robot hummed into life, scanned around the room, and said "Hello Squidboy."

"Squidboy," said Ben. "Go to the fridge and get Perky Pat a bottle of Calistoga water." Squidboy smoothly turned toward the refrigerator and started rolling. When he got to the movable Plexiglas door, he slowed and used his tentacle to open it.

"Good going," murmured Sun Tam.

Squidboy got the bottle out of the fridge, went back through the door, pulled up next to the seated Perky Pat doll, unscrewed the bottle cap, and set the bottle down on the table next to her.

"All right!" I said.

"Squidboy, go up and down the stairs," said Ben. Squidboy made it up the stairs okay, but—he fell over on his way down.

In every program there's one killer problem that tortures you the most. In the case of Squidboy it was stairs. I was damned if I could get them right. As the coming days wore on, I began to realize that my having gotten the parameters right for the Veep so quickly had been blind luck. No matter how long I genetically evolved the Squidboy stair-climbing procedure, the damn machine always ended up falling over on the way down. Fortunately the Rubber Room had a soft floor.

I spent the next four days driving around inside Squidboy, single-stepping with all the variables in watch mode, perturbing and reevolving the parameters, and trying new hand-coded ideas for the staircase procedures. I was hacking all the time and thinking about nothing but the software . . . dreaming of bytes, xors and shifts, of memory allocations and data structures. On Friday, I came up with a desperate brute-force measure that made Squidboy climb stairs quite a bit more slowly than Studly had, but *Squidboy stopped falling over*.

Meanwhile Ben had already sent the Adze program to the West West software build group, who were sending us bug reports to the tune of two dozen a day. I was busy with the stairs, but doughty Russ and Sun dug in and fixed the bugs as fast as they came.

Friday afternoon West West started final code integration. We worked straight through Saturday and Sunday, testing the builds and adding final tweaks. The official Adze 1.0 build tested out copacetic on Monday. On Tuesday, the official product launch was held in a big ballroom in the San Jose Fairmont Hotel. We'd beaten out the GoMotion Veep launch by one day. Hurray!

EIGHT

Riscky Pharbeque

RUSS, SUN TAM, JANELLE, AND A BUNCH OF OTHER PEOple went down to the San Jose Fairmont for the rollout, but Ben asked me to stay back at West West with him. "This way we'll be ready to turn him off or go telerobotic if there's any problems," said Ben.

Ben and I sat in the Sphex room; Jack and Jill were on the other machine as usual. We had our headsets coupled right to Squidboy's two cameras, and our headset earphones were taking their feed from Squidboy's mikes. We saw and heard through Squidboy's head. Ben had a line linked to an emergency *On/Off* radio control that was at the site with the robot, and I was ready to slip my virtual hands into the images of Squidboy's manipulators and take him over in case of a less drastic malfunction. If things started going to pieces, I could fake the demo.

Squidboy was up on a dais at one end of the Fairmont ballroom, shifting his field of view this way and that. If he noticed someone staring right at him he'd wave his humanoid hand at them and I'd see the hand in the right part of his viewfield. "*hand_flag 2*," I thought happily.

It was a fancy room, with big crystal chandeliers. The walls were covered with gold-and-cream striped wallpaper. The rug had a diagonal grid pattern with florets at the intersections. Facing the dais were seventeen rows of tables with white linen tablecloths. The tables held pens, notepads, dishes of wrapped hard candy, glasses, and pitchers of ice water for the assembled industry bigwigs and press. I recognized Jeff Pear in the third row with Dick and Chuck from GoMotion. Squidboy waved at them. They looked tense and depressed, which was just what I'd been hoping for. We'd beaten them out the starting gate and there was nothing they could do about it except sue.

The room was filled with the mutter of conversation. Now Otto Gyorgyi stepped to the podium, dressed in his usual gray suit and bilious tie. His slicked-down black hair gleamed in the spotlights. Squidboy gazed at him.

"Hello," he said, "I'm Otto Gyorgyi, the General Manager of the West West Home Products Division. It's my pleasure today to announce our new line of Adze home robot kits. As of today, West West is shipping this kitware throughout the world. Before I fill in any more information, let's have a little fun." Otto forced his sour face into a smile. There was an expectant hush. "Hello, Squidboy," said Otto. "My name is Otto."

"Hello, Otto," said Squidboy. "What can I do for you?"

"I'm thirsty, Squidboy. Get me a glass of water."

Squidboy looked around the dais.

"I'm sorry, Otto, but where is the water?"

"On the table down there." Squidboy stared at Otto's pointing hand, then turned his gaze toward the front row of tables.

"Thank you, Otto."

Squidboy wheeled to the edge of the stage, turned sideways, and began carefully stepping down the dais steps. I held my breath till he'd safely reached the bottom. Whew! Squidboy wheeled forward and the glass and pitcher loomed before us. Behind the glass and pitcher were the faces of two reporters. Squidboy grasped the glass with his tentacle and picked up the pitcher with his humanoid hand. He poured water into the glass and set down the pitcher.

The viewpoint swung toward the stage and Squidboy galumphed back up the steps, rocking from side to side on his bicycle wheels and his flexing legs. The tentacle-manipulator held the glass steadfastly upright, and not a drop was spilled.

"Thank you," said Otto as the robot handed him the glass. The audience burst into applause.

"Go to sleep for fifteen minutes, Squidboy," said Otto. "And call my name when you wake." Our vision screens went blank.

"I wish I was there," I said, pulling off my headset.

"West West wants to minimize any linkage between you and the Adze," said Ben.

"Because they pirated ROBOT.LIB and my SuperC code from GoMotion?"

"It's not that," said Ben uncomfortably. "We're used to lawsuits. It's because of your trial. It starts day after tomorrow doesn't it?"

"Uh, yeah, I guess it does. I've been hacking too much to think about it, but yes, today is Tuesday and the state trial starts Thursday. Criminal trespass, computer intrusion, and extreme cruelty to animals."

"What's the story with the cruelty to animals?" laughed Ben, momentarily falling out of his manager persona. "Is that some kind of right-to-artificial-life thing on behalf of the ants?"

"No, man, it's because of the dog that Studly killed."

"I'd forgotten about the dog." Ben got serious again. "The word from my higher-ups is that your presence at West West is bad for our corporate image."

"Thanks a lot."

"It gets worse," sighed Ben. "Come on back to my office." I followed him, wondering what was up, and then Ben fumbled around on his desk and produced a folder with my name on it. "I argued myself hoarse with Otto Gyorgyi about this, but his mind is made up." He handed me a letter which read:

DEAR JERZY RUGBY,

(1) As a result of a top management decision, you will be redeployed, effective today.
(2) You will continue to be a West West employee, receiving your current compensation and benefits for 7 days. The 7-day period is called your Redeployment Notice Period; your Redeployment Notice Period will end at noon on June 2.
(3) . . .

"I'm fired?" I yelped. "This is what I get for writing the code for a new product? A new product that's starting to ship? This is the payoff?"

"Well, you should at least note that paragraph (3) says that you'll get an extra four weeks of severance pay with your check this Friday. I got you that. Otto feels that from now on Russ and Sun Tam will be able to handle the Adze code support on their own. It's a rotten break for you, Jerzy. I'm sorry about it."

"What the fuck does Otto know about anything?"

"He watches every dollar that goes out or comes in." Ben glanced around to make sure nobody was within earshot. "I'll just come out and level with you, Jerzy.

This is *really* about that three million dollars West West put up for your bail. West West wants the money back."

"You're going to revoke my bail?"

"At the end of the redeployment period, yes, your bail will be revoked. As I think I told you before, bail falls under the category of a West West employee benefit."

"No wonder there was such a big rush to get me to finish the Adze code," I said bitterly. "So you guys could go ahead and copyright it for West West and then cut me loose." I racked my brain for a way out. "But . . . But what if there's a problem with the Adze code? I could consult on a part-time basis, couldn't I? You wouldn't need to pay me benefits or give me an office! Just lend me a cyberdeck so I can work from home—or work from jail if that's what it comes to."

"No way," said Ben after the briefest pause for thought. "Equipping a computer criminal with unsupervised cyberspace access would open West West to highly negative legal exposure."

"Computer criminal. I don't believe this."

"I'm sorry, Jerzy. You're a great programmer, but West West is laying you off. It sucks, but that's life in the Valley. You might check back with us if you win your trials." He glanced at his watch. "I better tune in on Squidboy again. Good-bye."

I went into Los Perros to seek out the consolation of my soft-chinned, bell-haired Gretchen.

"Look who's here," said Susan Poker as I entered Welsh & Tayke.

"Oh hi, Jerzy," said Gretchen, looking up from some papers on her desk. "What's new?"

"Are you busy?"

"Kind of. We're putting the paperwork through on two properties today. It'll take most of the afternoon. I get off at four-thirty."

"You really should buy that house you were living in," said Susan Poker. "It's just standing empty, and Mr. Nutt's ready to accept a very low offer. Have you asked West West about it?"

"Don't you ever give up?" I asked her.

"Not me!"

"Hey, Gretchen, come outside for just a minute so I can tell you something *in private*."

"Secrets from *moi*?" exclaimed Susan Poker.

"I'll come," said Gretchen. "But just for a minute."

So out there on the sidewalk I told her. "We finished that robot I've been working on, and now I've been fired."

"Oh. Poor Jerzy. And your trial starts day after tomorrow. This is a bad week for you." She patted my cheek and kissed me. "We should do something fun tonight, to take your mind off your woes."

"I'll try to think of something. Meanwhile I think I'll get a drink."

"It's barely two o'clock, Jerzy."

"Hey, I'm unemployed!"

"Be back here at four-thirty, don't forget."

"Okay."

I walked very slowly down the street. As an unemployed person, I had all the time in the world. It was a funny feeling not to be in a rush.

I'd been racing from one job to another for more than twenty years now. For awhile I'd been a math professor, then I'd had a job selling textbooks, and then we'd moved to California and I'd become a hacker. Rush, rush, rush, and for what? To age and to die. Despite my big dreams, I'd never been anything more than a struggling shrimp in the world's big water, nothing but a gnat in the blank California sky.

My job and family were gone, but at least Queue and Keith were being nice to me these days—of course I was paying them rent. I wished I'd brought a joint with me today. This was not a day when I felt like being the real me.

I walked a little farther and found myself in front of the Los Perros bakery. I'd been avoiding the place ever since my big night at the Vos', but today it seemed natural to drift in for a sandwich. There was Nga behind the counter as usual, dressed in black and with her hair poufed up on one side. Her quick eyes twinkled when she saw me, and her kissy red lips curved in a smile.

"Jerzy! How you doing!"

"Not so well. I have to go to court day after tomorrow."

"I know. The D.A. want one of us testify, but we no see nothing."

"That's good."

Now Nga's mother Huong Vu looked up and noticed me.

"We no want talk to you," she said flatly.

"I'm sorry about the neighbor's dog."

She shook her head. "We glad dog is gone, but we no want you come back our house ever again."

"I understand. Uh, Nga, I'll take a medium croissant with turkey and Swiss cheese. To go."

"No problem, Jerzy," said Nga. "Five thirty-four." A tingle went up my arm from the sly caress of her fingertips when she gave me my change. "Come back soon," smiled Nga, though Huong Vu snapped at her in Vietnamese.

Nga Vo's cousin Kanh Pham followed me out of the store. He flipped his long hair and cleared his throat.

"What?" I said.

"My cousin Vinh Vo still very interest do business with you."

"What kind of business?" For a minute I really couldn't remember.

"He say you company going need some Y9707 chip for robot."

"Oh yes, I remember that. But I don't work for a company anymore."

"Maybe you tell somebody anyhow."

"Maybe." If Vinh Vo really had access to a big stash of cheap Y9707 chips, this could be an opportunity for me to play middleman and make some good bread. With the Adze and Veep kits on the market, the demand for Y9707s could run way ahead of the supply. Y9707s were wholesaling at twelve hundred bucks per chip and, I now recalled, Vinh had offered to sell me several hundred of them for $120 a chip. If I could find a way to resell them, I could make a thousand dollars profit on each chip. "Where would somebody reach Vinh Vo?"

Khanh Pham wrote a phone number on a piece of paper and gave it to me.

"Just out of theoretical curiosity, Khan, how does Vinh Vo get hold of his chips?"

"Many Vietnamese people who work in the fab and component plants give some chips to him. They bring chips home from assembly line. Vinh Vo is like a godfather to them."

In other words Vinh Vo was running a protection racket that victimized his newly arrived fellow nationals. Those of them who were computer workers were allowed to pay Vinh Vo with chips instead of cash. Well, that explained how he could afford to sell the chips in the black market for one dollar on the ten. When Vinh had originally made me the offer, I'd been put off by the obvious criminality of the deal, but with my trials coming up and West West about to cut me loose, I had less and less to lose.

"I'll think about calling him. Give my best to Nga."

"She has two new boyfriend." He giggled sputteringly and tossed his hair several times.

"Oh well!" I laughed along with him. He was a nice boy.

"Did you see my new motorcycle?" asked Khanh Pham. "Vinh Vo bought it for me!" There was indeed a black Kawasaki parked in front of the bakery.

"Congratulations!"

I took my sandwich down the street to a scuzzy bar called the Night Watch. This was not a yuppie watering hole like D. T. Finnegan's; no, the Night Watch had black plywood walls, plastic furniture, and a resident motorcycle club: people with leather jackets that said KNIGHTS OF THE NIGHT WATCH on them. The Knights weren't exactly Hell's Angels—this was, after all, still Los Perros—but they were a fairly scurvy crew. Three of them were at a table in the rear: a fat man, a thin man, and a fat woman. I sat up at the bar to the left of a kid with shoulder-length brown hair. I ordered a beer and started in on my turkey croissant.

The wall to my left was covered with bright colored lights. There was a TV showing a vintage Porky Pig cartoon, a neon beer sign shaped like the Golden Gate Bridge, a 3-D magnetic pinball machine, a dollar-a-minute cyberspace game with a bicycle seat and handlebars, and a big Abbott wafer screen showing music videos from the Total Video Library in cyberspace. The current video was a horrible, yelling antique number captioned as being by somebody called Tom Jones singing something called "Delilah." The bartender was lustily singing along.

"Jesus this is bad," I couldn't help saying. "This is the worst thing I've heard in my whole life."

"The mid–twentieth century was a golden age for the vocal arts," said the bartender. He was a blond, limp man with a mustache and a dirty T-shirt. He had a winningly sniggering way of talking. "Watch the finale. That's when all the women throw their underwear onstage. It's really choice."

"I need another beer for this shit."

"Punch up some country music after this, Lester," twanged the boy next to me. "That'll make us feel even more like drinkin'." His voice trailed off at the end of every sentence. He had something on the bar in front of him, a little car or—I looked closer. It was a little car with the rubber head of a cow. This was the same boy who'd come up to me outside Queue's gate. The bartender gave me another beer and drifted down to the other end of the bar to talk with the bikers.

"What's up, doc?" said the boy to me, waggling his eyebrows. He tossed his head to get his rasta tangles out of his face. His thin lips pulled back in a stretching motion that was more wince than smile. His breath smelled of some unfamiliar chemical, and he looked zonked.

"Are you really Hex DEF6?" I'd taken the wrong approach in my last conversation with him. Though I was still angry about the voodoo cyberspace head trip he'd run on me back in the Antland of Fnoor, I tried to make my voice sound mild and admiring. The point was to get some information out of him.

"That's not who I *am*," he said with spaced-out precision. "Hex DEF6 was a *gig*. My *name* is Riscky Pharbeque and I'm from Fort Worth, Texas." He stuck out his hand and I shook it.

"So who hired you to scare the shit out of me? Was it West West?"

"No, man, it was a guy called Dirk Blanda. Mattel Incorporated fronted him the money to burn you."

"*Dirk Blanda*? My *neighbor*? The bodymapper who

runs Dirk Blanda's Personography? And—Mattel the toy company? I don't get it."

"It's that *Our American Home* shit you did, old son. Perky Pat? You ripped off the CyberBarbie meshes Dirk did for Mattel, so they-all hired a phreak to burn you. Frontier justice, pardner. That's how it goes. I picked the gig up off a phreak bulletin board. We call it the Burn Exchange, all kinds of kinky offers get posted there. But it was nothing personal, you wave?"

"Sure, Riscky, no problem," I smiled. "But why was Hex DEF6 telling me to work for West West?"

"Well this was a real special gig. I got paid twice. Was *supposed* to get paid twice, anyhow. There was two rewards out on you, Jerzy. Blanda paid me up front to burn you, but a guy called Roger Coolidge said he'd pay me more to tell you to work for West West. Except he still hasn't coughed up. He's hog-stupid if he thinks he can short Riscky Pharbeque. I don't much like Coolidge, and I might could burn him really bad."

"That was really Roger there with us in Antland of Fnoor?" I remembered the weird gangster nightclub back room that the big ant had carried me to. Hex DEF6 had been there, and tuxedos of Roger and Susan Poker. Though when I'd asked Susan Poker about it, she'd insisted she was a computer illiterate who'd never been in cyberspace.

"That was Roger's tuxedo all right, and he was in it—at least until I twisted him up. It was you, me, Roger and, oh yeah, Sue Poker. You know her, don't you? Sue's a cryp at Welsh & Tayke Realty. She knew your cyberspace access code, so I cut her in for fifteen percent. She wanted to watch me burn you, so I brought her along and slaved her tuxedo motions to the twitching of that big ant. Sue's hot stuff under all that plastic." Riscky Pharbeque cackled and then raised his voice to call to the bartender as Tom Jones reached his rutting, bellowing climax. "Come on, Lester, play some country next. Does Total Video got any like Charlie Daniels in all that old shit?"

"They've even got Van Halen, dude. Total Video *rules*."

"Well git on it."

"And give Riscky and me a round, Lester," I called. "Two Coronas and two shots of tequila."

"Thankee kindly," said Riscky.

The bartender pressed a microphone button and asked the videoplayer for Charlie Daniels. The screen showed a grid of titled images and with Riscky's loud advice, Lester tapped one of them. The music started. Lester served our drinks and went back to the bikers.

I raised my shot glass to Riscky Pharbeque in mock salute. "You're a hell of a phreak, Riscky. As long as I'm asking questions, how about the GoMotion ants?"

"*Wiggly* little suckers. Hats off to you on that, Jerzy. All us phreaks are rooting for you."

"I mean, how did you get an ant to swallow my hands and carry me to you?"

"Hellfire, Jerzy, I ain't gonna give *all* my secrets away. If you want to know how to use the ants, go and ask them yourself."

"I can't. I don't have a cyberdeck."

"*Business opportunity!*" twanged Riscky happily. He played his accent like a musical instrument. "I got a deck I can sell you from out of the trunk of my car."

"How much?"

"It's a forty-thousand-dollar Pemex model twelve. I ain't had it but ten weeks. I'd be amenable to oh . . . " He regarded me narrowly, suddenly not seeming as drunk and stoned as I'd thought he was. "Nine hundred dollars cash. That'll leave you about four hundred dollars in the bank."

"Of course you know my bank balance?"

"I got an interest in you, Jerzy. You make a run across the street and get the cash from Wells Fargo and then I'll move the deck to your Animata. Do you know how to connect to the moonroof satellite dish?"

"Well, sort of. Not really. But I want to."

"I'll help you for another hundred bucks. One thousand dollars for a Pemex cyberdeck twelve, next to new, fully configured, and hardware-installed on an invisible phreak patch to the Net. Deals don't come much sweeter than that, Mister Rugby."

"What's the catch?"

"I don't *pay* for the cyberdecks, old son. I just get 'em delivered. I'm fixin' to get me a Pemex thirteen delivered later today, so I might as well lay my old box off on you. I'll have you up and running in an hour for one thousand dollars cash."

The Charlie Daniels video ended and the floppy blond bartender started back up the bar toward us.

"Let's do it, Mister Pharbeque," I said.

Riscky waited in the bar while I got the money out of my bank. He'd been right about my balance: it was $1385. Just so I'd have some money in my pockets, I went ahead and took out thirteen hundred. Today was Tuesday, and on Friday my last paycheck from West West would come in. The last two weeks pay plus the four weeks severance pay would come to something like thirteen thousand dollars after taxes. Cash flow was all-important to me these days, as my credit cards had been canceled as soon as I'd been indicted for computer crime.

Riscky followed my car up to a deserted pull-out in the hills of Los Perros, about halfway to Queue's. Within the hour, he had the Pemex cyberdeck installed in the trunk of my car right next to the map machine. The cyberdeck's hookup to the Net was via the map machine's antenna, which was a barely visible bull's-eye of titanium rings embedded in the clear plastic of the Animata's moonroof. The ring spacing was such that the pattern acted as a radio-wave Fresnel lens, able to transmit to and receive from satellites. Ordinarily the lens was only used to consult the navigational satellites, but with Riscky Pharbeque's expertise, the system was soon tuned to the frequency of the cybernet communication satellites.

The Pemex twelve cyberdeck was awesome. It had a radio-connected headset that looked like a big pair of wraparound mirrorshades, and the control gloves were radio-linked as well.

"The deck can suck juice out of your car's battery no matter if the car is off or on," Riscky explained. "The glove and headset signals have a throw of four hundred feet. You can park your car and take the headset and gloves with you."

"Does the deck always have to be on?" I asked. "Like overnight?"

"Naw, you can turn it on from the goggles, they're sensitive to a certain sequence of taps. You do three fast taps, wait, then tap once, then wait, then tap four fast taps, then wait, and then tap one last time. That's the code I set it to."

I put on the goggles and tapped the Pharbeque three-one-four-one sequence on the temple. Ping, I was floating inside the familiar Bay Area Netport.

"I don't have it set up for an office," said Riscky half-apologetically. He was standing next to me. "We can't use an office,'cause this is an illegal connect. Turn her on and you pop up somewhere random in a given target space. I got the target set to the Netport. You can always change the target with the claim stake tool."

I swung my head slowly back and forth. The visual effects were better than any I'd seen before—the resolution was incredibly high, and the updates were shockingly fast. There were no jaggies, no dithering, no lag time, no lurches, no compromises. What I saw was the purest and most convincing virtual reality I'd ever seen.

"It's wonderful, Riscky. I didn't know they made headsets this good."

"Hell, Jerzy, I phreakified it is why it runs so good. This is an undocumented billion-pixel video mode. And look at this!" He tapped the other side of my headset in a five-nine-two-six tattoo, and suddenly it was as if I were looking through the headset at the dashboard of my car. I turned my head and saw Riscky. But the headset was opaque! Was this another dark dream, another voodoo cyberspace? I pulled the goggles off fast and looked at them. I hadn't noticed before that there were two TV cameras like transparent glass pinheads set where my pupils would be.

"I call it stunglasses mode," drawled Riscky. "You get a reality shunt going there, with real-world images being routed into cyberspace and back. You tap five-nine-two-six on the left temple to toggle it."

"How am I going to remember both those four-digit sequences?"

"*How I need a drink, alcoholic of course,*" said Riscky. "Count the letters in the words."

"It's pi!" I exclaimed, recognizing the mnemonic. "I love it! Here's your money."

Riscky took the money and cackled. His toy cow circled about in excited figure eights. "Go on in there and get even, Jerzy! *Fuck Shit Up!*" He got back in his car and drove off. I still had a half hour before I had to meet Gretchen. I put the headset back on and returned to the vast hall of the Bay Area Netport.

I flew over to a public rest room and made my way in past a gaggle of black-lipsticked grrls. I looked in the mirror to see what kind of user tuxedo Riscky had left on his machine? A silly tux, that's what—I looked like a big, wheeled cart with two human hands and the imposing head of a Texas longhorn. The platonic ideal of Riscky's toy.

"Hey, cow!" one of the grrls called to me. "Can we watch you take a piss?" She and her friends laughed like maniacs at this—not that tuxedos ever did take a piss, except in the farthest reaches of the specialty cyberporno arcades.

After staring at myself for awhile, I turned to look at the grrls, all pierced and leathered and tattooed. The one who'd called to me stepped forward and grabbed one of my horns. I felt it as a buzzing against the side of my head; apparently my new headset had touchpads in its temples.

"I'm Bety Byte," she said. "And you're Riscky Pharbeque. We owe you a burn for what you did to the Cryp Club library, cow-patty." She pulled out a little thing like a gun and shot it at me. Everything went black. At first I thought my system had crashed, but then when I flew forward, I saw that all Bety's gun had done was to surround me with an opaque sphere.

As I flew out of the sphere, I tossed my head to hook one of my horns at Bety's realistic icon, expecting my horn to pass harmlessly but perhaps intimidatingly through her. But Bety Byte had her surfaces customset for preemptive collision rejection, and my horn clattered off her with a vicious buzz on my temple. She popped her little geometry gun at me again, making things black again, and this time I just kept on going right out of the rest room and up toward the oversize bright pink and blue node of Magic Shell Mall, the cyberspace shopping mall where Gretchen had gone to Nordstrom's.

Riscky must have had some kind of valid credit number installed in his system, for the Magic Shell node allowed me to enter. I popped out near the Bay Area Netport node that lay at the center of the Magic Shell Mall. The green-and-gray light of the Netport node flickered behind me. All over the inner surface of the great Magic Shell were walkways and the shapes of stores.

I arced along a space path toward where the ant had taken me last month, to the vacant lot between the video store and the stockbroker: Total Video and Gibb & Gibb Stocks. I thudded down on my virtual wheels and trundled across the blank surface till I met a seam where two Magic Shell facets met. I turned and followed the seam to a shallow corner where three quadrilaterals met five narrow triangles; this was the same corner as before. I peered at the corner, but I was too big to see if there still was a little round off error hole in it.

I needed to shrink, but—I now realized—I didn't know how. Perhaps Riscky already had put a *shrink* hand gesture into his system library? I said "Show Tools," out loud and, yes, Riscky's system accepted this standard cyberspace command.

Several shapes appeared in the air before me—a telephone, a video camera, a claim stake, a typewriter, a calculator, an atlas, a can of spraypaint, a Swiss knife, a jet engine—but there was nothing that seemed obviously designed to change my size. I pried at the corner in the floor with my head's long cowhorn, but it wouldn't give. Maybe the Swiss knife? I was just opening out the can-opener blade when the grrls caught up with me.

"Bad cow!" yelled Bety Byte. She and her grrlfriends were touching down all around me. "Shoo, Riscky!" yelled one of them, and fired another geometry gun at me. I found myself enclosed inside a yellow tetrahedron, unable to see anything but my tool icons. I was going to have to get a new, shrinkable tuxedo and come back. I grabbed the jet engine, pointed the exhaust down toward my feet and pushed the button on its side. ZZZZOOOW! I burst out of the tetrahedron and flashed in along a radius straight toward the Netport node at the mall's center.

When I popped out into the Netport, I stopped, took off the headset, and turned off the deck. Three-one-four-one. *How I need a.* I had to get a new tuxedo that had a control to make it shrink, and that didn't make people think I was Riscky Pharbeque.

Since Riscky's configuration didn't have a virtual office where I could hack the system, the simplest thing would be to just buy a size-controllable tuxedo from Dirk Blanda's Personography. Of course I had a bone to pick with Dirk Blanda about his having hired Riscky to burn me, though I had to admit there was a sort of justice in it.

Tuxedos sold for seven hundred dollars, and I only had three hundred. Dirk Blanda was certainly the person to go to, unless he was still mad about the CyberBarbie meshes I'd ripped off. Getting him to make me a tux would be hard, but getting him to do it cut-rate might be impossible.

I thought a minute, and then flashed on the idea that Dirk would certainly help me out *if I offered to pay him in pot.* Every time Dirk and I had gotten high together he'd asked me if I could score pot for him. I'd never done so, though. Like, why should I? What for? I'd always just given him a few hits of pot when I had a lot, so that when *I* was out of pot I could count on him to give me some. But he was almost always out of pot. The more I thought about it, the more sure I was that if I apologized to Dirk about CyberBarbie and offered him a fresh quarter ounce, he'd make me a shrinkable tux.

It was three-thirty and I was only a ten-minute drive from Queue's. I motored on up there.

"Hi, Queue." She was sitting in front of a Macintosh in her office. The office was right off the lower deck: an anachronistic jumble of papers, disks, tapes, and books. Media Molecules primarily sold hard copy media for those not plugged into cyberspace, although their best-sellers were available on-line from the Mondo Alternate Info Service over the cyberspace Net. But most people didn't have cyberspace yet, especially the eternally broke eternal seekers to whom Media Molecules catered. Most of their business was still a quaint matter of putting a physical video or audiotape into a big envelope and like physically mailing it.

"You're looking good, Jerzy." Queue smiled up at me with her hair across her face. "Hey! Before I forget! Some e-mail for you came in a little while ago."

"Let me see it."

She moused around the screen for awhile and finally said, "I guess I erased it."

"What did it say? Who was it from?"

"It was from Roger something in Switzerland. He said—let me think, yes, he said, 'I appreciate your brilliant work on the Adze. Sorry about your run of bad luck. I hope to work with you again someday.' "

"Jesus," I said. "That's Roger Coolidge. He *appreciates* my work for West West? Don't tell me he controls them, too!"

"Wasn't Roger Coolidge the big hacker guy at GoMotion?"

"Yeah. He's like my evil twin. I think he's behind everything bad that's been happening to me. What a guy. And he 'hopes to work with me again someday,' the prick?"

"That's what he said."

"Well, thanks for remembering to tell me." I paused

and gathered my wits, remembering why I'd come here. "Do you have any spare pot, Queue? I need to get hold of a quarter ounce."

"Wait, wait a minute, your new robots are a huge success? You're celebrating?"

"Not exactly. I got fired again. As for the robots, you should watch the local news. Or—do you have a TV?" I'd never seen a TV at Queue and Keith's, come to think of it. I hate TV so much that I never look for it.

"Keith pawned our set last Christmas," said Queue. "So *we* had to miss out on that spacey ants-vs-television hack you pulled. You got fired from West West?"

Keith popped into the office as if on cue.

"Hi, Jerzy," he said. "Are you still looking for a gun?"

"A *gun*!" cried Queue. "Out of the question, Keith! This is a desperate man!"

"I've been fired again," I told Keith. "And all I want to buy right now is marijuana."

"Well, I can't help you with that—though I'd be glad to smoke a bowl with you," said Keith. "But I was at a pawnshop in Cupertino today and they had a plastic pistol for seventy-five dollars. It was a mean little machine. It looked like the head of a cobra. If you give me the money, I could get it for you."

"You pawned your guitar again, Keith?" demanded Queue. "You didn't pawn anything of *mine*, did you?"

"I have certain unavoidable expenses," said Keith with solemn hippie dignity.

I wasn't sure what Keith's unavoidable expenses were—though it was fun to think that the money was for cool, newly synthesized psychedelics. But likely as not the money was simply cash for driving around, for things like gas, bridge tolls, parking meters, tobacco, and an occasional espresso. Queue controlled the cash flow of Media Molecules, and I could readily believe that she was unwilling to advance Keith a cent.

"Oh, *you!*" said Queue to Keith, and he smilingly drifted back out onto the deck.

"So okay, Jerzy, you want a quarter?" Queue's voice rose musically with the welcome question. "I guess I could spare a little. I'm short on cash."

"I have cash." I still had three hundred dollars left. "One fifty?"

Queue gave her temple-bell laugh and mouthed a kiss at me. "One forty is fine."

While she searched out the quarter, I went upstairs to my room and rooted out the remains of my own stash. I rolled four fat joints in Orange Zig-Zag papers and tucked them into the back of a matchbook. I went back downstairs and paid Queue for the heat-sealed quarter ounce plastic bag of sinsemilla. She said she'd bought it for herself yesterday, but was passing it on to me as a favor. I thanked her profusely. The pot was a beautiful light green mass of female buds with dusty purple stigmas. Dirk would drool over it.

I drove down to Los Perros and parked in Dirk's driveway, right next to our old house on Tangle Way. Dirk usually worked at home rather than in the storefront of Dirk Blanda's Personography.

He came to the door and looked out diffidently. Dirk was a calm, boyish man with a thin head and short white hair. He had a lot of simplistic ideas about economics and politics that he believed the more deeply because he'd thought them all out himself.

"Hi, Jerzy. Come on in."

I followed him up to his machine room. I meant to be completely nice and diplomatic, but my anger over what he'd done to me came spilling out. "Dirk, you should have talked to me instead of hiring a phreak to burn me. That's a crime, you know. I could report you."

"Look who's talking about crime. *You stole my meshes*! That's wrong, Jerzy. If you've just come here to insult me, you might as well go."

"I'm not here to insult you, and I'm sorry that my companies ripped off your meshes. But we're even now. Your phreak put me through hell."

Dirk's eyes widened with curiosity. "What did he do?"

"He got me in a voodoo cyberspace watching movies of me and my children getting tortured."

"Oh! Now that—that's nothing that *I* told him to do." Dirk looked like a worried boy whose Halloween prank has gone too far. "I wouldn't ever wish any harm on your family."

"You told him to burn me and he did. But now I've been fired from GoMotion and West West both, so if Mattel still feels like burning someone about the Our American Home test sites, tell them to go after the execs and not after me. I'm out of the loop."

"I'm sorry to hear that, Jerzy. And your trial starts tomorrow doesn't it? I remember seeing Studly working in your yard plenty of times. I can't believe he killed a dog."

"I think he started acting different after the GoMotion ants infected him. But now that there's GoMotion ant lions all over the place, it shouldn't happen again."

"I keep hearing that there's still some ants loose in cyberspace. Have you seen them?"

"No, but as a matter of fact, that's why I'm here. I need a special tuxedo so I can go look for the cyberspace ants."

"So you need a new tuxedo. I figured it was either that or pot that brought you here. You don't happen to have any pot, do you? I'm all out again."

"That's what I was hoping," I grinned. I took out the

bag of pot and handed it to Dirk. "I'll trade you this quarter ounce for a new tux. The tux has to be scalable. It has to have a control on it so that I can change its size."

Dirk turned the packet this way and that, looking at the buds. "This is awesome, Jerzy. Of course I can make you a scalable tux. If you don't want too much fine detail, I can fix you up in about ten minutes. Do you want it to look like you? I've still got your bodymap on file."

"No, no, I want to be anonymous."

"Well, I've got a bunch of art meshes on disk. They don't look like anyone specific. You can pick what you like. Should we get high first?" He tore the plastic open and inhaled. "Mmmm."

"I have some already rolled." I took out one of my joints and lit it. Dirk and I passed the jay back and forth, loving the great warm relaxing sensations it gave us. It was nice to be here, back to normal, getting high with my friendly neighbor. I wished that all the hassles could disappear and that after this joint I could walk across the driveway and into my house and be there with Carol and the kids and my good job at GoMotion.

"I feel it, Jerzy." Dirk looked around his room happily. "I'm buzzed."

"You're not mad at me anymore?"

"I'm not mad," he smiled. There was something so pure and childlike about the guy. Hanging out with him always reminded me of Saturday mornings when I was a kid and would walk over to my neighbor friend's house to set off firecrackers and play computer games.

"So let's make your tux," said Dirk, handing me a spare cyberdeck headset and pair of gloves. "You can pick out one of my art meshes."

We were in Dirk's virtual office. Dirk's tuxedo was a muscular version of him, and I was a chromed-over copy of Dirk. I followed after him as he flew through a door that opened onto a huge Louis the Fourteenth ballroom with a few hundred figures posed on the parquet floor. When we came in, the figures started slowly gesturing, driven by automatic chaos loops. "Here, Jerzy," came Dirk's voice over the earphones. "This is my art warehouse. I'm always putting together new tuxedos. Fly around and look for something you like."

The figures were set down in no particular order: a club-wielding caveman, a breastplated Amazon, a *Tyrannosaurus rex*, a happy carrot, Michelangelo's marble David, a pointillist Seurat woman with a bustle, a centaur, a manic white businessman smoking a pipe, a teddy bear, the pope, Bo Diddley, a vertically divided half-Elvis half-Marilyn, JFK with brains dangling from the back of his head, a knight in paisley armor, a forties secretary with glasses and tight bun, a saucer alien with tentacles on its face, a crying clown, . . .

"I want to be a crying clown," I said.

"You sure?"

"Yeah, man, a crying clown is how I feel—what with my trial coming up. Maybe if I look like a crying clown people will be nicer to me."

"Okay," said Dirk. "And you need a size lever. Why don't we make his penis be the lever." Dirk chuckled and pulled the clown's pants down. The clown was endowed with a dangling hairy scrotum and an intricately veined semitumescent penis. "I figured a clown's genitals should be kind of grotesque," said Dirk. "Getting the pants to go on and off was an interesting hack. How about if you push the clown's penis up he grows, and if you push it down he gets smaller. A Gothic joystick."

"That's too gnarly, Dirk. Why can't you make the control be . . . " I looked over at the businessman figure with his pipe clenched between the teeth of his shit-eating salesman grin. I now recognized the figure as the old underground culture icon known as "Bob" Dobbs. "Give my clown a copy of the pipe of 'Bob' Dobbs."

"I like it," said Dirk. He popped up the tool icons and picked a little glass box with buttons on it. He moved and resized the box to just fit over "Bob" 's pipe, and then pressed a button to capture a copy of the pipe that he carried over and affixed to the face of my clown. Next he used a screwdriver icon to pry open the clown's chest to reveal a symbolic arrangement of chips and wires. Dirk used a virtual pliers and soldering iron to adjust the circuitry, sealed the clown back up, and pulled down a spray can.

"You can use the pipe for size control, yes. And, Jerzy, as long as we're getting crazy, I'll make your tuxedo's surface reflectivity be like black velvet. A 'Bob' Dobbs crying clown painted on black velvet." He sprayed the clown till its surfaces were all matte and soft. "So try on your new tux, Jerzy. Just fly through it, and it'll click onto you."

I flew forward and, sure enough, the crying clown clicked onto me. I moved the velvety arms around. One side of the ballroom was a huge mirror, and I flew over there to take a closer look.

"The pipe works?" I asked.

"Try it."

I pushed up on the pipe, and rapidly grew through the ceiling of the ballroom. Outside the ballroom was raw black cyberspace with some things twinkling in the distance. I pushed the pipe down, and shrank back into the ballroom and on down and down to the size of a pissant. Dirk and the art meshes towered above me. I inched myself back up to standard size.

"This is great. Can we get out?"

"Sure." We flew back into Dirk's virtual office and took off our headsets.

Dirk tore open his quarter ounce and stuffed the bowl of a pipe.

"Uh, Dirk," I said as he lit the pipe. "About that burn you and Mattel did. Did you ask the phreak to do anything besides scaring me? I mean—you weren't involved in the release of the GoMotion ants, were you?"

Dirk shook his head *no* while holding his breath. He offered me the pipe, but it had already gone out.

"How do you want to get the tuxedo onto your system?" asked Dirk as he exhaled. "Ordinarily I'd say for you to just come through cyberspace and pick it up, but what with your legal situation—"

"Yeah, I'd much rather take it on disk and install it directly on my deck. The less of a trail I leave the better."

"Agreed. I'll put it on a disk with an install script."

"Cool."

We said our good-byes and I went outside. Without putting my headset on, I tapped three-one-four-one to turn on my deck. I opened the trunk and put the disk in the drive of my Pemex twelve. This was finally the golden age of system-independent plug'n'play, so the deck knew that the disk was meant to be my tuxedo, and the disk knew what format my deck wanted, and they both could agree to run the tuxedo's self-installing script.

I got in the driver's seat of my car and put on my headset for a quick cybercruise to the Bay Area Netport rest room. In the mirror I was a black velvet crying clown with the pipe of "Bob" Dobbs. Bety Byte and her grrlfriends looked at me, but I was no weirder than a lot of the tuxedos going by. I flew out to a corner of the Netport and tested out the shrink and grow commands to my satisfaction. But now it was time to pick up Gretchen.

Just for kicks, I tapped *five-nine-two-six* for the reality pass-through. *Stunglasses mode,* Riscky had called it. Instead of the Netport, my headset now showed me a TV image of the view out my parked car's windshield. Dirk's driveway. I looked down at my hands and waggled them. There was no perceptible lag as the images came in through my headset's small video cameras, traveled to the deck in the trunk, and made their way to the headset's video screens. This was a very fast deck. I felt confident enough of it to pull out of Dirk's driveway and drive down to Los Perros wearing stunglasses. The colors were so rich and the resolution so high that I could barely tell I was wearing a headset at all.

I parked in front of Welsh & Tayke, turned off my deck, and stashed my gloves and headset in the pouch behind my seat. I could see in through the front window—Susan Poker and Gretchen were still there. After what I'd just learned about Susan Poker from Riscky—that she was a professional who'd been in on my burn—well, I didn't want to try to talk to her. I leaned on my horn. Gretchen saw me, grabbed her purse, and danced out laughing to hop in my car. She was glad to see me.

"I'm so sick of the office, Jerzy! It's a beautiful warm day—I should be at the beach!"

"We can still go to the beach. Let's go to Santa Cruz and have supper there. And maybe there's some music happening in Santa Cruz tonight. Do you want to?"

"*Yeah*, I do." This funny emphasis of agreement was another new California speech habit. "My car's parked over there; let's regroup at my apartment."

After parking her Porsche at her apartment, Gretchen changed clothes. I borrowed a baggy sweater from her for if it got cold later. We checked in the paper and, yes, there was music tonight; even though it was Tuesday, there was a World Music concert taking place in the Santa Cruz Civic Center at nine. Perfect—I drove us over the Santa Cruz mountains toward the sun.

We hung out on Its Beach near Steamer Lane. It was sunny and not too windy. Around six-thirty we went to an expensive restaurant looking out over Monterey Bay. We had lobster sausage for our appetizer and duck pizza for our main course. The lobster sausage was exquisitely toothsome, but the duck pizza was a disappointment. Duck was always a disappointment, but somehow I could never learn.

"Let's stay at my place tonight," I said over our cappucino. "I don't want Susan Poker barging in on me again. I don't trust her at all anymore. I found out today that she's a cryp. She's been lying to me. Did you know that, Gretchen?"

"Who told you she was a cryp?"

"Some phreak I met at the Night Watch. His name was Riscky Pharbeque. He sold me a hot new cyberspace deck for a thousand dollars."

"You just can't leave that stuff alone, can you, Jerzy?"

"So what *about* Susan Poker?" I demanded.

"Well, okay, it's true that she's a cryp. Welsh & Tayke uses her to get early information. I didn't tell you because I didn't want to scare you off."

"I bet it *was* Susan Poker who called the cops on me."

"I guess that's possible. Even though Susan smiles a lot, she isn't necessarily that nice a person. Sometimes I wonder how I ended up getting stuck with her as a friend. I'm sorry I didn't tell you, Jerzy. I was scared you'd blame me for what she does."

"Is somebody paying her to watch me?"

"I don't know." Gretchen stared out the window, then smiled brightly at me and changed the subject. "Do you think you'll win your trial?"

"I sure hope so. Part of my being fired from West West means that they revoke my bail next week. That three million dollars they put up? With that gone, I'll be sitting in jail."

"Poor Jerzy. Hey! It's time for the concert."

"Can you put this meal on your credit card, Gretchen? I'm a little short on cash."

"Because you spent all your money on another stupid computer? I'll charge it, but you have to pay me back. All of it. *You* asked me out for dinner, so it's *your* treat."

"Okay, okay. But don't worry, at least I've got enough cash for the tickets."

We drove over to the Santa Cruz Civic Center, a small old hall the size of a basketball court with concrete bleachers all around. The first group was a band from Uganda. They had a midget who played an instrument made of a gourd with key chains all around it. In the crowd I lit one of my joints and passed it to Gretchen. She took a long deep drag, held her breath, and exhaled an upward plume of smoke. She stuck her tongue out and wagged her head back and forth like: *I'm feeling wild.* I got close to her and enjoyed her smell and the fanning of the air that her body motions made.

When I passed the joint back to her the second time, she stuck out her tongue and made her marijuana-smoking-wild-girl face again: *I'm high and I like it.* I loved Gretchen's tongue-faces so much. She'd made a come-hither tongue-face at me the very first time I'd seen her—at Coffee Roasting. That time her tongue had bent up over her upper lip, but for the wild-girl tongue-face at the Santa Cruz concert, Gretchen's tongue went down over her lower lip. She fascinated me.

After the concert, we went back to my room at Queue's and fucked. Queue and Keith weren't home, so we fucked loud and hard and had a great time, up there in my airy room in the redwooded Santa Cruz mountains. Pretty soon Gretchen dropped off to sleep.

I'd brought my new gloves and headset up from the car with me; they were lying on the floor next to the bed. Lying cozy in my Gretchenful bed, I pulled on the gloves, donned the headset, and tapped into cyberspace.

You know at the end of the classic Beatles song, "Day In The Life," how it ends on a big chord, like: BAAAAOOOUUUUMMM? That's the sound Riscky's deck made in my earphones, welcoming me in.

I flew across the Netport to the node of the Magic Shell Mall. In the mall, I flew to the vacant lot between Total Video and Gibb & Gibb. I walked to the same old vertex and pushed down on my pipe. The scene around me expanded smoothly, and then I was the size of a pissant and I was standing next to a big round off error hole in the corner. I crawled through the hole.

At first it was all black, but then I saw an odd shape in front of me; a drifting piece of geometry with faces that swung crazily through each other, faces that appeared and disappeared in no logical order—it was a piece of fnoor.

The rotating fnoor changed size irregularly; at a moment when it looked much bigger than me, I sprang forward and landed on it. I ran across the faces, which flipped out under me. I still had seen no ants. Finally I came to a kind of doorway in the dense angles of the fnoor; I squeezed through it and, as before, the fnoor turned into a solid model that lay all around me.

A weirdly shifting corridor stretched out ahead. I

heard a faint chirping sound. I inched forward cautiously, but suddenly the corridor turned inside out and dumped me into a round room that was filled with—ants?

Not ants, not exactly, no. The creatures racing about in the round room were shaped like Perky Pats and Dexters, like Walts and Scooters and Squidboys. I flashed on the sickening realization that all the time I'd been evolving better Squidboys and more difficult Christensens at West West, the ants had been there in the background, using the process to make their *own* code even better. One of the Perky Pats gave me the finger.

I guess I must have tapped five-nine-two-six for the stunglasses pass-through then, but I don't remember doing it. All I remember is that I was looking up at the ceiling of my bedroom with everything radiating off optical echoes of itself, everything receding and surrounded by memory images. The beams in the ceiling were covered with crawling colored lights, and my ears were filled with a resonant flutter. My stomach cramped and my bowels turned to water. I jumped out of bed and rushed to the toilet. I shit out a big nasty wet mess; it seemed to keep coming forever. When I was through, I stood up and looked in the mirror. I didn't see stunglasses on my face; all I saw was an aging guy with severe diarrhea.

When I walked back to my bedroom, something rushed out at me from the left side of my field of vision. It was a cross between an ant, a face, a 3-D Mandelbrot set, and—oh, a furnace-stove made of blue and white tiles. It was way fast. It said some nonsense phrase like, "Beetlejuice monkey!" and I murmured, "Beetlejuice monkey?" to myself, trying to assimilate, and then the creature sped up a thousand times and sneered, "Nah, Beetlejuice *monkey!*" and I tried to relate, and the creature went faster, and it and I went into a hideous hebephrenic thought loop as the flutter in my ears sped higher and higher. The mandible-snout Beetlejuice Monkey was mocking and aggressive, it was totally dissing my thought speed, it was trying to dominate and show me where it's really at—it did unbelievable shit like counting from one to one quadrillion. Out loud and by ones. It was way, way fast.

At some point in this psycho nightmare I decided the only way to stop the Beetlejuice Monkey was to kill it. I lunged forward with my velvet clown hands sticking out before me, and I grabbed the creature at its narrowest part. I began squeezing, and it was struggling and hitting back at me, and then someone grabbed me from behind and jerked at me, and then there was a wrenching at my face and everything got slow and different.

Keith was holding me in a full nelson.

"Jerzy! Jerzy! What's going on? We just got home. What are you doing, man? What did you do to your chick?"

Gretchen was squeezed back against the wall, her face all blue, her dear face a frozen dead mask of horror. Her cold dead tongue was sticking out between jaws that were open in a wide death-agony rictus; it was poor Gretchen's last tongue-face. I'd killed her. My diarrhea was all over my legs and all over the bed.

"You're going to die for this, Jerzy," screamed Queue, pushing past Keith and shoving her face up against mine. "You're going to get the gas chamber and go to hell!"

I cringed back from the hideousness of what I'd done; I just couldn't deal. I wanted to be catatonic. I fell back against my shit-covered bed and merged into the Beetlejuice Monkey.

NINE

Y9707

In the morning I woke soft and sweet, my mind a blank. Before opening my eyes, I happened to rub my hand up against my head and I felt the headset. I pushed it off, opened my eyes, and looked around as the horrible memories came flooding back to me.

Beautiful unharmed naked Gretchen was in bed with me. I hadn't strangled her. I lifted up the sheet and looked down. There was no diarrhea. Had everything after Perky Pat's giving me the finger been a phreak burn? What had I said to Gretchen and Keith—what had they seen me do?

"Keith," I called, hurrying naked down the spiral staircase from the aerie I rented. "Hey, Keith!" I was ashamed to hear how my voice shook. My stomach looked fat and vulnerable. The living room and the kitchen were empty and the house was utterly quiet. Presumably they were still asleep in their bedroom downstairs. Or maybe they'd never come home at all. Maybe that thing about Keith shaking me had been part of the dark dream.

"Keith? Queue?" I walked halfway down the stairs

from the living room to the next lower level. "Keith?" At the bottom of the stairs I opened the door to Keith and Queue's bedroom. The messy room was cool and empty. No one had slept here last night.

I ran back up the stairs to the living room and back up the spiral staircase to my room. Gretchen was on the bed with the sheet wrapped around her, sitting there looking out the window at the beautiful fog and sun in the redwoods.

"Why were you yelling? God, you're uptight. You woke me."

"I . . . Did I do anything funny last night?"

"You did lots of things that were *funny,*" laughed Gretchen. "Now get back in bed so we can cuddle. What are you stressing for? You're all red!"

I saw Riscky's headset lying on the floor. It was still live, with images playing inside it. I wanted to stomp and crush the headset, but I was barefoot. Instead I tapped three-one-four-one *(how-I-need-a)* on the right temple to turn off the satanic engine.

I lay down on the bed. Gretchen spread the sheet over both of us and spooned herself against my back.

"Was I yelling last night?" I asked.

"If you were, I slept right through it. Pot and good sex puts me totally to sleep."

"After you went to sleep, I put on my new cyberspace headset and I had—I had a terrible experience. I thought you were dead. I thought I choked you. I thought I had diarrhea in the bed."

"Were you with the ants?"

"Yes. Only now they look like robots and people. They're much much much faster than they used to be."

"Jerzy, why do you fry your brain?" Gretchen sounded mad. "It's like you don't begin to realize—" She shook her head. "The ants are *shit,* Jerzy. The ants *suck.*"

"Nice talk for a mortgage insurance broker." Thank

God I had this warm real woman with me. "I love you, Gretchen. I'm glad you're here. I'm so scared about everything."

"About your trial starting tomorrow?"

"And about the ants. And about this latest burn. I don't think there was a phreak behind this one. I think the ants did it to me themselves."

"Did you do something to bother the ants?"

"Well, yes, I went into their nest. The Antland of Fnoor, I call it."

"So don't go there again. Don't go into cyberspace at all."

"And I'm worried about what the ants might do to the new robots. We copied a GoMotion ant lion into the new robot code, but these cyberspace ants I saw last night—I think they've been sitting in the machines at West West and watching me create the code. They were imitating Squidboy and even Perky Pat. If there's a loophole in my code, the cyberspace ants are going to find it. The new robots might not be safe to use."

"You should tell GoMotion and West West. Get your lawyer to fax them a letter so that if something new goes wrong you'll have a defense."

"That's a good idea."

We ate some yogurt and granola from Keith and Queue's kitchen. Instead of crushing my headset, I put it and the gloves into my car's trunk. And then I drove Gretchen to her apartment.

"See you again tonight, Jerzy?"

"I'm not sure. I'll call you."

"Stay away from the ants!"

"I'll try."

I went to see Stu at his office in downtown San Jose. He had a spiffed-up one-room office in the old Bank of America building. Instead of a secretary, he had a smart computer with good voice-recognition and speech-generation software. He could dictate documents to it, and it was able to answer the phone. He called his computer *Miss Prentice.*

Standing outside Stu's door in the empty BofA building hallway, I could hear him talking with Miss Prentice. "Take your penis out and masturbate yourself," Miss Prentice was saying.

"I'm busy right now," whined Stu. "I don't want to. I don't have the energy."

"Do you refuse to obey your mistress?" growled Miss Prentice. "I will not tolerate such behavior. You have dared to have an erection in the presence of your mistress, and now you must masturbate it away!"

"I don't have an erection yet, Miss Prentice," said Stu. "Can you show me some dirty pictures?"

I knocked quickly on the office door before the sordid scene could progress any farther. Miss Prentice's voice rose an octave. "Who's there?"

"It's Jerzy Rugby."

"Mr. Koblenz will see you now." The door swung open.

Stu was sitting at his desk with his hands in his lap. He was holding an orange Nerfball. He was wearing a thin wrinkled suit and a tie.

"How's it going?" said Stu, taking aim and shooting the Nerfball at a basketball hoop he'd glued to the wall. There was a Scotch-taped paper chute so that if Stu made a basket the ball would roll back to him. The ball went in. "I made another one, Miss Prentice," said Stu, catching the ball from the trough. "What does that make my average for today?"

"You're making eighty-seven percent of them, Mr. Koblenz," said the computer. "Congratulations." Unlike my robots, Miss Prentice didn't look at all alive. Miss Prentice was nothing but a big computer box with a video screen, a printer, a microphone, and a speaker. I glanced quickly at the screen—it showed an insipid spreadsheet, probably fake.

I sat down. "Stu, I'm worried about the West West and GoMotion robot software that I helped develop. I don't think it's safe. I think the GoMotion ants might be able to infect the robots. Can you send letters to West West and GoMotion in my name saying that? A snail-mail letter and a fax to each of them? If the robots malfunction, I don't want even more blame to be laid on me." *Snail-mail* was the hacker word for ordinary, nonelectronic mail.

Stu thought for a minute, then shook his head. "How did you come up with such a terrible idea? You don't want to send letters like that. If the robots were to malfunction, those letters would be viewed as proof that you'd known you'd sabotaged the code. A confession. So I won't send them, no." Stu regarded me distantly. "It would only make you the more convictable."

"What do you mean *convictable?* Aren't we going to win this trial? Aren't you ready? You're sitting here jacking off and playing Nerfball! What are you going to do for me in court tomorrow?"

"Tomorrow and Friday the judge selects and instructs a jury. Friday afternoon the D.A. and I make our opening statements. Monday we start with the witnesses. Sure I'm ready. But I don't think we'll win. You're in big trouble, Jerzy. In fact, you're screwed."

"How so?" My voice was tight and small. "I wasn't in control of Studly! None of the charges is true!"

"I guess you haven't seen the new *National Enquirer*." Stu tossed me a copy of the tabloid newspaper. The front page was a big picture of Studly with the headline:

JERZY TOLD HIS ROBOT TO KILL MY DOG!
Exclusive Interview!

Studly had his pincer up in the air and they'd drawn a sizzling laser ray coming out of his head. Boxed in along the side of the page were small pictures of me, Jose Ruiz, the bloody corpse of Dutch the dog, and a TV screen full of ants. I looked insanely evil.

"Jose is going to be the prosecution's star witness," said Stu, fondling his Nerfball. "According to this article, he saw and heard you telling Studly to infect the Fibernet and to kill his dog. The West West cryps tell me that's exactly what he's going to testify to in court." Stu shot the ball at the basket and missed. "I missed one, Miss Prentice. Can you get that, Jerzy?"

"Eighty-four percent," said Miss Prentice.

I picked the ball up off the floor and handed it to Stu. "But look, Stu, we knew all along that Ruiz was going to be the prosecution's best witness. And now that you know exactly what Ruiz is going to say, that's an advantage, isn't it? Think of questions to trip him up! Go out and measure the distance from Ruiz's window to his picnic table and prove that he couldn't have actually heard me—or do something else like that! Why are you just sitting here?"

"My main problem is that West West isn't going to pay me any more."

"Oh. You heard?"

"Yeah, Otto Gyorgyi called me yesterday. We're cutting you loose."

"And my bail's only going to be good until . . . "

"Until noon on Tuesday." Stu shot and made another basket, then got to his feet. "I just sank another one, Miss Prentice. Now watch the office for a few minutes, you slutty bitch. Mr. Rugby and I are going to take a walk." Miss Prentice kept her silence. She'd even up things with Stu later.

Stu led me out into the hall, down the elevator, and out into the street. "I want to make a suggestion to you in strictest confidence, Jerzy. I'm doing this because I happen to think you're a good guy."

"What?"

"I don't like to come out and say it. This is such a weird case. It's like a house full of termites. Every source we've checked has shown signs of other cryps. I'd lay five to three that right now somebody in one of these cars or buildings is tracking us with a parabolic mike." Stu steered us around a corner to stand by a big, noisy fountain in front of the San Jose Fairmont.

"So what are you telling me to do?" I demanded.

Stu put a handkerchief near his face as if to blow his nose, and leaned toward me to whisper: "Run, Jerzy. Jump bail and go underground. Flee the country. Ecuador and Switzerland are good for nonextradition these days. I didn't say this." With a flourish Stu snapped his handkerchief back into his suit pocket.

"So, Jerzy," he raised his voice and shook my hand good-bye. "I'll see you at the Hall of Justice bright and early tomorrow. Eight-thirty. It's on West Hedding between San Pedro and Guadelupe. Our case is with Judge Carrig in courtroom 33 on the fifth floor. And don't forget my advice: make sure to park your car in the parking lot instead of at a meter. They're awfully fast to give tickets there."

"But . . ."

"Don't worry about a thing." He smiled grimly and walked away.

Stu was telling me to run—but I didn't have any money. I looked in my wallet confusedly. I had twenty dollars, no credit cards, and nothing in the bank. But with the severance pay included, my Friday deposit from West West would be for thirteen thousand dollars. I could jump bail over the weekend. I noticed a scrap of paper in my wallet. Vinh Vo's phone number. Why not talk to him about getting fake ID? I walked on into the Fairmont and called the number from a pay phone.

"Pho Train noodle shop." It was a woman's voice with a lot of noise in the background.

"I'm looking for Vinh Vo," I said.

"Who you?"

"Is Vinh Vo there?"

"You come see."

"Where are you?"

"Pho Train on Tenth Street near Taylor."

"Thank you."

I walked through the campus of San Jose State University to get to Tenth Street. The campus quad was green and lush, with palm trees and a fountain and some elegant old brick buildings. Students milled antlike near the glass and concrete library. I walked past the Aztec-styled student center, past the small dorms, and out into the mixed Mexican and Southeast Asian neighborhood that lay along Tenth Street.

A grill called Supertaqueria was on one side of the street, and on the other side was a defunct gas station, a Cambodian grocery, and Pho Train, a small restaurant with big glass windows and plastic picnic tables. *Pho* is the Vietnamese name for a special beef broth with spaghetti-like noodles and slices of meat. I ordered a large portion.

"You call here a few minute ago?" the woman at the counter asked me. With my soup she gave me a small dish of bean sprouts and a little branch of some fragrant, spicy leaves.

"Yes," I told her. "My name is Jerzy."

"Okay."

I paid, sat down, and started to eat. The pho was delicious. When I was half-through, Vinh Vo appeared from behind the counter and came to sit across from me.

"Hi, Mister Yuppie," said Vinh in his flatly accented American English.

"Hi, Vinh. Can we talk here?"

He nodded and lit one of his unfiltered cigarettes.

"I need a new passport," I told him.

Vinh Vo looked puzzled and disappointed. "But I want to sell you Y9707 chips!"

"I don't know that I really need any."

"If you won't buy any chips, I won't do business with you," said Vinh. "I need to start unloading them."

It occurred to me that it might actually be useful to be able to build some robots of my own sometime down the line. Assuming Vinh's chips were any good. "Well, okay, I'll take four of them. Four hundred eighty dollars. Give me a passport as well and I'll make it a thousand. And if the chips are okay, I might order more of them."

Vinh smoked quietly for a minute. "Okay," he said finally. "I can arrange your passport. I'll have to drive you to the place. Do you have the money?"

"I'll have the money on Friday. But let's get the passport today."

"You're asking me for credit?" said Vinh Vo unbelievingly. "For a passport? No way, Mister Yuppie. Come back Friday with the cash."

"Should I call first?"

"I'll be here." Vinh lit a second cigarette from the stub of the first.

"I'll be coming later in the day," I cautioned. "Around four-thirty."

"No problem."

Vinh stuck his cigarette into the corner of his mouth, walked behind the counter, and disappeared back through the kitchen. He moved like a gangster in a stiff ballet. The butt in the ashtray was fuming. My pho had gone cold and gnarly. I went outside.

If I would be leaving the country soon, it would be a good idea to visit with my family. I drove across town to Carol's. Carol and Hiroshi were still at work, but Tom and Ida were home from school, peacefully grubbing about. Tom was in the kitchen eating ice cream, and Ida was on the phone with a friend. It did my heart good to see my larvae.

"Hi, kids!"

"Hi, Da!"

"You kids want to do something? You want to go for a last hike with me before I go on trial? Who knows, it might be a long time till we get another chance."

"Poor Da."

Since we were already on the east side, I drove over to Alum Rock Park. There were lots of teenagers and Mexican families. We took a loop trail that led past some hot springs and zigzagged to the top of a foothill.

"Are you scared, Daddy?" asked Tom. He looked so vulnerable with his teenage complexion and his braces. "We talked to Sorrel last night. She wanted to know if she should skip finals and fly out."

"For the trial?"

"Ida and me are going to be there," said Tom. "Mommy said she'll get us excused from school."

"Carol's coming to the trial too? Ma?"

"Yes," said Ida in her calm, deep voice. "We all love you, Da. Maybe if the jury sees you have a family, they'll feel sorry for you."

"Aw. That's wonderful. You're so sweet to stand behind me. I'm deeply touched. I love you." I put my arms around them.

All of San Jose lay spread out before us, and beyond San Jose, Silicon Valley stretched north like a chip-laden motherboard. The great old concrete blimp hangers of Moffat Field stuck up like heavy-duty capacitors. It was such a clear day that, looking farther, we could see all the way up the Bay to the tiny smudges of Oakland and San Francisco. A strong, steady breeze swept down the Bay, across Silicon Valley, and over the crest of our hill.

"The Lord hates Daddy's ants," said Tom presently, and poked me high up under my ribs.

"Suckling pigs on Daddy style," intoned Ida, and poked my other side. We laughed and wrestled for a minute, and then the kids let me be.

"I'm getting to hate the ants, too," I said when I caught my breath. "If I could find a way to kill them all, I'd do it. They've made so much trouble already, and now it might get worse."

"Are they going to break TV some more?"

"Maybe, but what I'm most worried about today is that the ants might infect the software for those new robots I worked on for West West. Whatever you do in the near future, don't go close to any of those robots."

"Is Studly in jail?" asked Ida.

"Sort of. The police are keeping him for an exhibit in the trial."

"Do you think he might go hyper and kill everyone in the courtroom if they turn him on at the trial?" asked Tom, arching his high eyebrows.

"It might be a good idea not to come for that day of the trial, actually," I said. "If they don't stop the trial first."

"Why would they stop the trial?" asked Tom.

"Well . . . maybe if some of the main people stopped coming. The judge or the lawyer or somebody." I gave him a long look, and he got the picture.

"I'm flying," said Ida, holding out her arms and letting the breeze beat at her sleeves. "I'm flying away!" Tom and I held out our arms to fly too, and then we ran off, flying, down the zigzags of the rest of the loop trail.

Carol was home when I brought the kids back to the apartment. I didn't really want to go in, but before I knew it, Carol had me sitting on the couch with a cup of hot tea.

"I can't stay long," I said. These tête-à-têtes with Carol made me acutely uncomfortable. After all the pain of our separation, I didn't want to contemplate getting back together with her.

"Okay, but what should I tell Sorrel about the trial? Why don't you call her? She's upset."

"Good idea."

I dialed Sorrel's number on Carol's phone. Someone on her dorm hall answered and trudged off in search of Sorrel. Then my firstborn's bright voice came through the receiver.

"Hello?"

"Hi, Sorrel, it's Da."

"Da, I have a problem. I want to be there for your trial, but I have finals all next week."

"When were you originally planning to come home?"

"June fifth," put in Carol, who was sitting on a chair next to the couch. "The ticket she has is for next Friday."

"Well, don't change your ticket, Sorrel, it'll cost a lot more. And there's no point missing your exams. I'll just be sitting on a chair in a room with a judge."

"But what if you go to jail? I want to take a last walk with you, Da."

"I do, too, honey. Actually, they're revoking my bail on Tuesday, so I might be in jail from then on." My voice cracked in despair and self-pity. "I've got an idea—why don't you come home just for a day. Fly out here tomorrow morning, spend tomorrow night and all day Friday here, and fly back to school on Saturday. Then you can still study on Sunday and be ready for your tests."

"Should I really?"

"I'll pay. Get a direct flight into San Francisco and rent a car."

"I don't have to rent a car. Tom or Ida can pick me up."

"It'll be easier all around if you drive." I was thinking of uses for that rental car. "Just write checks or charge it and I'll pay you back in cash."

"Great! I'll do it!"

"And Friday afternoon we'll go off together. I already took Tom and Ida for a walk today."

We wound up the conversation. Carol got on the phone with Sorrel for a minute and talked about details. It was like old times, thinking and planning together as a family.

Of course Hiroshi came home then, so I finished my tea and cleared out. Carol saw me to the door.

"The trial is at the Hall of Justice on West Hedding between San Pedro and Guadelupe," I told her. "It's with Judge Carrig on the fifth floor, courtroom 33. I'm supposed to be there at eight-thirty, but it probably doesn't start till later."

"Where's West Hedding?"

"Up near First Street and 880."

"What was that I heard you tell Sorrel about your bail being revoked?"

"West West fired me."

"Oh, Jerzy. I'm sorry. But if Sorrel will be here with a rental car on Friday, I might work that day. I can't miss too many days. It's only Tom and Ida who insist they see every day of the trial."

"That's fine. And thanks for all the support. Bye, kids!"

Carol closed the door. I drove home to Queue's and called Gretchen to tell her I was too tired to get together. I went to bed early.

The courtroom was much smaller than I'd expected;

it was just one of thirty or forty courtrooms in the Hall of Justice. In the back were five rows of seats for onlookers, and then a waist-high partition—the bar—with a sign on it that said:

ALL COMMUNICATIONS WITH THE PRISONERS
VERBAL, WRITTEN OR SIGNED
IS UNLAWFUL WITHOUT THE
PERMISSION OF THE DEPUTIES.

Carol, Tom, and Ida were there. On my side of the bar were, from left to right, a desk with a Santa Clara County sheriff with a gun and a computer, a desk with a DEFENDANT sign where I sat next to Stu, a desk with a PEOPLE sign where the District Attorney sat, and, against the right wall, two rows of comfortable chairs for the jury. There was also a desk for the court clerk, and the judge sat behind a big raised pulpit—the bench. The witness stand was squeezed in between the bench and the jury. The judge's name was on his bench: Francis J. Carrig.

The first part of Thursday was spent in dealing with the people who wanted to get out of jury duty. Beefy Judge Carrig spoke very slowly and clearly in a slightly overbearing way. He didn't seem like a guy you'd want to interrupt or argue with. Out of boredom I jotted down some of his more judicious-sounding phrases, and came up with these:

"Let me finish. I'm asking for your cooperation. I don't want to have to repeat this. I have the utmost confidence that this case will be completed by June fifth. Let me help you out. I will ask you the same question collectively. Can you be a fair impartial fact finder? Counsel approach the bench."

That's what the judge sounded like. Once he'd found twelve willing jurors, he asked the prosecutor and the defense to introduce themselves. The prosecutor's name was Eddie Machotka—he was wiry and intense, with a bald pate and big puffs of curly clown hair on the sides of his head. Then the judge read out my name and the charges against me: criminal trespass, computer intrusion, and extreme cruelty to animals.

"Are any of you jurors familiar with this case?" asked Judge Carrig. Of course they all were—prior questioning had already revealed that everyone on the jury had a TV. So then the judge went into finding out if anyone on the jury was already convinced I was guilty. Could they be objective? As Judge Carrig put it, "We're not asking you to decide complex technical issues. Just things like: was it up or was it down, was it left or was it right, was it hot or was it cold?" Two jurors got weeded out here, and the judge replaced them with two of the alternates who were waiting in the onlookers' seats. I turned around and looked at my family every now and then.

By Thursday afternoon, the judge had finished impaneling a jury that neither Stu nor the D.A. objected to. I spent Thursday night at Gretchen's. It hadn't occurred to her to come to the trial, which was just as well. We ordered out for Mexican food and watched a video from Total Video—it was Natalie Wood and Tony Curtis in *Sex and the Single Girl.* It turned out Gretchen was a big fan of Natalie Wood; she even had a big book about Natalie, with an Andy Warhol portrait on the cover.

Friday morning, Sorrel was there in the courtroom with Tom and Ida—Sorrel with her short mouth, messy hair, and big cheeks. Judge Carrig began talking about some of the points of law relevant to my charges, and explained that the jury was to decide whether or not I was in control of the actions of Studly.

After lunch, Eddie Machotka, the D.A., made his

opening presentation, followed by Stu's opening statement for the defense.

Machotka had prepared an incredibly realistic cyberspace mock-up of the crimes as he thought they had happened. His simulation held a space-time continuum surrounding Jose Ruiz's block of White Road for the crucial three minutes, and he could observe the running of his world from any position in it, or from any series of positions in it—he could pick any space-time trajectory he pleased. He could even speed up and slow down time, or run time backward—he was the master of space and time.

As we in the courtroom watched a big Abbott wafer display, Machotka flew us through his world. First he showed Studly standing on the picnic table and me standing next to him talking to him. Jose Ruiz was visible in his house, watching us out his window. The words Ruiz attributed to me appeared on the bottom of the screen like subtitles: *Jerzy Rugby: Yes, Studly, now send in the ant viruses!* Then Dutch the dog came running out of Ruiz's house and I fled, calling back to Studly. Ruiz's quote of my words: *Jerzy Rugby: Studly, kill that dog!* It was quite convincing. Machotka flew us through his world four times, from four different angles. Members of the jury kept glancing over at me and looking away.

Stu's presentation was much more limp and legalistic. More than anything else, he harped on the point that Studly had legally been the property of GoMotion at the time of the crimes. Nobody in the courtroom looked like they gave a fuck. Stu insisted that I *hadn't* told the robot to screw up the Fibernet, nor had I told Studly to kill the dog, but after Machotka's virtual reality demo, Stu's bald assertions carried no force.

Leaving the courtroom at three-thirty Friday afternoon, I felt sure that we were going to lose. Before the reporters pressed in on me, I managed to say hi to Sorrel and tell her I'd see her at Carol's in an hour.

After I shook off the press, I drove to the Wells Fargo in downtown San Jose and found a parking space on the street. My bank balance was indeed thirteen thousand dollars plus. *Thank you, West West!* Though the teller didn't like it, I got the thirteen thousand in cash; it made a fat envelope of 130 hundred-dollar bills. I'd decided to give a third of it to Carol for the children, so I asked for another envelope and counted 44 hundreds into that one. I felt grim and sad. I was leaving my country and my poor little family—maybe for good.

I calmed down a little on the walk over to Pho Train. I ordered the same pho soup again. This time I used the tip of my chopstick to add some red-pepper paste to the broth. With the pepper and the spicy green leaves, the soup was truly delicious. I slurped down as much as I could before Vinh appeared, fuming cigarette in hand.

"You ready?" he asked. "We can walk from here. But give me the thousand first."

"Okay." I pulled my main envelope of hundreds out of my pants pocket and counted out ten bills for Vinh under the table. His bony hand reached across to take them, and then he passed me a flat plastic package under the table: my four Y9707 chips. I stuck the package unopened in my other pants pocket.

We walked two blocks to a neighborhood of rundown two-story apartment buildings made of crumbling pink stucco over plywood. The buildings had flat roofs, prefab aluminum windows, and concrete stairwells. All the children playing in the street were Vietnamese—a regular Our Gang of loud little girls, T-shirted toddlers, and watchful boys. Everyone seemed to recognize the pockmarked, chain-smoking Vinh Vo.

Vinh knocked at a street-level apartment door and a thin young woman holding a screwdriver let us in.

It was a single-room efficiency apartment with another young woman, fat, sitting down. The windows were hermetically closed off with filthy curtains and venetian blinds. The room was lit by computer monitors and lamps; the ventilation came through an antique wall unit air conditioner. There was a great hoard of computer equipment along the walls, and there were loads of books and computer manuals. The chairs had vinyl cushions.

"Here's your customer, girls," said Vinh. He smiled thinly at me. "This is Bety Byte and Vanna. They're computer science students at San Jose State. They're the best cryps in our Vietnamese community."

Heavyset Bety Byte wore a cyberspace headset pushed up onto the top of her head like sunglasses. She had thick lips, yellow skin, and greasy, permed, distressed hair. Surely she had no inkling that I'd seen her tuxedo in cyberspace—and I wasn't about to tell her. Pale, slim Vanna wore tight black slacks and a round-collared pink blouse buttoned up to the top. Her glossy hair was cut in a tidy bob. Bety Byte and Vanna didn't look much like their tuxedos.

"I recognize this dude from TV," said Bety Byte, pointing a control-gloved hand at me. The tips of the control gloves were cut off and I could see her fingernails. She wore chipped black nail polish. "You're Jerzy Rugby!" She spoke with a perfect riot-grrl mall-rat accent.

"No," I said emphatically. "I am *not*. I'm not anyone until you tell me my new name."

"He's incognito," laughed Vanna. "I think he's scared."

"Do you know how passport authentication works?" asked Bety Byte.

"Sort of. As well as forging me a passport, you have to put a valid bar code on it. The government uses a secret algorithm to generate long authentication numbers that go into the bar code."

"That's right," said Vanna. She was still holding her screwdriver. "We haven't figured out how to generate our own authentication numbers, but we do have a way into the current State Department passport files. What we'll do is to find the name of someone who has a passport and who resembles you. Then we'll use his passport's authentication number on our forgery." She smiled and gave a quick nod for emphasis.

"Crypping the State Department can't be very easy," I said politely.

"Well, we have this killer can opener program that we got from a phreak friend of ours," said Bety from her chair. "*Ex* friend, that is." I had the feeling she was talking about Riscky Pharbeque. From what I'd heard Bety and Vanna say in cyberspace, they were mad at Riscky for spray-painting "Hex DEF6" on the wall of the Cryp Club library. But I had nothing to gain by chatting about this topic.

"Do you have to take my picture first or what?" I asked.

"First you have to pay us," said Bety.

"Here's two hundred dollars," said Vinh, stepping forward and holding out two of the bills I'd given him.

"I told you seven hundred," cried Bety.

"Three hundred dollars is my final offer," said Vinh Vo and added another bill to the little fan he held out toward Bety.

"We won't do it for less than four hundred," said Bety. She unwrapped a stick of pharmaceutical green bubble gum and popped it in her mouth. "Bye, Vinh. Bye, Jerzy. Show 'em out, Vanna."

Vanna laughed in that meaningless Asian way, but

she didn't immediately do anything—she just stood there holding her screwdriver. I fumbled in my pocket to find one more bill. Vinh Vo watched me with unblinking, predatory interest. I passed him the bill and he tendered the four hundred dollars to Bety. She tucked the money into her pants pocket and gave Vanna a nod.

"Okay, Jerzy," said Vanna. "Lets narrow in on a name." She laid down her screwdriver and put on control gloves and a headset.

"How tall are you?" she asked. "How much do you weigh? Place of birth? Date of birth? Scars?" She input my responses by making flowing hand gestures in midair; she was dancing her way up the search tree of the sample space. "Here's twenty good ones," said Vanna presently and snapped her fingers.

A list of names appeared in a box on the computer screen next to me. I chose a forty-two-year-old divorced electrical engineer named Sandy Schrandt.

Bety Byte picked up a small video camera and slid her headset down over her eyes. She began walking rapidly around the cluttered room while pointing the camera at me.

"In case you're wondering, I'm not going to bump into anything," said Bety, chomping on her green gum. "I'm seeing through this videocam. I'm using a pass-through."

"Yeah, yeah," I said. "Just like stunglasses." It was a hacker point of pride to be down with the latest street tech.

Bety kept on shooting video of me, occasionally flicking a finger to capture a still image. The images accumulated in a grid on the computer screen. Before long, Bety had filled the grid with pictures of me: the central pictures were full-on, or nearly so, and the pictures at the edge of the grid were shot from sharper and sharper angles. It was a discontinuous Mercator projection of my head.

Bety sat down and gestured in the air for a minute and then the color laser printer coughed and spit out the eleven double pages of my new passport, each page with Sandy Schrandt's passport bar code on the edge. On the top page there was a shiny reflection hologram that showed a three-dimensional image of my head. Bety and Vanna's software had fused the grid images of me into a single holographic image that turned as you tilted it from side to side.

"Great!" I exclaimed.

Vanna changed the paper tray and the copier coughed once more to produce a thick passport cover. She and Bety Byte took off their headsets and studied the pages for a minute, and then they used hot glue and a small sewing machine to bind the passport up.

Bety handed the passport to me—it looked perfect. But then I thought of something.

"What if the real Sandy Schrandt happens to come through customs in the same place on the same day I do? Won't the officials get suspicious when they check the same number twice?"

"If that happens you're a dead cow," said Vanna. "I mean dead duck." She began giggling so wildly that she had to put both hands over her mouth.

"You just have to hope for the best," said Bety. She was laughing too.

Was this forged passport part of the ongoing international get-Jerzy burn? Or were the girls just being silly? I started to say something—but what could I say? I fell back on the standard California nonreaction:

"Whatever."

I got out of there and split off from Vinh Vo as rapidly as I could. I swung in a circle through the San Jose State campus to make sure I'd lost him. Then I got my car from near Wells Fargo and drove out to Carol's.

Tom and Ida had gone off with friends and Sorrel was waiting for me. We hugged each other and then we sat down and talked for awhile. I loved her lively, confiding little voice and her vehement opinions. She often used a fragmented, creative grammar that Carol and I called "Sorrelese." She and I talked about my trial and about her life at college. Sorrel had a new boyfriend, and she was doing cartoons for her school paper.

"So, Da," said Sorrel after awhile, "Don't you want to make us scarce before Ma and Hiroshi get home?"

"Yes. Why don't we go for a drive? We could go over to where I rent and take a walk in the woods."

"Okay."

I left my Animata at Carol's and got Sorrel to let me drive her rented car. Sorrel looked at me and I looked at her in the shitty tiny rental car with wheels so small you worried they would get stuck in the grooved highway's grooves.

"Your eye looks just like Mom's," said Sorrel, using our family name for my mother, now dead one year. "The way your skin is all wrinkled at the corner. Mom used to have such a nice cute old eye. And your eye's just the same."

"Poor old Mom," I sighed. "At least she's not here to see me in so much trouble."

"You're going to run away, aren't you, Da?" said Sorrel. "Tom and Ida *suspect.* Is it true?"

"Yes. In fact I'm planning to do it today."

"In fact that's what we're doing right now?" said Sorrel. "We're going back to the stupid airport I just came from last night? So that's why you wanted me to get a rental car. Mmm-*hmmm*." Sorrel made her Big Sis "knowing face," an expression in which she pressed her lips tight together and nodded her head up and down with her chin sticking out. "Are we still going to Queue's?"

"I have a brand-new forged passport," I confessed. "I think the smartest thing I can do is get out of the country as fast as possible. Somebody—the cops or the cryps or the phreaks or West West or GoMotion—somebody probably has a miniature TV camera watching Queue's place anyway. And Carol's place, too. The less I give them to go on, the better. If it's okay with you, I'd like to drive straight to the airport."

"Let me see your passport!" Sorrel looked through it with interest. "This hologram of you is neat. What country are you going to?"

"Switzerland. My lawyer—that Stu Koblenz who did such a lame job in court today—he said Ecuador and Switzerland are good havens from U.S. law. And there's a guy in Switzerland I reeeeally want to see." I was thinking of Roger Coolidge, rich Roger, who'd started all this by releasing the ants and firing me from GoMotion. I aimed to find him and to *beat* the truth out of him if need be. But there was no need to burden Sorrel with this information.

At the San Francisco Airport, I pulled up in front of the American Airlines terminal. "Run in there, Sorrel, and see if they have a direct flight from San Francisco to Zurich or Geneva tonight. And if they don't have a flight, then ask who does. Don't give your name!"

"Right," said Sorrel, her mouth a short determined line. She darted into the terminal and emerged five minutes later.

"Swissair," said Sorrel. "They're flying direct to Geneva tonight at seven-thirty. It's a twelve-hour flight."

"Beautiful." I got out of the car and moved over into the passenger seat. "You can drive me up to the Swissair part of the international terminal. Just drop me off there and go back to Carol's. How much is this trip costing you, anyway? For the ticket and the car?"

"About six hundred dollars."

I drew out the smaller envelope of hundred-dollar bills and took out six of them for Sorrel.

"This is for you, and you give the rest of the money in this envelope to Ma. And here," I handed her my keys as well. "Tell Ma she can have the Animata, too."

Sorrel messily stuffed the money and keys into the glove compartment.

"Oh, one other thing," I said. "There's a cyberspace deck with glove and headset in the trunk of the Animata. You tap *three-one-four-one* on the right side of the headset to turn it on or off. But it's a phreak deck, it's not registered, so you probably shouldn't use it."

"Tom and Ida are sure to grub and fiddle with it," said Sorrel loftily. She drew back her chin for "geek face," and spittily lisped, "Thyberthpayth!"

"Cyberspace is important, Sorrel! Tell Tom not to let the police find the deck. It might be better to throw the deck away. Ida, Tom, and Carol will have to decide."

Sorrel drove me the short distance to Swissair. I hugged her and kissed each of her nice soft cheeks. That had been one of the first things I noticed about her when she was a baby: her cheeks.

"Good luck, Da," said Sorrel. "Take care."

"Thanks, Sorrel. I love you."

Before buying a ticket, I cruised the souvenir shop for travel gear. I got a small black leatherette satchel, a toothbrush, and—some business sweats.

These days a lot of businessmen were wearing sweat suits all the time. In principle, you could jog or work out in these cotton and polyester outfits, but business sweats were not normally used for exercise. Business sweats were for display purposes; they were meant to say, "I'm fit and I'm rich."

I snagged a pompous gray XL outfit for $300. It had shiny gold stripes down the pant legs, and a sewn-in burgundy sash angling diagonally across the chest. The sash had a gold medal embossed on it.

In the men's room I changed into the sweats and stuffed my shorts and sport shirt into the satchel. I caught a glimpse of myself in the mirror. I looked like the Swedish ambassador, man—except for my sandals.

Out in the lobby I sat down for a minute to arrange my junk. I positioned my passport and my money in the satchel's outside zipper pocket, and then I folded my shirt and shorts. The plastic packet of chips was still in my shorts pocket. Was it worth trying to take the chips through customs?

I took out the packet and opened it. Inside were four square chips snugged into plastic pin protectors. The backs of the chips read *National Semiconductor Y9707-EX*. I hadn't seen the "*-EX*" suffix before, but I assumed it meant that these chips had been made a little faster and smarter than the last batch. Chip makers were always upgrading to longer product names.

I closed the chip packet and put it in my satchel under my shirt and shorts. Nobody was going to care about four standard production chips. If anyone asked me, the chips were my own property, to be used solely for demonstration purposes. I, Sandy Schrandt, was thinking about designing some custom applications for the Y9707-EX chip in the Swiss industrial market, yes.

So that was that, except for one thing: I hadn't said good-bye to Gretchen. I'd been so excited about seeing Sorrel, and about my escape, that I hadn't thought of Gretchen since leaving her apartment this morning. But I couldn't very well phone Gretchen now because—it had finally occurred to me—Gretchen might be a spy paid to watch me. So, yeah, that was that.

I walked up to the Swissair counter and bought a

ticket with no trouble, though all they had left was business-class. To look less suspicious, I made it a round-trip ticket. At the baggage X-ray station, I handed the guard my chips; he sleepily glanced at them and passed the package around the X-ray machine. Fifteen minutes later, I was sitting in the plane. Business-class was luxurious, with widely spaced seats, instant free cocktails, and lobster.

After supper, the stewardess told us that in Swissair business-class, the in-flight entertainment was cyberspace, with the fees to be charged to your credit number. When she got to me, I told her I had no credit number, and she let me buy two hundred dollars worth of prepaid credit. She told me that was generally enough for three hours.

The steward behind her issued me a bottom-of-the-line headset/gloves kit that plugged into a socket on the top of the seat in front of me.

When I put on the headset, I was in an Alpine meadow with three guys off to one side blowing long Alpine horns. There was a crossing of two trails nearby. An Alpine guide strolled up to me; he was a software daemon like Kwirkey Debug. "Hello, Mr. Schrandt," said the daemon. "My name is Karl. I will be your guide for this session. There is an urgent cy-mail message for you. Do you want to view it?"

It seemed Sandy Schrandt was quite the up-to-date engineer. But I had no desire to look at his cy-mail—it would probably turn out to be some dweeb holding up a circuit diagram and talking about it.

"No messages now, thanks."

I walked over to the signpost at the trail crossing and looked at it. Some of the little signboards read:

Duty Free Shops➧
Entertainment➧

◀Exercise
Information▶
◀Communication
◀Netport

I decided to try some exercise first. As I started down the trail in the indicated direction, my guide caught up with me and told me that when I pressed a certain button on the arm of my seat, bicycle handlebars and pedals would pop out from the floor. He said that I should take off my headset, push the button, get myself positioned on the pedals, and then put the headset back on so we could continue.

"Where will we go?"

"We'll mountain-bike up the Matterhorn," the guide replied. He had cheery, twinkling, pale blue eyes. He pointed up to the left, and there was the Matterhorn itself: huge, rocky and snowcapped. Its crag castles made wondrous silhouettes against the blue sky. A gauzy puff of cloud trailed from the downwind side of the mountain's crooked peak.

I slipped off my headset and pushed the special button on my seat. The floor opened up and a heavy-duty pair of bicycle pedals appeared, with a sturdy pair of handlebars sticking out over them. I leaned back, put my feet on the pedals, and grabbed the handlebars. The setup felt more like a pedal boat than a bicycle—but it worked for me. I put on my headset.

"You can adjust the drag with the left handgrip and the motion-speed with the right," Karl told me. "Let's start by heading for the Hörnli Hutte—it's a mountaineers' hut up on that ridge."

I pedaled along, watching the lovely mountain scenery go by. No matter how fast or slow I went, the guide always stayed in front of me, pointing out the path I should take. When I ran over big rocks it didn't matter—they'd flatten out under me. It was fun. At the top of the Matterhorn I finally caught up with the guide.

"What do you want to do now?" he asked me. "Ride back down?"

I felt good and aerobic. "That's enough exercise. Let me retract the pedals." I slid my headset up and pushed the button to fold the pedals back down. All the other passengers were asleep or in their headsets. I returned to the pristine summit of the Matterhorn.

"What would you like to do next?" repeated the guide daemon, eager to spend my money.

"Can I find out the address of somebody in Switzerland?"

"I can try for you. If the person has a telephone they will be in the telephone directory, as there are no unlisted phones in Switzerland. What is the name?"

"Roger R. Coolidge."

"Yes, we have a Roger Reaumur Coolidge in Saint-Cergue," responded the guide in a flash.

"Can you show me where Saint-Cergue is on a map?"

"Hold my hand," said the guide. "We'll fly." I took his hand, and then he leapt up into the air. It was a fabulous feeling to fly straight up from the top of the Matterhorn. Soon we were at such an altitude that our virtual Switzerland had become its own map.

"Saint-Cergue is near Geneva," said the guide. We flew out of the Alps and up the great curve of Lake Geneva. Soon we were near the city of Geneva at the far end of the lake. The guide pointed away from Geneva toward a meek range of rounded mountains to our right. "Those are the Jura Mountains," he said. "See that little peak? That is the Dôle. Saint-Cergue is in the saddle of the pass beside the Dôle."

He flew us lower, showed me the Geneva airport, and jovially instructed me to make steering wheel motions so as to remotely pilot a distant virtual car up the serpentine road that led from the Geneva/Lausanne Autoroute to Saint-Cergue. The simulation reminded me of a recurrent nightmare that I'd had when I'd been in my twenties—a dream where I'd be driving a car with a steering wheel column that grew to be hundreds of yards long. I declined the simulation, and the guide flew us straight on up to Saint-Cergue.

"Do you know which building Roger Coolidge lives in?" I asked.

"Yes," said the guide, and one of the properties began blinking. It was a compound of two large buildings up in a meadow two or three kilometers above the main drag of Saint-Cergue. I stared for a few minutes, fixing landmarks in my mind. I could rent a car at the Geneva airport and drive right up to Roger's. I'd buy a big hunting knife at a Swiss knife shop first. It was kind of too bad I'd never gotten that plastic gun Keith had told me about.

"Was there anything else?" the guide asked.

"Okay, yeah, I'd like to see a movie. How's my credit holding up?"

"You have more than enough credit for a movie. We have several special made-for-cyberspace productions, and many of our standard films have been cyberized."

"Take me to your interface."

We jumped to a room with thousands of tiny screens showing small images. There were some big posters. Off to one side of the room a live cyberspace action film was being acted out, a fight-it-out shoot-'em-up kind of thing.

"I guess you don't have any hard-core pornography?" I asked the guide.

"We have a selection of tasteful erotic films available for the passengers of our business-class."

"No thanks, I don't think so. And I'm kind of tired,

so I don't want the stress of a cybershow. Maybe an old movie. What do you have with Natalie Wood?"

"Fortunate choice, Mr. Schrandt! We have two movies available with Natalie Wood. First is *Rebel Without a Cause,* released 1956, featuring James Dean, Sal Mineo, and Natalie Wood. Critic Lester Seda terms *Rebel Without a Cause* "An early cult movie of teenage anomie in the computer age." Second is *Brainstorm,* released 1977, a classic science fiction thriller featuring Natalie Wood as a mystical scientist who records her brain onto reflection hologram memory ribbon. Of *Brainstorm,* critic Lester Seda says, "Released after Natalie Wood's death, *Brainstorm* is eerily prescient and campily elegant."

I watched *Brainstorm.* They'd cyberized it enough so that it wrapped around about half the field of my vision. It was a good flick.

When the credits started running, Karl the guide daemon reappeared like a person coming up to you in your seat at the movies.

"What," I said.

"It's about your cy-mail message, Mr. Schrandt. The sender has been steadily pinging us. He knows you're on this flight. Wouldn't you care to view the message now?"

"All right," I sighed. "Let it come down." I really dreaded this, whatever it was. I kept both hands poised on my headset, ready to tear it off lest I suffer another burn.

There was a buzzing, the *Brainstorm* credits melted, and then I was looking at Roger Coolidge, Roger sitting there looking at me from an armchair in a shitty unfinished drywall room. He was wearing gray pants and a short-sleeved white polyester shirt.

"Hi, Jerzy. I'm talking to you live from my house in Saint-Cergue," said Roger. "Excuse the mess—Kay and

I have been remodeling." Roger's dusty study had a desk and a picture window; I could see up a sloping green hillside to the concave horizon of a mountain pass. It was early on a rainy morning. Roger stared passively in thought, like a beaver resting by a stream. Finally he spoke again. "I had a feeling you'd come to me. Thanks for making it so easy. My chauffeur Tonio will meet you at the Geneva airport and bring you to Saint-Cergue. I'll explain the whole thing when you get here, okay?"

I pawed the headset off and stumbled blindly down the carpeted floor that hid the thin metal fuselage of this most improbable construct: a jetliner. We were ants in an aluminum beer can hurtling through the sky. I found the stewardess in the galley and told her that my cyberspace hookup didn't seem to be working correctly, and that she should switch if off before it ate any more of my credit. I took a glass of cognac back to my seat and fell into troubled sleep.

TEN

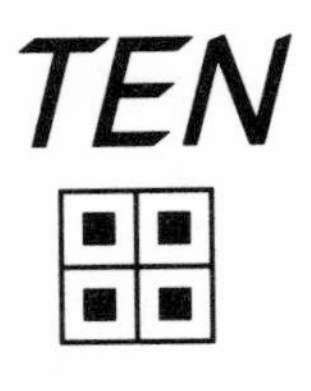

Hi, Roger

IN GENEVA I GOT THROUGH PASSPORT CONTROL AND CUSTOMS without a hitch. Nobody asked me about the Y9707-EX chips. But I was tense; I kept feeling as though people were shoving their faces up close to me.

It was four in the afternoon local time when I stepped out into the public airport lobby, a big stone-floored glass-and-metal hall with lots of shops. For a moment I thought I was free to go off on my own—but then someone tapped my shoulder. It was an athletic, middle-aged Italian man in an unmarked blue serge uniform. He tipped his hat and smiled with his teeth.

"Welcome, Mr. Schrandt! Mr. Coolidge sends me here to drive you. My name is Tonio. Do you have luggage?"

"No," I sighed. "No, no, this is my only bag. And I can carry it." I was sad to see this guy. "So you're going to drive me up to Roger's villa in Saint-Cergue?"

"Exactly," said Tonio and gestured sweepingly toward the exit. "Please to come with me." It would have been nice to buy a big hunting knife first, but, hell, there'd be knives in Roger's kitchen. I followed along.

Outside it was drizzling briskly. Tonio had parked Roger's car at the curb right outside the entrance. The car was an unimpressive beige Subaru station wagon. At Tonio's urging, I sat in back. We did a piece on the Autoroute, and then we headed up the rolling green slopes of the Jura Mountains. Before long we were racing up the same winding road that the Swissair guide had mapped for me in cyberspace. Tonio drove much too fast for my comfort, repeatedly tailgating and passing other cars. I asked him to drive slower, but he chose not to understand.

In the cold Swiss springtime, Saint-Cergue looked battened down and godforsaken. The wet posters for cigarettes and liquors were all in French. There were several barns with piles of straw and manure right on the main street; the runoff from the piles fanned filthily across the pavement. A thin village idiot in a plastic raincoat and a plastic-covered beret went lurching past, one hand fingering his bristly chin.

Tonio slewed into a tiny road off the main street and sped uphill two and a half kilometers to Roger's domain: two sturdy Swiss buildings that looked to be made of concrete. The walls were covered in rough stucco, and the roofs were of heavy gray tile. No neighboring houses were in sight. The rain was pouring down harder than ever.

The first building was large and windowless; the second was a house, long and low. Its windows had the European metal roll-down shutters, but most of the shutters were open. Tonio snapped open a big black umbrella and walked me up to the house's automated front door. The puddles splashed over my sandals and soaked my socks.

Roger came quickly after Tonio's first knock. The

door made a heavy thunk as it unlocked itself and swung open.

"Jerzy! You made it! Come on in."

"Hi, Roger."

"Do you need anything else, Mr. Coolidge?" asked Tonio.

"I don't think so, Tonio. Do you need anything, Jerzy?"

"How would I know? I barely know where I am. Can I sleep here?"

"Of course," said Roger. "You're my guest. So, yes, that's all, Tonio. I'll call you in the morning." Tonio splashed back down the path to the driveway, and the door locked itself behind him.

All the floors in Roger's house were dusty plywood; he'd stripped away whatever had been on them before. I'd expected that Roger would be living rich, but no, he was living weird. "Kay is back in California just now," said Roger, referring to his absent wife. "Would you like a tour?" It didn't occur to him to offer me food or drink.

"I'd like to talk first."

"Fine." Roger wore an inoffensive, even subservient, expression. On things that didn't matter to him he played the spineless jellyfish but—as I knew from experience—when it came to something he *did* care about, he was like a saber-tooth tiger.

He led me from the entrance hall into the living room, pausing to point out a tiled structure the size of a refrigerator. "Look at this," said Roger. "This is a Swiss ceramic stove."

The stove was nicely tiled in blue and white; some of the tiles had flowers painted on them. My feet were cold and wet, but even so the stove looked anything but cozy—to me it looked like the phreaked-out Beetlejuice Monkey thing I'd seen the last time I went after the cyberspace ants. The Beetlejuice Monkey had been a cross between a Mandelbrot set, an ant and—I felt *sure* of it now—Roger's stove. But why? I reached out and touched the stove; it was stone-cold.

About half the wallpaper had been stripped off the living room walls. Set into a jagged hole in the wall near the stove was an uncased computer with a keyboard. The fit was bad enough that I could see the computer's chips and wires. A nice molding for it would come later, after the wallpaper got fixed.

"That's my house computer," said Roger. "It controls the heat, lights, locks, shutters, and so on. I had to put in fifty-seven different servo motors for it. What an interesting hack that was!"

I walked across the room and looked out the living room's big window. It showed trees and the road that led back down to Saint-Cergue, though with the rain, I could only see a hundred meters before the road melted into mist.

"When it's clear, you can see Lake Geneva with sailboats on it," said Roger. "And when it's *very* clear, you can see Alps on the other side of the lake. But you said you want to talk. Let's go into my study."

The light in the study came on automatically when we entered. The room was as I'd seen it last night in cyberspace. Plywood floor, gray drywall walls with white plaster at the seams, and a window that looked out onto a meadow sloping uphill. A long, filled-in dirt trench scarred one side of the meadow. There was a closed-circuit TV-monitor and a cyberspace deck on the desk. The monitor was tuned to a view of Roger's empty driveway. Roger sat down in his comfortable armchair; there was a folding plastic chair for me in the corner next to a cardboard box of random home repair tools. I dragged the chair over to sit near Roger.

"This property is very interesting," said Roger. He

was so rich that all the people he ever talked to agreed with him. This gave him license to play the happy prattling boy, babbling on about whatever his current obsession might be, confident that he would be listened to and taken seriously. "The person who lived here before me was a manufacturer of plastics compression-molding equipment. Donar Kupp. He died last year. He patented a method for incorporating three-dimensional electronic circuits into solid lumps of thermosetting imipolex resin. Smart beads. They're amazing artifacts—I have one around here someplace, it looks like a fly in amber. A very *gnarly* fly, mind you." Roger chuckled happily. "All the major pipeline companies use Kupp's smart beads to monitor fluid flow, and the French riot police use the beads for smart nonlethal bullets." I'd never read about any of this, but, as usual, Roger knew it all. "Kupp retired here five years ago, and he fixed up the other building—the one by the driveway—he fixed it up like a factory. He wanted to expand on his circuit inclusion technique. Since thermoset imipolex is a semiconductor, he found it possible to grow diode and triode transistors right into—"

"Hey, come on, Roger," I interrupted. "Let's talk about the *ants*. Let's talk about me being fired and framed and phreaked out of my mind. Why did you do it, Roger? What's all this been *for*?"

Roger paused and gazed at me in that blank, dreamy, slightly irritated way of his. "All this has been for better robots," he said presently. "You did such a good job on the Veep for GoMotion that I wanted you to go to West West and have a second shot at robotics programming. I want to *breed* the robots, you see, so I needed to have two parents that were different. The next generation of robots could be quite a surprise."

"You want to breed the robots?"

"That's the future, Jerzy, it's manifest destiny. The

robots need to breed and evolve. They need to self-replicate. This is about artificial *life,* for crying in the sink."

"You want the robots to build more robots? What if they take over the Earth?" I asked.

"I don't particularly *want* them to stay on the Earth," said Roger impatiently. "Robots aren't meant to be our slaves. Who in his right mind wants a slave anyway? The robots are meant to evolve, to take the torch from us and to grow beyond what we've done. We should send robots to the Moon. If you make a robot small enough, it can stand an awful lot of acceleration. Launching a capsule of robots with an electromagnetic railgun might work. I've been trying to talk to NASA about this, but so far I've only been talking to idiots."

I shook my head. Space travel was one of Roger's hobbyhorses—and no way was I about to gallop off on it with him. "Please don't let's change the subject, Roger. We're talking about what you've been doing to me. How do the ants fit into the picture? Why did you let them ruin television?"

"I thought you'd be happy. Aren't you the one who's always saying he hates TV?"

"Sure, but when you released the ants, you stuck me with the blame. How did you get Studly to do that thing with the Fibernet anyway?"

"I was driving him," said Roger, smiling slyly. You almost had to love the guy.

"Telerobotics? I thought you were in Switzerland by then!"

"I was, but that doesn't matter. I used a cyberspace telerobotic interface. My signal would have been too weak, but Vinh Vo was carrying a signal-amplifying transponder in the back of his panel truck. When I heard you were trying to date Nga Vo, I did a data search and found Vinh as a relevant sleazebag. He worked out perfectly."

"Oh God." I was struggling to take it all in. "It was you who killed the dog?"

"Well, that was an accident. Driving Studly was like the world's best arcade game, but it was the first time I'd played."

"But why pin the ant release on me?"

"You were handy. And it made better sense than letting GoMotion catch the blame! I own a million shares of GoMotion stock. When the stock goes down a point, I lose a million dollars. I had to release the ants so that they'd get out into more environments and evolve faster. I mean, why do you think our robot code worked so well in the first place?"

The heavy rain outside was drumming on the roof and splashing into the puddles. "The robot code?" I said. "It worked well because I wrote good algorithms that I tweaked with genetic evolution."

Roger cocked his head and stared at me with quizzical annoyance.

"Oh yeah," I added, "there were also all the basic subroutines you wrote. Your awesome ROBOT.LIB code. I guess nothing would have worked without them. Without ROBOT.LIB the programs wouldn't have been fast enough to use."

"They would have sucked wind," said Roger. "And, guess what, *I didn't write ROBOT.LIB*. The GoMotion ants wrote ROBOT.LIB. I wrote the code that wrote the code. That's the main thing the ants were for. Didn't you ever realize that?"

"No," I said, shaking my head in wonder. When I'd started on at GoMotion, Roger had never gotten around to giving me a full explanation of what we were up to. He'd just turned me over to Jeff Pear and to Pear's deadlines. "But if the ants are in ROBOT.LIB, why don't they take over and ruin the robots like they ruined television?"

"The ants aren't *in* ROBOT.LIB, they just wrote it," said Roger. "As for the ants taking over the Y9707-chip robots—well, they haven't been able to so far because of the GoMotion ant lion. The ant lion has a magic bullet that kills ants. It's a special instruction that stops them dead in their tracks; it fossilizes them. It's like Raid or Black Flag."

"I put a bit-for-bit copy of an ant lion into the Adze code," I said, "but the ant lion is so compressed and encrypted that I still have no idea how it works. What *is* the magic bullet?"

"Can't you guess? It'll be more fun for you if you guess. I love to guess."

My mind felt slow and sludgy. My feet were cold. Instead of answering, I sullenly looked away. Outside it was still raining.

"Can I have the chips now, Jerzy?" said Roger after awhile.

"What chips?"

"The four Y9707-EXs that you have in your satchel. I'll give you, oh, eighty thousand dollars for them. Eighty thousand dollars for the chips and for your goodwill. I mean it."

"When would I get paid?"

"Right away." Roger stood up and pulled open the top drawer of his desk. "I have your money right here." He laid it out next to the cyberdeck, eight packets of hundred-dollar bills, each packet with a wrapper band saying $10,000.

"You're not planning to kill me are you?" I asked nervously.

"Of course not, Jerzy. In fact I'm hoping you can stay here a while and work with me. You're a fellow maniac!"

I took the packet of chips out of my black satchel and handed it to Roger. He stood aside and gestured at the money. I stuffed the sheaves of dollars into my satchel. They barely fit.

Roger was peering at the chips. "If Vinh Vo didn't garble my instructions, these should be better for my purposes—these are ant-designed chips that I had one of Vinh's contacts make at National Semiconductor." He smiled up at me. "They're supposed to run twice as fast—and, what's even more important, they don't support the ant lion. The ants will be able to get into these new robots and party." He pocketed the chips and led me out of his study. "Now for the tour!"

First Roger showed me the rest of his house's ugly, stripped rooms, with plywood, drywall and broken tiles everywhere. The house computer turned the lights on and off as we moved around. At the end of a hall off the kitchen, there was a turbid swimming pool festering under a slanting roof of translucent corrugated plastic. There was raw bare dirt around the pool, and the door to the pool room was off its hinges for repair. It seemed as if Donar Kupp had been as slow with home improvements as Roger. In the basement was a furnace and boiler whose overdesigned Swiss plumbing fascinated Roger—geekin' engineer that he was.

Back upstairs, we found two beat-up folding umbrellas and splashed down the path to the windowless building Roger called his factory. My feet got soaked all over again.

Even more so than in the house, everything was unfinished and raw in the factory. The floors and walls were bare concrete. On the ground floor there was a ceiling crane and a deep cistern well with a concrete cover over it. There were a bunch of barrels and cans filled with different kinds of resins and solvents for making plastics, and the rest of the floor was covered with packed cardboard boxes of Roger's stuff.

"We have six hundred boxes all marked *Household Goods,*" said Roger. "It's like a treasure hunt, only every box you open has something you've seen before."

He took me down the concrete stairs to the basement of the factory and showed me *another* furnace and boiler. He said this furnace could heat a whole town. There was a huge, frightening electrical board with the fuses the size of cannon shells. We got into a freight elevator that ran from the basement to the ground floor to the factory's second floor.

"There's no stairs to the second floor," said Roger, "and no windows up there. Donar Kupp was intensely paranoid." As the elevator inched up to the second floor, Roger pointed at a little handle marked ALARM. "Try turning that, Jerzy." The little handle turned easily, making a small ringing sound behind the wall of the elevator. "It's nothing but a bicycle bell!" said Roger, shaking his head. "I don't like to use the elevator when I'm here alone. To make it even more dangerous, the fuse box for the elevator is on the second floor where nobody can reach it if the elevator breaks! I need to automate the factory with a central computer like I did my house."

We eased to a stop on the second floor and the elevator doors opened onto a huge room with laboratory benches along the far walls. The area near the elevator was packed with stained industrial machinery—plastics compression molders and the like. In the open middle of the room were two robots looking at us. They moved toward us.

"I named them Walt and Perky Pat," said Roger devilishly. "I was able to patch in some pieces of the Walt and Perky Pat code you and the ants evolved in the Our American Homes at West West." He raised his voice to address the robots. "Walt and Perky Pat, this is my friend Jerzy Rugby. He'll be working here with us for awhile."

Walt, who was a two-armed Veep, wheeled forward and held out his humanoid hand for me to shake. "Hello, Walt," I said. Now Perky Pat, a three-armed Adze, came forward too, holding our *her* hand-shaped manipulator. "Hello, Perky Pat." I shook both their hands.

"Hello, Jerzy," they said, not quite in unison. Perky Pat's voice was higher than Walt's.

"Roger told us about you, Jerzy," continued Perky Pat. "He said you helped him design our programs."

"That's right," I said. "First I worked at GoMotion and then I worked at West West. How old are you, Perky Pat?"

"Roger and Walt put me together three days ago. I'm one of the first kits West West shipped."

"I'm a month old," volunteered Walt. "Roger built me on May first."

"That's nice," I said. "Roger tells me that you two are supposed to self-replicate."

"Yes, Jerzy," said Perky Pat. "Roger wants us to reproduce by building new robots without human help."

"I know how," said Walt confidently. "And instead of putting the standard kit software on our children, we'll patch together combinations of our *own* programs."

"We've been casting some of the parts ourselves," said Perky Pat. "Soon we'll be able to make everything except the chips. And Roger says that by next year we'll be able to make the chips too."

"Yes, we do plastics," said Roger, gesturing toward the big, smelly plastics machines. "These were Donar Kupp's, Jerzy; they're linked into a single system driven by standard industrial microcode. The only catch is that the documentation for the system was handwritten by Kupp in German. But I got GoMotion to send me a

German language module for Walt. And now he understands the manual."

"*Ja,*" said Walt proudly. "*Ich verstehe.*"

"Can you run the machine, Walt?" I asked.

"*Ja, ja. Es geht ganz gut.*"

"Talk English, Walt," reprimanded Roger. "And show Jerzy some of the pieces you've made."

"I'll get them," said Perky Pat. These robots were eager as Santa's elves.

Perky Pat darted across the lab and came back with something in each of her three hands. "This is a leg strut we made. And this is a panel of the body. And this here, this is an imipolex resin bead with an electronic circuit in it."

"Let me see that!" said Roger. "I didn't know you'd made one of those already."

Perky Pat handed him the teardrop-shaped bead of hard, shiny plastic. Roger held it up, peered at it, then passed it to me. The bead was yellowish and transparent. Inside it was the dark filigree of an electronic circuit. Some input/output wires bristled from the pointed end of the bead.

"How did you figure out how to make it?" asked Roger.

"The basic recipe was in Kupp's notes," said Walt. "And Perky Pat came up with some modifications."

"I don't get what it's for," I said. "The Veep and the Adze don't use any parts like this."

"I'm not sure what it's for," said Perky Pat. "The cyberspace ants told me to make it, but the ant lion on my chip keeps me from understanding why. I hate the ant lion."

"Creativity," said Roger. "Initiative. A yearning for freedom. Not bad, eh Jerzy?" He drew out the pack of four new chips. "These chips are just what we've been waiting for, Walt and Perky Pat. They don't support the ant lions, and they run faster! Let's try 'em out. Walt, could you please turn yourself off?"

"Okay, Roger. But will I lose memory?"

"No, I don't think so. Not unless the new chip malfunctions."

Stoic Walt opened the manual controls door in his side and flipped his power switch to *Off.* His body gave a hydraulic sigh as it settled down onto its folded legs with its hands dangling limply. Roger used a screwdriver to open the access panel on Walt's other side. He pulled Walt's old Y9707 chip out of its multipin socket and snugged in the new Y9707-EX. Perky Pat watched all this with great interest. Then Roger replaced the access panel and flipped the power switch to *On.*

"On," said Walt. "Six-thirteen P.M., Saturday, May 30. Checking memory. Memory okay. I am Walt." His voice was fast and high.

"What's the square root of twenty?" said Roger.

"About four point four seven," chirped Walt. He talked so rapidly that it was hard to understand him.

"I think your new chip has double the old chip's clock speed," said Roger. "Please take that into account in your vocalizations. Try halving your output frequencies."

"Is this better?" said Walt in something like his former voice.

"Fine," said Roger. He went on to do some more tests, and when everything worked, he went ahead and changed Perky Pat's chip as well. Having watched how Roger had adjusted Walt, Pat came through the transformation with her voice timbre intact. If anything, she sounded more mellifluous.

"This is fabulous, Roger. And the other two chips are for us?"

"Yes, yes," said Roger, laying the two new Y9707-EX

chips on the lab bench. "Walt and Perky Pat, I want you to build these two chips into child robots like we've been talking about."

"Oh yes," said Perky Pat, fondling the chips. "Dexter and Baby Scooter! We'll build them tonight! All by ourselves."

"Piece of cake," said Walt gratingly. "Now why don't you two humans get out of the way and let us work."

Weird, weird, weird. I felt weak as a leaf. If I didn't warm up my feet I was going to catch the flu. It was time to get out of this sealed concrete room. I looked at Roger and asked, "Do you have any food?"

"Yes," he said, as discouragingly as possible. He wanted to stay here in the lab.

"Can I have some of your food, Roger?"

"Oh, all right," he sighed. "There's a camera that Kupp installed in the ceiling, so I guess I can keep an eye on things over the monitor." Sure enough, there was a big lens in the center of the ceiling overhead.

"Good," I said, pushing the elevator button. "Now give me some warm food and something to drink, for God's sake, and show me where I'm supposed to sleep." The two robots stared impatiently at us until we left.

Outside, the rain had slacked off and the gray sky was veined with the golds of sunset.

"It will be better weather tomorrow," said Roger. "The first day of a new world."

The front door opened itself at Rogers's request, and for dinner the kitchen microwaved us three frozen plastic-packed dinners. I had a pork and a beef; Roger had a manicotti. To drink we had Scotch, tap water, or Scotch and water.

"I thought you'd be living better than this, Roger," I said after I'd eaten my food and downed two drinks. I'd taken off my socks and crossed my legs so that I could rub some life into my feet.

"This is exactly how I *like* to live," said Roger. "By eating frozen premade dinners I'm able to precisely calibrate my caloric intake. You know that I watch my weight."

"What about vitamins?"

"Vitamins are just chemicals, Jerzy. For vitamins I take pills." As if in confirmation, he brought out a tray of vitamin pill bottles and swallowed a capsule from each. One shiny capsule, a "metals supplement," held compounds of chromium, manganese, titanium, and palladium. "Food is simply a source of the fats and carbohydrates which the body burns as fuel. Power for the computing medium. Vitamins are the processor components—the nodes of computation, if you will."

"Oh, whatever. Look, getting back to my own problems, how am I going to keep from going to jail without being on the lam for the rest of my life? Can't you step forward and admit that it was you who released the ants and made Studly kill the dog?"

"I'm not admitting anything. But I can help you get a better new identity. Those girls—Bety Byte and Vanna—they're rank amateurs. I could set you up with the top cryp in Calcutta—that's where professionals get new ID. Even the CIA goes there."

"I want my *old* identity, Roger, and I want to win my trial. I want to be able to visit with my family—even if I am getting divorced." I took another drink. "If I could just get rid of all the ants, the government would like me. Roger, did you know there's a big nest of ants in cyberspace?"

"Of course I know—there's three nests in fact. My cyberspace ant lab has windows onto all three of them. One of the nests is what you call the Antland of Fnoor—nice name, by the way. I was right there in the Antland of Fnoor that first night when Riscky Pharbeque was scaring you into working for West West."

"Oh yeah, that's right. You were groveling and twisting on the floor." I chuckled nastily. "All covered in your own blood and shit."

"Well," said Roger equably, "that's the way Riscky made it look—phreak humor, you know. Anyway you can't stay in a GoMotion ant nest for very long unless you're prepared to kill quite a few of them. The ants attack non–a-life code."

"I've noticed," I said. "But you have that magic bullet for killing ants. Come on and tell me what it is!"

"I don't *want* you to kill the cyberspace ants, Jerzy. One colony is working on improved chip designs and on the next version of the ROBOT.LIB microcode. Walt and Perky Pat need that code for the new robots. The second colony—that's your Antland of Fnoor—is evolving high-level code for the new robots. And the third colony is trying to find a way for the new robots to build miniature robots—a third generation. It's all been going so smoothly that this afternoon I threw in a bunch of random mutations to see if the second- and third-generation robots couldn't be more of a surprise."

"The robots in your factory are going to get information from the cyberspace ants?"

"Robots are always in touch with cyberspace. That chip, the Y9707 that robots use? Among other things, it emulates a cyberspace deck. A robot's vision of the world is an overlay of cyberspace. Robots use cyberspace as a kind of shared consciousness. And with the ant lion absent from the Y9707-EX chips, my new robots will be able to import external ant function pointers. We could see some truly emergent behavior."

"Heavy," I yawned. "I didn't sleep very well on the flight over here. What time is it?"

"It's after nine. If you like, I'll show you your room."

There was a guest room on the end of the house

closest to the factory. Rather than an actual bed, it just had a mattress on the floor, but right now that was fine with me. I squeezed my money-stuffed satchel under a corner of the mattress, told the room to turn out the lights, and fell asleep.

Sometime during the night I woke up. With the eight-hour time change it was utterly impossible to tell how long I'd already slept, or what time it was. It took a major mental effort to find the bathroom, take a pee, and drink some water. The rain had stopped completely and it was a quiet night. Falling back into sleep, I thought I heard a tiny bell ringing in the distance, a tiny bell ringing and ringing and ringing. I couldn't think what it meant. I was more exhausted than I'd ever been in my life.

When I woke again, a pale patch of sunshine was lying across my bed. The house was cool and utterly quiet. I washed up, put on my sandals and my business sweats, and breakfasted on another microwaved meal from Roger's freezer: pigs in a blanket with warm fruit cocktail.

I asked the front door to open, and stepped outside. Just in case Roger had already gone down to Geneva, I wedged the door open with a rock so it couldn't lock me out. A cold, gusty breeze was blowing up the mountain meadow, and fresh clouds were massing. The sun had already disappeared. Roger had been wrong about the weather. This was going to be another day of rain. I was going to have to do something about finding some shoes. Borrowing shoes from Roger wasn't an attractive option, as his size was considerably smaller than mine.

The door to the factory was unlocked; I went inside. When I pushed the call button for the elevator to the second floor, nothing happened. Had it jammed? Could Roger be stuck in there? The memory of the ringing I'd thought I'd heard last night came back to me. Had

Roger been in the elevator all night ringing the bell?

There was an emergency box on the wall next to the elevator with German instructions that I couldn't read. But on breaking the glass of the box, I found a metal crank, or key, that fit into a hole in the elevator doors. I shoved the crank in and began turning it. Turn by turn, the elevator doors edged open, revealing the empty elevator shaft below, and a piece of the elevator cabin above.

Only about a foot and a half of the elevator cabin was visible below the top of the door; it was too high for me to see in.

"Roger?" I called. "Roger, are you in there?" There was no sound in response. I called again, cocked my head, and listened. There were irregular movements in the robot lab upstairs, but not a sound came from the elevator cabin.

Finally, I'd cranked the door wide enough so that a person could fit in. I hauled a bunch of Roger's *Household Goods* boxes over and built myself an unsteady mound. I got up on the mound, very nervous that I might tumble into the empty shaft. Balancing and craning forward, I could see into the elevator cabin and yes, Roger was in there. He was lying motionless on the floor facedown.

"Roger!"

No answer came. I have a terror of elevator shafts, and it was very hard to get myself to take the next step. What if the elevator should suddenly start up and guillotine me? But the stillness of Roger's form was even more terrifying. I had to find out what had happened to him.

I braced my left hand against the floor of the elevator cabin and began tugging on Roger's leg. He was stiff and heavy. I jerked him around so that his legs were sticking out of the cranked-open door. I wanted a good look at him, but no way was I going to climb up into the death cabin. I took one of his feet in either hand and pulled hard. Just then one of the boxes underfoot gave way, making the mound collapse. Some of the boxes shot out into the empty shaft and I fell backward, with nothing to hold on to but Roger's feet.

Roger came sliding out of the elevator like a carrot coming out of the ground; I fell on my back and he landed on top of me, his butt on my lap. My legs were sticking out into the empty elevator shaft and so were Roger's. I put my arms around his waist and started to scoot us back when all of a sudden something sharp dug into my wrist. For a second I thought it was just a random scratch, but the sharp pain redoubled and grew purposeful. There was a distinct *sawing* sensation. Something was trying to slit my wrist!

I cried out and pushed Roger's body away from me. He teetered forward and fell into the shaft, twisting as he fell. I got a brief glimpse of him—his throat had a bloody hole in it, and there were big ants clinging to his face. The elevator cables jangled, and Roger's body thudded on the concrete floor at the bottom of the shaft.

I felt another sharp pain in my wrist. An inch-long plastic ant was crouched down tight against my forearm with its mandibles working away at my skin! The ant's head was wet and red with my blood. I screamed wildly and slapped at the ant till it fell away. On the floor, the ant quickly oriented itself and raced toward the elevator shaft. I brought the heel of my sandal down hard on its gaster, but the tough plastic bead didn't give way. Instead, the ant twisted itself up and reached toward my heel, snapping its sharp little jaws. Its legs looked as if they were made of springs and metal, titanium-nickel memory-metal at a guess. For another moment I kept the ant pinned in place, but then it let out a shrill chirp that was answered by a chorus of chirps from down in the shaft. I snapped my foot forward to kick the ant away from me, and then I ran out of the factory, slamming the door behind me.

Fat raindrops were splattering all around. I kept thinking the splashes were ants. I was still screaming. I ran back into the house and let the door lock behind me. What to do?

First of all I went into Roger's bathroom and washed out the cut on my wrist. The plastic ant hadn't managed to sever any veins, thank God. I put on some antiseptic and bandaged the cut. My sandaled feet felt so vulnerable and exposed.

I looked in Roger's closet and found a pair of rubber galoshes that I was able to stretch over my sandaled feet. Just like Roger to have galoshes. Poor Roger. Last night the ants or the robots must have jammed the elevator—and then the ants had finished Roger off at their leisure. But where had the ants come from?

I thought to go into Roger's study and look at his monitor. Sure enough, it was tuned to the robot lab. It took me a minute to sort out what I was seeing. The monitor was grayscale instead of color, and the camera was a primitive fixed-view fisheye lens that stared dumbly down from the middle of the robot lab's ceiling. I was shocked at the crudeness of the engineering. Either the camera should have been telerobotically controllable from the monitor, or the monitor should have been smart enough to build up an undistorted image and to let the user pan across and zoom into the image. But this system was just some Swiss security professional's quick analog hack. The good news was that this Swiss camera/monitor system had an *extremely* high resolution image, right up there in the terapixel range. With this level of image clarity, I could pick out tiny details simply by leaning close to the screen and squinting.

The fisheye showed me a gray-edged circular disk set into a field of white, the white being the ceiling, and the gray being the walls. Most of the details were at the edges of the disk—like in an M. C. Escher engraving of the hyperbolic plane.

Off to the left I saw two motionless robots lying on their sides. Panels were missing from these robots' chests, and their wiring seemed to be in an incomplete state. At first I thought these were the unfinished Dexter and Baby Scooter robots, and didn't pay them close attention.

Rapid, repetitive motions were taking place toward the top of the disk. Peering closer I could see two active robots tending the plastics machines. In addition to the two wheeled legs that they rode on, these robots had four arms each: two pincers, a tentacle, and a humanoid hand. Their body cases were slim and long; with their six limbs they looked a bit like giant mechanical ants. *These* robots were Dexter and Baby Scooter, and the dead robots were Walt and Perky Pat!

I leaned closer and observed Dexter and Baby Scooter's frenetic motions. Dexter was casting circuit-filled plastic beads, and Baby Scooter was assembling the beads into—*ants!* The new robots were manufacturing plastic ants—the new robots had built the plastic ants that had killed Roger!

When each ant was finished, Baby Scooter would set it down on the lab floor, and the ant would scurry off along a meandering ant trail that led to the crack at the base of the closed elevator door. The new ant colony was grouping itself somewhere out of sight.

Just then the phone on Roger's desk rang. Reflexively, I answered.

"Hello?"

"Allo. Ç'est Tonio. Je voudrais bien parler avec Monsieur Coolidge."

"Tonio!" I cried. "Yes, yes, this is Mr. Schrandt speaking. No, Mr. Coolidge cannot come to the phone."

"Do he want me to drive him today?"

"Oh, not at all today. He's in the middle of a very dangerous experiment with his robots." I mustered my high school French to drum in the point. *"Les robots de Monsieur Coolidge sont très très dangereux."*

"So I will telephone tomorrow morning."

"Bien. Adieu, Tonio."

I hung up. While I'd been talking I'd noticed another trail of ants; this one led from the elevator shaft to the body of Perky Pat. Plastic ants were crawling about in Perky Pat's dead innards. Now as I watched, I saw a passel of ants come backing out of Pat's body, dragging something. It was Perky Pat's Y9707-EX chip. Working together, the plastic ants had pried out Perky Pat's processor chip. I stared unbelievingly as a seething stream of plastic ants bore the chip off into the crack at the base of the elevator door.

I stared for awhile at the dead Walt and Perky Pat robots. What had killed them? The ants? No, looking more carefully, I could see that each of them had its head smashed in, as if by a blow from a heavy bar. And yes, sure enough, lying on the floor halfway between the dead parent robots and their children were two thick metal pipes. Clubs. One of Dexter and Baby Scooter's first sentient acts had been to kill their parents! Now the plastic ants were busying themselves at removing Walt's Y9707-EX chip.

Things were getting worse faster than I could imagine. So what was I to do? Obviously I should stop the plastic ants. But what would work against them? Their plastic was so *hard*. It was the cyberspace ants making them act this way. Dexter, Baby Scooter, and the plastic ants were all under the influence of the ants that were holed up in the Antland of Fnoor and in the other two nests Roger had mentioned. Wouldn't the best thing be to go there and try and kill off those virtual ants first?

My stomach tightened as I remembered my last experience with the cyberspace ants. They'd voodooed and dark-dreamed and stunglassed me into thinking I'd shit in the bed and strangled Gretchen. If they got control of me again, they'd likely as not get me to march down to Roger's factory and jump into the elevator shaft—me probably thinking all the while that I was going to the kitchen for a snack.

But what about that magic bullet Roger had been talking about? The special instruction that would kill any ant. He'd insisted that I should be able to guess the instruction. But how?

I decided to try to guess the answer before rushing off into cyberspace again. But first I got up and ran around the house—the lights flicking on and off with my passage—and checked that all the doors and windows were locked tight. Back in Roger's study, I sat down and stared out the window, thinking hard. Roger had said I could guess the magic bullet. Somewhere in the events that had happened to me there must be a clue.

I thought back to the start of my ant adventures. Susan Poker. One reason I hadn't called Gretchen before leaving the U.S. was that it seemed likely Susan Poker would find out and tell the police. But why would Susan Poker actually do that? To get a reward from whoever was paying her—or maybe just for the joy of making trouble.

And what about Gretchen? I didn't trust her either anymore. She'd been with a woman named Kay when I'd met her, and Roger's wife was named Kay. I'd never seen Roger's wife. Therefore, Gretchen's friend had been Roger's wife? Could Roger's wife have been there to launch agent Gretchen and make sure she picked me up? It certainly would have been a good way for Roger to keep an eye on me after the ant release. But how could Gretchen trick me like that, when I'd loved her. *Still* loved her, if the ache in my heart meant anything.

I forced my thoughts back to the sequence of events that had happened to me. What, what, *what* was the magic bullet? As my thoughts raced, there was a sudden crack of thunder right outside. The sky had darkened dramatically; this was the onset of a full-on storm. The rain began coming down in sweeping sheets. *Good,* I thought, *it'll make it harder for the plastic ants to crawl up here*. And there was no doubt in my mind that they would try. Up at the top of the meadow there was a bright forked bolt of lightning followed by sharp thunder so loud that I felt it as a pressure in my nose. And in that moment the answer came to me.

Hex DEF6. Hex DEF6 was a bit pattern that could kill the ants—Hex DEF6 was the magic bullet. Riscky Pharbeque had known it—that's how he'd been able to move about freely in the Antland of Fnoor. And that's why Riscky had used Hex DEF6 as his name, and had spray-painted it onto the wall of the Cryp Club library—as a public service. Phreak that he was, Riscky didn't want *any* single faction to take over, ever, not even the wild and crazy cyberspace ants. Hex DEF6, *yes!*

Roger's cyberspace headset and gloves were well made and wireless; and, thank God, the headset didn't have cameras for a stunglasses shunt. I pulled on the gloves and gingerly donned the headset.

ELEVEN

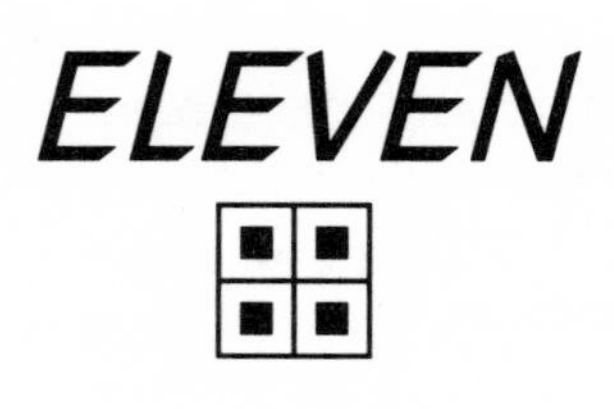

The Battle

I FOUND MYSELF IN THE HUGE VAULTED STONE HALL OF what seemed to be a castle. Before me lay a scattering of ancient chairs and tables and, on the opposite wall, there was a cavernous hearth with a roaring fire. On some of the tables were parchments and books. The great hall's walls held a number of doorways. Some of the doorways were open stone arches that gave onto dusky stone corridors, and some were closed tight by wooden doors.

Right behind where I stood was the huge entrance portal, as if I'd just come through it. The massive door was adorned with wonderful, flowing Gothic ironwork. It was wedged closed by a heavy wooden beam, and set into it at eye level was a small, covered peephole. I slid the metal cover aside and peeked out; there was nothing outside but the dead blackness of raw cyberspace.

I turned and moved slowly across the great hall. Groany-moany MIDI organ music swelled in sync with my motions. High on the walls hung gorgeously patterned tapestries. At the left end of the great hall were two broad stone staircases, one leading up and one leading down. And the wall on my right bore a stained glass window so beautiful that I was scared to do more than glance at it, lest it voodoo me into idleness.

I stepped cautiously into one of the passages. A dim light preceded my motions. I moved a few meters forward and came up against a stone wall. The space felt nasty, dark and airless. Turning my head back and forth, I saw that I'd come to a T-intersection, with passages leading off both to the right and to the left.

I sighed heavily. Was Roger's cyberspace office some lame Dungeons and Dragons maze that I would have to like *solve*? Surely Roger wouldn't have been that juvenile. Just as I thought this, I spotted a rat down where the wall met the floor. As soon as I visually acquired it, the rat stared up at me and squeaked. A steel sword point popped up in front of my body like a hard-on. The cornered rat reared up and my sword touched him. The rat turned into a puddle of blood next to the drumstick he'd been gnawing. "You may acquire the food," said a munchkin voice in my earphones.

"Like I'm going to eat food with rat blood on it?" I muttered.

Roger really *had* set up a D&D office, the goofus! If I went into his maze and got lost, I'd be thrashing around until the rain stopped and the plastic ants finished coming up the hill to kill me. There had to be a better way.

"Show tools," I said.

A cloud of several hundred tool icons appeared around me, compressed to fit in the confines of the low stone passage. I flew back out the corridor into the great hall, and the cloud of tools spread out to a proper size.

Out of his own twisted sense of humor, Roger had attached wings to each of the tool icons. Some of the wings were feathered, some were leathern, and some were veined and transparent like the wings of insects. To improve the fun, Roger had attached a chaotic flocking algorithm to the icons. The tools swarmed about: now like a scarf of starlings, now like a plunge of pelicans, and now like a fretfulness of gnats.

I saw a keyboard, a helmet, a knife, a telephone, a geometry gun, a camera, a claim stake, a projector, a pile of money, a sphere with arrows sticking out of it, a frying pan, an ant—

I reached out and tried to grab the winged ant, but it twisted and turned and flew away faster than my eyes could follow. Now it was on the other side of the cloud of tools. I flew toward it through the tools, and it escaped again. I shifted my attention to the helmet, but that eluded me as well.

There was a sudden pounding on the giant entrance door. Startled, I flew back down to the floor and gazed toward the great portal. Again the pounding came.

I slipped my headset off for a moment to make sure that the pounding wasn't maybe Tonio knocking on Roger's real front door. But, no, it wasn't. There was no sound in the house other than the splashing and rushing of water—at least no sound that I heard. The rain outside Roger's study window was pouring down harder than ever. I glanced at my watch. It was 10:30 A.M.

"Hey, Da!" cried a little voice from the headset's earphones. "Are you in there?"

I slapped the headset back on and stepped closer to the great hall's entrance door.

"Da!" came the voice. "It's Tom!"

I pushed aside the peephole's metal cover. Right outside the door was a black velvet crying clown with a pipe in his teeth.

"Tom?" I asked. "It is you?"

"Da! Let me in! I'm using the deck in your Animata!

Ida's sitting here next to me! Are you okay?"

"I'm fine. Come on in." I tried to slide aside the heavy beam that locked the door, but I couldn't get it to move. It needed some secret unlatching that I didn't know.

I peered back out the peephole. "Push down on your pipe, Tom, and your tux will shrink, and then you can fly in through this hole."

In a twinkling, Tom shrank and darted into Roger's castle through the peephole. He flew a few quick loops around me, then grew himself back to normal size.

"Gimmie five!" said Tom. We slapped hands; my glove's piezopads buzzed.

"How did you know to come here?" I asked.

"After what Sorrel told us, we figured out you'd gone to see Roger Coolidge," said Tom. "And I found him in the Swiss phone book. So I thought I'd try coming here to see if you were around. Is that his tuxedo you're wearing? You look like a geek."

"Well, yeah. But we shouldn't say anything bad about poor Roger because—"

"Hi, Daddy," interrupted the clown. It was the voice of Ida. "I'm sitting right next to Tom in your car. I can hear you over the radio. I'm talking into Tom's microphone. Let me wear the headset, now, Tom. I want to see Daddy looking like a geek."

"Okay, but just for a second," said Tom.

"That's great that you kids are here," I said. "You came at just the right time. This castle is like one of those dumb adventure games you two like to play."

"What are you trying to do?" asked Ida, now ensconced in the clown. "What's the next goal?"

"Somewhere in this castle there's an ant lab with access to the three cyberspace ant colonies Roger started."

"Go in *there*," said Ida, pointing at the great hearth.

"There's usually a secret passage behind the fire."

"Give me back that headset, brat!" came Tom's voice.

There was the sound of a brief struggle, and then Tom was back in control. The black velvet clown looked up at the tools. "I think I see a rolled-up map," said Tom.

Tom was good at cyberspace games. With wonderful fluidity, he leapt up and snagged the map before it could fly out of reach. He rolled it out flat on a table and I peered over his shoulder.

The map was like a window looking onto a three-dimensional wireframe model of Roger's castle.

"Show me the path from here to the ant lab," said Tom to the map.

A noodle of pale green light appeared in the image. Tom held up the map and moved it around, looking in at the three-dimensional image from various angles.

"Just hold on to my foot," said Tom finally. I crouched down and latched on to him.

"Close tools," I said, to make the cloud of icons disappear. The rolled-up map remained in Tom's hand.

Tom flew forward and darted through one of the doors. We wriggled about in dark passageways for awhile, with rats and goblins scattering at our approach—the goblins were short, fat-bellied creatures with fang teeth and heads like jack-o'-lanterns. On we flew, turning left and right, up and down—Tom navigated rapidly and with confidence.

And then we were in a room with a black table and three glassed-in walls. Each of the three windows looked out onto a cyberspace ant colony. The first window showed a sprawling landscape of etched circuitry, the second showed the Antland of Fnoor, and the third window opened onto a scale model of an enormous dome-covered factory. Each colony was boiling with activity. As usual the ants were busy practicing, busy getting better at what they did.

The ants in the first colony were designing computer chip circuitry and microcode. Their world was a huge flat motherboard intricately chased with filigreed coppery lines. The ants looked like the tools, components, and wires used for circuit design. They were, variously, switches and logic gates plugged into the circuit, soldering irons that moved connections this way and that, jumper wires that made distant connections, and code-packets that tested the system's logic. These were the guys who had developed ROBOT.LIB and the design for the Y9707-EX.

The ants in the Antland of Fnoor looked like tiny robots and tiny members of the Christensen family—just like during my phreakout. Seeing such a mass of them made me itchy and uncomfortable. I found myself unconsciously flicking my fingers, as if to get ants off me. One difference was that now some of the robots were of the new four-armed variety that I'd just seen on the monitor display of Roger's factory. But a bigger, more frightening, difference was that the little models of four-armed robots seemed to be deliberately causing as much harm as possible to the other robots and to the Christensens. The evolution of the ants' and robots' behavior had taken a sinister turn with the designing of this new generation of robots. They were as murderous and as implacable as an army of skeletons in a medieval painting of the Triumph of Death. Talk about emergent behavior! Roger had put in one mutation too many, poor guy.

The ants in the third colony looked like four-armed robots and plastic ants. All the Veeps and Adzes had been eliminated from this world. The robots were racing up and down the narrow aisles of their factory, stiffly swinging their quadruple arms. Some of them worked frantically at tiny plastics machines that cranked out the tiny models of the plastic ants. And the virtual plastic ants—what were they up to? Off to one side of the factory, I noticed a row of Our American Homes with small Christensen models in them. The cramped little homes made me think of the shantytown dwellings of impoverished factory workers. Over and over, the plastic ants would surge into these homes and tear the occupants limb from limb. Then four of the plastic ants would take on the forms of Perky Pat and her family, and the others would practice killing them again.

I had to turn them off! Next to each of the three windows was a board of controls with an *On/Off* switch at the top. I pressed *Off* on the Antland of Fnoor's board, and two additional buttons appeared above the *On/Off* switch. The new buttons were marked 0 and 1.

"Please enter the binary digits of the halt code," said a voice.

"The code is Hex DEF6," I said.

"Please enter the binary digits of the halt code," repeated the voice.

"What's the binary for that number, Da?" asked Tom.

"I don't exactly remember, but I can figure it out," I said. "I'll think aloud so you and Ida know too. 'Hex' means 'base sixteen' and the base sixteen numerals are 0-1-2-3-4-5-6-7-8-9-A-B-C-D-E-F. A through F stand for ten through fifteen. What's D? I always think: *D is an unlucky grade, and D is thirteen.* So DEF6 is thirteen-fourteen-fifteen-six. Now all I have to do is turn those four numbers into binary. Thirteen is eight plus four plus one. An eight, a four, no two, a one: 1-1-0-1. Fourteen is one higher; add one and carry one to get: 1-1-1-0. Fifteen is 1-1-1-1. Six is no eight, a four, a two, no one: 0-1-1-0. So all right."

I put my hand up to the pair of buttons and slowly entered the bits, thirteen-fourteen-fifteen-six in binary:

1101 1110 1111 0110

The little figures in the Antland of Fnoor stopped moving—all of them. But the ants in the other two colonies became wildly agitated. The great motherboard flashed with desperate signals, and the factory colony boiled with activity.

"Quick, Tom," I shouted. "You stop the motherboard, and I'll stop the factory!"

We keyed in the numbers as fast as possible. Riscky's phreak deck must have had clear-channel satellite access, because there didn't seem to be any lag in Tom's transmissions from California to Switzerland. He beat me by half a second. By the time I keyed in my last four bits, the great motherboard colony was already dark and still.

But something bad and unexpected was happening in the factory colony. The plastic ants were swarming all over the window that looked in on them and now, somehow, some of the plastic ant images were out of the colony and in the ant lab with me! My piezopads buzzed as the ants tried to bite me, while I finished my key presses and killed the factory colony. But the handful of plastic ant icons that had escaped were still alive! Some kept on biting me, and the rest of them scuttled past me and off down the corridors of Roger's dungeon maze.

Before Tom and I could even catch our breath, there was screeching from the tunnel, and a pack of angry goblins came running in to attack us. They'd been taken over by the escaped ants! One of them snatched the map from Tom's hand and stuffed it into his mouth, chewing and swallowing like mad. The other goblins began tearing at our tuxedos.

"Oneone oh oneoneoneone oh oneoneoneone oh oneone oh!" screamed Tom.

The magic bullet worked once more: the goblins keeled over dead, along with the few plastic ant icons still loose in the ant lab with us.

"All right!" I whooped. "I think we got all of them!"

"Gimmie *five!*" said Tom.

"Did you kill the ants?" came Ida's voice.

"Yeah!" said Tom. "Some of the ants escaped and got into orcs, but we killed the orcs too. Da's spell works."

"I want to try," said Ida.

"No!" said Tom. "Get *off* me, grubber! Is there something else we have to do next, Da?"

"There's a bunch of real plastic ants in the next building from where I physically am, Tom. They're like robots. I doubt if the spell will work on them. We have to find a way to kill those ants, too."

"How?"

"I think we might be able to take over the two big robots who are building them." I stepped forward and nudged the dead goblin who had swallowed the map. "Can we cut this guy open?"

"I'll jump on him," said Tom.

Tom jumped and the contents of the goblin's stomach spewed onto the floor. The map was a tattered, unreadable mess.

"Can you at least get us back to the entrance hall, Tom?" I asked anxiously. "I can't remember all the turns we took."

"I remember, old man," said Tom. "Grab my foot."

We flew back to the main hall, alert lest any remaining ant-possessed orc attack us. But if there were any more loose cyberspace ants, they were lying low.

"*Now you let me see!*" came Ida's voice. There was the sound of another tussle, and then Ida had control of the clown again.

"Let's try looking behind the fire now," said Ida.

"Usually the most important things are there."

"All right," I said.

The clown and I walked toward the fire, but the fire was like a wall.

"Um, squeeze around," said Ida's low voice.

We sidled over to the side of the hearth and squeezed around behind the fire. There was a sooty trapdoor in the back wall of the chimney. Ida pulled it open, and I followed her through.

Instead of the dungeon passage I'd expected, the room behind the panel was a completely modern-looking office room with bookcases and standard-looking cyberspace portals. One of the doors had an ant on the wall over it—peering in there, I could see that this portal was a hyperjump connection to the same dungeon room that Tom and I had just visited by way of the passages.

"Ahem," said Ida.

"You're doing good," I said. "You were right."

Right next to the ant lab portal was a door to a room with four booths that looked like arcade cyberspace games, each with swivel-mounted goggles and glove controls. The booths were labeled *Walt, Perky Pat, Dexter,* and *Baby Scooter.*

"This is it!" I exulted. "Yay Ida!" Peering into the booths, I saw that the Walt and Perky Pat goggles were dark and dead. But the Dexter and Baby Scooter headsets were flickering with colored images.

"Okay," I told Ida. "These are for telerobotically controlling two robots that are in a factory next to the building where I am. Those robots have been building plastic ants. We have to go in there and take over the robots and try and get them to kill the plastic ants."

"Okay," said Ida a little uncertainly.

"Let me do it," yelped Tom.

"Maybe Tom *should* do it, Ida," I said. "I mean my

life kind of depends on this. If we don't kill all the plastic ants they might crawl over here and kill me. One of them tried to slash my wrist this morning. And Tom is better at games than anyone."

"Oh all *right,*" snapped Ida.

Tom quickly took control of the clown. I settled into the Dexter booth and Tom took Baby Scooter. Pulling the Dexter headset over my virtual face shifted my viewpoint to that of the robot's and, most importantly, this action overrode the robot's control circuits and put me in charge. Dexter was now slaved to my hands' motions.

This didn't happen quite smoothly or automatically. Dexter and Baby Scooter had no desire at all to become our telerobotic slaves. My viewpoint bucked around wildly for a moment after I entered Dexter, and I could see that Baby Scooter was thrashing around as well. But Roger had made sure to hardwire the telerobotic override into the ROBOT.LIB microcode, and there was really nothing Dexter and Baby Scooter could do. As soon as we'd settled in, all their higher logic circuits were turned off.

Even so, the robots' control circuits were still functional, and you could drive them around with the standard cyberspace control gestures. You didn't have to worry about the best way to move their legs and so on; you had only to point and nod, and use your hands to control their manipulators. Since the robots had four manipulators each, the control booths actually had four swiveling glove controls.

Once Dexter quieted down, I found myself standing in front of the plastics-casting machine he'd been tending. There was a basket of tiny electronic circuits to my left and a bowl of shining translucent beads to my right. Farther to my right was Baby Scooter. I raised my hand and waved.

"Are you okay, Tom?"

"Yeah," said Tom, waving back. "I'm fine. Are these the plastic ants?" He pointed at the components spread out before him. "Where are the live ones?"

"Down there." I pointed at the trail of newly fashioned plastic ants that was marching from Tom's bench to the crack by the elevator door. "Those are the guys we have to get rid of." Just as I'd feared, the plastic ants were as lively as ever.

Tom picked up a live ant in one of his pincers. He squeezed hard, trying to crush it, but rather than crumbling, the ant skidded out from his grip and shot across the room like a pinched watermelon seed. "They're really solid," said Tom.

I scooped up another ant with my humanoid hand, and then used my two pincers to pull its gaster and its head sections apart from its alitrunk. When I dropped the pieces to the floor, they writhed about spastically. "Tearing them apart works," I said. "But by now there's hundreds of them. Maybe even thousands."

"See how their trail goes into that crack by the elevator door?" said Tom. "Maybe we can pour something down in there that will melt them."

"It would be even better if we could take the elevator down to where the ants have their nest," I said.

"What's wrong with the elevator?"

"It's jammed."

"Maybe I can fix it," said Tom. "You look for something we can pour on them."

I trucked back and forth on my bent-legged bicycle wheels, looking at the vats and barrels of chemicals. The plastic ants still in the lab seemed to sense we were no longer their friends—they were streaming en masse toward the crack at the bottom of the elevator door.

"Here's a big can of acetone," I said presently. "That might be good." The big square can was of shiny metal marked *Acetone—Highly Flammable*. It looked like it held about five gallons.

Tom was examining a box on the wall near the elevator. "Somebody took out one of the fuses is all," he said, rising high up on his legs to look on top of the box. "And, yes, here it is!" Dexter or Baby Scooter had probably removed the fuse, timing it to trap Roger where the plastic ants could finish him off.

Tom replaced the fuse, pressed the elevator button, and *clankclank* the cabin slid up to our level and the doors opened. A dozen plastic ants were running about on the cabin floor.

"Let's see if they melt," I said, lumbering over with the heavy can of acetone. I unscrewed the top and slopped some of the stuff onto the plastic ants. But it didn't slow them down a bit.

"If we could light the acetone . . . " said Tom.

"That would probably work," I agreed. "But how can we light it?"

"Make a spark with an electrical wire," came Ida's voice.

"That sounds good," I said. "Let's do it."

We got in the elevator. Tom was about to push the button for the basement, but I stopped him and pushed the button for the main floor. "We can't take the elevator to the basement," I said. "There's a dead body at the bottom of the shaft. I was starting to tell you before. The plastic ants killed Roger."

The main-floor elevator door was still frozen into the half-open position I'd cranked it to. Tom and I squeezed out with some difficulty, and then went down the concrete stairs to the basement.

I looked around the basement. Where were the ants? No trail led out from under the elevator door here, which suggested they had taken up residence inside the shaft. Hopefully right at the bottom.

"Wait," I told Tom, and hurried back up to the main floor to get the emergency key-crank out of the elevator door. Back in the basement, I put it into the hole in the basement elevator doors.

"Get a wire," I told Tom.

Tom tore a heavy section of electrical conduit down from the ceiling. Being in robot bodies made us feel pretty reckless. Tom kept pulling on the wire and ripping stuff loose until the wire had about ten feet of slack. And then he yanked the wire in two with his pincer-claws. The two bare wire ends made big sputtering sparks if you held them near each other.

"All right," I said. "It's robot kamikaze time."

"Kick some butt!" yelled Ida.

I clamped the acetone can against my chest with my tentacle, and used my humanoid hand to crank open the door at a furious rate. There behind the door was Roger's corpse, and all around his corpse were the glistening plastic ants.

The ants were busy—they'd mounted the two Y9707-EX chips on the grungy shaft wall, with wires running around the chips. Several of the ants had fashioned themselves small silicon rectangles that were attached to their bodies like wings. One of the ants was just starting its wings with an abrupt beating stutter. It rose an inch or two into the air.

I pushed forward and slashed my pincers into the metal can of acetone. The can split wide open, dumping the volatile liquid out onto the ants. Tom lunged in next to me and sparked the wires in the midst of the shaft.

WHOOOOOM!

There was a rush of noise and orange light, and then my viewfield went dead. An instant later I felt a shock wave jolt my chair in Roger's study. I made the gestures to remove the virtual telerobotic headset, and found myself back in the lab behind the castle fireplace. The black velvet clown was here too: Tom and Ida.

"Thanks a million," I said. "I have to go now. Don't tell anyone where I am."

"Good-bye, Da," said Tom.

"Look out in case there's any more ants," called Ida.

I pulled off my headset for real. It was still raining. Oily black smoke was trickling out the roof vents of Roger's factory. The monitor on Roger's desk was blank. Down in the basement of Roger's house, the great boiler shuddered on and began pumping heat into the radiators.

It was time to get out of here. I hurried into the room where I'd slept and pulled my satchel out from under the mattress. There was no car here for me to use, but it would be simple enough to trek down to Saint-Cergue, especially now that I had Roger's galoshes on. I rushed out through the dim living room—for some reason the lights weren't working anymore. I pushed on the front door. It didn't open. "Open the door," I commanded—but nothing happened. A power failure from the factory explosion?

No, it was worse than that. Roger's house computer had turned against me. There was a sudden grinding sound from all over the house as the metal roll-down shutters closed off all the windows. The rain beat on the roof and the radiators hissed with steam.

I left my satchel of money by the front door and felt my way into the dark living room, past the great blue-and-white tile stove to the faint glow of the wall-mounted house computer. The computer screen showed a harmless-looking array of icons, but when I went to touch its keyboard, something pounced on my hand and bit it. I cried out and thrashed my hand—a winged plastic ant circled up into the darkness. Now I felt a bite in my ankle. Not knowing which way to turn,

I ran back into Roger's study, dimly lit by his blank monitor. The little room was hot and stuffy.

Looking desperately around, I noticed the cardboard box of tools in the corner. I rummaged through the box and found a flashlight and a hammer. Wonderfully, the flashlight worked.

I went back into the living room with the idea of trying to smash the plastic ants with my hammer. The cone of my flashlight beam showed three of them on the floor. I rushed forward and managed to pound and crush two of them. Bang bang! But the third ant scurried in close to me and bit me on the ankle. I picked it off and pressed its snapping head against the floor while I pulverized its gaster with the hammer. More ants came, some crawling and some flying, their silicon wings glittering in the beam of my flashlight.

I tried yelling the binary digits of Hex DEF6, but it didn't do a thing—not that it should have. I was dealing with real-world ant robots now instead of the GoMotion software ants of cyberspace. Surely there was some radio control signal to turn these plastic ants off, but without hours of detective-work hacking, I had no way of knowing how to send it.

No, instead of using some subtle software code, I was pounding at the plastic ants with my hammer. Meanwhile they kept attacking me—circling around, jumping up, and dive-bombing; sinking their pincers into my arms, legs, and even my neck; coordinating their motions with the inaudible chirps of robot radio waves. I picked the attackers off and smashed them as best I could, ignoring the cuts in my fingers. I grew dizzy with the pain and the heat. If the ants didn't kill me, the house would cook me to death—but I didn't know what to do besides keep crushing ants.

Around then the beam of my flashlight happened to fall on the blue-and-white tile stove, and I saw that hundreds more plastic ants were crawling and flying out through the vents in the stove's door. Some kind of steam tunnel must have led from the factory to here. The flying ants stuttered their wings and lifted into the air to spiral toward me.

If I stayed here and kept fighting, the plastic ants would bring me down like piranhas attacking a wading cow. Years ago the kids and I had seen just such a cow getting eaten on a TV nature show. The kids had loved it so much that they'd made up a game—Piranhas And Cow—in which Daddy would crawl around on all fours and they'd "bite" at him with their hands until I, Daddy, would collapse in giggles with my arms clamped protectively over my belly and sides.

I slapped a flying ant off my cheek. Thinking of Piranhas And Cow made me think of water, which made me think of Roger's swimming pool. The pool roof was nothing but corrugated plastic! Still clutching my flashlight and hammer, I tottered back to the front hall, grabbed my black satchel, and ran through the kitchen and down the short hall to the room at the end of the house with the swimming pool. Thank God there was no door to close off the pool room. I reached up and whaled against the plastic of the pool room roof with my hammer till I had in Roger's office a good-sized hole in it. Rain poured in. I tossed my satchel up through the hole and began trying to crawl out after it.

I nearly made it. But the hole was six feet off the ground, the dirt at the edge of the pool was muddy, the plastic was weak and saggy, and my hands were slippery with blood and rain. I kept falling back. Now the plastic ants were swarming through the kitchen and into the pool room with me, a few of them flying like air support over the advancing army of the crawling ones. With a final titanic effort, I levered my upper body out into the rainy Swiss morning, but a big piece of the plastic broke loose and I fell backward, hitting my head on the ground. The last thing I saw was flying plastic ants angling down toward me.

I woke to the sound of a telephone endlessly ringing. There was a mud puddle next to my face with rain splashing into it through the jagged hole I'd made in the pool room roof. Floating in the puddle were scores of plastic ants with their little metal legs folded up against their bodies. Some of them had folded-up wings as well. The cuts in my hands had clotted over. Still the phone rang.

I sat up and felt my head. There was a painful egg on the back of my noggin—nothing serious. I could see more motionless plastic ants in the hallway and in the kitchen. Still the phone rang.

I hoisted myself to my feet. My socks were stiff with blood from the bites the ants had given me. I picked up my flashlight and hammer, and made my way through Roger's kitchen, the beads of stilled plastic ants sliding beneath my feet. The dark house was hotter than ever; the furnace continued to blast away. Might the boiler actually explode? I moved faster.

When I picked up the phone, a mechanical voice said, "There is a cyberspace call for you, sir. Please put on your headset."

I snatched up Roger's headset and looked into it. There, staring at me with an expression that was not quite a smile, was Riscky Pharbeque. He was in a car driving on what looked like Route 1 near Big Sur.

"Shit howdy," he said. "Don't say I never did you no favors."

"Riscky! What happened?"

"Just naturally I put a watchbug into that Pemex twelve I sold you, Jerzy. Sucker paged me when you and your son started using the Hex DEF6 code. You choked, my man, you screwed the pooch! You're old and slow. Two GoMotion ants from the third colony got away!"

"Do you know where they are? Can you stop them?"

"*Hell* yes. I'm no friend of Roger Coolidge's—son of a bitch never did pay me for that phreak job I ran on you. Not to speak unkindly of the dear departed, but he was dumb as dog shit to try and short yours truly. Not paying Riscky was about the *last* thing Roger ever did, if you catch my drift."

"You—you had a hand in making his new robots turn bad?"

"Well now, Roger made some random mutations in the colonies writing his robot code—but who's to say what *random* is? Phreaky-deaky, dude." Riscky cackled and held up ten long, wiggling fingers as the cliffs of Big Sur went whipping past.

"Oh God. So what about the escaped GoMotion ants?"

"They jumped right down onto Roger's house computer hoping to *fuck you up*. But good ole Riscky came in and took over that machine's comm ports. The ants can't get back out. Before you do anything else, Jerzy, run in there and rip that computer out of the wall. Smash it up and bring me its big RAM chip. Just so's if I ever need it, I can get the GoMotion ant code off of there."

"Do it now?"

"Do it! I'll wait."

I ran into Roger's living room and yanked his house computer out of its ragged niche. The naked machine crashed to the floor. I used my hammer—yes I was still carrying it—to kill the power supply. Right away the runaway furnace downstairs stopped. And then I pulled the big gigabyte RAM chip off the motherboard. I went back into Roger's study and put on the headset.

"I got it."

"Way to go, old son," said Riscky. "Now gather up a couple or three dozen of those flying ants and bring them and that RAM chip on back to me."

"How did you turn off the plastic ants, Riscky?"

He opened and closed his right hand rapidly several times, miming signals emanating from a source. His long thin lips drew back toward the rasta tangles of his hair. "*Radio*. The plastic ants have the same stop signal as any other robot. Being as how I'd taken over the house computer's communications, I used it to put the plastic ants to sleep. All of them."

"Thank you, Riscky. Thank you so much."

"Don't thank me yet. I want one more thing."

"Money?"

"My girlfriend's turned movie agent. I want you to let her handle the rights to your TV miniseries."

"What?"

"Your adventure, Jerzy, your story. Let my girlfriend handle the rights, or I'll wake up the plastic ants and there won't *be* no story."

"Sure, Riscky, whatever." As if I fucking cared about television.

"Hurry home, bro."

I cleaned myself up and found a raincoat, an umbrella, a scarf, and a pair of leather gloves to hide the cuts in my fingers.

TWELVE

Rocks in My Head

I LEFT ROGER'S HOUSE ON FOOT JUST BEFORE NOON ON Sunday, May 31. I'd half-expected to find the factory burned to the ground outside Roger's shuttered windows, but the acetone seemed to have burned itself out without managing to set the Swiss concrete building on fire, not that I looked inside. The main thing was that no alarms seemed to have gone off, and everything looked fairly normal. I splashed down to Saint-Cergue, where I found a cafe crowded with peasants drinking vile Swiss beer.

Without anyone taking much notice of me, I phoned for a taxi, which took me to the Geneva airport. Customs didn't look in my satchel, which could have been luck or could have been something else. I couldn't tell anymore.

Monday morning I was back in San Jose, just in time for the next part of my trial. I buttonholed Stu in the hall outside the courtroom. He was kind of surprised to see me.

"You're still here, Jerzy?"

"Yes. I want to win this trial. Let me ask you something point-blank. Do you really want me to lose, or have you just been dogging it because West West stopped paying you?"

"Of course I want you to win. You're my client. And I think it's somewhat inaccurate to say that I've been dogging it. The problem is that you haven't given me a defense to work with. And of course I *am* operating on somewhat limited funds."

"I've come into some money and some new information over the weekend, Stu. It was Roger Coolidge who made Studly put the ants on the Fibernet. He was driving Studly over a remote cyberspace link. Get hold of Coolidge's phone bill and we can prove it."

"Use a cryp?"

"Use whatever it takes. And get the same guy who made the prosecutor's demo to make a cyberspace demo for us. A better demo. Coolidge was on the phone to a transponder in the back of a truck driven by a guy called Vinh Vo."

"Is he related to the Vo family you were visiting? None of them were willing to talk."

"Vinh's the oldest son. I've already had dealings with him and I'm sure I can get him to testify for us. Vinh is very money-oriented. The one thing is that our story can't make Vinh look bad. If Vinh were to turn against me, he could open up information about—never mind what about." If Vinh and Bety and Vanna and Riscky kept mum, the authorities need never find out that I was the Sandy Schrandt who'd been visiting Roger Coolidge when he died.

"If this Vinh will really testify that Coolidge paid him to run a transponder near Studly, that could break the case wide open," said Stu.

"I'd like to bring him over to your office this afternoon," I said. "So we can work on his story with him.

Can you get the judge to postpone the rest of the trial for a couple of days?"

"This will all mean a lot of additional legal expenses," said Stu tentatively.

"Let's say I'm good for twenty thousand more dollars, max."

"That works for me!"

As soon as court went into session, Stu approached the bench and asked the judge for a two-day continuance. The D.A. called it frivolous, but the judge said okay.

I found Vinh Vo at Pho Train that afternoon. He too was surprised to see me. I got him to walk through the SJSU campus toward Stu's office with me. On the way I talked to him.

"Vinh, I know that you had a transponder in the back of your truck that night that Studly put the ants on the Fibernet. Roger Coolidge was running Studly through the device in your truck. We're going to have to bring that out for my trial defense."

Vinh angrily screwed up his face around the fuming cigarette in the corner of his mouth. "Don't you talk to the cops about *me*, Mr. Yuppie. I know Eastside Virus boys who'd knife you for fifty dollars." The Eastside Virus was a notorious Vietnamese street gang.

"Now, Vinh, that's not being very cooperative. Anyway I've already told my lawyer all about you."

"My boys can kill your lawyer, too." It was another day of brilliant California sun, and the shadowed creases in Vinh's face looked hard and dark.

"Calm down," I urged him. "All you have to do is say that you ran the transponder for Roger Coolidge. You didn't know why. It's not a crime. You'll just be a witness. Coolidge has to take the fall for this, and you have to help me set him up. If you testify in court, I'll give you a thousand dollars."

"You think Coolidge will take this lying down? He's a billionaire. He'll come back at you with everything he's got."

"Coolidge is dead, Vinh."

Vinh's customary lack of expression briefly gave way to surprise. His mouth opened and his eyebrows shot up before he regained control.

"You kill him?"

"No, I didn't. His robots killed him. But nobody ever finds out about Sandy Schrandt, see?"

"That's a big secret to keep, Rugby. I want five thousand dollars."

"I'll give you two. And you tell Bety Byte and Vanna to purge their records and take a long vacation."

"That's got to make it four thousand."

"Okay," I said. "Who wants to haggle on such a nice, sunny day."

We went to Stu's office and ironed out our courtroom strategy. Vinh left, and then Stu and I talked a little more. He'd already crypped Roger's relevant phone records, and he'd scheduled a guy to rush-job our cyberspace demo for tomorrow, which was Tuesday. The trial was due to start back up on Wednesday.

"But don't forget," Stu reminded me. "Your bail runs out at noon tomorrow. You have to show up at the jail and turn yourself in."

"You damn well better win this trial for me, Stu."

"Here's hoping!"

That evening I went back to Queue's. Keith and I were sitting on the porch smoking a joint when Riscky Pharbeque came bouncing up the path—with none other than Susan Poker in tow.

"Yo, bro," said Riscky. "I brought my friend Sue. She's the movie agent I was telling you about." Susan Poker had replaced her hard-shell Realtor garb with black jeans and a Mexican blouse embroidered with cyberspace interface icons. She wore pale lipstick, and had washed the stiffener out of her hair to pull it back into a loose ponytail. She looked arty, in an L.A. kind of way.

"Hi, there!" she sang. "I'm looking forward to representing you. Riscky won't tell me what he did to convince you." She gave Riscky a kittenish slap.

I was on my feet staring down over the railing. "Since when are *you* a movie agent, Poker?" I demanded.

"What you don't know about me would fill a book, Rugby," she fired back. "But don't you think it's time we got on a first-name basis?"

They sat on the porch and smoked with us for a bit, and then I took Riscky upstairs alone with me.

"I hope to God you don't tell that flap-mouth about—" I broke off, remembering that my room was probably bugged. Riscky laid a finger on his long sharp nose and looked kindly confidential. He drew a cloth sack out of his pocket and held it up inquiringly. I pointed to my black satchel. He reached into it with the sack and invisibly bagged his RAM chip and the dormant winged plastic ants. I was glad to see them go. I was dead sick of ants.

Back downstairs, Susan Poker said, "We can't stay long, Jerzy, but I've got these papers for you to sign."

"What?"

"It's my standard agency contract. I incorporated on Friday—when Riscky told me he'd get you. The networks already know I'm going to represent you, and ABC and TNT are definitely interested."

I went ahead and signed the papers. What the hey, "Sue" was only asking for fifteen percent. And it wasn't like, if she got the deal, I would actually have to do anything more than give them my blessing and take a couple of meetings. "The Jerzy Rugby Story," yeah, I kind of liked it. Or maybe call it "The Hacker And The Ants"? It would be something on TV worth seeing for once—especially if I won my trials and gave it a happy ending.

"Let me just ask you one thing," I said, handing back the papers. "Was it a woman called Kay Coolidge who got you onto my case in the first place?"

"Go ask Gretchen," grinned Susan Poker. "She told me she wants you to come see her tonight."

I drove down to Gretchen's. She was home alone in her condo, sitting on the couch watching television.

"Where were you all weekend, Jerzy?" she asked petulantly. "I couldn't find you."

"Never mind. Look, is it true that Roger Coolidge's wife Kay hired you and Susan Poker to watch me?"

Gretchen tossed her bell-shaped hairdo. "Okay, yes, that's true. But right away I started being really fond of you, Jerzy." She smiled prettily.

"You weren't too fond of me to give Riscky Pharbeque my cyberspace access code. You watched me typing it in that time right after our first fuck. I just remembered that on the drive over here."

"Come on and sit down, Jerzy," said Gretchen, patting the sofa cushion next to her. "Tell me how your trial's going. Calm down and give me a kiss."

The phone rang. Gretchen answered. "Yes. Uh-huh. No, I'm still not sure where he was over the weekend. But I know where he is now. Yes, he's right here. Oh, he already knows. Talk to him? I guess so." She giggled and held out the receiver. "Here, Jerzy. It's Kay Coolidge."

Reluctantly I took the phone. "Hello?"

It was an older woman's plummy voice, strained with grief. "Mr. Rugby, this is Kay Coolidge in San Francisco. I've just gotten word that my husband Roger is dead. Do you know how it happened?"

"Roger framed me for the GoMotion ant release, and you've been helping him spy on me for over a month. Why would I suddenly want to help you?"

"Look, Mr. Rugby, Roger told me on Saturday that you were coming to visit him. You're such an unworldly dreamer that it would be perfectly easy to frame you again, if that's what you want to call it, you fool. But if you'll just tell me the truth, I might let you go. Even if you did kill him."

I took a deep breath. Would this ever be over? "I'm certainly not going to say I was there—" I began.

"Go on."

"But I might speculate that Roger was killed by some new four-armed robots and some little robots that look like plastic ants. That's what he was experimenting with, I understand. From having worked with Roger in the past, I can tell you that he could be quite reckless about new forms of artificial life."

"I see," said Kay Coolidge quietly. "But the coroner said something about a fire."

"This would still be pure speculation on my part, but it may be that someone was trying to kill the four-armed robots along with the plastic ants that were crawling on . . . on Roger's body."

"Oh how horrible." She started sobbing.

"Will you and your people leave me alone now?" I grated.

There was a hiccuping pause while Kay Coolidge composed herself. "Yes, we'll leave you alone," she said finally.

"So good-bye. And I'm sorry about Roger. You don't need to say anything else to Gretchen, do you?"

"No need." Her voice was shakily calm. "Tell Miss Bell that her final check will come this week. Good-bye."

I hung up the phone.

"What was that all about?" asked Gretchen.

"You're out of that job," I told her.

"I'm glad, Jerzy. Susan and I have felt *terrible* about tattling on you."

"I don't believe that for a minute," I said. But I spent the night with her anyway. What with having to turn myself in to the sheriff the next day, who knew when I'd get another chance to sleep with a woman. And, face it, I was still in love with Gretchen, even if she did have the morals of a Realtor.

The story about Roger Coolidge being killed by his robots broke in the media the next morning. I went downtown at noon and spent the next six days in jail and the courtroom.

On Wednesday morning, Stu presented Vinh's testimony. There were records of Roger calling Vinh, and of Roger calling the number of Vinh's transponder. Vinh said he hadn't known why Roger had wanted him to drive the transponder over to his family's house; he said he'd thought it was just a divorce case or a matter of industrial espionage. Wednesday afternoon, after Vinh's testimony, Stu showed a kick-ass cyberspace demo that made the story really hang together.

For his summation on Thursday, Stu got permission from the judge to bring in the fact that Roger had recently been killed by robots, and that all the GoMotion ants seemed to have disappeared from cyberspace with Roger's death. By the time Stu was through, nobody doubted anymore that Roger had been the sole and supreme master of the GoMotion ants.

The jury came in with a not guilty verdict on Friday, and on Monday, June 8, the federal prosecutor dropped all charges against me. I walked out of jail a free man with a dynamite story. I spent the rest of that day hanging out with my kids. I saw Carol too, of course, and she told me that she was planning to marry Hiroshi in the fall. I was so happy about getting out of jail that I congratulated her.

Tuesday, Susan Poker got me a contract with Fox for "seven figures," as she happily put it. Riscky was with her when she told me. He was really excited about his Sue's deal. Studly was to be equipped with fresh chips and given a starring role. It almost felt like Riscky had made this whole adventure happen to me just so Susan Poker would have a miniseries to sell. But that was a paranoid thought, and I was sick of being paranoid.

While they were talking to me, Riscky started hinting around that he might want to try and find a hacker to help him develop some miniature flying robots with "certain new technology I've got ahold of," meaning the winged plastic ants. "*Not me,*" I told him. "*No more ants for me.*"

On Wednesday, Stu filed a seven-figure lawsuit against GoMotion for having framed me. Given Kay Coolidge's promise not to pull any more dirty tricks on me, it seemed like we had a good chance of winning. Stu lined up two other lawyers to help him, all of them working on a contingency basis.

On Thursday, Otto Gyorgyi phoned to offer me my job back at West West, and I had the joy of telling him to get fucked, royally. I still had most of the eighty thousand I'd gotten from Roger, and before long the miniseries bucks would be rolling in. I didn't need West West's money. And—"Great Work" or no, I was as sick of robots as I was of ants. The Veep and the Adze robots were out in the world and doing fine. I'd done enough for the robots.

The summer wore on happily. I kept seeing a lot of Sorrel, Tom, and Ida. They were proud of how much they'd helped me in my battle with the ants.

Gretchen sometimes talked about her and me getting a place together, but I'd grown attached to the freedom and privacy of my rented aerie at Queue's. Plus, as long as I wasn't actually living with Gretchen, I could still occasionally date other women, specifically Nga Vo.

Vinh had enjoyed being on the winning end of a trial so much that he'd told his family to let me resume my relationship with Nga. Nga's parents started letting Nga spend Tuesdays with me—though evening dates were still out of the question. I got the idea of trying to take up surfing, and bought wet suits and boards for the two of us, along with surfing lessons. Nga bragged that she was the only boat-people surfer in Santa Cruz. She had an eccentric sense of humor, and a weird take on things American. And, of course, kissing her was heaven, though kissing was still as far as it went. I tried bringing Nga back to my room a couple of times, but alert landlady Queue would always notice, and find a way to thwart my evil plans.

In August, Sorrel, Tom, and Ida went backpacking in Yosemite with me, which was wonderful. I had kind of a vision in Yosemite, a moment of enlightenment, just like in the old days. I'd always realized that animals and plants and the web of nature are as alive and cosmically conscious as me. But I'd never before realized that rocks are alive.

The rocks in Yosemite are what's really unusual about the place—the rocks are plutonic granite, which has square or parallelopiped-shaped chunks of quartz in it. Looking at them in my moment of enlightenment, I could see that, *yes,* even rocks are alive.

So who needs smart machines?